Lynne Graham was born in Northern Ireland and has been a keen romance reader since her teens. She is very happily married, to an understanding husband who has learned to cook since she started to write! Her five children keep her on her toes. She has a very large dog, who knocks everything over, a very small terrier, who barks a lot, and two cats. When time allows, Lynne is a keen gardener.

Michelle Smart's love affair with books started when she was a baby and would cuddle them in her cot. A voracious reader of all genres, she found her love of romance established when she stumbled across her first Mills & Boon book at the age of twelve. She's been reading them—and writing them—ever since. Michelle lives in Northamptonshire, England, with her husband and two young Smarties.

THE INNOCENT'S FORGOTTEN WEDDING

LYNNE GRAHAM

HIS GREEK WEDDING NIGHT DEBT

MICHELLE SMART

MILLS & BOON

First Published in Great Britain 2020
by Mills & Boon, an imprint of HarperCollins*Publishers*
1 London Bridge Street, London, SE1 9GF

The Innocent's Forgotten Wedding © 2020 by Lynne Graham

His Greek Wedding Night Debt © 2020 by Michelle Smart

ISBN: 978-0-263-27809-5

MIX
Paper from
responsible sources
FSC™ C007454

This book is produced from independently certified FSC™ paper
to ensure responsible forest management.
For more information visit www.harpercollins.co.uk/green.

Printed and bound in Spain
by CPI, Barcelona

THE INNOCENT'S FORGOTTEN WEDDING

LYNNE GRAHAM

CHAPTER ONE

MILLY'S HEARTBEAT SPEEDED UP with excitement when she saw Brooke's name flash across the screen of her cheap mobile because it had been a while since she had heard from her famous and glamorous half-sister.

When Brooke phoned, however, it meant that Brooke *needed* her and that truth more than made up for Brooke's often cold and seemingly critical attitude towards her. Milly loved being needed and, in any case, deep down inside, Milly was convinced that her sister *cared* about her even though she might be too proud to admit it.

After all, why else would Brooke confide in her about so many private things if she did not, at heart, see Milly as a trustworthy friend and sister? Furthermore, aside of each other, neither one of them had a single living relative. Nor was it surprising that Brooke would need her services again when her life was in such turmoil, thanks to that dreadful possessive tyrant of a man she had mistakenly married. What sort of a man would try and come between Brooke and her career? What sort of man would divorce a wife as beautiful and talented as Brooke simply over ugly rumours that she had had an affair?

'He won't listen to a word I say!' Brooke had wept when she'd confided in Milly. 'He set me up because he wants rid of me. I'm convinced he *paid* that creep to lure me into a hotel room and lie about having sex with me!'

'Brooke?' Milly exclaimed warmly as she answered her phone.

'I need you to pretend to be me for a few days.'

'A few...*days*?' Milly stressed in dismay, for that request went far beyond anything her sister had asked of her before. 'Are you sure I'll be able to manage that? I'm OK until people speak to me and expect me to be you!'

'You'll be holed up in a fancy hotel in the heart of London,' Brooke told her drily. 'You won't be required to talk to anyone but room service. You won't need to leave the room at all.'

Milly frowned. 'For how long?' she pressed anxiously.

'Five or six days. That's all,' Brooke informed her briskly.

'I *can't*, Brooke,' Milly protested apologetically. 'I've got a job and I don't want to lose it.'

'You're a waitress, Milly, not a brain surgeon,' her half-sister reminded her tartly. 'You can pick up casual work anywhere at this time of year. And if it's a matter of me paying your rent *again* for you, I'll do it!'

Milly flushed and subsided again because it was

true, she could find another job relatively easily, and if Brooke made up her loss of wages to cover the rent on her bedsit as well, she had no grounds for complaint either. When it occurred to her that she had ended up sleeping on a friend's sofa the last time she'd needed help to cover her rent, she suppressed the memory. Brooke had forgotten to give her the money she had promised but Milly felt that that oversight was her own fault because she had been too embarrassed to remind Brooke. She couldn't help but shrink from highlighting the financial differences between her and her sister, and wasn't one bit surprised that Brooke had always refused to be seen in public with her or invite her into her more exciting world even briefly, except in Milly's guise as a lookalike. What else could she expect? Milly asked herself ruefully. In truth, she was lucky to have *any* kind of relationship with her sibling at all…

Brooke had first sought out Milly when she was eighteen and fresh out of a council home for foster kids. Milly had already known that she was illegitimate, but she had been shocked by what her newly discovered half-sister had to tell her—well, shocked and initially repulsed by Brooke's view of the circumstances of her birth. But then, slowly, she had come to understand Brooke's feelings of betrayal and had forgiven her sister for her offensive wording.

'Your mother was the slut who almost broke up my parents' happy marriage!' Brooke had told her sharply.

To be fair to Brooke, Milly's mother *had* been the

other woman who slept with a married man, inflicting considerable suffering on that man's innocent wife and child. Brooke and Milly's father, William Jackson, a wealthy wine importer, had had a long-running affair with a model called Natalia Taylor and had threatened to leave his wife over her.

Sadly, a heart attack had taken William's life when Brooke was fifteen and Milly was nine. Natalia had died in a bus crash only a couple of years later and Milly had ended up in council care, where she had remained until she reached eighteen. At first meeting, both young women had been taken aback by the likeness between them, for they had both inherited their father's white-blonde curly hair and dark blue eyes. Milly, however, had had a large bump in her nose and somehow the features that made Brooke a stunning beauty had blurred in Milly's case, putting her into the pretty rather than beautiful category.

It had been Brooke's idea that she could use Milly as a stand-in either to avoid an event she considered boring or, more frequently, to mislead the paparazzi that dogged her footsteps and who occasionally followed her places where she didn't want to be seen or photographed her with individuals whom she didn't wish to be seen with. Brooke was obsessed with airbrushing and controlling the public image she wanted to show the world.

In the same way she had pointed out that Milly couldn't help her unless she was prepared to go that extra mile and have her nose 'done' so that it mirrored Brooke's far more elegant nose. At first, Milly had said a very firm no to that idea, not because she was fond of her less than perfect nose but just because it was hers and she was accustomed to her own flaws.

Brooke had had a huge row with her over her refusal and Milly had been devastated when her half-sister had cut off all contact with her. When Brooke had called her again six weeks later, Milly had been so grateful to hear from her that she had agreed to the surgical procedure and before she could change her mind she had been whisked into a private clinic and her nose had been skilfully enhanced to resemble Brooke's. Once that had been achieved, expert make-up had completed her transformation.

The first time Milly had pretended to be Brooke to enable her sister to evade a boring charity event, she had been terrified, even dressed in her sister's clothes and made up to look like her, but nobody had suspected a thing and, for the first time in her life, Milly had felt like an achiever. Brooke's gratitude had made her feel wonderfully warm inside and the second time, when Milly had had to simply step out of a limousine and walk into a shop while Brooke was many miles away, she had felt even better. She had discovered that it was fun to dress up in expensive clothes and pretend to be someone she was not and there had been very little fun in Milly's life before Brooke entered it.

And with Brooke in her current predicament, struggling to deal with her broken marriage, Milly knew that she should definitely go that extra mile for her sister. 'Where will you be while I sit in this hotel?' she asked curiously.

'Having a very discreet little holiday, so I'll need your passport,' Brooke advanced. 'I daren't travel on my own.'

And Milly frowned at that reference to her passport but could only smile at the mention of a holiday. A holiday was exactly what her poor sister needed at this stressful time in her life and if Milly roomsitting in some fancy hotel was all that was required, it would be utterly selfish of her to refuse to help. 'OK. I'll do it.'

'You can only bring one small bag with you. I've packed a case for you, and you can change into my clothes in the car,' Brooke informed her. 'I'll do your make-up in the car too. I'm better at it than you are.'

After Brooke had arranged to pick her up, Milly straightened her hair and threw her passport, fresh underwear, a couple of books and a range of craft items into a bag before heading out. It was a filthy wet day and she didn't step out onto the pavement until she had her umbrella up to protect her hair for Brooke's hair was always a perfect blonde fall without even a hint of curl.

First, however, Milly took ten minutes to walk down the street and quit her waitressing job in a local café, mentioning a family emergency. She hated letting people down, but Brooke had been right, she would probably find another job quite quickly, she reasoned, guilty at having let an employer she liked down at short notice. But, my goodness, Brooke *did* deserve a holiday after everything she had recently been through and if she could help her sibling achieve that, then she could be proud of herself because family needs came first, family should *always* come first, she thought ruefully, regretting that neither of her parents had lived by that truth.

Brooke looked amazing when Milly glimpsed her inside the limo, all groomed and flawless in a black jacket, a tomato-red sheath dress and very high-heeled stilettos. It was likely, though, to be a struggle for her sibling to get out of that dress in the back of the limo, no matter how spacious it was, Milly ruminated.

'Quick, get in!' Brooke snapped at her. 'We can't be seen together!'

'What about the driver?' Milly asked in bemusement as the passenger door closed to seal the two women into privacy.

'I pay him well to keep quiet!' Brooke fielded, snapping shut the privacy screen between the front and the rear seats. 'Now help me out of this dress… Oh, yes, don't forget that I need your passport too.'

'It has to be against the law for you to travel on my passport,' Milly muttered uncomfortably. 'Do you *have* to borrow it?'

Brooke settled furious dark blue eyes on her. 'I don't have a choice. I'll be traced if I travel under my own name. With your name, I'm nobody, and nobody is the slightest bit interested in me or where I go.'

Reluctantly accepting that reality, Milly handed

over her passport and proceeded to help her sibling out of her tight dress.

'Good grief, I don't see you for a couple of months and you let yourself turn into the ugly sister. Your nails are awful!' Brooke complained, snatching at one of Milly's hands to frown down at the sight of nails that were an unpainted and modest length. 'I'm always perfectly groomed. When you're checking in, keep them hidden and get a manicurist to come to the room and fix them before you check out again!' she instructed impatiently.

'I'm sorry,' Milly muttered, choosing not to point out that she couldn't afford to have her nails done professionally. Brooke regarded expensive treatments in the beauty field as essential maintenance and never ever considered the cost of them. 'When do you think you'll be back?'

'Hell…you're putting on weight again too, aren't you?' Brooke said in frustration as she urged Milly to breathe in to enable her to get the zip up on the fitted dress.

Milly had been born curvier and almost an inch shorter than Brooke and she didn't respond. She knew she wasn't overweight but since meeting Brooke, who was thinner, she had deliberately dropped almost a stone so that she could fit better into her sister's clothes. Unfortunately, that had meant avoiding all her favourite comfort foods and reining in her love of chocolate. Beside her, Brooke kicked off her shoes and began to dress in jeans and a long concealing top, bundling her hair up under a peaked cap. Digging into her bag she produced moist wipes and began to wipe off her make-up.

'It's like being a spy,' Milly remarked with helpless amusement.

'Don't be so childish, Milly!' Brooke snapped impatiently. 'Have you any idea how much is riding on this holiday I'm having? This is too important to joke about. I'm meeting someone while I'm away who may put my name forward for a film part.'

'Well, it's exciting for me,' Milly confided with a little wrinkle of her nose and a look of guilty apology. 'Sorry. I expect it'll be pretty boring stuck in that hotel room though, so this is the fun part.'

'You'll need my rings…for goodness' sake, don't lose them! I may need to sell them somewhere down the road,' Brooke admitted stiffly, threading her wedding and engagement rings off her long manicured finger and passing them over. 'That *bastard*, Lorenzo! He could have slung me a few million for the sake of it, but he stuck to the letter of the pre-nup. I'm not getting a penny I'm not due. Still, he'll just be a bad memory a few years down the road. My next husband will be a fashion icon or an actor, *not* a banker!'

Disappointed by her sister's bad mood, Milly donned the rings and slid her feet into the shoes while Brooke passed her bag and jacket over. 'Do you think that when you come back we could spend an evening together?' she asked hesitantly.

'Why would I want to do that?' Brooke demanded.

'It's been ages since we spent any real time together,' Milly pointed out quietly. 'I would really enjoy that and maybe talking over things would make you feel better.'

'I'm feeling fine.' Brooke snapped open the privacy screens and lifted her make-up kit before pausing to communicate with the driver and telling him to speed up because she didn't want to check in late for her flight. 'When I first went looking for you, I was curious about you. But I'm not curious any more. I've been very good to you too, sprucing you up, fixing your face. What more can you expect from me? It's not as though we could ever be friends, not with your mother having slept with my father while he was still married to *my* mother. Do you realise that my poor mother tried to *kill* herself over their affair?'

Milly paled at that new revelation and dropped her head. 'I am so sorry, Brooke, but I've been hoping that in time...well, that we could get over that history because we're still sisters.'

Brooke pushed up Milly's chin to outline her mouth with lip liner. 'Smile...yes, that's the ticket. There is no getting over the fact that your mother shagged my father and I don't do friends. Friends let you down and talk behind your back.'

'I wouldn't *ever*!' Milly protested.

'Well, you haven't so far,' Brooke conceded grudgingly. 'And you've been very useful to me, I'll agree. But we have nothing in common, Milly. You're poor and uneducated and you wouldn't even be able to talk properly if I hadn't sent you to elocution classes. You knit and you go to libraries. What would we talk about? I'd be bored stiff with you in five minutes.'

Milly paled and stiffened and called herself all kinds of a fool for running blindly into such abuse. She had closed her eyes too long to Brooke's essential coldness towards her, hoping that Brooke would eventually accept her as her sister and leave the sins of their mutual parents behind her in the past where they belonged. But for the first time, she was recognising that Brooke was as angry and resentful now about their father's affair as she had been when she'd first met her. Brooke tucked away her make-up kit and told the driver yet again to speed up, the instruction sharp and irritable in tone.

The rain had got so heavy that it was streaming down the windows and visibility was poor. It was a horrible day weather-wise, Milly conceded wryly, suppressing her hurt at being labelled boring. It was true that she and her sister had little in common apart from their paternity and their physical likeness to one another. Evidently, however, Brooke didn't feel an atom of a deeper connection to her because of their blood bond. When Brooke had confided in her about her problems, had it meant anything to her at all? Possibly, Brooke had grasped that Milly was trustworthy in that line and unlikely to reveal all to some murky tabloid newspaper. Or maybe Milly had just been there at the right moment when Brooke had needed to unburden herself.

'This will be the last time I stand in for you, Brooke,' Milly said quietly but firmly. 'If I'm honest, I kind of wish I'd never started it.'

'Oh, for heaven's sake, why do you have to start

getting difficult right now?' Brooke demanded wrathfully.

'I'm not being difficult and I'm not about to let you down,' Milly responded tautly. 'But once this is over, I won't be acting as your stand-in again.'

Brooke flashed one of her charming smiles and stretched out her hand to squeeze Milly's. 'I'm sorry if I've been short with you but this has been such a frantic rush and I'm living on my nerves. We're almost at your hotel. Make sure you don't get into any conversations with staff. I never chat to menial people. Stay in your room and eat there too and don't eat any rubbish. I am known for my healthy eating regime and I have an exercise video in the pipeline. You can't be seen after you've checked in. People will understand. They know my marriage is over and I wouldn't look human if I wasn't seen to be grieving and in need of some private downtime...'

Milly was not fooled by that fake smile or the apology. She could see that she was only receiving it because Brooke was scared she would pull out on her at the last minute and it saddened her to see that lack of real feeling in the sister she had come to care deeply for.

Their driver was travelling fast when he suddenly jammed on the brakes to a jolting halt to make a turn. Milly peered out at the traffic. There was a large truck coming through red stop lights towards them and she gasped in fear.

Beside her Brooke was shouting at the driver and as Milly braced herself and offered up a silent prayer she tried to reach out for Brooke's hand, but her sister was screaming and she couldn't reach her. There was a terrible crunch on impact that jarred every bone in her body and then she blacked out in response to the wave of unimaginable pain that engulfed every part of her. Brooke… *Brooke*, she wanted to shriek in horror, because her sister had released her seat belt while she was changing…

Lorenzo Tassini, the most exceptional private banker of his generation and a renowned genius in the field of finance, was in an unusually good mood that morning because his soon-to-be ex-wife had finally signed the divorce papers earlier that day.

It was done. Within a few weeks, Lorenzo would be free, *finally* free, from a wife who'd lied, cheated, slept around and created endless embarrassing headlines in the newspapers. Brooke hoped to build an acting career on the back of her notoriety. Lorenzo might despise her, but he blamed himself more for his poor judgement in marrying her than he blamed her for letting him down. In retrospect, he could barely comprehend the madness that had taken hold of him when he had first met Brooke Jackson, a woman totally outside his wide and varied experience of the opposite sex. Lust had proved to be his downfall, he reflected grimly.

Brooke's white-blonde beauty had mesmerised him but the two years he had been with her had been filled with rage, regret and bitterness, for the honeymoon period in their marriage had been of very short duration. The ink had barely been dry on their marriage licence before he'd realised that his dream of having a wife who would give him a happy home life was unlikely to come true with a woman who had absolutely no interest in making a home or in having a child or indeed spending time with him any place other than a noisy nightclub.

But then what did *he* know about having a happy home life? Or even about having a family? Indeed, Lorenzo would've been the first to admit his ignorance in those fields. He, after all, had been raised in a regimented Italian palazzo by a father who cared more about his academic triumphs than his happiness or comfort. Strict nannies and home tutors had raised him to follow in the footsteps of his forebears and put profit first, and his dream of leading a more normal life in a comfortable home had died on the back of Brooke's first betrayal. All that foolish nonsense was behind him now though, he assured himself staunchly. From now on, he would simply revel in being very, very rich and free of all ties. He would not remarry and he would not have a child because ten to one, with his ancestry, he would be a lousy parent.

The police called Lorenzo when he was on the way out to lunch. He froze as the grim facts of the crash were recited. The driver was dead, one of *his* staff. The other passenger was dead. What *other* passenger? he wondered dimly, reeling in shock from what he was hearing. His wife was seriously injured, and he was being advised to get to the hospital as soon as possible. He would visit the driver's family too to offer his condolences, he registered numbly.

His wife? Seriously hurt? The designation shook him inside out because he had already stopped thinking of himself as a husband. But in an emergency, he was Brooke's only relative and if she was hurt, she was entirely *his* responsibility, and no decent human being would think otherwise, he told himself fiercely. Without hesitation, he headed straight to the hospital. He had stopped liking or respecting his wife a long time ago, but he would never have wished any kind of harm on her.

The police greeted him at the hospital, keen to ask what he might know about the other woman, who had died. According to the passport they had found, her name was Milly Taylor, but he had never heard of her before. The police seemed to think that, with it being a wet day, Brooke might have stopped the car to give some random woman a lift, but Lorenzo couldn't imagine Brooke doing anything of that nature and suggested that the unknown woman might be one of Brooke's social media gurus or possibly a make-up artist or stylist because she frequently hired such people.

He wondered if the accident had been his driver's fault. Consequently, was it *his* fault for continuing to allow Brooke the luxury of a limo with driver? Although the pre-nup Brooke had signed had proved ironclad in protecting his assets and his fortune, Lorenzo had been generous. He had already bought and given Brooke a penthouse apartment in which to live and had hesitated to withdraw the use of the car and driver as well until she had officially moved out of Madrigal Court, his country home. And Brooke had stalled about actually moving out because it suited her to have staff she didn't have to pay making her meals for her and doing the hundred and one things she didn't want to have to do for herself. *Madre di Dio*...what total nonsense was he thinking about at such a grave moment?

The police reassured him that the accident had not been his driver's fault. A foreign truck driver had taken a wrong turn, got into a panic in the heavy traffic and run a set of stop lights, making an accident unavoidable.

Brooke, he learned, had a serious head injury and he was warned by the consultant neurosurgeon about to operate on her that she might not survive. Lorenzo spent the night pacing a bland waiting room, brooding over everything that he had been told. Brooke had facial injuries. The tiny glimpse he'd had of her before she went into surgery, he had found her unrecognisable and he was appalled on her behalf because he had never known a woman whose looks meant more to her. He would engage the very best plastic surgeons to treat her, he promised himself, shame and discomfiture assailing him. As long as she was alive, he would look after her in every way possible, just as if she were *still* a much-loved and cherished wife. That was his bounden duty and he would not be tried and found wanting in a crisis.

When he learned that she had come through the

surgery he breathed more freely again. She was in a coma. Only time would tell when she would come out of it or what she would be like when she came round, because such head traumas generally caused further complications and even if she recovered she might be different in some ways, the exhausted surgeon warned him. Furthermore, Brooke was facing a very long and slow recovery process.

He was given her personal effects by a nurse. He recognised her engagement ring, the big solitaire he had slipped on her finger with such love and hope, the matching wedding band he had given her with equal trust and optimism. He swallowed hard, recognising that he was at a crossroads and not at the crossroads of freedom he had expected to become his within weeks. Brooke was his wife and he would look after her and support her in whatever ways were necessary. In the short term, he reflected tautly, he would put the divorce on hold until she was on the road to recovery and capable of expressing her own wishes again.

CHAPTER TWO

THE WOMAN IN the bed was drifting weightless in a cocoon, her awareness coming to her in weird broken flashes.

She heard voices but she didn't recognise them. She heard sounds like bells, buzzes, and bleeps but she didn't recognise them either. And she couldn't move, no matter how hard she strained her will to shift a finger, wriggle a toe or even open her eyes. Her body felt as heavy as lead. And then she heard one voice and, although she didn't recognise it either, she clung to it in her disorientation as though it were a lifeline.

It was a man's voice, deep and dark and measured. It made her listen but at first she couldn't distinguish the words, and even when she began picking up stray words she couldn't string them together into a coherent sentence or think about what the words meant. Maybe it was a television, she thought, wondering why it was constantly tuned to a foreign channel because early on she identified a faint but very definite foreign accent that stroked along his vowel sounds like silk, sometimes softening them, sometimes harshening them. Time had no meaning for her while she listened to the voice.

And then there was the music that came and went in the background. It was the sort of music she had never listened to before, mainly classical. But occasionally she heard birdsong or the surge of waves on the shore or even noises she imagined might be heard in a jungle, as if someone had compiled a diverse sound collection just for her. She loved the birdsong because it made her feel that if she could only try a little harder to wake up, she would waken to a fresh new day.

Lorenzo studied his wife while he stood at the window of her room. Superficially, if one discounted all the machinery and the tubes, Brooke looked as though she were simply asleep, her cascade of white-blonde curls tumbling off the side of the bed in a glorious curtain. They called her, 'the sleeping beauty' in the high-tech care home he had moved her to when the hospital could do no more. She had moved from the coma into a vegetative state and there was no sign of recovery after fifteen months.

Fifteen months, Lorenzo conceded, driving a long-fingered hand through his luxuriant black hair, for fifteen crisis-ridden months, his life had revolved around her treatment. Fifteen months during which she had been in and out of Intensive Care, in and out of surgery, both major and minor, and now she was repaired, broken limbs mended, cuts and bruises healed, her face restored by the very best surgeons and daily physiotherapy keeping her muscles from wasting… but still, she wasn't *fixed*.

Fixing her every problem, banishing the physical damage caused by the accident and readying her for a return to the living had kept Lorenzo going, even when the hopes of the medical staff had begun to fade. He could not let her go, he could *not* allow those machines to be switched off, not while there was hope, and he was fortunate that he was wealthy enough to fly in specialists from round the world, only unfortunately all of them had different opinions on Brooke's prospects of recovery. He had never been humble but it was finally beginning to dawn on Lorenzo that he was not omnipotent and that she might *never* be fixed and might never open her eyes again.

He sat down by the bed and scored a forefinger over the back of her still hand. Her nails were polished, just as her hair was regularly washed and styled. They had wanted to cut her hair short but he had simply brought in a hairdresser to take care of it instead, just as he had brought in nail technicians. It was what Brooke would've wanted, although he had told the hairdresser to stop straightening her hair and leave the natural curls. He knew she would never have agreed to that change and if he accidentally brushed a hand through those glorious tumbling white-blonde ringlets he felt guilt pierce him.

'I *did* love you once,' Lorenzo said almost defiantly in the silent room.

And a finger twitched. Lorenzo froze and studied

her hand, which remained in the same position, and he told himself he had imagined that movement. It wouldn't be the first time that he had imagined such a thing and he was being fanciful.

It bothered him that Brooke was so alone and that he was her sole visitor aside of the occasional specialists. He had never realised how isolated she was until after the accident when paparazzi had tried to sneak in and catch pictures of her but not one single friend had shown up. There had only been cursory phone calls from her agent and various other people engaged in building her career and those enquiries had soon fallen off once the news that she was in a coma spread. The fame she had gloried in had, sadly, proved fleeting. There had been a burst of headlines and speculation in the wake of the crash but now she seemed to be forgotten by everyone but him.

Early the following morning, alarm bells rang and lights flashed from the machinery by the bed. The woman came awake and went into panic, eyes focusing on an unfamiliar room and then on the arrival of two nurses, their faces both concerned and excited at the same time. She clawed at the breathing tube in her throat because she couldn't speak and the women tried to both restrain and soothe her, telling her over and over again that the doctor was coming, everything would be all right and that there was nothing to worry about. She thought they were crazy. Her body wouldn't move. She could only move one hand and her arm felt as if it didn't belong to her. How could she possibly have nothing to worry about? Why were they talking nonsense? Did they think she was stupid?

The panic kept on clawing at her, even after the doctor arrived and the breathing tube was removed. He kept on asking her questions, questions she couldn't answer until she couldn't hide from the truth any longer. She didn't *know* who she was. What was her name? She didn't *know* why she was lying in a hospital bed. She didn't have a last memory to offer because her mind was a blank, a complete blank. It was a ridiculous relief to receive an approving nod when she evidently got the name of the Prime Minister right and contrived to name colours correctly.

'What happened to me?' she whispered brokenly, her breath rasping. 'Have I been ill?'

'You were in an accident.' The doctor paused there, exchanging a glance with the staff surrounding the bed.

'What's my name?' she asked shakily.

'Your name is Brooke... Brooke Tassini.'

The name meant absolutely nothing to her, didn't even sound slightly familiar.

'Your husband will be here very soon.'

Brooke's eyes widened to their fullest extent in shock. *'I have a husband?'*

For some reason, the nurses smiled. 'Oh, yes, you have a husband.'

'A very handsome husband,' one of the women added.

Brooke stared down at her bare wedding finger. She was married. Oh, my goodness, she was married.

Did she have children? she asked. No…no children as far as they knew, they said, and a tinge of relief threaded through the panic she was only just holding at bay. Then she felt guilty about that sense of relief. She liked children, *didn't she*? But it was scary enough to have a husband she didn't remember—it would be simply appalling if she had contrived to forget her children as well.

Lorenzo stood outside in the corridor studying the middle-aged doctor babbling at him. And it *was* babble because the care-home staff were not accustomed to their comatose patients waking up and excitement laced with frank worry had taken over.

'It's post-traumatic amnesia, perfectly understandable after a serious head injury. You need someone more qualified than me in the psychiatric field to advise you on her condition, but I would warn you not to tell her anything that might upset her more at the moment. I wouldn't mention yet that other people died in the accident or that you were…er…splitting up at the time of the crash,' the doctor muttered hurriedly, visibly uncomfortable with getting that personal. 'She's in a very high state of stress as it is. Try to calm her, try to keep it upbeat without divulging too much information.'

Lorenzo had been in an early board meeting when the phone call came. He had been so shocked by the news that Brooke had recovered consciousness that he had walked out without a word of explanation. Now that he was on the brink of speaking to her again, he was, for once, at a loss. Brooke didn't *remember* him? Could he believe that of a woman willing to use anything and everything to create a furore in the media? What better way to spring back into the public eye than with an interesting story to tell? When he had first met her, such suspicion would have been foreign to him and momentarily he was furious that he had to consider that she could be faking it. But he had learned the hard way that Brooke was a skilled deceiver.

The door opened and Brooke froze against the pillows, her chest tightening as she snatched in a breath. And there he was in the doorway and there was nothing familiar about him. Indeed, it immediately occurred to her that no normal woman could possibly have forgotten such a man.

He stood well over six feet tall, wide-shouldered, lean of hip and long of leg, and he wore a dark pinstriped suit with a blue tie and white shirt. And he was, undeniably, absolutely breathtaking in the looks department. His hair was black and cropped short and it was the sort of thick springy hair that a woman wanted to run her fingers through. His bronzed features were all high cheekbones and interesting hollows, dissected by a narrow blade of a nose, while his wide sensual mouth was accentuated by the faint dark shadow of stubble surrounding it. His eyes, deep set and very dark and framed with lashes lush as black fans, were even more arresting and resting on her now with a piercing gleam. She could feel her skin heating because that appraisal could have stripped paint.

No, he *couldn't* be her husband, she decided immediately. He had to be some sleek, highly qualified consultant come to suss her out. Instinct seemed to be telling her that her husband would be a much more ordinary sort, maybe a bit homely, a bit tousled, but when his wife woke up after being in a coma, he would, at least, be smiling with relief and happiness. This guy didn't look as if he smiled very often. He was downright intimidating even in the way he stood there, radiating raw masculinity and authority.

'Brooke…' he murmured without any expression at all, walking in and shutting the door behind him and then those amazing eyes were locking to her again and it was a challenge to breathe. 'How are you feeling?'

Her heart was hammering so hard with nerves she felt her throat close over, her already sore throat, still tender from the removal of the breathing tube. But when he spoke, she froze in wonderment because his voice was familiar. 'I know your voice… I *know* your voice!' she gasped with a sense of attainment. 'In fact it's the first thing I've recognised since I woke up… but I don't recognise you. Who are you?'

'Lorenzo Tassini.'

'I'm *married* to *you*?' Brooke yelped in open disbelief.

Lorenzo's brows drew together. He was trying very hard not to stare at her because she was a vision of natural beauty, this woman he had married who had only shown him the ugliness she kept hidden on the inside. With her dishevelled hair hanging across her shoulders, framing her entrancing heart-shaped face, and those huge incredible dark blue, verging-on-violet eyes, she looked utterly angelic. And different, startlingly different, because he didn't think he had ever seen Brooke without her cosmetic enhancements. Brooke would climb out of bed at dawn to put her make-up on, no matter how often he had told her she didn't need it to look good.

But, of course, there were differences in her appearance. She was thinner, for a start, painfully thin in spite of the nourishing diet she had been fed by tube. She looked frail and somehow younger. The surgeons had restored her to perfection, but his acute gaze had already spotted the changes. Her mouth seemed a little wider, a little lusher in its pout, her nose shorter, less defined, and her eyes, those beautiful violet eyes were as bright and inquisitive as a bird's. And he had never ever seen such an expression on Brooke's face before. Brooke rarely showed emotion of any kind but, right now, he was seeing uncertainty, shock and intense curiosity fleeing across her face and it was a novelty for him to be able to interpret her feelings.

'Yes, you're married to me,' he confirmed flatly, recalling the doctor's warning, striving to abide by it when his conscience wanted him to throw the truth out there and be damned for it because he wanted no more lies between them. But if he told her about the divorce, he would lose her trust, her ability to depend on him, and she *needed* him right now. She needed to trust that he would not harm her and that she could rely on him because he knew there was no one else to take his place.

Brooke swallowed painfully and closed her eyes. A headache was beginning to pulse behind her brow. She was ridiculously tired for someone who had only been awake for a couple of hours.

'Would you like a drink?' Lorenzo prompted, lifting the glass with the straw in it.

'Yes…thanks.' Her eyes flickered open again and she sucked eagerly on the straw, the cool water easing her throat. 'I've got so many questions.'

'We'll answer them one by one.'

'But why don't I remember *you* when I remember your voice?' she exclaimed in frustration. 'How long have I been here? Nobody would tell me.'

'You've been here over a year.' Lorenzo watched her eyes round in further disbelief and once again savoured the newness of being able to read her face. 'After the first few weeks, when you failed to come out of it, the prognosis wasn't optimistic, so it is a source of great satisfaction for me to see you awake.'

'It *is*?' Brooke repeated, brightening in receipt of that acknowledgement. 'Then why don't you show it?'

'*Show* it?' He frowned.

'Smile, look happy. You walked in here looking like the Grim Reaper,' she told him, reddening at her boldness in being that blunt. 'I feel so alone here.'

Ramming his ever-present doubts about Brooke's veracity to the back of his mind, Lorenzo closed a hand over her limp fingers. 'But you're not alone.'

'Sit down beside me…here, on the bed,' she heard herself urge.

He looked as startled as if she had suggested he get into the bed with her and she stiffened in mortification. Instead of doing as she asked, he backed away and sank into the chair by the window. He was very reserved, she decided, adding to her first impression of him, not a guy who relaxed or who was easy with informality. It was impossible to imagine that she had ever been in bed with him and, at the thought, her face burned.

'How long have we been married?' she pressed.

'Three years now.'

Then, she had *definitely* been in bed with him, Brooke realised, and she would have squirmed with embarrassment had she had the ability to move normally. But nothing was normal about her body or her brain throwing up random embarrassing thoughts, she conceded ruefully, and nothing was normal about their situation either, and it had to be causing Lorenzo equal discomfort that he had a wife who didn't remember him.

'I'm sorry about all this. I'm sorry I don't know you and that I've caused you all this trouble.'

'You haven't caused me any trouble whatsoever,' Lorenzo lied, wondering what was wrong with her because Brooke's view of the world was generally one-sided. She didn't consider other people or their needs. She valued those around her strictly in accordance with the benefits they could bring her. She could be charm personified to get what she wanted but would then dispense with a person's services the instant she achieved her objective. But, of course, he reminded himself darkly, he *was* valuable to Brooke at this precise moment when she had nobody else to fall back on.

'It's kind of you to say that but all these months I've been lying here like a rock and I must've been the most awful worry for you,' she mumbled, her words slurring.

'I think you need to rest now,' Lorenzo told her, rising from his seat. 'I need to make arrangements for you to be moved to a more suitable facility where you can convalesce.'

Her head heavy, she turned her eyes back to him. 'I just want to go home,' she whispered weakly.

'I'm afraid that's not an option. Right now, you need a rehabilitation programme to regain your strength and medical support to deal with your amnesia,' Lorenzo explained smoothly.

'How did we meet?' she muttered drowsily, her brain spinning on and on, in spite of her exhaustion, wanting answers to countless questions.

'At a party in Nice. I was there on business.'

'You're a businessman?' she slurred.

'A banker,' he advanced.

'I don't like banks,' she mumbled, and then thought in surprise, Where did that thought come from?

Brows pleating, Lorenzo paused at the door to look back at her searchingly. 'Why don't you like banks?'

With an enormous effort she opened her eyes again and there he was, standing directly below the lights, his hair blue-black, his eyes transformed into liquid-gold pools of enquiry. He looked devastatingly handsome and she smiled at him sleepily. 'I don't know. It was just a random thought that came out of nowhere,' she admitted.

'Go to sleep, Brooke,' he urged. 'I'll see you tomorrow.'

'No kiss goodbye?'

Lorenzo froze at what struck him as an almost childlike question, which was laughable, he told himself, for anyone acquainted with Brooke's past history. 'No kiss. You're too sleepy and I like my women awake.'

'That's mean,' she mumbled.

Lorenzo stood at the foot of the bed watching her sleep. He should've been on the phone looking into convalescent facilities. He should've been seeking out a top psychiatrist to treat her. He should've told her that he wouldn't see her tomorrow because he was flying to Milan for an international banking conference. But he did none of those sensible things. He stood and he watched her sleep, feeling guilty at leaving her but all the while thinking in rampant disbelief that he might have married Brooke, but suddenly he was feeling as though he didn't know *her* either. Everyone had layers, he told himself irritably. Maybe this was how Brooke was when she was unsure of herself and no longer knew who she was. Restored to her fantastic wardrobe and her make-up and her headlines, she would once again become the woman he remembered.

* * *

Brooke sank into a seat in front of Mr Selby, her psychiatrist, and stowed the stick she was using. After a physio session she was always very sore and the slight limp she still had made her clumsy as she tired towards the end of the day, but she didn't complain because just being able to walk again felt like a precious enough gift.

'How have you been over the last few days?' the psychiatrist enquired over the top of his eccentric half-moon glasses.

'Great, but no flashes, no memories yet,' she said uneasily. 'Everything still feels so strange. Lorenzo brought me this giant metal case of cosmetics to replace the one that was destroyed in the accident and I think he was expecting me to be ecstatic, but I couldn't identify half the stuff in the box. I used a bit of it for his next visit. I didn't want him to think his present was a disappointment.'

'You seem to care about Lorenzo a great deal,' her companion remarked.

'Surely that's healthy when I'm married to him?' Brooke replied.

'Of course, you've been forced to depend on him, but it will be even more healthy for you to embrace a little independence as you recover your physical strength.'

Brooke's nod of acknowledgement was stiff. Over the past two months, she had learned just to let advice she didn't relish pass over her head. Everyone she met in the rehabilitation centre seemed to want to give her advice. She had dealt with surprise after surprise since her arrival. She had discovered that she was married to an extremely wealthy man and piece by piece she had learned that, before the crash, she had been a minor celebrity, a known fashion icon and often a source of media interest.

Those revelations hadn't felt natural to her and hadn't seemed to fit in very well with the quieter, less confident image she had slowly been developing of herself. But when she asked Lorenzo when she could go on the Internet to research her own previous life, he had insisted that it would be the wrong thing to do and that her memories would have a much better chance of returning if they weren't forced.

'What will I do if the memories never come back?'

'You will rebuild yourself. You've been very lucky. Your injury was severe, but you have no other on-going problems,' Mr Selby reminded her bracingly.

Except a husband she *still* couldn't remember, a reality that tormented Brooke every time he visited her. But he wasn't able to visit her as often as he had hoped because he was an exceptionally busy banker, who went abroad several times a month. And her initial impression of Lorenzo had been spot on in its accuracy. He *was* very reserved. He rarely touched her in even the most fleeting way. It was a little as though she had an invisible force field around her, she conceded with a regretful grimace. Obviously he was deeply uncomfortable with the fact that she didn't remember him but his hands-off approach wasn't helping her to feel any closer to him. It was a subject she needed to tackle…and soon, she told herself ruefully.

He hadn't walked away while she was in a coma, so why was he keeping his distance now? Did he love her? Did he still find her attractive? Or was their marriage in trouble?

She agonised over the options in the giant box of make-up because he was coming to see her that evening. She even leafed through the totally impractical garments he had had brought to her, which hung in the wardrobe, and selected a dress because greeting Lorenzo in the yoga pants that she wore for physio sessions hadn't got her anywhere. Lorenzo was used to a fashion queen, so she would strive to please and maybe that would warm him up.

Her skin heating at that enterprising thought, she did her face and put on the electric-blue dress that she thought was hideously bright, almost neon in shade, but presumably she had bought it and liked it once. She slid into it and then embarked on the matching shoes. She wasn't supposed to wear heels yet but she wouldn't be moving around much, which was just as well because the shoes pinched painfully at the toes.

Lorenzo stepped out of his chauffeur-driven limo and studied the modern building with disfavour as he braced himself for another visit to his wife. If she didn't recover her memories soon, he was likely to be forced to the point of telling her the truth about their marriage. And the psychiatrist had warned him that Brooke wasn't ready to deal with that reality, that he had become her 'safe place' and if that support was suddenly withdrawn, it might well disrupt her fragile mental state and send her hurtling back into panic mode, which would set back the recovery process.

He was already in major conflict with his lawyers' warnings. They didn't take a humane approach to the situation he was in, merely cautioning him that frequent visits to his estranged wife would only convince a judge that granting him a divorce would get in the way of what could be viewed as a potential reconciliation. And he didn't want to do that, no, he definitely did not *want* to stay married to Brooke. There had to be a hard limit to his compassion and care. But that wasn't what was really bothering him, was it?

He wanted her: that was the *real* problem. In fact, he lusted after her more, it seemed, than he had ever lusted after her. Why? Because she was different, *so* different he couldn't believe it sometimes and, quite ridiculously, he *liked* her now. How was that possible? Logic told him that he was seeing Brooke as she might have been before the lust for fame and the infatuation with her own beauty had taken hold of her. Even more shockingly, Brooke *au naturel* was a class act.

Only he didn't *think* it was an act any longer because he was convinced that the woman he remembered could never ever have carried off that outstanding mix of artless naivety and innocence she showed him. In short, Brooke was all sorts of things she had never been before with him…caring, unselfish, undemanding. She had made him like her again, but he was determined not to be sucked back into that swamp a second time, he reminded himself grimly. She was recovering well and soon he would be able to cut their ties again and slot her into that penthouse apartment.

Lorenzo strode in and Brooke leapt upright at speed, wanting him to see that she had made the effort, wanting him to see that she was truly getting back to normal...*and* ready to go home.

'You look...more like yourself this evening,' Lorenzo commented as she regarded him expectantly.

Her violet eyes, bright with what he recognised as excitement, unsettled him.

'I think I'm ready to leave here...to come home,' she told him urgently. 'I'm sure it would be better for me to be in a familiar place. They're very kind to me here but I'm going crazy cooped up like this and it's so boring and uneventful. Your visits are the only highlights in my week.'

With difficulty, Lorenzo mastered his consternation. 'I'll speak to your doctors tomorrow. We don't want to rush into anything. After all, you couldn't even walk two months ago.'

'I'm getting stronger every day!' Brooke argued. 'Why don't you see that?'

'I *do* see it,' Lorenzo countered levelly. 'But until you recover your memory, it's too risky.'

Brooke's hands coiled into tight fists, the sudden burst of temper that ignited inside her an explosion of the frustration she had been fighting off for days. 'Am I going to stay here for ever, then, as a patient?'

she exclaimed angrily. 'Because I've already been told, and you must also know, that I might *never* get my memory back!'

Lorenzo gritted his teeth. He did know that, but he had confidently put the warning to the back of his mind because every time he saw her, he expected to see her change back into the woman he remembered. 'Sit down,' he urged. 'We'll discuss this calmly.'

Brooke dropped down on the side of the bed. Lorenzo studied her. She had been all built up to ask him to take her home and now she was upset, and he felt as if he was being cruel even though he knew that he had no other choice. Sitting there, she was a picture with her tangled ringlets half concealing her piquant face, the faint pout of her luscious pink mouth, the long length of her legs displayed to perfection in that dress and those shoes. A punch of lust tightened his groin and he tensed, willing back his desire, fighting for control. The yoga pants had driven him crazy, showing every curve, every indent, but Lorenzo wasn't easily tempted, not where Brooke was concerned, and he had fought that reaction every rigorous step of the way. He stood by the window gazing out at the tranquil courtyard garden in the centre of the building, striving to calm himself.

'Before the accident…' Brooke began hesitantly. 'Our marriage was in trouble, wasn't it?'

At that moment she didn't want the positive answer she suspected to be her new reality. Even so, she felt she still had to ask and had to be strong enough to confront such an unwelcome truth because, in that scenario, pretending wasn't fair to either of them.

Disconcerted, Lorenzo froze in position. 'What makes you think that?' he enquired in a deliberately mild tone.

'It doesn't take a rocket scientist,' she framed a little unevenly. 'You never touch me unless you can't avoid it. You never mention anything personal and if I ask questions in that line you stall. You don't want me home either. Just be honest, Lorenzo. I *can* take it. And then, just go home or back to the bank because you seem to work eighteen hours a day.'

Lorenzo almost ground his teeth in frustration. It would have been the perfect moment to speak had he not had to consider her condition. He glanced across at her and saw the tears shimmering like sunshine on water in her eyes.

Angrily aware of the tears prickling, Brooke dashed them away with an impatient hand. 'Stop treating me like a child, stop choosing your words. I'm twenty-eight years old, for goodness' sake, not a little girl! It's bad enough not remembering stuff, but it's a *torment* to be sitting here wondering all the time what sort of relationship we have…'

In disconcertion, Lorenzo strode forward just as she leapt up in haste, determined not to cry in front of him. 'Just go home!' she told him fiercely as she headed for the door and the sanctuary of the patients' lounge. 'I'll see you another day—'

But she tried to move too fast in the high heels and her weaker leg flailed and tipped her over. She was within inches of crashing down painfully on the hard floor when Lorenzo snatched her up, lifting her clean off her tottering feet and settling her down in front of him in the circle of his arms. The scent of him that close was like an aphrodisiac to her senses, an inner clenching down in her pelvis instantly responding. She closed her arms round his neck because she had decided that if he couldn't even kiss her, obviously he no longer felt attracted to her, and she would get her answer to how he felt about her one way or another.

Lorenzo collided with her wonderfully unusual eyes and, involuntarily, he bent down and kissed her, damning himself for even that momentary surrender. But he was too clever by half with women not to guess that she was giving him the green light to test him. One brief kiss and nobody was catching it on camera, he reminded himself, and then her soft, succulent mouth opened invitingly under his and suddenly all bets were off because the taste of her went to his head and his groin like a bushfire licking out of control.

She tasted like…she tasted like… His primal nature threatened to take over, almost made him forget that since she had lost her memory this was their *first* kiss as far as she was concerned. Quite deliberately he tried to rein himself back. But Brooke was still blown off her feet by the explosion of passion Lorenzo delivered with his mouth. His lips were hard and urgent and demanding, somehow everything she had been craving without realising it for endless weeks, and he crushed her to his tall, powerful frame.

It was off-the-charts exciting.

Her hands bit into his broad shoulders to keep her upright while the intoxicating chemistry of his mouth on hers left her breathless and dizzy and afflicted with all sorts of reactions that felt entirely new to her. Of course, they couldn't be new to her, but her heart was racing and her nipples became tight and almost sore in their sensitivity beneath her clothes. At the apex of her thighs, there was a burn, a sort of pulsing ache that inflamed her senses and, against her abdomen, she could feel the literal effect she was having on Lorenzo as well and somehow that shocked her when it shouldn't have done.

Indeed, for Brooke, Lorenzo's sizzling kiss was the first true gift she had had in all the weeks of her frustrating convalescence while she worried and wondered about who she truly was and wondered even harder how Lorenzo wanted her to behave. She was in constant conflict, struggling between what little she knew about her past self and the newer and equally unknown self that often prompted her to behave differently. But that kiss restored her equilibrium. It was *acceptance*, it was proof positive that her husband *still* wanted her and that she had been fretting herself into a state about nothing.

As he lowered Brooke down onto the bed and broke their connection with a slight shudder of recoil, Lorenzo was reminded very much of a saying a teacher of his had been fond of recounting to him: 'between a rock and a hard place'. 'Damned if you do, damned if you don't,' struck him as more apt. Still, what was one kiss? he reasoned wrathfully, instantly going into damage-limitation mode and stepping back from her. He was awesomely aware of the arousal he couldn't hide below the finely tailored trousers, the coolness he couldn't yet slide into place, and so furious with himself for succumbing to her again that his lean brown hands clenched into fists.

Lorenzo had once liked to pride himself on being an unemotional man like his late father but the unemotional man who had married Brooke had discovered otherwise. He had felt *tortured* by the endless dramas and he had shut that weak and disturbing part of himself away again, closed it down, re-embraced his calm, his control, his...sanity. He wasn't going back there, no, not even for the sake of honour or decency!

'That was wonderful.' Brooke gave him a huge smile, utterly impervious to his feelings at that moment. 'I feel so much better about us.'

'Good,' Lorenzo gritted between his perfect teeth, because it felt like another nail in his coffin that she had come alive in his arms as she never had before. He was in shock, he conceded, acknowledging the fact that Brooke had never kissed him back that way in their entire acquaintance, had never shown him an atom of the desire he had assumed she had for him when he married her. He shook his handsome dark head slightly as though to clear it. She was *so* different, but hadn't the doctors warned him of that possibility?

He trained his dark deep gaze on her. 'I'm not an emotional man, Brooke.'

'You don't really need to tell me that. It's kind of obvious,' Brooke pointed out. 'You've never shown me any emotion in your visits and it worried me about us but obviously we managed to get married anyway and right now I can see how tense you are.'

Lorenzo was starting to feel like the accused in the dock. 'I'm not tense,' he insisted.

But the tension was engraved in his lean, darkly handsome features, Brooke recognised with relief. Lorenzo might be locked up tight in his reserve, but he had shown her wonderfully strong emotion in that kiss…*hadn't he*? Or had that only been sexual hunger? And why didn't she know the difference? The way she seemed to just know other things? Like the names of the seasons, the days of the week? She swallowed hard, afraid to get carried away by her expectations of him, afraid to expect too much.

'Will you bring me home this week?' she just asked him baldly. 'I'm ready even if the doctors fuss about the idea. I can't stay here for ever…unless that's what you'd prefer?'

That anxious question shot through Lorenzo much like a whip because he could see the stress and the level of concern she was trying, very poorly, to hide from him, and he marvelled all over again at the complete absence of her once unrevealing shuttered expressions. 'Of course not,' he responded by rote. 'I'll speak to them.'

Content to have received that response, Brooke slid off the bed and walked over to him. 'I won't be any trouble to anyone. It's not like I'm depressed or mentally troubled in some way. I've only lost my memory. I just want my life…' *and* my husband, she added inwardly, 'back.'

Suddenly, Lorenzo found himself smiling at the almost enthralling prospect of reuniting Brooke with her wardrobe, her jewellery and her precious scrapbooks and files of headlines and articles. Nothing surely was more likely to revive her memory than her possessions and her media triumphs? What the hell had he hoped to achieve when he kept her in a sterile medical environment? Deprived of everything she valued and enjoyed in life? Nothing in the private clinic was familiar to her and nothing here would appeal to her tastes. In such a place there was no stimulation that could help her to recover her memory. *Sì…* He would take her to her supposed home and in all likelihood she would recover there and remember that she hated him. He could bear a few more weeks—*couldn't he?*

Even more enchanted by his rare smile, Brooke went pink. She had virtually thrown herself at him and, while it had taken a lot of initiative to act that way with him and had felt horribly pushy, the ploy had indisputably worked. As long as she didn't mention their marriage or love or anything of that nature, Lorenzo could handle it, but for the first time she was questioning what in their marriage or in his background had made him so uncomfortable about ordinary feelings.

CHAPTER THREE

IN THE LIMOUSINE that wafted her down the long drive-way towards the giant building that sat at the bottom, Brooke sat wide-eyed with wonder but striving to conceal the fact. It seemed that she was married to a man who was very much wealthier than she had understood, and that was a shock too. But acting shocked got old quickly and she was slowly trying to learn how to school her face into less revealing reactions every time she got a surprise about herself. This was *her* life, after all, she reminded herself soothingly, *her* home.

And Madrigal Court was gorgeous, she thought helplessly, as the sunlight glinted off the rows of windows and the old brick with its intricate designs and so many chimneys—a country house that must've been hundreds of years old. Tudor? she wondered with a frown, disconcerted to find that term popping up in the back of her brain. Seemingly she knew more about old buildings than she had assumed, or could it have been a memory? She was desperate to recall something concrete: an event, an image, a face, a fact, anything really, she acknowledged ruefully, but so far there had been nothing and that had to be incredibly frustrating for Lorenzo.

Without even thinking about it, she reached for his hand because she had been so very flattered that he had taken a day off to share her homecoming with her. She was extremely conscious that he worked very hard and for very long hours and she thought that might have been why she had concentrated equally hard, it seemed, to make a separate role and career for herself. Clearly, Lorenzo had married a strong, independent and confident woman and Brooke was desperately trying to shore up those traits in herself.

There would be no clinging, no whinging, when he disappeared abroad for days at a time, no mention of the truth that she missed him terribly when he was gone. He wouldn't want to hear that kind of stuff and he would be disappointed in her. And hadn't he had enough disappointment already, sufficient to end many a marriage, she reminded herself, when his wife wakened and didn't know him from a stranger in the street?

Totally shocked by that gesture, Lorenzo flicked a covert black-lashed glance down at their linked hands and breathed in deep and slow to embrace calm. His enthralling vision of her walking into her wardrobe and shrieking in delight, 'I'm home!' still refused to retreat. But this new version of Brooke didn't shriek, and her voice was low-pitched, just one of the many, many changes in her that unsettled him. It was almost as though she had had a personality transplant, he mused. *Per Dio*, she had *cried* when he told her that her parents had passed away before he met her and that she had no other relatives, nobody, who could fill in the blanks of the memory loss she was enduring now. Of course, there might be photos of her family somewhere in Brooke's stuff, he reflected hopefully, because he knew that would please her.

At her request, he had retrieved her wedding ring from the home safe and she had threaded it on as though it were something special, not the plain band that she had originally dismissed as 'not very imaginative'. Nothing that didn't glitter with valuable jewels had once incited Brooke's admiration.

She listened to his advice now as well. She hadn't asked for a phone or even the Internet again, which impressed him as being even more weird, for Brooke had *lived* on her phone. How could she not be missing it? Of course, she didn't know *who* or what she had to miss, did she? Lorenzo's lean bronzed face hardened. Not least the very married film star who had recently had an aide contact Lorenzo to enquire after his wife's health, evidently having heard a rumour that Brooke was recovering from the accident. Lorenzo suspected there had been an affair between them, but he reminded himself that Brooke's sex life was, thankfully, no longer any of his business. They might remain legally married but there was nothing deeper involved.

Brooke walked up the worn stone steps into the

house and smiled at the middle-aged man opening the door for their arrival. 'And you are?'

'Stevens, madam,' the older man supplied in surprise.

'Thank you,' she said quietly, moving indoors and stopping dead to take in the big imposing entrance hall made cosy by the low fire burning in the ancient fireplace to one side. 'Oh, this is beautiful!' she claimed, startling Lorenzo.

'You hated this house,' Lorenzo heard himself murmur in soft contradiction. 'You wanted a modern home, a McMansion. I refused to move because this was my mother's family home and, although I never knew her, I enjoyed the knowledge that she had once lived here.'

'*Hated* it?' Brooke exclaimed in disbelief, spinning round to look at him. 'I don't think that's possible.'

Watching her flounder with uncertainty as soon as she had spoken and accepted that such a former attitude was perfectly possible, Lorenzo registered his error in being that honest and at speed he strode over to a door to throw it wide. 'Lots of married couples have different tastes.' He dismissed that hint of contention smoothly. 'This room is more your style.'

What style? Brooke almost asked for every piece of furniture was gilded and the drapes, the upholstery and even the carpet were pristine white. Even the vase of flowers on the low table was filled with white blooms. In her opinion, it was stark and uninviting, but it certainly gave a striking effect.

'And this is you...' Lorenzo indicated the large

professional photograph on the wall in which she posed on the same sofa for a *Dream House* magazine interview she had, according to him, given only weeks before the accident.

Brooke stared in fascination at the woman in the photograph and her fingers went up to pluck uneasily at her loose ringlets as she studied that smooth straight fall of hair in the image. 'I should be straightening my hair!' she gasped suddenly.

'I like it natural,' Lorenzo dared to impart.

'Honestly?' she queried tautly as she stared at that flawlessly groomed, almost inhumanly perfect image with a sinking heart. It was undeniably her, but it was *not* the version of her that she was currently providing him with.

'Honestly.'

In that moment, Brooke felt overwhelmed. Coming home was proving more of a challenge than she had expected. Was it possible that the head injury had altered her tastes? She supposed it was. When she had expressed her concern about such changes to Mr Selby, he had been very reassuring, never failing to remind her that she was lucky to be alive and relatively unscathed as if the loss of her every memory from childhood was something she simply had to accept. And perhaps it was, and there was nothing less attractive than self-pity, she told herself fiercely, moving back into the hall.

'Let's go upstairs,' Lorenzo urged. 'I'll show you your room.'

Your room, Brooke noted. 'Don't we share?'

Lorenzo cast her a lazy, careless smile because he was fully rehearsed on that answer. 'You like your own space and you often took your stylist up there to decide on outfits. Sharing wasn't practical.'

'You know more about my life than I know about yours,' Brooke couldn't help commenting.

'I don't think that there's anything in the world of finance that would interest you,' Lorenzo parried. 'Unless, of course, you've decided to set up a business or something of that nature.'

'Not just at the minute, no,' she quipped, breathing in deep.

So, separate bedrooms, little wonder Lorenzo was so physically detached from her and prone to treating her as though she were a friend rather than a wife. Even though they lived in an enormous house, they didn't seem to share much as a couple. Not a bed, not taste, not their lives. It was unhealthy but perhaps Lorenzo liked his marriage that way even if it didn't appeal to her, she ruminated worriedly. How had she let the man she loved move so far from her in every way?

Obviously she loved him. She couldn't believe that she would have married him for any other reason. His money, his giant house and his servants all made her feel intimidated. But *he* didn't intimidate her, he made her…happy. Mr. Selby had urged her to think about whether or not that was just her insecurity talking and had asked her how she could possibly still love a man she didn't remember. But she knew that she did in the same way she knew that the sun would rise in the morning. She had remembered Lorenzo's voice and it was the *only* thing she remembered, which to her signified and proved his overwhelming importance in her life.

Brooke walked into another blindingly white room, but this time it was a bedroom and she decided that the absence of colour did give a certain feel of tranquillity.

'And then there's your favourite place,' Lorenzo proclaimed, casting wide another door.

Brooke froze on the threshold of an amazing dressing room. But it was so big, so packed with stuff it didn't really qualify for that description. Racks and racks of shoes and bags lined the walls in glass cabinets. Rails and rails of zingy, colourful garments hung in readiness. It was a feast of conspicuous consumerism, a rebuttal of the 'less is more' mentality, and she thought, Oh, dear heaven, I'm greedy and extravagant and spoilt rotten! And then a calmer voice switched on inside her, reminding her that being a fashion icon had sort of been her job. She forced herself deeper into the room to browse through the clothes, hoping for something to jar her memory, glancing at labels and surprised that she only recognised the household names of famous designers that everyone knew. In the general knowledge sense, her fashion antenna seemed to be running on an empty tank.

'Of course, you'll have to throw it all out.'

Brooke whirled, violet eyes huge. *'Throw it out?'* she gasped incredulously.

'Because everything in here is old and out of fashion now.' Lorenzo tossed out that award-winning lure with deep satisfaction because he had already worked out how best to occupy his soon-to-be ex-wife. 'Your wardrobe is out of date. You'll need to start from scratch again and replace it all.'

'But that would be horribly wasteful,' Brooke framed in disbelief, fingering through a rack of jeans, searching for an ordinary pair but finding only slashed, sparkly or embroidered ones, marvelling that her former self had apparently never succumbed to a desire to simply wear something comfortable.

'It's the way that you live.' Lorenzo shrugged, brilliant, thickly lashed dark eyes cynical and assured. 'Every season you start again, so I imagine you'll be shopping until you drop for weeks.'

Brooke nodded jerkily since it seemed to be what he expected from her. 'It seems a very extravagant way to live,' she remarked uneasily.

'I can well afford extravagant,' Lorenzo intoned, wondering why she wasn't one bit excited at the prospect of shopping, wondering why she looked kind of lost standing there in the middle of the room, rather like a little girl contemplating a giant dress-up box that frightened her. This was Brooke's world, from the fashion magazines piled on the coffee table to the immaculate shoe collection. And she *didn't* recognise any of it, he acknowledged grimly.

At least now, she could explore her life, Brooke reminded herself, for there had to be personal things tucked away somewhere within the two rooms, surely photos of her late parents and that kind of stuff, she reasoned as Lorenzo departed. As for the fashion end of things, she clearly wasn't able to become a fashion icon again in her current state of mind and she would just have to move on from that and find something else to keep her busy. Reinventing yourself was all the rage these days, she reminded herself dully. It was not as though she had a choice when she couldn't imagine wearing a see-through lace dress or jeans that exposed her bottom cheeks.

That reflection, however, threw yet another obstacle into her path. Almost certainly that more audacious woman was the woman Lorenzo knew and had chosen to marry. Brooke paled at that acknowledgement. A *sexier* woman. Was that the common denominator at the heart of her marriage? That together sexier Brooke and more reserved Lorenzo meshed like magnets? Was that why Lorenzo was now so distant with her? Because she wasn't putting out the right vibes any longer with her clothing and her manner? Well, she was just going to have to fake it, wasn't she?

What do you know about being sexy? she asked herself limply. But she had to *know* those things to make such daring clothing choices! She relived that kiss and a slow burn reignited low in her pelvis and she shifted restlessly. Maybe she was sexier in bed than she imagined and when it happened it would all just come seamlessly together for her…but what if it didn't? What if her apparent stock of general knowledge didn't include the bedroom stuff? What if she lay there like a graven image and freaked him out? And why was she even having these thoughts, she asked herself, when to date even getting a kiss out of Lorenzo had entailed practically falling on him? Maybe *she* was the partner who made all the sexy, inviting moves, she thought anxiously, and if that was true, the onus would be on *her*…

Perhaps Lorenzo had simply been waiting to bring her home, she reasoned, and tonight, when she was tucked up in bed, he would visit?

CHAPTER FOUR

'I'D LIKE SOME details about the accident,' Brooke declared over dinner two weeks later.

'I don't think that's a good idea,' Lorenzo informed her lazily.

For the first time ever, Brooke wanted to slap her husband for still treating her like a vulnerable child to be protected from every ill wind. 'I disagree. Since I wasn't driving—I mean, you told me that—who *was* driving?'

'An employee. I'm afraid that he died,' Lorenzo told her smoothly.

Brooke lost colour and stilled. 'Oh, how dreadful! I should go and see his family. Will you give me the address?' she pressed.

'He didn't have a family as such. He lived with an elderly mother. I've ensured that she is financially secure. You don't need to get involved,' Lorenzo assured her.

'I think the least I can do is visit his mother to offer my condolences,' Brooke responded firmly.

Lorenzo almost rolled his eyes at this new caring, sharing display of Brooke's. He compressed his hard mouth. Every time he saw her, she annoyed him by being so beautiful, so...*tempting*. There she sat, hair foaming in ringlets and cascading round her like some cartoon mermaid, triangular face bare of cosmetics, violet eyes bright and friendly and natural and, in truth, she remained drop-dead gorgeous. Yet she was wearing jeans, simple plain jeans, and flat shoes. She was another almost unrecognisable incarnation of Brooke and one he didn't intend to waste time on because the transformation wouldn't, *couldn't* possibly last. Inevitably, her indomitable will, her piranha-fish appetites for sex, media exposure and money would resurface and he, for one, would be a great deal happier.

He didn't want to be reminded of that treacherous kiss in the clinic when he had inexplicably contrived to overlook all the other men she had betrayed him with. Of that kiss, it was enough to recall that she had burned him alive and filled him with a hunger he refused to satisfy. He was even more astonished that she could *still* have that effect on him. Only days before the accident he had enjoyed the definitive proof that he was completely impervious to her looks and her seductive wiles. He could only suppose that being forced into a protective role for so long with his estranged wife had somehow softened his previous hard shell of cold disinterest. After all, he had never been the kind of foolish man who returned to explore his worst mistake and that was what Brooke genuinely was to him: *his worst mistake*.

'Do you want the full story of the accident? Even if it's distressing?' he prompted, reminding himself that keeping such secrets from her wasn't doing anything to help her adapt to her return to the land of the living.

Feeling a little threatened now and worried about what he might have held back from her, Brooke nodded urgently. 'Yes.'

'There was another woman in the limo with you and she died as well. We don't know what she was doing with you because, although I looked into her history before the funeral, I couldn't see anything relevant that would have brought you together that day.'

Brooke's smooth brow furrowed. 'That's a puzzle. Who was she?'

'She was a waitress in a London café, although she'd quit her job that same day, quoting a family emergency, but when I investigated it turned out that she had no family and there was nothing of interest about her,' Lorenzo recounted with a fluid Italian shrug of dismissal. 'I suppose we'll never know what she was doing in the car with you that day unless you regain your memory.'

Brooke was troubled by the discovery that some mystery woman had been with her on the day of the crash. She had already discovered a severe absence of personal possessions in her bedroom. She had waded through a dozen files packed with press clippings and some rather suggestive headlines, depicting her with other men in nightclubs, but she hadn't found a single picture of her parents or indeed of anyone else.

Her life, evidently, had been lived solely through the media and nothing else had much mattered to her, and that saddened her because her previous existence now seemed shallow to her and empty of real purpose.

As for her marriage, she ruminated regretfully, it didn't appear to be much healthier than her lifestyle had been because she barely saw Lorenzo except at the dinner table. When she had made the effort to rise at dawn to breakfast with him, he had not seemed remotely appreciative of her company and had buried his nose back in the *Financial Times*, the one and only media publication that came to the house.

It was ironic that she had actually been spending more personal time with her husband when he had been visiting her at the clinic. Now that she was back home, he was perfectly polite and pleasant, but it was almost as if she didn't really exist on his terms, which was weird, *wasn't it*?

But everything was weird in their relationship, she conceded wretchedly. Why didn't he sleep with her? Why didn't he want sex when popular parlance suggested that men always wanted sex? What was wrong with her? Or what was wrong with their marriage? She had tried to ignore the signs that something was not quite right but after a fortnight of being treated like a house guest rather than a wife, Brooke felt that she could no longer disregard suspicions that were a deep source of concern to her. After all, if Lorenzo didn't want her any more, what was she doing living in *his* house? Obviously she could only be uncomfortable with the fear that she wasn't truly welcome below the roof of the place she had mistakenly assumed was her true home.

'Why do you never take me out anywhere with you?' Brooke asked with a directness she had not dared to utilise with Lorenzo before.

Lorenzo glanced up from his plate, beautiful dark deep-set eyes shrewd and level, and she experienced that same maddening little prickling of awareness that his gaze always evoked and her heart started to thump faster inside her tight chest. 'We've always had separate social lives. And, unhappily, if we *are* seen in public together, you would be mobbed by the paparazzi because you are the former beauty maven who has now returned from the dead and many people are very curious about you. I don't like press attention in my private life…however, you do.'

'Oh…' Brooke breathed, crushed by those truths delivered so instantaneously. 'You think there might be headlines?'

'I *know* there would be. Brooke…' Lorenzo sighed and lounged back in his chair, devastatingly good-looking and infuriatingly calm. 'There have been cameras waiting at the foot of the drive to catch a photo of you since the day I brought you home. If you'd even once gone shopping, you would've seen them there. Maybe you don't feel like having that media attention right now?'

'I don't,' she confirmed.

'But it's still a very large part of who you used to be,' Lorenzo reminded her. 'And the paps aren't going to give up and go away any time soon.'

Having dealt that final blow, Lorenzo left for the Tassini Bank while Brooke retired to her white bedroom to read a book she had bought online about Italians, seeking in some small way to redress her ignorance of her husband. But there seemed little point reading about how Italians highly valued their families and seeking such a trait in Lorenzo. He was diligent in assuring that her medical needs were covered with regular online sessions with Mr Selby and physio sessions with a personal trainer, but his care never ever got more personal than that. She was fed, housed, clothed, medicated and that was that.

Along with jeans and casual tops, she had bought a dress, low-necked, short and scarlet in hue, and high heels. She viewed the more decorative fitted outfit as a move forward, a first step in becoming the woman whom Lorenzo obviously expected her to be. Now, sadly, she wasn't even sure she would have the nerve to wear it because he had shut her down again.

Two other people had died in that accident and *she* had survived. She was much luckier than she had ever appreciated, and she knew that her first outing would include a visit to the driver's mother and a respectful call at the cemetery to the grave of the woman who had been with her that day. Maybe she had been a friend, Brooke reflected sadly, for she could hardly have failed to note that she didn't seem to have friends in the way that other women had. Hadn't she liked other women? Hadn't other women liked her? The lack of a friend or relative to turn to sometimes made her feel very alone…

Blasted self-pity, she told herself off firmly, and returned to her book while wondering if she had the nerve to wear that dress for dinner and whether Lorenzo would even notice what she wore, because he didn't seem to look at her that much.

Just then, however, when she was least expecting it, the door literally burst open and she jerked bolt upright on top of the bed, her violet eyes wide with surprise.

The very image of innocence, Lorenzo thought in a rage as he strode across the room to slap the newspaper he had bought for that purpose down on the foot of the bed. The lurid headline ran: *She Doesn't Know Who She Is!*

He was furious with himself most of all for starting to trust her again even though he knew she was a liar and a manipulator. It wasn't like him to lose his temper, but when he had seen that newspaper headline, he had felt betrayed, and then he had wondered *why* he felt betrayed when Brooke was only doing what she had always done in seeking to shape her public image and stoke press interest. He should've been better prepared, should've expected such behaviour from her. It was his own fault that he felt as though she had deceived him. When, after all, had he begun to forget what kind of a woman she was?

'I should've guessed that you'd have your own more direct but *sly* way of dealing with the media!' Lorenzo fired down at her.

Brooke was frozen to the spot in disbelief by his behaviour because Lorenzo had never once raised his voice to her before. But at this moment, he was ferociously angry with her and it showed in every honed, hard lineament of his lean, darkly handsome features. 'Go on...look at the article and tell me you're not responsible for this outrage!' he challenged with contempt.

Trembling, Brooke lifted the tabloid newspaper, shaken to see the photo of her in the blue dress she had worn at the clinic now adorning the front page. She recalled the friendly nurse who had asked if she could take a picture on her phone. Brooke had said yes, had believed that it was the dress that the woman was interested in. She hadn't known enough about safeguarding herself from such exploitation to say, no, sorry, she conceded in dismay. So, it *was* absolutely her fault, just as Lorenzo believed, that that picture was in a newspaper.

'Obviously it was more than your vanity could bear to have the press speculating that you could be scarred or in a wheelchair!' Lorenzo bit out in raw condemnation. 'You tell me you don't want media attention and then you do...*this*? You give an interview to them? *Madre di Dio*, why the hell am I acting surprised?'

'An interview?' she whispered, turning the page with shaking fingers, intimidated more than she liked to admit by his sheer dark fury. There was more volatile emotion than she had ever thought he possessed emanating from him and lacing the atmosphere with brutal tension. Unfortunately, it wasn't how she would've wanted to discover that he was

much more emotional in nature than he was prepared to show.

'*Sì*, an interview. While I'm busy hiring extra security to *protect* you, you're still feeding the fire to
gain the attention you crave from your admirers!'

Brooke took a mental step back from the toweringly
tall, dark man raging over her and concentrated on the
article. She was quick to recognise that stray com-
ments she had made and medical info that should've
been kept confidential had been cobbled together and
leaked in the form of an interview that had been faked.
'I didn't give anyone an interview, Lorenzo. I did let
one of the nurses take a photo of me and I'm sorry
she gave it to the press, but I didn't exactly know who
I was supposed to be then or that I shouldn't allow
that,' she confided uncomfortably. 'Read it properly
and you'll see I'm telling the truth. It's a *fake* interview.
I wouldn't want people to know that I'm suffering from
amnesia because that's embarrassing—'

'Unfortunately for you,' Lorenzo countered gla-
cially, 'I already know that I can't trust a word you
say because you're a gifted liar. You lie about the
most ridiculous things and then shrug indifferently
when the truth comes out. I've never been able to
trust you!'

While Brooke had contrived to remain calm and
in control while Lorenzo vented his wrath over a
naïve mistake she had made, those words fell on her
like hand grenades that exploded on contact with her
shrinking body. In shock, she drew up her knees and
hugged them. All her natural colour had gone into re-

treat while her tummy stirred sickly. She had told her husband lies and he had found her out in them? *She* was a liar? It dawned on her then that for the very *first* time Lorenzo was giving her what he deemed to believe was the absolute truth about herself, yet only raw anger had drawn that honesty from him. For just a few minutes he had forgotten to treat her like someone too delicate to handle reality.

All of a sudden, she was being forced to face the fact that, regardless of how hard she had tried to explain away her husband's cool attitude towards her, their relationship *did* have problems. Indeed, Lorenzo saw her as a liar he couldn't trust. Shaken and appalled by that revelation, she rocked back and forth where she sat, struggling to deal with that new sobering knowledge.

Lorenzo stared down at her and then he blinked and the explosive rage that had powered him, most ironically a rage that had never once seized him with Brooke before, vanished as though it had never been. Stricken by what he had dumped on her in a temper, he came down on the side of the bed and hauled in a deep shuddering breath, cursing his lack of control and the damage he had inflicted. She looked so small, so lost, so unlike the woman he remembered, the woman he needed to *bury* and forget about because *that* version of Brooke might never return, he finally acknowledged.

'I'm sorry. I shouldn't have lost my temper,' Lorenzo conceded heavily and reached for her hand.

'When I saw that paper, a fuse just blew somewhere inside me *and*—'

'We're both living in a very stressful situation,' Brooke pointed out in a wobbly undertone. 'It's sure to be affecting you as well.'

Lorenzo didn't feel that he was in a stressful situation because naturally he was in possession of facts she had yet to learn. But he did feel guilty, horrendously guilty for shouting at her, condemning her and causing her distress. When her hand pulled away from his, rejecting that hold, he was disconcerted by that withdrawal.

'You don't need to pretend any longer, Lorenzo,' Brooke sighed in explanation. 'You've let the cat out of the bag. We don't have a good marriage, which actually explains *a lot*.'

Unprepared for that far-reaching conclusion being reached at such speed, Lorenzo hesitated only a moment before reaching across the bed and bundling her small resisting figure into his arms and settling her down across his long muscular thighs with an intimacy he had never dared to embrace before. 'No, it only explains that I have a terrible temper, which I usually manage to keep in check,' he breathed as he heard her swallow back the sobs making her tremble within his grasp. 'It doesn't mean anything.'

'But you said I was always telling lies and that you couldn't trust me!' Brooke sobbed outright.

Lorenzo was usually very fast at thinking on the back foot, as it were, but a quicksilver tongue somehow evaded him when he had Brooke struggling to hold back sobs in his arms. *He* had done that; *he* alone had distressed her to that extent. Yet she had borne every unsettling, scary development bravely from the outset of her recuperation. Even so, he had, and for the second time, reduced her to tears. He felt like a complete heel. When had he become so tough, bitter and selfish that he only went through the motions of giving her a roof over her head while at the same time utterly ignoring her presence in every other way? Of course, she had noticed that he wasn't behaving like a husband, of course she had become anxious about it.

'Did I lie about money?' Brooke whispered chokily. 'I mean, I can see by that wardrobe that I was kind of a bit...spendthrift.'

Lorenzo seized on that option with intense relief. He was rich enough to support a thousand spendthrift wives but rows over extravagance and lies concerning that extravagance were far less damaging to her self-image than the truth would be. 'Yes,' he confirmed, relieved to feel some of the jerking rigidity in her small frame drain away. 'Nothing I couldn't deal with, but you kept on doing it.'

'Well, I won't any more,' Brooke whispered shakily, the worst of her crushing anxiety draining away. 'I promise you, absolutely promise that I won't tell you any lies or spend too much money. There's no limit on those credit cards you gave me, is there?'

Lorenzo breathed in deep and slow. 'I don't think we need to worry about that now. You've only spent a couple of hundred pounds since you arrived,' he reminded her ruefully. 'Believe me, you can be a lot more spendthrift than that. I don't want you worrying about that either.'

'Maybe getting married to someone with money like you have sort of went to my head and I got carried away,' Brooke suggested thoughtfully.

Lorenzo registered the one salient fact that he should have shared with her sooner. 'No, you weren't penniless when I married you—your father left you a decent trust fund. He was an affluent wine importer and you were an only child.'

Brooke focused huge violet eyes on him as she flung her head back. 'I have money of my own?' she exclaimed incredulously.

'Yes, although we agreed when we married that I would take care of all the bills.'

But Brooke was still gripped by amazement that she had her own money. 'That really surprises me because I don't feel like I've ever had money. I suppose that sounds weird to you when I obviously have, but everything like the staff here and the limousines and the grandeur makes me feel…overwhelmed,' she finally confided. 'I assumed it was because I hadn't had time yet to become accustomed to your lifestyle.'

'Your parents weren't rich, only comfortably off,' Lorenzo suggested, the feel of her body heat, the brush of her breasts against his shirtfront and her proximity combining to increase the hard arousal thrumming at his groin and remind him of just how long it had been since he had had sex. As gently as he could, he scooped her up, rose upright and laid her back down on the bed. 'You should rest. I upset you.'

Brooke sat up again. 'I'm fine now. The nurse that took that photo was called Lizzie and if you read the supposed interview, you can see it's just put-together stuff aside of the amnesia.'

Lorenzo lifted the paper he had slapped down in front of her and spread his free hand, long brown fingers flexing. 'My temper went off like a rocket. I didn't read it and I'll inform the clinic about the nurse.'

'I don't want her to get in trouble!' Brooke protested.

'She sold a photo of you and revealed confidential medical facts. The clinic needs to protect their patients,' Lorenzo murmured smoothly, still incensed by the condemnation he had immediately laid at his wife's door and the distress the episode had caused her.

The distress *he* had created by jumping to conclusions without proof and venting freely. He swore to himself that it would be the very last time he awarded blame to her on the basis of her past sins. He really hadn't thought through the extent of the responsibility he was taking on in bringing her back to what had once been her home. And now he was stuck fast, neither married nor divorced, his own life in limbo alongside hers…

And for how long could he tolerate that injustice?

Lorenzo returned to the bank. Brooke went out to the garden, which she loved, strolling along gravel paths, enjoying the sunlight and the flowers and greenery all around her. A little dog bounded out from below the trees and began to bark at her. Brooke laughed because it was a tiny little thing, a mop of tousled multi-shaded brown hair on four spindly legs.

'Now who do you belong to?' she asked, settling down on a bench when natural curiosity brought the dog closer. He jumped up against her legs, more than willing to invite attention. She petted him, lifted him and discovered that *he* was a girl and laughed again, letting her curl up on her lap and settle there.

The gardener nearby, engaged in freshening up a bed with new plants, glanced across the sunken garden at them in apparent surprise. When she moved on, the little dog followed at her heels and she said to the gardener. 'Who does the dog belong to?'

'Topsy's yours, Mrs Tassini,' he said without hesitation and she realised that her amnesia was no longer a secret, if it ever had been, in the household.

Only a slight flush on her cheeks, Brooke walked on before stooping to pet the little animal. Her dog had found the way back to her and she smiled, delighted to discover that she had a pet and that she liked animals. It was uplifting to learn that there had been a positive side to the self she no longer remembered because so far she only appeared to be finding out negative stuff, she conceded ruefully, thinking about the extravagance and the lies that had clearly damaged her marriage. At the same time though, it was better to be forewarned that there could be further obstacles ahead, she reflected ruefully. What else had she done that she would be ashamed to find out?

At least, Lorenzo had resisted the very human urge

to just dump all her mistakes on her at once, she thought fondly. That had been generous of him in the circumstances. He was doing everything by the book and shielding her from unpleasant truths. How could she not love a man like that?

Brooke dressed for dinner that evening with greater care than usual. Finally, she surveyed her reflection in one of the several mirrors in the dressing room and something strange happened. For a timeless instant as she gazed into the mirror, she became dizzy and she saw another woman. No, it wasn't *another* woman, she realised with a spooked shiver of reaction, it was herself clad in a black jacket with her hair straight and wearing a different red dress. She had been sitting in the back of a limousine. She blinked rapidly and realised that she had *finally* remembered something from the past and she couldn't wait to tell Mr Selby about that promising little glimmer.

It wouldn't be worth mentioning it to Lorenzo though, would it? Just as she hadn't thought to mention that none of the ravishing shoes in the cabinets even fitted her any longer because evidently her feet had grown a little fatter and those shoes pinched like the devil. A tiny little flashback that only involved seeing herself and that showed her nothing important wasn't worth telling Lorenzo about. Even so, it was a promising start to a complete recovery.

Lorenzo was still upstairs when she arrived in the dining room and she walked out onto the terrace that overlooked the garden, wondering if it would be acceptable to suggest that they ate outside during the

summer months because the evenings were so beautiful and she did love the fresh air. Careful in the high
heels that she was still a little wobbly in and with
Topsy in tow, because the little dog hadn't left her
side all day, she descended the steps that led down
to the garden and roved along a path that led into a
shrubbery backed by natural woodland. Topsy went
scampering ahead and then started barking so ferociously that she almost levitated off the ground.

'Topsy,' she began to say and then, before she
could gather her breath, a man leapt out of nowhere
in front of her and gave her such a fright that she
screamed.

And screamed again, backing away in absolute
terror, every natural instinct on high alert, her heart
thundering in her ears with fear. The man threw up
his hands in apparent disbelief and then two men appeared from behind him and pulled him away.

An arm snaked round her quaking figure from
behind. 'Are you all right?' Lorenzo's very welcome
and familiar voice enquired, and relief made her sag
like a ragdoll in his arms. 'I was in the dining room
when I heard you scream. I've never moved so fast
in my life!'

'Who was he?' she prompted shakily. 'What did
he want?'

'A paparazzo chancing his arm,' Lorenzo imparted. 'Didn't you notice his camera?'

'No… I thought… I thought he was a rapist or
something,' she contrived to explain unevenly, her
breath still see-sawing in and out of her raw throat.

'That's what I assumed. I didn't think about this being a garden and how unlikely that would be, which was stupid.'

Lorenzo's dark eyes glittered with wildly inappropriate appreciation of that explanation for Brooke's reaction to a member of the press and he made no comment, seeing for himself that she was still pale and trembling with fright. He closed an arm round her to direct her back indoors. 'You can blame me for this frightening experience as well,' he told her instead in an exasperated undertone. 'I was about to double our security before I saw that newspaper headline this morning and then I *forgot*.'

'You're allowed to overlook stuff occasionally,' Brooke told him, still struggling to get her breathing under control. 'Anyway, how can it be *your* fault when it's obvious that my love of attracting publicity caused all this nonsense?'

'It wasn't wrong for you to like attracting publicity,' Lorenzo countered levelly. 'That was your world. I shouldn't have given you the impression that it was a bad choice, because it wasn't for you.'

But it was a bad choice for anyone married to you, Brooke completed inside her head, for everything about Lorenzo implied that he was a very private man and the last man imaginable to enjoy that kind of exposure. Clearly, her past self hadn't much cared about that, and she had continued to relentlessly pursue her own goals. She was twenty-eight years old and could scarcely blame that decision on immaturity. She had put her media career first, *not* her marriage.

'Topsy!' she called, and the dog raced over to her, long silly ears flopping madly, tongue hanging. Without hesitation she scooped the little animal up and started telling it that it was a great little watchdog while Lorenzo looked on in disbelief.

Brooke didn't *like* animals, but some nameless admirer had gifted her the puppy when handbag dogs were in vogue. She had brought the dog home and abandoned it in the kitchen and, as far as he knew, had never looked at it again. Lorenzo decided it was time for him to have another chat with her psychiatrist and ask how it was possible that his wife could be displaying entirely new personality traits as well as different tastes. Brooke wasn't even eating salads any longer, never mind fussing about her diet. She no longer used the gym and barely touched alcohol aside of a glass of wine at dinner. The changes were piling up to the extent that he no longer knew what to expect from the wife he would once have sworn that he knew inside out.

'Would you like a drink after that…er rather unnerving encounter?' he asked calmly.

'No, thanks. But thanks for being there this morning and this evening to ground me,' Brooke murmured in a rush, staring up at him with a great burst of warmth rushing and spreading through her veins, because she was grateful, *so* ridiculously grateful that Lorenzo existed and that she was married to him. He was her rock in every storm.

'I wasn't there for you this morning in the way I should've been,' Lorenzo corrected with a sardonic twist of his beautiful shapely mouth, tensing as that warm look in her eyes somehow contrived to arrow straight down to his groin. 'I attacked you, misjudged you.'

Determined violet eyes connected with his. 'But I forgive you.'

'Too easily,' Lorenzo chided, trying to keep some distance between them while he was as hard as rock and throbbing with arousal.

Brooke realised that she was literally backing him into the wall and she laughed in surprise, wondering if Lorenzo was always so slow on the uptake, so businesslike, so prone to saying and doing only the right thing that he couldn't even grasp when his wife was coming on to him! She lifted her hands and ran them up over his ribcage over the shirt below his tailored jacket, sensitive fingertips learning the lean mouth-watering musculature hidden beneath, and she stretched up and literally face-planted her mouth on his.

Two very masculine hands sank into her mane of ringlets and held her fast and she smiled against his parting lips, her mouth opening eagerly for the plunging urgency of his. It was everything she remembered from the clinic, a chemical explosion of sheer hunger and demand. Oh, yes, her husband *wanted* her all right, she savoured with pleasure, he only needed encouragement while she needed no encouragement whatsoever when keeping her hands off him was more of a challenge. Her body was coming alive with a host of sensations from the tightening of her nipples, to the swell of her breasts, to the aching hollowness that tugged at the heart of her.

There was a sound somewhere behind her and Lorenzo yanked her back from him as though he had been burned. Stevens was muttering an apology and Lorenzo assured him that dinner *right now* was fine.

Her face hot as hellfire, so hot she wanted to die for a split second, Brooke retreated to her designated dining chair and grasped her wine glass with new fervour. She couldn't look at Lorenzo, she absolutely couldn't look at him in that instant, she was so mortified by her own forward behaviour, but honestly, it was as if he were a magnet that pulled at her until she couldn't resist the charge any more. She was convinced that she had never felt desire so strongly before…and yet how could that be?

Lorenzo infuriated her then by acting as if nothing had happened. He asked her about her day and her enjoyment of the garden. Slowly, painfully, her equilibrium returned. It wasn't *his* fault that she wanted him to be the sort of guy who said to hell with dinner and carted her off to the nearest private spot to take advantage of her willingness…*was it*?

CHAPTER FIVE

IT WAS NOW or never, Brooke challenged herself, because on a deep inner level she was cringing about what she was about to do.

The many mirrors in her dressing room showed a slender figure garbed in a white satin and lace nightdress. Wearing it felt weird because Brooke was convinced that, at heart, she was a pyjama girl rather than the fashionable, sexier image she was sporting, but, going by the decorative lingerie collection in the dressing room, her past self had never given way to the weakness of putting comfort first. Pyjamas weren't sexy though and she *needed* sexy, needed it desperately, she acknowledged apprehensively, because in spite of reading the book she had found in the bedside cabinet on 'how to thrill your lover,' she *still* felt as if she didn't have a clue!

After all, suppose Lorenzo *rejected* her? How would she ever rise above that humiliation? She breathed in deep. Her need to have a normal marriage, added to the desire she definitely felt for him, was motivating her and what was wrong with making a major effort? Why would he reject her when he kissed her as though his life depended on it? she asked herself, striving to bolster her flagging courage as she ranged closer to the connecting door between their bedrooms and reached for the handle. The blasted door was locked! She couldn't believe it, and so afraid was she of losing her nerve altogether that she stalked straight out of her bedroom and walked down the corridor to let herself into his room with a fast-beating heart.

She couldn't believe her luck when she heard the shower running in the en suite. In one frantic leap she made it into the bed and hit the lights on the wall to plunge the room into darkness. Maybe that was a little too cowardly, she reasoned with a grimace, because that amount of self-consciousness wasn't sexy either. Stretching up, she put the lights back on and surveyed his bedroom décor, which was much warmer and comfier in ambience than her own stark white bower of rest.

Brooke was still all of a quiver, like a real scaredy-cat. She shrank at the prospect of being confronted by Lorenzo's shock, surprise and, ultimately, his rebuff. But if he said no, he would have to explain why not, wouldn't he? And then another little piece of the mystery of their marriage would fall into place, so, at the cost of her dignity, she would find out more even if he did dismiss her.

Lorenzo was in a dark brooding mood as he stepped out of the shower and snatched at a towel to dry off his hair. It was a challenge for him to believe that sharing a roof with Brooke could wind him up like a clockwork toy with sheer lust. How had that happened? *When* had that happened? It was damned near three years since he had experienced that hunger and then Brooke had woken up after the accident and somehow that primal urge had come back with a vengeance, engulfing him without reason or logic. It infuriated him.

When Lorenzo strode naked out of the bathroom and saw her lying in his bed, the last chain of restraint snapped inside him and set him free. Suddenly he had had it with self-discipline and had it with continually hearing his legal team's warnings in the back of his mind and all he could think about was that there were no cameras in his bedroom and he could do whatever the hell he liked with the woman he had married. Brooke was still his wife. He wanted her and *she* wanted *him*. If he kept it that simple, he didn't need to even think about anything else, and it *was* simple, basic sexual instinct and nothing more.

'I th-thought...' Brooke stammered, peering in awe at him over the top of the duvet, striving to grab up some bad-girl sass from somewhere down deep inside her, so deep she couldn't find it. She felt like a woman who had never been in a man's bed in her life and that was unsettling her more and increasing her nerves.

'Great minds think alike,' Lorenzo quoted, all smooth and dark in tone like the finest chocolate laced with that delicious accent of his.

And he smiled at her, he actually *smiled*, and

the charisma of that smile set her heartbeat racing and released butterflies in her tummy. In an abrupt movement, Brooke pushed back the duvet with valiant hands and sat up against the pillows, the worst of her nerves conquered by the suspicion that she could have looked as though she was hiding in his bed like a little kid. A deep heat assailed her face when she registered that he was naked, absolutely naked, all bronzed and hair-roughened and aroused naked, and her mouth ran dry.

'So,' she breathed shakily. 'You're not going to throw me out?'

Lorenzo tilted his tousled and damp dark head to one side and sent her a smouldering appraisal from dark glittering eyes that speared her where she sat. 'You want me?'

Unnerved a bit by the change in his attitude, Brooke nodded jerkily like a marionette.

'Say it,' Lorenzo commanded, needing to hear the words because he knew she didn't remember being with him before and that for her this was her first time with him.

'I want you,' Brooke practically whispered, so hard was it to get sufficient oxygen into her struggling lungs.

'*Dannazione...* No, I'm not going to throw you out,' Lorenzo told her thickly.

'I want us to have a normal marriage,' she muttered tightly.

'It's been a long time since we had normal,' Lorenzo admitted.

'But why *is* that?' she pressed.

'That's not something we want to get into at this moment,' Lorenzo growled, tossing aside the towel still clutched in one lean brown hand and climbing into the bed.

Brooke felt almost as if she couldn't breathe with Lorenzo that close, the heat of his body warming hers even before he touched her, and then his wide sensual mouth crashed down on hers and breathing began to seem a much overrated pursuit as every sense she possessed flew off on a wild and wonderful trail of discovery. The very scent of him, soap, designer cologne and clean male, overwhelmed her and the minty taste of him against her tongue was delicious. As for the actual feel of that long, lean, hot, heavy body pressing against hers, it invoked a delirious wriggle closer from her hips while she pushed her breasts against the hard wall of his chest.

Great minds think alike.

She loved that phrase, which suggested that he had been waiting for her. Maybe this had always been their way—she came to him—and the idea no longer bothered her because he was pushing the welcome mat out with irrefutable enthusiasm.

Think about what you're doing.

The words sounded somewhere in Lorenzo's brain like an alarm bell but he suppressed them fast. He was way past caring *how* Brooke had contrived to make him want her again. He was fed up with being sensible when she drew him now on a very primitive level that kept him awake at night, wondering, fantasising about a woman who only eighteen months earlier he could not wait to kick out of his life. He stressed too much about making mistakes, he told himself impatiently. For once he would just go with the flow and do what seemed entirely natural.

Without ceremony he stripped off the nightdress and her breath caught in her throat again as she looked up at him. He had such beautiful eyes, lustrous gold in the lower lighting and framed by dense black lashes that curled up at the ends. Breathless, she lay there entranced until his warm, sensual mouth sealed to hers and a great swoosh of heat rushed up through her as a large masculine hand curved round a plump breast, the thumb rubbing at the sensitive tip until she gasped. Instantaneously she wanted more and when he utilised his mouth instead to suck at the swollen bud, she marvelled that even amnesia could make her forget such distinct sensations.

The tug on her nipple set alight the burn between her thighs, the pulsing liquidity that turned her to mush. She pushed against him in helpless need and he laughed softly, even that sound surging through her like an added aphrodisiac. She ran her hands down his sleek, satiny back with new confidence, smoothing over a lean flank, mentally recalling the book that had specified 'firm, assured' as the most desirable touch and wondering how on earth she could've forgotten something so basic as how to make love to her husband. However, when she touched him, he froze, and she jerked her fingers away again in swift retreat from that daring.

'No…no, don't back off,' Lorenzo positively purred in her ear, returning her small fingers to their former destination and revelling in her enthusiasm. 'I *like* being touched.'

Confidence renewed, Brooke stroked her hand along that smooth velvety skin, fascination powering her in her exploration of all that made them different. But a little of her attention seemed to go a long way and, before she got very far, Lorenzo was spreading her across the mattress like a starfish and she was a little nervous of that position until he began to work his path down her splayed body employing both his mouth and his hands to investigate her curves. The warm damp feeling at her core increased exponentially, leaving her craving his touch to an extent that was almost unbearable to her straining body.

'You've been driving me crazy with hunger for weeks,' Lorenzo growled, kissing a deeply intimate trail up her inner thigh, reducing her to uneasy little twists and jerks of a curious but self-conscious nature.

'Have I?' she pressed, half an octave higher, the words strangling in her throat as he ran his tongue over her most sensitive area, and her hands snapped into fists of restraint because she wanted to sink her fingers into that tousled dark hair of his.

'Every time I look at you, I want you,' Lorenzo grated, stringing a line of kisses across her quivering belly.

'Doesn't show!' she gasped, ridiculously grateful that she had gone leaping into his bed and weak with relief because Lorenzo didn't show things, didn't usually talk like this to her. Evidently, he needed a certain level of intimacy to get comfortable enough to share such truths.

He dallied between her thighs, making moves that drove her to the outer edge of hunger, and every nerve ending was screaming for release and then it happened, in a magical great whoosh that exploded through her being like a shooting star, a drowning absolute pleasure that drenched every limb and left her with a sense of shock that anything could feel that physically good.

That achieved, Lorenzo shifted over her with an intense look of hunger in his dark glittering eyes and it made her feel like a million dollars and as if every path in her life were paved with solid gold. Her heart clenched because the more she found out about him, the more she wanted him, and it was a heady moment that made her eyes prickle with tears, making her blink and turn her head away as his hands slid beneath her hips to tilt her up to him.

And in the next moment, he surged into her ready body, although her body didn't react as though it had been ready for that masculine invasion. It hurt, it hurt *a lot* and almost startled Brooke into crying out, but she mercifully managed to hold onto the cry that almost parted her lips because she was sure that that would have spoilt everything. He would have blamed himself for causing her pain when surely the only reason she had suffered pain lay in the reality that it had been well over a year since she had had sex. And that wasn't anybody's fault, she conceded ruefully.

It was a relief when the discomfort ebbed entirely, and she was able to lose herself again in the intimacy. Her heart began to pound with every lithe thrust of his body over and inside hers, excitement climbing, breathlessness ensured as she wrapped her legs round his lean hips and savoured the sweet throbbing pleasure engulfing her. The hunger came back, urging her body to shift up to his, and little sounds escaped her without her true awareness since it was a passion beyond anything she thought she could ever have felt. The excitement was overwhelming, all-consuming and she wanted more and more until she rose against him on a feverish wave of wild pleasure and another orgasm took her in a rush of high-wire energy.

'Wow,' she whispered in the aftermath, flaking out back against the pillows, limp and drained but secretly triumphant as well because she had achieved exactly what she had set out to do.

'Incredible,' Lorenzo commented, collapsing down beside her out of breath while he dimly wondered how sex could possibly be so different with her that even her behaviour had changed, and he felt as though he was with a different woman. Yes, he was definitely going to see Mr Selby for the question and answer session that he badly needed. Although he doubted if he would mention their new intimacy because that was private...wasn't it? Was *anything* between them private now? he asked himself in disbelief at the concept.

'I'm not on the pill,' Brooke murmured with a sudden stab of anxiety, for she suspected that the very last thing they dared risk in a marriage that appeared to need rebuilding would be a child. 'Did you—?'

'You have an IUD,' Lorenzo assured her while it dawned on him that, even so, he should have taken precautions because she had been with other men. On the other hand, while in medical care she had been saturated with every antibiotic known to man.

His contraceptive omission, however, was another concern that he was in no mood to deal with. It was, after all, a reminder of the true state of play between them and he suppressed the thought of it because if he thought about it too much, it would drive him crazy. The entire situation was *already* driving him crazy, he acknowledged as he questioned the secrecy he had been urged to embrace for her benefit.

But *was* it for her benefit?

Would she have slept with him were she herself?

And without warning, Lorenzo was snatched back into a black and white world with no forgiving shades of grey again. Brooke had hated him when he demanded a divorce and hadn't once spoken a civil word to him during their time apart when he had been forced out of his own house by her infidelity into a city apartment he had hated.

'We shouldn't have done this!' Lorenzo exclaimed with startling abruptness, feeling as though he had taken unfair advantage of her even though *she* was the one who had issued the invitation. 'You're not yourself…you don't know what you're doing.'

Brooke was galvanised out of her comfortable relaxation while thinking how weird it was that he had known she was on birth control when she did not. Even so, it was something she could live with until he said what he did, which filled her with a sensation very close to panic because she did not want him regretting what they had just shared. 'No, *no*, it's not like that!' she argued fervently.

'It is exactly like that,' Lorenzo contradicted gravely. 'I don't *like* that it feels like that but facts are facts.'

'No! You're not allowed to think like that now!' Brooke told him almost fiercely as she scrambled up and literally perched on top of him like a naked nymph, he reasoned in wonderment as arousal kicked in again for him with shocking immediacy.

'Why not?' Lorenzo breathed almost bitterly. 'I took advantage of you.'

'No, you didn't!' Brooke protested, leaning over him, her hands planted either side of his head on the pillows, the twin peaks of her luscious breasts brushing his chest. 'I got into *your* bed, for goodness' sake! I wanted you and we had a great time and that's all there is to it!'

Lorenzo blinked at that hail of keen protest and gazed up into vivid violet eyes and a flawless heart-shaped face surrounded by a tangle of platinum curls. His hands went up before he even knew it himself and he tasted her pouting pink lips like a man starving for that particular flavour. Need surged through him stronger than ever, a bone-deep driving need that threatened to unnerve him.

'I think I'm falling in love with you again, Lorenzo,' Brooke declared.

Lorenzo froze as though she had paralysed him. It was an interesting response from a husband in receipt of such a proclamation, she acknowledged unhappily.

'You can't love me…you don't know me,' he told her levelly.

'I beg to differ. It's almost three months since I came out of that coma and throughout that time you have been my biggest and best support team,' Brooke countered strongly. 'I have got to know you. I have got to see how you put me and my needs first *every time*. I have been here while you lived through a profoundly challenging situation with me and still took nothing for yourself. So please don't tell me that I *can't* love you because I don't know you. I do know what I've seen and how it makes me feel. I'm *definitely* falling for you.'

Lorenzo took a deep breath and parted his lips as if he was about to say something. But then he closed his mouth again and tugged her back down to him. 'Whatever,' he breathed, urgently conscious of her curvy body moving over his groin. 'I still want you.'

'Nothing wrong with that,' Brooke assured him, her colour rising headily as he gazed up at her full of blatant sexual intent.

'*Dio…cara mia,*' Lorenzo ground out, all self-discipline beaten down, even that affectionate label extracted from him by the encouraging feel of her in his arms. 'So, I'm free to live out my every fantasy, then?'

'Pretty much,' she whispered, barely recognising herself from the shy, uncertain woman she had been a mere hour earlier.

'I have quite an appetite built up,' he warned her thickly.

'It seems I have too,' Brooke whispered, recognising the hot tight sensation in her pelvis for the desire that it was this time around and ever so slightly proud of herself for no longer feeling either so ignorant or insecure about her own body. Lorenzo wanted her; indeed he had said that every time he looked at her, he wanted her. Why hadn't she had the perception to see that for herself in the man she had married? Why was her brain so dense where he was concerned? Why wasn't there even a glimmer of natural insight?

Stashing away her increasing frustration with her inability to remember what she needed to remember, Brooke fell into Lorenzo's blazingly sexual kiss, every concern about her ability to be sexy laid to rest. She was enough for *him* and really, at that moment, that was all that mattered to her or seemed the least bit important. He settled her down over him and raised her hips and, seconds later, she realised that it was all beginning again as he eased into her slow and sure, controlling her every movement in an innately dominant way while touching her in a way that sent her flying off the planet again within minutes. Exhausted then, she rested her head down on a smooth brown muscular shoulder and smiled dizzily.

Lorenzo surveyed his wife over breakfast with a faintly dazed light new to his shrewd dark gaze. There she was, curled up in a chair being all affectionate, playful and teasing while munching on toast and feeding Topsy pieces of crust. Brooke didn't eat carbohydrates; Brooke treated carbs like poison. He had never known her to be affectionate or playful either, even before he had married her. Within the hour, he was meeting with her psychiatrist in search of advice.

'Yes, I think it's perfectly possible that she could be a *very* different person without that celebrity frame of reference that was once so crucial to her self-image,' the older man declared with confidence. 'There are documented examples of cases of this nature but I'm afraid I can't tell you how to proceed. That is *your* decision, but I suspect it may soon be time to tell her that you were pursuing a divorce before the accident.'

Lorenzo mulled that challenging suggestion over on the way to the Tassini Bank for a board meeting and he grimaced. Last night they had had sex. Today he admits they're in the midst of a divorce? He breathed in slow and deep and groaned. That wouldn't work. He would sense the right moment to tell her when it arrived, he reasoned, recognising that he didn't want to rock the boat or cause her distress. It was still his role to be supportive, *not* destructive.

On the other hand, he was equally aware that he would never consider *staying* married to Brooke— he could not pardon either her lies or her infidelity. And that acknowledgement plunged him straight back into the same, 'damned if he did' and 'damned if he didn't' scenario...

* * *

Quite unaware of Lorenzo's thorny dilemma, Brooke was getting dressed to go out, which was something of a challenge given the glitzy nature of the contents of her dressing room. She knew that she didn't have to wear black to offer condolences, but it seemed a matter of respect for her to wear something other than a party outfit. She chose a navy pencil skirt and a silk striped top but she couldn't get the skirt to zip up and had to take it off again and accept with a wince that she had evidently put on weight. A pair of loose dark palazzo pants replaced the skirt. As she left the house for the first time since her arrival, she felt stronger and braver and relieved that she had finally got the gumption to do what she felt she had to do to lay her accident to rest in her own mind.

Lorenzo's PA at the bank had sounded surprised when Brooke phoned her but had been happy to pass on the address and the details she knew about the driver and the passenger who had died in the crash. Brooke bent her head out of view when she saw the cluster of paparazzi at the foot of the drive. Lorenzo's disdain for their interest in his wife had been palpable and she marvelled that she had married a man who cherished his privacy when her own interests had clearly pushed her in a very different direction.

The driver's mother was delighted with her gift of flowers and pleased to have the chance to talk about her late son. She referred several times to the substantial tips that Brooke had regularly given her son and

Brooke smiled, relieved to hear that she had been generous. Visiting Milly Taylor's grave, however, put her in a more sombre mood. Although enquiries had been made, only the young woman's former employer had claimed to know her, and that café would be Brooke's final destination.

The gravestone was simple. Brooke set down her floral offering and sighed, wondering if the woman had been a friend. It would make sense that she had had *one* friend, wouldn't it? But would she have made friends with someone from such a very different background? What would they have had in common?

The café was within walking distance of the cemetery and she had asked her driver to pick her up in half an hour. On the way there she passed a newsstand on the pavement and something caught her eye on a front page. She paused to lift the magazine. It was her face and across it was splashed: *Divorce or Reconciliation?*

'You need to buy it to read it,' the vendor told her irritably and she dug into her purse for the cash, her face heating.

She stood in the street reading the article inside and shock went crashing through her in wave after wave. Her tummy succumbed to a queasy lurch and she felt dizzy. Suddenly everything she had believed she knew about Lorenzo was being turned on its head! And equally, everything she had believed she knew about herself was being torn to shreds. Rumours of affairs? Yes, she had seen those photos of her in nightclubs with other men, but she had assumed those men were work contacts or social connections, had never dreamt *that*…?

And Lorenzo had a business trip to Italy, for which he was leaving that very evening, and he would be away for a week. If she wanted the chance to speak to him, she couldn't afford to wait, no, she needed to see him immediately…

CHAPTER SIX

'YOUR WIFE'S HERE to see you,' Lorenzo was informed an hour later at the bank.

Taken aback by that unexpected announcement, because Brooke had never once in all the time he had known her come to see him at the bank, Lorenzo rose from behind his desk.

Brooke entered and the instant he saw her face he knew that something was badly wrong. Her eyes had a sort of glazed look and she was very pale, her stance as she paused uncertainly halfway towards him stiff and unnatural.

'What's wrong?' he asked quietly. 'Although possibly I should be asking you what's right. This *is* the first time you've emerged from the house since you left the clinic.'

'I shouldn't have come here…er…where you work,' Brooke muttered in belated appreciation of what she had done in her distraught frame of mind. 'I should've waited until you came home, so I'm going to just do that and we can talk before you leave for the airport.'

Lorenzo hauled out a chair from the wall before

she could leave again. 'No, sit down. I can see that you're troubled about something. Tea? Coffee?'

'A coffee would be good,' she conceded flatly, hoping the caffeine would cut a path through the tangled turmoil of her emotions and miraculously settle her down at a moment when she felt as though the floor beneath her feet had fallen away.

She *was* too dependent on Lorenzo, she acknowledged with a sinking heart. Lorenzo was irreversibly stitched into everything she had thought and done and worried about since she had first wakened from the coma. Since awakening, she had built an entire life around him, and the idea that their marriage was simply a cruel mirage cut her off at the knees and left her drowning in a sea of insecurity and regrets.

The coffee arrived in record time and she was relieved to have something to occupy her hands as she cradled the bone-china cup and marvelled that it was a cup instead of a beaker. That random thought brought a wry smile to her lips. In truth, she recognised, she was eager to think about anything other than the giant chasm that had opened up beneath her feet.

'I went to see Paul Jennings's mother this morning,' she revealed as an opening.

Lorenzo leant back fluidly against the side of his desk, embracing informality for her benefit while both his exquisitely tailored dark suit and her surroundings screamed huge influential office and very powerful occupant. He was gorgeous, she conceded rather numbly, and it was hardly surprising that she had become attached to the idea that he was *hers*. Any woman in her circumstances would've done the same thing, she told herself bracingly. Not only was he gorgeous and sexy and terrific in bed, he had been a rock for her through every step of her recovery process. Whatever the truth of their marriage was, she still owed him gratitude for his generosity.

'Yes, my PA mentioned your plans. I thought it was great that you were finally emerging from the house,' Lorenzo commented. 'So, what went wrong?'

'Oh…nothing went wrong,' Brooke assured him tautly. 'I bought a magazine because I saw my face on the cover.'

'Dio…' Lorenzo bit out, tensing. 'I should've foreseen that you might do something like that.'

Quite deliberately, Brooke lifted her chin, her violet eyes clear and level, giving no hint of the turmoil inside her. 'You can't protect me from everything, Lorenzo…and you shouldn't be *trying* to protect me from the truth,' she told him tightly. 'If it's true that we were getting divorced before the accident, you should've told me weeks ago.'

Lorenzo shifted a lean brown hand in a sudden imperious movement that sought to silence her as he took a step forward.

'Of course, I know *why* you didn't tell me because someone like Mr Selby or some other clever doctor warned you that it might be too much for my battered little brain to handle,' Brooke framed steadily, ignoring his gesture. 'But I disagree with that kind of overprotective attitude because I'm back in the real world now and I *have* to adjust to it, no matter how tough or destabilising it is. I'm not a child.'

Lorenzo surveyed her, feeling strangely appreciative of her control and dignity in a very taxing situation, two responses that he had least expected from her. Brooke had always been more about hysterics and ranting and blaming everybody but herself when anything went wrong. He breathed in deep and accepted the inevitable. The truth was out and he couldn't deny it. 'We *were* pursuing a divorce at the time of the crash,' he admitted levelly.

'Why?' Brooke asked baldly.

Lorenzo studied her. She looked tiny in that chair and she was as white as a sheet. How was he supposed to tell the woman that she now was that she had played away with multiple men, indeed any man who suggested that he could advance her goal of breaking into the screen industry? Lorenzo had never had the slightest difficulty in delivering bad news. Indeed, it was integral to his role as a banker, but when it came to shattering the woman seated before him, he just couldn't drop the ugly truth on her at that moment. The divorce would've been a big enough blow to a woman who had told him that she thought she might love him only the night before. Never mind that that professed love was simply an assumption brought on by her amnesia. She was still being very brave and he admired that, and bad news was never *quite* as bad if it emerged piece by piece over a lengthier period of time, he told himself grimly.

'We were ill-suited, different goals, different outlook on life,' Lorenzo responded. 'I wanted children but you didn't. I wanted a home. You only wanted an impressive backdrop for your photos. Divorce was inevitable.'

Brooke nodded valiantly. 'And…er…the men, the affairs?'

'Rumours,' Lorenzo asserted valiantly. 'But I didn't enjoy the rumours.'

Brooke bent her head but breathed a little easier at that release from her biggest fear: that she was capable of that kind of betrayal and of cheating on him. 'Of course not,' she agreed flatly. 'Even without my memory, I can see that the woman I was and the man you are weren't a good match.'

Lorenzo had gone very quiet. He was thinking hard and fast, wondering whether to take her straight to that penthouse apartment he had bought her to cement their separation back into place. In rapid succession he pictured her there alone and potentially lost and he recoiled from that image while questioning his own sanity.

'And I really shouldn't be living in your home any more,' Brooke completed quietly, raising the point she knew she had to raise to set him free from feeling responsible for her.

Lorenzo's black lashes dropped down over his glittering eyes and every muscle in his lean, powerful frame jerked rigid. He *couldn't* let her go, at least, *not just yet*, he reasoned fiercely. She wasn't fit to be abandoned to sink or swim and that might not strictly be his business any more, but he still *felt* as though it were. Right now, a separation would be premature.

'I have a better solution,' he heard himself say before he had even quite thought through what he was about to say, a divergence from habit that shook him even as he spoke. 'I suggest you accompany me to Italy this evening.'

'To Italy?' Brooke gasped as if she had never heard of the country before, so disconcerted was she by that proposal at that particular moment.

'Yes, it would be good for you to escape the paparazzi and the publicity and enjoy some breathing space. You're a UK celebrity, pretty much unknown—' he selected that last word tactfully '—in Italy. We'll be left alone, free of this constant media speculation. A break is what we need.'

Brooke lifted her head, her heart, which had slowed to a dulled thud, suddenly picking up speed again. 'We?' she queried in a near croak.

'*We,*' Lorenzo stressed with vigour, some of his tension ebbing now that he could see a provisional way forward out of the current chaos.

'But we're getting a divorce,' Brooke reminded him shakily.

'The divorce has been on hold since the day of the crash. A few more weeks aren't going to make much difference at this point,' Lorenzo informed her with assurance. 'We can separate or divorce at any time. Let's not allow past decisions to control us in a different situation. Let's be patient a little while longer and see how things progress. Your memory may yet return.'

Brooke was plunged deep into shock all over again, the price of having been thrown from one extreme to yet another. She had come to his office to confront him with her heart being squeezed in a steel fist of pain. She had believed that their marriage was an empty charade already all but over and that it was her duty to finally set Lorenzo free, even though she loved him. She remained absolutely convinced that, even though she had made a mess of their marriage, she *still* loved him.

But to her astonishment, Lorenzo was reacting in an utterly unexpected way by offering her a second chance at their marriage. Wasn't that what he meant? For goodness' sake, what else *could* he mean? He didn't want to immediately reclaim his freedom as she had assumed. He was willing to wait…he was willing to continue living with her as her husband. A shaken, shuddering breath forced its passage up through her constrained lungs because relief was filling her almost to overflowing, liberating all the emotions that she had been fighting to suppress since she read about their divorce proceedings in that awful gossipy magazine. Her eyes stung horribly and flooded. She blinked rapidly, warding off the tears and hastily sipping at her cooling coffee.

Lorenzo reached down and rescued the shaking cup and saucer to set it aside, and scooped her up into his arms. It wasn't pity driving him, he told himself with ferocious certainty, it was a crazy, impossible mix of lust, responsibility, sympathy and fascination with the woman she now was. He was taking her to Italy with him. It was a done deal.

'I'm sorry,' she briefly sobbed against his shoulder before she got a grip on herself again and glanced up at him with a grimace of apology. 'It was the shock. I was *expecting*—'

'Keep it simple, like me,' Lorenzo urged. 'I'm practical and calculating and very typical of the male sex. I'm expecting you in my bed at night.'

An indelicate little snort of laughter escaped Brooke then, drying up the tears at source. 'Is that so?' she mumbled, a sudden shard of happiness piercing her.

'You haven't even asked me yet what *I* did wrong in our marriage,' he reproved. 'The mistakes weren't all on *your* side. I worked long hours, left you alone too much and only took you to boring dinner parties where everyone was talking about finance. You weren't happy with me either.'

'We'll see how Italy goes,' Brooke murmured softly. 'As you said, we can choose to part at any time, so neither of us need to feel trapped.'

'You're feeling trapped?' Lorenzo demanded without warning, an arctic light gleaming in his beautiful dark eyes.

'No…' Brooke toyed with a button on his jacket, striving not to flatter him with too much enthusiasm. 'I don't feel trapped at all. Maybe I've grown up a bit from the person I was before the crash. Obviously I've changed. I don't seem to want people with cameras chasing me. I seem to have lost what seems to have been an overriding interest in fashion and clothes… gosh, I'm going to be forced out shopping if you're taking me travelling. A lot of the clothes, and particularly the shoes, don't fit me now,' she confided ruefully.

'I'll organise someone to come to the house this afternoon and kit you out. I'll postpone the flight until early tomorrow morning,' Lorenzo informed her arrogantly. 'But that means I'll have to work late tonight… OK?'

'OK,' she agreed breathlessly.

Lorenzo stared down at her heart-shaped face while a *what-the-hell-am-I-doing?* question raced over and over through his brain. He concentrated instead on that luscious pink mouth and the ever-present throb at his groin and bent his head to taste those succulent lips.

Brooke fell into that kiss like honey melting on a grill. Her insides turned liquid and burned. It happened every time he kissed her, a shooting, thrilling internal heat that washed through her like a dangerous drug, lighting up every part of her body. She wanted to cling, but she wouldn't let herself, stepping back with a control that she was proud to maintain after her earlier emotionalism.

She reddened as she connected with his brilliant dark eyes, which packed such a passionate punch. Maybe this very hunger was what had first brought them together and kept them together even when their relationship didn't work in other ways. Sadly, it was a sobering thought to accept that sexual attraction might have been the most they had ever had as a couple and all she had left to build on.

Obviously, naturally, she wanted more, she reflected ruefully. She wanted him to *stop* feeling as responsible for her as a man might feel about a helpless child. She wanted him to see and accept that she no longer needed to be handled with kid gloves, that she was an adult and able to cope with her own life, even if it did mean losing him in the process. And possibly that was what it *would* mean, she conceded unhappily, bearing in mind that their marriage had apparently been rocky from the start.

Yet where had the ambition-driven woman she had been gone? Where had all the knowledge she must have accumulated from the fashion world gone? Why didn't she care now about what style was 'in' and what was 'out'? Why was she most comfortable in a pair of ordinary jeans? Where now was the brash confidence that had fairly blazed out of the magazine cuttings in her press scrapbooks? Those were questions that only time, or the recovery of her memories, would answer. But facing up to more challenging situations alone would probably strengthen her and do her good, she told herself fiercely. She resolved to make that visit to the café to ask about Milly Taylor on the drive home. Perhaps that would help her work out what the connection had been between two ostensibly very different women.

The café was also a bakery and Brooke waited patiently until the queue of customers had gone and the older woman behind the counter looked at her for the first time. The woman's eyes rounded, and she paled, stepping back as though she had had a fright.

'*Milly?*' she exclaimed shakily, her hand flying up to her mouth in a gesture of confusion as she stared at the younger woman. 'No, no… I can *see* you're not Milly, but just for a moment there, the resemblance gave me such a shock!'

Brooke's brow pleated as she asked the woman if they could have a chat. 'I'm Brooke Tassini. Milly died in the crash that I was injured in. You seem to think I resemble her… I've lost my memory,' she explained with a wince. 'I'm still trying to work out who Milly was to me.'

'Brooke? I'm Marge,' the middle-aged woman said comfortably as she moved out from behind the counter. 'When I get a better look at you, the resemblance isn't as striking as I first thought it was. But Milly had the same long curly hair and the same colour of eyes. Look, come and see the photo of her.'

Brooke crossed the café to scrutinise the small staff group photo on the wall, but it wasn't a very clear picture and she peered at the smiling image with a frown because she could see the extraordinary similarity of their features and colouring. 'When she was working here, did she ever mention me? I'm wondering now if she could be some distant relation, a cousin or something?'

'Milly didn't ever mention you,' Marge told her apologetically. 'She was a quiet girl. To be honest, I don't think she *had* much of a life outside work and she only worked here for a couple of months. I got the impression that she had moved around quite a bit, but I was still surprised that morning when she chucked her job in, because she had seemed content here. She said she had to quit because she had a family crisis.' Marge made a face. 'She seemed to forget that according to what she had once told me, she didn't *have* a family.'

'Oh…' Brooke breathed, acknowledging that she was no further on in her need to know who her companion had been and why they had been in the limousine together. The resemblance, though, that was a new fact, something that hadn't come out before, possibly because Marge wasn't in the right age group even to know who Brooke Tassini was or what she looked like, she reasoned while thanking the woman for her time.

As she walked to the door to leave, a startling image shot through her brain and for a split second it froze her in her tracks. In the flashback a man was standing over her where she sat in the café and shouting drunkenly at her while Marge flung the door wide to persuade him to leave. Brooke tried to hang onto that snapshot back in time, frantic to see more, know *more*. But nothing else came to her and embarrassment at the time she had already taken out of Marge's working day—Marge, who was already serving a new queue of customers at the counter—pushed her back out onto the street again in a daze.

Why did she never remember anything useful? she asked herself in frustration. Obviously she had visited the café at some point, presumably to see Milly, and Marge hadn't remembered her, which wasn't that surprising in a busy enterprise. What did still nag at Brooke, though, was the resemblance that Marge had remarked on and she had seen for herself. That was a rather strange coincidence, wasn't it? But how could it relate in any way to why that woman had been with her in the car?

CHAPTER SEVEN

BROOKE WAS RELAXED and calm on the drive from the airport in Florence.

Even the crack of dawn flight had failed to irritate her because the change of scene was a relief and an escape from her repetitive and anxious thoughts. Those exact same thoughts had threatened to send her out in search of more gossipy magazines that would enable her to find out additional stuff about her marriage. Aware of that temptation and the futility of such an exercise, when she already knew as much as she needed to know for the present, she had made herself concentrate instead on the selection of a capsule wardrobe with the stylist, who had arrived at Madrigal Court the previous afternoon. It had been a disappointment, though, that Lorenzo had come home so late that he had evidently chosen to sleep in his own room.

The crisp white and blue sundress she wore was comfortable in the heat of an Italian summer. It was neither edgy nor trendy but it was elegant and flattering, skimming nicely over those curvy parts of her that she was beginning to suspect were a little *too* curvy. Was a tendency to gain why she had once watched her diet with such zeal? But she had been too thin when she emerged from the coma and was now content to be a healthy weight, she reasoned. In any case, Lorenzo had been with her when she was flawless in figure and physically perfect and, clearly, it had done nothing to save their marriage. Now she had scars and more curves and neither seemed to bother him, although, to be fair, the scarring was minimal, thanks to the expert cosmetic surgery she had received, she acknowledged gratefully.

'Have I ever been to this house of yours before?' she asked Lorenzo.

'No. I tried to bring you here a couple of times, but it never fitted your schedule. There was always some event, some opening or fashion show that you couldn't miss.'

'Did you grow up in this house?' she prompted with curiosity.

Lorenzo surprised her by laughing, amusement gleaming in his lustrous dark golden eyes. 'No. I bought and renovated it. Sometimes, I forget how little you know about me now. I grew up in a splendid Venetian palazzo on the Grand Canal with my father.'

'No mother around?' she pressed in surprise.

'No, sadly she died bringing me into the world. She had a weak heart,' Lorenzo volunteered. 'And I don't think my father ever forgave me for being the cause of her death. He told me more than once that she was the only woman he had ever loved and that I had taken her from him.'

'But that's so unjust. I mean—'

'Do you think I don't know that?' Lorenzo sent her a wryly amused glance at her bias in his defence. 'He was a self-centred man. My mother wanted a baby and took the risk of getting pregnant against doctor's orders and I got the blame for it. I believe my father could have adjusted quite happily to *not* having a son and heir. Maybe a daughter would've brought out a softer side to him…who knows? He died last year, and we never had a close relationship.'

'That's so sad, such a waste.' Brooke sighed regretfully. 'I wish my parents had lived long enough for you to meet them and then you could have told me something about them.'

'Being without family never seemed to bother you. I think that it was natural for you to be a loner.'

'Is that why you think I didn't want children?' she asked abruptly.

Lorenzo expelled his breath in a measured hiss. 'No, you had multiple reasons for that. The effect on your body, the risk to your potential career, the responsibilities that would eat into your ability to come and go as you pleased.'

Brooke nodded, getting the message that in the past she had *definitely* not wanted a child. Evidently, her career had meant everything to her and that tough decision surprised her because she had found herself watching young children visiting their relatives in the clinic and had easily and quickly warmed to their presence. But Lorenzo had to know the woman he had married best, particularly now that he was no longer glossing over the more sensitive subjects simply to keep her in the dark and supposedly protect her from herself. But how on earth was anyone to tell her how to cope with a self that she, increasingly, didn't like very much?

'Did I tell you that I didn't want a family before we got married?' she pressed.

'No,' Lorenzo framed succinctly. 'Knowing *that* I wouldn't have married you but, to be fair, you didn't lie about it either. Later, I realised that you had merely avoided saying anything that would've committed you.'

Brooke still saw that as sly, just as he had once labelled her, but she said nothing because the picture of their marriage she was getting was still better than the blank she had had before, even if the more she learned, the more she suspected that saving such a troubled relationship could be a steeper challenge than even she had imagined.

'Why are we even talking about this?' Lorenzo demanded with wry amusement. 'The last complication we need now is a child.'

'Yes,' she agreed a little stiffly because it was true: they had quite enough on their plate with her amnesia. 'So, what happened to the Venetian palazzo you grew up in? Or didn't you inherit it?'

'I did inherit. I converted it into an exclusive boutique hotel. I had no personal attachment to the place.

My childhood memories aren't warm or fluffy,' he admitted.

'I wonder if mine are,' she murmured ruefully.

'I should think so. The way you told it, you were an adored only child.' Lorenzo closed a hand over her restive hands where they were twisting together on her lap. 'Stop fretting about what you don't know and can't help.'

'I've had a couple of flashbacks!' she heard herself admit rather abruptly. 'Mr Selby thinks that's very hopeful.'

Lorenzo frowned in disconcertion, annoyed that she hadn't told him first. 'What did you remember?'

'Only an image of me seated in a limo and one of me in that café where Milly Taylor worked and where I must have gone to meet her. Not very helpful or interesting,' she remarked with a sigh.

'But promising,' Lorenzo commented, wondering why he didn't feel more excited over the prospect of her reclaiming her memory and, consequently, her life. Was it possible that after so many months he had reached some stage of compassion fatigue and disappointed hopes where he was simply guilty of secretly wishing that his life would return to normal?

Dannazione, why didn't he just admit the truth to himself? This current version of Brooke was his unparalleled favourite. He was in no hurry to reclaim the original version. As she was now, she was likeable, desirable and surprisingly appealing. Naturally he preferred her this way, he conceded with gritty inner honesty, no great mystery there. Only a masochist would have craved the old Brooke. What was wrong with being truthful about that? The woman he was with now was neither the woman he had married nor the woman he had been divorcing.

Brooke peered out of the windows as the limo drove up a steep twisting lane hedged in by dense trees and her eyes widened with appreciation as the lane opened out to frame the rambling farmhouse that sat on top of a gentle hill, presiding, she suspected, over a spectacular view of the Tuscan countryside. 'It's a beautiful site,' she remarked.

'It's remote,' Lorenzo warned her as he climbed out of the car. 'You may find it quite isolated here while I'm away on business.'

'I think I'll be fine,' Brooke declared, waiting for the driver to open the car and bring Topsy's travelling carrier out. She bent down to release the little animal, accepting the frantic affection coming her way with a wide grin. 'I can go for walks with Topsy, sit out and read, maybe even do a little exploring.'

'I'm not planning to work *every* day,' Lorenzo told her with a sudden flashing smile. 'I don't want you going too far on your own, so save the exploration until I'm here and it will be much more comfortable for you.'

Topsy bouncing at her heels, Brooke walked into the house, violet eyes sparkling with pleasure at everything she saw. Her hand stretched out to brush the weathered pale sun-warmed stone of the house as if she couldn't resist its appeal. 'I love old things,' she told him cheerfully.

Lorenzo stoically resisted the urge to contradict her with his superior knowledge of her tastes. 'She's discovering herself again,' the psychiatrist had told him. 'Give her that freedom.'

'When did you buy this place?' she asked.

'Long before I met you. I wanted a home base in Italy, and I assumed I would use it for holidays but, to be frank, I've hardly been here since the renovation project was completed.'

Brooke gave his shoulder a playful mock punch. 'Because you work too hard,' she pointed out, gazing around the rustic hallway and caressing the smooth bannister of the old wooden staircase that led up to the next floor.

'You used a designer, didn't you?' she guessed, moving from doorway to doorway to study the pale drapes and the subtle palate of colours employed to provide a charming and tranquil backdrop to antique rustic furniture and comfortable contemporary sofas.

Lorenzo laughed, his lean dark features extraordinarily handsome in that moment as he stood in the sunshine flooding through the open front door. 'How did you guess?' he mocked.

'Whoever you used was really good,' Brooke was saying appreciatively when a sparely built older man appeared in the hallway and greeted them in a flood of Italian.

'This is Jacopo. He and his wife, Sofia, look after us here,' Lorenzo informed her, closing a hand round hers to urge her towards the stairs. 'When would you like lunch?'

'Midday? After our early start, I'm quite hungry.' She shot an uncertain glance up at his lean dark face, ensnared by vibrant and lustrous black-lashed golden eyes that left her breathless.

Lorenzo informed Jacopo and led her upstairs. 'Sofia likes a schedule to work to. She's a great cook.'

'Did I ever cook for you?' Brooke enquired.

'Never.'

Her brows lifted in surprise. 'I wonder why not. I like reading recipes, which makes me think that I must've enjoyed cooking at some stage of my life,' she told him, walking into a breathtaking bedroom as complete in charm and appeal as the ground-floor reception areas. Turning round, her head tilted back to appreciate the vaulted ceiling above, she sped through the door into the corner turret room to laugh in delight when her suspicions proved correct and she discovered a deftly arranged circular bathroom. 'It's a wonderful house, Lorenzo. Was it a wreck when you found it?'

'A complete ruin,' he confirmed. 'I loved the views and the old courtyard out the back, which was completely overgrown. I didn't really appreciate how much potential the house itself had or, indeed, how large it was. We certainly don't require the half-dozen bedrooms we have here.'

The doors had been secured back on a balcony on the opposite wall and she strolled out, relieved the ironwork was thick enough to prevent a nosy little dog from sliding between bars and falling, because there was no use pretending, she thought fondly, Topsy wasn't the brightest or most cautious spark on the planet. Seconds later she was so enthralled by the view of the Tuscan landscape, she simply stared.

A hint of early morning mist still hung over the picturesque walled stone village on a nearby hilltop and somehow it almost magically enhanced the lush green of the vines and fruit orchards in the valley below. Ancient spreading chestnut trees marked the boundary of the garden, the turning colour of their leaves hinting that autumn was on its way. 'It's really beautiful,' she sighed.

The only outstandingly beautiful object in his vision at that moment, Lorenzo acknowledged abstractedly, was her, a foam of curls falling naturally across her bare shoulders in a white-blonde mass, the pretty, surprisingly simple blue dress only adding to the fragile femininity that she exuded and the slender, shapely legs on view. Hunger stabbed through him as sharp and immediate in its penetration as a knife and he strode forward.

Brooke relaxed back into the warmth of his lean powerful frame as his hand came down on her shoulder, a roaring readiness within her taut body to do whatever it took to ensure that their relationship had a fighting chance of survival. His sensual mouth dropped a kiss down on her other shoulder and she trembled, her body coming alive as though he had pressed a magic switch, and by the time he shifted his lips to the considerably more sensitive flesh of the slope leading up to her neck, her hips were pushing back against his in helpless response.

The zip of her dress eased slowly down and he

spread the parted edges to run his mouth down over her slender back and she wriggled and jerked, learning that she had tender spots she had not known she possessed. The snap of her bra being released unnerved her when she was standing out in the fresh air, *in public*, as she saw it, even though it was a very rural area. She spun in his arms.

'I don't want anyone to see me,' she mumbled nervously, suddenly wondering if that reaction was a passion killer as he looked down at her in seeming surprise at her inhibitions. 'I mean, there might be… er…workers in the vines or something.'

Lorenzo laughed soft and low and swept her up into his arms as if she were a lightweight, when she knew she was not, and carried her over to the bed. He skimmed off her bra with almost daunting expertise. Her violet eyes shot up to lock to his lean bronzed face. 'You must've been with an awful lot of women,' she heard herself say, and five seconds later cringed at that revealing observation, her face burning as hot as hellfire.

Taken aback, Lorenzo looked down at her in surprise. 'The usual number before we married,' he conceded.

'And not…er…*since*?' Brooke prompted, unable to stifle that question. 'I mean…we were separated… and then I was in a coma for well over a year…'

'I haven't been with anyone else since the day I married you,' Lorenzo spelt out with a level of precision that disconcerted her even more. 'I don't break my promises.'

A controversial topic, she recognised uneasily, but she was impressed nonetheless by that steadfast fidelity that many men would surely have forsaken during a legal separation. It was one more gift to appreciate, wasn't it? In one statement he had both surprised and delighted her, affirming her conviction that they might still have a marriage worth saving. He had not turned to another woman for either sex or consolation and that said so much about the sort of guy he was. She wanted to tell him that she loved him again, but she swallowed the words, which would strike him as empty when she didn't have the luxury of even recalling their past relationship.

'We're getting too serious,' Lorenzo told her with a sudden flashing smile that didn't quite reach his gorgeous eyes.

'Blame me,' she muttered ruefully. 'I was the one asking awkward questions.'

'You should feel free to say whatever you like to me,' Lorenzo told her, backing away from the bed to slam the door shut and shed his jacket, his tie and his shoes in rapid succession.

Brooke swallowed hard, wondering why she always felt so shy with him, wondering why she wanted to cover her bared breasts from view. She *had* to be accustomed to such intimacy. That she could be innately shy in the bedroom, after all, went against everything she had so far learned about herself. Women who were shy or modest about showing their bodies didn't wear teeny-tiny shorts and incredibly short skirts, she reminded herself impatiently.

There was nothing shy about Lorenzo either, she acknowledged as he strolled, buck naked, back to the bed like a very, *very* sexy bronzed predator, all lean, rippling muscle and hair-roughened thighs. Just looking at Lorenzo almost overwhelmed her because she still experienced a deep, abiding sense of wonder that such a rich, powerful and important man had married her. Yet where did that low self-esteem come from? She was supposed to be so confident, a woman in possession of a trust fund, both prosperous and successful in her own right. Had she always been scared on the inside and confident on the outside?

'*Dio*... I can't wait to get inside you,' Lorenzo growled.

That graphic assurance sent a flush running right up over her breasts into her face and that out-of-her-depth sensation that had grabbed her on the only night she had so far spent with him returned.

'What's wrong?' Lorenzo scanned the rapid changing expressions on her taut face. 'And why have you turned red?'

'I don't know,' Brooke gabbled, suddenly snaking free of the dress round her hips and kicking off her shoes to scramble below the sheets, desperate to be doing something rather than freezing guiltily beneath that far too shrewd and clever gaze of his. He picked up on her insecurities and it was not only embarrassing but also unnerving because it stripped away what little poise she retained.

'You're blushing!' Lorenzo laughed in apparent appreciation of that achievement.

'Did you have to mention it?' Brooke groaned. 'To me, being with you like this still feels very *new*. I know that's silly but that's how it is.'

'No, it's not silly. I'm being insensitive,' Lorenzo sliced in with lingering incomprehension at the concept of Brooke being embarrassed about anything on the planet. But he could see that, as far as she was concerned, she was telling him the truth and once again he marvelled at the transparency of her expressions.

'I'm the one out of step here with the norm, not you.' Brooke stretched up a hand to grasp his, trying to bridge the gap between them.

Lorenzo ceased trying to wrap his head around the inexplicable and came down on the bed to rub an appreciative hand over a succulent pink nipple and close his mouth there instead. When had she got so serious? When had *he* begun to behave as though what was only a temporary identity were the *real* Brooke? She was driving him insane again, only it was in a very different way from the first time around, he conceded fiercely. Here he was craving his almost ex-wife like an addictive drug. For the first time since the crash he wanted to walk away…and then her fingers tightened round his and she looked up at him and she smiled, and his thoughts evaporated as though they had never existed.

She stretched up, clumsily gripping his arm for support, and settled her ripe pink lips against his and the scent of her, the sweet delicious taste of her as her tongue darted against his, turned Lorenzo on so

hard and fast, he flattened her down to the bed with
two strong hands, his dominant nature taking over
with all the passion he had once had to restrain in
the marital bed. But there were no curbs now and he
could not resist that lure of being himself for the first
time with her or the temptation of not being with a
woman who lay back like a goddess inviting worship
and never touched him.

Brooke felt the change in him and welcomed his
passion, realising that she had almost frightened him
off with her insecurities. Her fingers delved into his
luxuriant black hair and smoothed down his high
cheekbones to the roughened blue shadow of stubble
that highlighted his wide sensual mouth. She gasped
as he dipped his head over her breasts and seized a
swollen pink crest and grazed it with the edge of his
teeth. She was *so* sensitive there that her back arched
and then his skilled hands were travelling lower, trac-
ing the damp cleft between her thighs, probing the
tight entrance, making her hips rock up and a low-
pitched cry part her lips.

'You're so ready for me,' Lorenzo husked in satisfaction, shifting position to roll her over and up
onto her knees.

Her whole body clenched in sensual shock as he
drove into her hard and fast. It was electrifying, every
skin cell and nerve ending in her body powering the
excitement that made her heart race and her breath
catch in her throat. Every sleek, powerful thrust of his
body sent sensation tumbling and cascading in seis-
mic waves through her quivering body and height-

ened the tight clenching low in her pelvis. Her internal muscles contracted and sent her careening with a cry into a climax that detonated like a bomb of sheer pleasure inside her trembling body. It felt so good tears of reaction burned her eyes and she blinked rapidly. But he wasn't finished, no, far from it, and as the pressure began to build and tighten unbearably inside her again, it only took one expert touch at the most sensitive spot in her body for another orgasm to fly through her in a violent storm.

Shattered, she collapsed down on the bed, while he groaned in satisfaction and his arms tightened round her, flipping her round so that his wicked mouth could tease her parted lips and then slide between, sending a quivering tremor through her drained length.

'Not moving for anything ever again,' she swore limply.

'The helicopter's picking me up at two but I'll be back by nine this evening,' Lorenzo intoned, brilliant dark eyes connecting with hers. 'Sleep this afternoon because you won't be getting much sleep tonight, *cara mia*.'

'Promises, promises,' Brooke teased, feeling wonderfully relaxed. 'You could be absolutely exhausted.'

Lorenzo smoothed her tumbled curls off her pale brow and curled her slight length close. 'I won't be too tired for you,' he intoned huskily, purposely closing off every logical thought and living in the moment. *She* was doing that and if he wasn't prepared to let her go yet, so must he.

* * *

Four weeks later, after Lorenzo had repeatedly extended their stay, Brooke stood back to study the table she had laid on the terrace at the side of the house. She was humming under her breath as she walked back into the kitchen to check the bubbling pots. Tonight, she was cooking because Sofia was away visiting her daughter but she wasn't quite as adept a cook as she had hoped when she first came up with the idea of providing dinner. Sofia, however, had given her some useful tips and some even more useful shortcuts and, with a little preparation and help behind the scenes beforehand, Brooke had felt able to tackle a simple menu.

She glanced at the tiny half-knitted garment that Sofia had left lying on the dresser. The older woman was knitting a cardigan for her first grandchild. Brooke picked it up, unable to explain why it had attracted her attention in the first place as she found herself scanning the intricate pattern, and then registered that she could name every one of the stitches used and even identify a mistake. She blinked and something tugged almost painfully deep within her brain. She shook her head again in surprise. So, she knew how to knit, like lots of other people, she acknowledged dismissively, and rubbed her brow until the tightness there began to evaporate.

As she walked back out to the terrace, a bout of unnerving dizziness made her head swim and her legs falter and she swiftly took a seat, lowered her head and breathed in deep and slow. She didn't know what was amiss with her and already planned to visit a doctor when they flew back to London the following day. She didn't think that the faintness or the headache were linked to her head injury, any more than the nausea that had assailed her at odd moments in recent days, but she thought it was time that she had herself checked out all the same. Perhaps she was coming down with some virus, she thought ruefully.

A slim figure in white cropped jeans and a vest top, she stood up again and studied the view of the tranquil patchwork of vines and orchards and fields that spread out beyond the garden boundaries. She had never dreamt that they would end up staying an entire month in Italy and the time had fairly raced past. Lorenzo had flown off to loads of business meetings but every other day he was at home, either working or taking her out somewhere, and their peaceful stay had done wonders for her state of mind.

Regrettably, she had experienced no further flashbacks, which was a considerable disappointment to her, but, on the balance side, she was sleeping well, eating well and generally felt much stronger. A lot of that related to her improved relationship with Lorenzo though, she conceded. He hadn't promised to make a special effort when he had said that they would see how their marriage went but he had definitely been trying.

Regardless of how busy he was, he had made time for her. She had drunk a glass of the local wine in the Piazza Grande in Montepulciano, strolled under the trees by the walls of Lucca, explored the labyrinth of underground caves in Pitigliano and wandered silent in appreciation through the gardens of Garzoni in Collodi. There had been dinners out as well in wonderful restaurants in Florence, but she had enjoyed the picnic in the orange orchard below the house even more because Lorenzo had surprised her with a sapphire pendant that took her breath away and had then made passionate love to her.

She had never felt so close to anyone as she felt to Lorenzo, and sometimes it scared her because she knew that she wasn't in a safe or settled marriage and that, at any time, Lorenzo could again decide that he wanted a divorce. When she allowed herself to think along those lines, her nervous tension went sky-high and so she tried to enjoy what they currently had without thinking too far ahead into the future. She didn't tell him she loved him now, no longer dared to be that confiding. Had she known the true state of their marriage, she would never have said it in the first place. She didn't want Lorenzo to feel trapped or that he couldn't tell her the truth, and her telling him that she loved him could only make him feel uncomfortable.

By the time the helicopter landed, Brooke had laid out the first course on the table and she stood back, smiling, as Lorenzo strode up the slope towards her, eye-catchingly gorgeous in his exquisitely tailored dove-grey suit, his luxuriant black hair ruffled, his spectacular dark golden eyes locked to her.

And, truth to tell, there was not a single cloud on Lorenzo's horizon at that moment and his lean, dark, serious face flashed into a smile at the sight of her waiting for him. It probably made him a four-letter word of a guy but he enjoyed the knowledge that his wife's world seemed to revolve entirely around him. She was a slender but curvy figure dressed entirely in white, her cloud of curls framing her piquant features, eyes purple as violets.

'I made dinner,' Brooke announced. 'But you have to sit down now.'

Lorenzo tensed. 'I was heading for a shower first—'

'You can't…if you do that the main course will be ready too soon and it will spoil,' Brooke told him earnestly. 'If you want to eat, it's now or never.'

Lorenzo grinned. 'I'll make a bargain with you. I sit down now to eat, and you join me in the shower afterwards…'

'That's a deal.' Brooke went pink and sank down at the other side of the table. 'Dig in. It's quite a simple meal but this timing thing is complicated.'

'I can't believe you've made a meal for us,' Lorenzo confided truthfully.

'It may not win any awards but I think I should be able to make a decent meal,' Brooke contended seriously. 'It's a basic skill.'

'How are you feeling about returning to London tomorrow?' he prompted.

'Kind of sad,' she confided, laying down her fork to finger the sapphire gleaming below her collarbone. 'I love it here and I've relaxed a lot more but we can't live cut off from the rest of the world for ever.'

'No, we can't,' Lorenzo agreed and, as he pushed

his plate away to indicate that he was finished, he lounged back in his chair and spread his hands. 'Why did you go to all this trouble for a meal? We could've eaten out. That's what I usually do when Sofia takes a night off.'

'It's our last night here.' Brooke shrugged in an effort to be casual and pushed back her chair to return to the kitchen. There she drained pans, whisked the sauce again and put the main course together on delicate china plates to take them out to the table.

'It looks great,' Lorenzo said softly.

'Wait and see how it tastes,' she urged.

He ate in deliberate silence, cleared the plate and then sent her a wicked grin of appreciation. 'That's it. You're on kitchen duty every night that I can spare you.'

'And how often would you spare me?' she enquired as she pushed her own plate away and went to fetch dessert.

'Not very often,' Lorenzo confessed, following her into the kitchen to tug her back against his lean, hard frame, his hands smoothing down over her hip bones to lace across her flat stomach. 'You have a much more important role to fulfil, *cara mia.*'

Insanely aware that he was aroused, she instinctively pressed back into him, loving the sudden fracture in his breathing and the way his fingers instantly slid up to the waistband of her jeans to release the button and delve down over her quivering tummy to the heart of her. 'And what would that role entail?' she prompted shakily, suspecting that he wasn't likely to let her make it as far as dessert.

Interpreting the damp welcome below her silk knickers, not to mention the encouraging gasp parting her lips, Lorenzo laughed appreciatively. 'I think you already know, *gatita mia*.'

'Well, you *have* to make a choice. Me...' Brooke told him, battling her hunger for him to gently step away and fasten her jeans, 'or the last course.'

Lorenzo snatched her back to him. 'I'm Italian... the woman wins every time.'

'Maybe *if* you're really, really good,' Brooke teased, 'I'll bring you dessert in bed.'

In answer, Lorenzo spun her round and kissed her with voracious hunger, his mouth crushing hers, one hand anchored in her mass of curls. Beneath that onslaught, she gasped and he wasted no time in bending down to scoop her up and head for the stairs. 'Bossy... *much*?' she taunted.

'You know you like it,' Lorenzo breathed with inherent dark sensuality, dropping her down on the bed and following her there to pluck off her shoes and divest her of the rest of her clothes.

'No, you undress first,' Brooke instructed, feeling daring as she pushed his jacket off his broad shoulders and yanked at his tie, her fingers deft on his shirt buttons. Pushing the fabric back, she spread her hands over the warm hair-roughened musculature of his chest.

Lorenzo vaulted off the bed to remove the rest of

his clothes. 'Off with the jeans and the top,' he commanded impatiently.

Brooke made a production of shimmying out of her tight jeans, sliding out one slender bare leg, then the next. Bending back, she released the hooks on her top and peeled it off over her head, her teeth tightening at the over-sensitivity of her engorged nipples as the air stung them. Her breasts had felt weird for several days, tender and swollen, and she had thought that had to be a sign of her menstrual cycle kicking in. Although she had had periods while she was still in the clinic, she had not had one since she left medical care and she knew that she would have to mention that to the doctor when she saw him as well. Possibly that IUD Lorenzo had mentioned was causing her problems, she reasoned wryly, and perhaps she would have to consider another method of birth control.

Lorenzo feasted his eyes on her with unashamed appreciation, his attention lingering on the luscious swell of her breasts. She must've put on weight and it really, really suited her, he acknowledged hungrily. 'I'm burning up for you—'

'Since when? You woke me up at six this morning,' Brooke reminded him helplessly, as always, almost astonished by his constant desire for her.

Lorenzo grinned and came down beside her. 'That was this morning and it was a lifetime ago, *bellezza mia.*'

'Will we still be like this when we go home?' Brooke heard herself ask in sudden fear that their new intimacy would somehow vanish when they left Italy.

'You're moving into my bedroom,' Lorenzo asserted.

'Am I?' Brooke smiled like a cat that had got the cream, reassured by that statement, that change in attitude that signified togetherness rather than separation.

'Are you thinking of arguing about that?' Lorenzo husked against her reddened mouth.

Her fingers speared into his black hair to draw him down to her, the same intense hunger firing through every atom of her being. 'No.'

A long while later, she lay in perfect peace in his arms and drifted off to sleep in a happy daze, which made the dream that followed all the more frightening because she wasn't prepared for it, couldn't *ever* have been prepared for the images that went flashing through her brain and made her scream so loud in the dark that she hurt her throat.

She saw the crash. She saw Brooke as she reached for her and failed to catch her hand, experienced the agony of knowing she had *failed* to save her sister, her only living relative. And in the shaken aftermath, when she must have regained consciousness for a split second, reliving that unimaginable pain and primal fear, she saw her knitting needles strewn in the smoking wreckage of the car…

'It's OK…it's OK…' Lorenzo soothed as she sat bolt upright in the bed, rocking back and forth, her head down on her raised knees as she sobbed. 'You had a nightmare. It's not real, none of it's real. *Dio*, you screamed so loudly I thought we were being attacked!'

But it was real, it was *very* real, Milly recognised, her frantic thoughts tangled and befogged by layer after layer of shock and growing disbelief. Somehow she had got her memory back, the memory she had once been so desperate to retrieve. Her true self had slipped back without fanfare into place during that nightmare, clarifying everything that had previously been a complete blank. But, disturbingly, reclaiming her memory and her knowledge of who she was had plunged her into an even more frightening world.

Brooke was dead and she was devastated by that knowledge, even though the last time she had been with her half-sister she had finally appreciated that Brooke was unlikely ever to accept her as a true sibling. But it was one thing to accept that, another entirely to accept that Brooke was now gone for ever and that their relationship could never be improved.

Her sister was dead and Milly had been mistaken for her. How had that happened? But the more she thought about it, the easier it became to understand. After all, she had been wearing Brooke's jewellery and Brooke's clothes and she had had facial injuries. The strong resemblance between the two women had gone completely unnoticed, presumably because Brooke had been seriously injured too. Her reddened eyes stung with fresh tears.

How on earth could she ever put right all that had gone wrong?

Lorenzo would be devastated.

Lorenzo didn't even know he was a widower. How could he? He had spent months looking after his injured wife's needs, caring for her because she had no one else and then, ultimately, living with and having sex with the woman he naturally believed to be his wife. But she *wasn't* his wife, she was a stranger, just as he had been a stranger to her when she first wakened out of the coma. Only, sadly, neither of them had recognised that reality.

Trembling, retreating fast from Lorenzo's attempts to soothe her, she hurried into the bathroom, for once taking no pleasure in her surroundings. She ran a bath as an excuse to stay there alone. Lorenzo appeared in the doorway, tall, dark and bronzed, and she chased him off again, telling him she just needed a warm bath and a little space to relax. Tears ran down her cheeks then as she sat in the warm water, all the mistakes she had made piling up on top of her, and she didn't know, she really didn't know *how* to go about telling Lorenzo the truth. He had said nothing was real in her nightmare, but he was wrong—it was all *too* real and the harsh facts could not be ignored. She had wakened from a nightmare to find herself entangled in a worse nightmare, because she was living her dead sister's life with a man she loved, who did not love her. Lorenzo was wrong: nothing was OK and it never would be again…

CHAPTER EIGHT

'DON'T TELL ME that you're fine again,' Lorenzo warned her in a raw-edged undertone, his lean, darkly handsome features set in stern lines as the limo wafted them through the London traffic from the airport. 'Obviously you're anything but fine. Something has upset you a great deal and it's time that you shared it with me.'

'We'll talk when we get back…er…home,' she told him shakily, in no hurry to get there and deal with his outrage, his disbelief and his belated grief.

Lorenzo had never been hers and her tummy lurched at the knowledge that everything that had happened between them had been based purely on his conviction that she was his wife. His *every* word, his *every* decision, his *every* caress had been bestowed on Brooke, not Milly, she reminded herself doggedly, shrinking guiltily from the knowledge that *she* had encouraged *him* into sharing a bed. Brooke had hated Lorenzo, she reminded herself, reluctantly thinking back to her sibling's conviction that Lorenzo was a possessive tyrant, who had unjustly accused her of infidelity in order to divorce her.

Obviously there had been a great deal of bitterness in their relationship by that stage. But Milly liked to think that, had Brooke seen how very supportive Lorenzo had been in the wake of the crash to the woman he believed to be his wife, she would have forgiven him for their differences. On that score, his behaviour had been above reproach. He could've walked away, let the divorce go ahead, leaving her to the tender mercies of the healthcare system and some legal executor. But Lorenzo hadn't done that. He had stood by the vows he had once taken...*in sickness and in health.*

Her head was aching again with all the stress of her feverish thoughts and she rubbed her brow, wishing foolishly that there were some miraculous way of avoiding what lay ahead of her. Obviously, she would have to leave Lorenzo's house and as soon as possible. Unfortunately for her, she had nowhere to go and not a penny to her name and no close friends either, because she had moved around too much to form lasting friendships.

It was a shame that she hadn't worked harder at the many different schools she had attended during her years in foster care, she reflected with regret. Sadly, the knowledge that she would inevitably be shifted to a new foster home and a new school with different exam boards and course content had removed any enthusiasm she had had when she was younger for studying. The continual changes had made her unsettled, undisciplined and distrustful of forging close relationships with anyone because, sooner or later, everyone seemed to leave her and move on.

Perhaps that was why she had repressed every qualm to stay friendly and involved with Brooke, generally accepting whatever treatment Brooke dealt out. She hadn't wanted to lose that all-important link with Brooke and had been eager to offer her half-sister all her love and support. Hadn't she clung to Lorenzo in much the same way? Pathetically eager to offer love even when he wasn't looking for it? Inside herself, she cringed for her weakness and susceptibility. But then had she *ever* been loved?

Her memories of her mother were very hazy because Natalia had died when Milly was only eleven years old, but Natalia *had* been affectionate and caring. Her father, however, had never paid her any attention when he visited them, hadn't seemed to have the slightest interest in her, she recalled sadly, although possibly his apparent indifference had come from his guilt at cheating on his wife. Had her mother not told her that William Jackson was her father, she would never have known because his name wasn't on her birth certificate. Although he had supported her mother financially, he had refused to officially acknowledge Milly as his daughter.

'We're home,' Lorenzo imparted flatly.

But Madrigal Court was *his* home, not hers, Milly ruminated, and immediately wanted to kick herself for that forlorn thought. Like many children raised by the state, she had always longed for a stable and permanent home. It was not a bit of wonder that when she had been deprived of her memory that deep-based need had surfaced and made her latch onto Brooke's home and husband like a homing pigeon eager to find a permanent roost.

'I'm afraid I can't understand how a bad dream can cause you this much stress,' Lorenzo breathed impatiently as he herded her into the pristine white drawing room and closed the door behind them. 'What on earth is the matter?'

Milly breathed in deep and slow to steady her nerves. 'I remembered the accident,' she admitted. 'And then my memory came back.'

Lorenzo paled and his lean, powerful frame went rigid. 'Just like that?'

'Just like that,' she confirmed sickly. 'But the real problem is that when I regained my memory I realised that I'm not the person everyone assumed I was...'

His brow pleated as if he was still trying to penetrate the meaning of that statement. 'What are you talking about?'

'I'm not Brooke Tassini, Lorenzo. I'm *not* your wife. I'm Milly Taylor.'

The fringe of his lush black lashes shot up over incredulous dark golden eyes and then he swung round and headed back to the door, pulling out his phone. 'That's not possible.'

'Where are you going?' she gasped.

Lorenzo compressed his lips. It was obvious to him that his wife was having some sort of nervous breakdown. He had not a clue how to deal with such an astonishing statement, but he was convinced that her psychiatrist would know. 'I'm contacting Mr Selby so that you can discuss this with him.'

'I don't want to see Mr Selby right now. I need to get things straight with you first,' Milly declared tautly. 'That's more important.'

'There *is* nothing more important than your mental health,' Lorenzo contradicted, sending her a censorious glance from his position by the door. 'Why did you keep quiet about this? Why didn't you immediately tell me what you were going through last night?'

'I had to get my head straight,' she protested. 'It was a big shock for me too and I feel terrible about everything that's happened. I don't know how the heck you'll ever sort out all the legal stuff.'

An imperious ebony brow elevated. 'What legal stuff?'

Milly dragged in another steadying breath. 'Brooke's... Brooke's dead, Lorenzo, and I've been declared dead but I'm still alive. That mistake will have to be rectified...*somehow.*'

Lorenzo was holding his phone so tightly between his fingers that he almost crushed it. Was she suffering from what he had heard referred to as a psychotic break? He studied her pale, rigid face, reading her distress. She really *believed* this stuff she was telling him, he registered in consternation: she had decided that she was not his wife, that she was the other woman in the car. Why would she do that?

'Brooke was my sister,' she murmured tautly.

'Brooke doesn't have a sister,' he overruled.

'Not officially. I'm illegitimate,' Milly admitted

stiffly. 'William Jackson had an affair that went on for years with my mother and I was born during their affair. He never recognised me as his child and never treated me as if I was his and I didn't know back then that he was a married man with another family. Brooke traced me and came to see me out of curiosity when I was eighteen and just leaving foster care. She was my half-sister...'

Lorenzo released his breath in a slow, measured hiss. He hadn't had Milly Taylor's birth and background checked out, hadn't considered her past relevant in establishing who she had been to his wife. He could not yet accept the enormity of what he was being told but he also could not imagine how or why his wife could have come up with such a detailed and fanciful story overnight.

'Brooke would've mentioned a sister.'

'She didn't tell anyone about me and was careful never to be seen in public with me. My very existence was...' Milly hesitated before forging on with a frown '...pretty much a source of resentment and annoyance to her. She knew about the affair and the amount of unhappiness it had caused *her* mother. My mother was dead by the time Brooke sought me out, but I suspect that the bitter anger she felt towards my mother transferred to me to some extent.'

Lorenzo was frowning. 'A half-sister? But that doesn't explain anything! If Brooke didn't like you or find you useful in some way, what would you have been doing in that car with her on the day of the crash? Nothing about this story makes sense!'

Milly stood up slowly, her violet eyes deeply troubled. 'I can help it make sense but you have to try to keep your temper.'

Lorenzo flung his arrogant dark head back and dealt her a scorching appraisal. 'Of course, I can keep my temper, but I still don't think you're going to be able to explain this nonsense, and discussing it as if it's true fact isn't helping the situation or you.'

'Brooke used me as her stand-in on several occasions,' Milly admitted starkly. 'We looked very alike, even more alike after I had had cosmetic surgery done on my nose,' she continued doggedly as Lorenzo continued to stare at her as though she had sprouted horns and cloven hooves. 'Brooke paid for the procedure and I didn't want to get it done but when I said no, she dropped me, and I was so desperate to hang onto our relationship that eventually I agreed.'

Lorenzo was frowning in disbelief. 'You looked alike? What was wrong with your nose?'

'It was too big. Nobody would have mistaken me for her if I hadn't agreed to the surgery. After that, she used me a couple of times to stand in for her at charity events where I didn't have to do much pretending. I'm no actress,' she confided tightly. 'Sometimes, she didn't want to attend events or she wanted to mislead the press about where she was and then she would phone me up and ask me to go in her place. She would give me her clothes and her jewellery to wear.'

His frown had laced his bone structure with hard lines of tension. 'You are telling me that you engaged in deception with Brooke to trick other people, including me?'

Milly bridled. 'That isn't how I saw it and you were never involved. I was just helping my sister out. Smoothing out her life when she was too busy to meet all the demands on her time,' she protested.

'You were deceiving people,' Lorenzo contradicted with glacial disapproval. 'If this far-fetched story is true, tell me where you were going on the day of the crash.'

Milly winced. 'I was to go to a hotel and stay there for several days pretending to be Brooke while she was away somewhere on holiday, having travelled on my passport. But, of course, we never got as far as the hotel or the airport...'

'She was using *your* passport?' Lorenzo demanded incredulously. 'But that's illegal! Where was she going?'

'I don't know. She didn't tell me,' Milly replied numbly. 'Sometimes she told me stuff, sometimes, she told me nothing. It depended on her mood.'

And that *was* a startlingly accurate description of Brooke's unpredictable, temperamental nature, Lorenzo conceded grudgingly, because in spite of all logic he was beginning to listen, beginning to put facts together to finally see a picture forming that could make some kind of sense. He could certainly check out whether a Milly Taylor had failed to turn up for her flight that day and he could look deeper into her background to see if he could establish an official link that would bear out her story.

From Milly's point of view, Lorenzo's attitude seemed oddly detached. He was dealing with the facts, avoiding the harsher realities of their situation, she suspected ruefully.

'Well, anyway,' she mumbled. 'That's what I was doing in the limo on the day of the crash. Brooke gave me the clothes she was wearing and her jewellery and I put them on while she got changed. I expect that is how I came to be identified as her.'

'You were unrecognisable,' Lorenzo admitted starkly, shifting his attention away from her as if he could no longer bear to look at her, his big, powerful frame rigid. 'You are telling me that my wife is dead, that she actually died eighteen months ago in the accident…'

'I'm so sorry. I'm sorry about everything that's happened!' Milly muttered in a driven rush of regret. 'If I hadn't been suffering from amnesia, I could have identified myself and you would have known the truth months ago…'

Lorenzo expelled his breath and raked a long-fingered brown hand roughly through his cropped black hair, his emotional turmoil palpable. 'Brooke is gone…'

'Yes,' Milly whispered, tears lashing her eyes. 'Do you believe me now?'

'Only once I have had time to confirm the extraordinary facts you have given me,' Lorenzo told her flatly.

Milly suppressed a shudder, feeling dismissed, sidelined, set back at a new and disturbing distance from him while he worked out whether she was a fantasist or a woman having a breakdown. All of a sudden everything had changed between them. Lorenzo was changing before her very eyes. It was as though their personal relationship had never happened, she acknowledged painfully. But then it had all been a lie, based on the false premise that Brooke was still alive, and at this moment Lorenzo was fathoms deep in shock and struggling to deal with the reality that his wife was dead. That was all he had the ability to consider right now and how could she expect anything more from him?

She studied his tall dark figure and the forbidding tension locking his facial muscles tight. It was selfish of her to feel rejected by his new reserve when she had no claim on him or his attention. She was nothing to him, never had been. Everything he had done for her had really been done for Brooke. On his terms she didn't really exist. And now that he knew that she *did* exist, he would never touch her again and would never look at her again as he once had.

And she had to deal with that reality and come back down to earth again, which would be challenging. After all, she had been living a kind of fantasy life with Lorenzo, a waitress from a very ordinary background, suddenly swept off into a billionaire's luxury lifestyle with private jets, servants and a level of wealth and comfort previously beyond her imagining. But it wasn't those expensive trappings she would miss, she conceded wretchedly, it would be Lorenzo.

Lorenzo, whom she loved to pieces, who didn't want her any more, who would never want her again. She felt as though her heart were breaking in two inside her and, tensing her slight shoulders, she compressed her lips, determined not to say or do anything emotional. Right now, Lorenzo didn't need that added stress and probably didn't even want to recall that he had had sex with her believing that she was his wife. No, the faster she got back out of his life again, the happier Lorenzo would be.

Lorenzo was looking back down through the months and marvelling that he had allowed the medics to silence his every misgiving about the woman who had come out of the coma. From her first wakening every atom of his ESP and intelligence had combined to send him continual warnings that Brooke's personality and character had apparently changed out of all recognition. He had listened to the doctors because it had naturally never occurred to him that the woman in the convalescent clinic could be anyone other than his wife.

Dio mio, she had been identified as his wife at the scene of the crash, presented to him as his wife when he was handed her jewellery for safekeeping before surgery. That an appalling mistake could've been made had not once crossed his mind or anyone else's. How could it have done when nobody had been aware of the striking resemblance between the two women? Of course, he hadn't had access either to her clarifying explanation about the nature of her relationship with Brooke. Brooke, indeed, had probably only latched onto her half-sister in the first place because of that resemblance, seeing how she could use that to her advantage. Milly had been acting as Brooke's stand-in, her *lookalike*. Distaste with her for having taken on such a deceptive role flared inside him, chilling his hard dark eyes to granite.

'I'll move out as soon as I can,' Milly muttered in a rush.

'Where are you planning to go?' Lorenzo lifted an ebony brow. 'Straight to the press to sell the story of the century for a fat price?'

Milly was aghast that he could even harbour such a suspicion and she turned white as milk, her violet eyes standing out stark against her porcelain skin. 'Of course not! I wouldn't do that to you or me.'

'Not even for the money?' Lorenzo prompted doubtingly.

Lorenzo's brain was awash with disconnected confused thoughts. He could not yet process what he had just learned. He struggled looking back through the long months with the woman he had believed to be his wife and accepting that she was an entirely different woman. And a stranger, his logic chipped in. A complete and total stranger. He grasped that he needed time and peace to come to terms with what he had just learned.

Milly went rigid, struggling to credit that only the night before Lorenzo had been making passionate love to her and holding her close in the aftermath as if she meant something to him. 'No, not even for the money,' she said sickly.

Lorenzo swung away from her as he could no longer stand to look at her. 'Pack,' he instructed grimly, recognising that he had to immediately get her out of the house if he was to avoid a sordid scandal. 'I have somewhere for you to live sitting ready for occupation and you might as well live there. Once I've checked out the information you've given me and consulted my lawyers, we'll sort this mess out.'

Pack?

Pure shock resonated through Milly and momentarily her head swam, and she felt dizzy. Evidently, he couldn't wait to get rid of her and the immediacy of his demand that she pack and move out disconcerted her. She might have told herself that he would want her to leave as soon as possible but her mind had yet to accept that idea. She hadn't been prepared for that change to take place so quickly and she blinked rapidly, her eyes dazed.

'I have nothing to pack. I don't own anything here,' she said flatly, because it was true when she didn't even own the clothes she wore because he had paid for everything.

'Don't be ridiculous!' Lorenzo growled. '*Anything* you have worn, *anything* that you have been using, is yours to take with you. Brooke is gone and she's not coming back.'

Milly nodded jerkily and quickly stood up, the dizziness she was still enduring dampening her face with perspiration. She felt ill, nauseous, but that was a weakness she had to hide. Lorenzo might be throwing her out but she was not about to play the poor little victim who couldn't cope. She had had enough of being weak and vulnerable while she was still in medical care.

As she opened the door to leave, Topsy hurled herself at her knees in greeting.

'You can take the dog with you too,' Lorenzo murmured. 'She's got used to you now. It would be cruel to separate you.'

But, seemingly, it wasn't cruel to kick out a bogus wife at such short notice, Milly reflected, heading upstairs with a straight spine, still battling to hold the dizziness at bay. Some sort of stupid virus she couldn't shake off, she thought wearily. As soon as she got settled, she would go and see a doctor, she promised herself. The clothes she had worn in Italy were still in the cases they had returned in and not yet unpacked, but even as she started to assemble the few items that she hadn't taken abroad with her, a maid arrived with empty cases for her to use. Lorenzo had already told the staff that she was leaving and her still-sensitive stomach rebelled to send her racing into the en suite to be sick.

Afterwards, she cleaned her teeth and with all the animation of a robot she went back to doggedly packing. She didn't have very much to show for her months in Lorenzo's life. She stripped off the rings, the diamond-studded watch and the sapphire pendant and laid them on the dressing table because they weren't hers, or at least had been gifts that weren't intended for her.

She might feel as though her life were over but, really, it was only beginning another phase, she tried to tell herself. Being hurt that Lorenzo wanted her out of his house was foolish. He had to mourn Brooke and adjust to the knowledge that the wife he had watched over for months while she was in a coma had not survived as he had believed. He had to draw a line under the past months and obviously he didn't want her around while he was trying to do that.

The cases were stowed in the limo and Milly climbed into the passenger seat, clutching Topsy to her like a tiny hairy comfort blanket. Lorenzo emerged last from the house, his lean, darkly handsome face wiped clean of emotion or any form of warmth, and barely a word was exchanged during the drive into London.

It was a fabulous apartment with its own private lift. Milly stood looking around her at the sea of crisp white furnishings and swallowed apprehensively.

'I had it decorated for Brooke,' Lorenzo breathed in a roughened undertone. 'She loved it.'

'It's spectacular,' she said woodenly, wanting him to leave so that she could ditch her game face. But at the same time, she was dreading the moment when he would actually leave and already wondering how long it would be before she saw him again.

'It's yours now. You can make any changes you want…at my expense,' he added impatiently when she glanced at him in astonishment. 'Legally, this will ultimately be *your* apartment.'

Milly frowned in bewilderment. 'How on earth could it ever be mine?' she queried.

'I signed it over to Brooke before the accident and, according to my lawyers, everything that once belonged to Brooke is likely to go to you in the end because I refused to take it. I don't want anything that belonged to her,' he confessed quietly. 'Of course, it will take weeks, if not months, to disentangle the legal threads concerning the misidentification that has been made and free up her funds. In the meantime I will ensure that you are financially secure. The apartment is serviced. The fridge should be packed with food.'

'I don't want your money,' she whispered and flinched inside herself because standing in an apartment he had bought, wearing clothing he had purchased and making such a statement struck her as absurd. But the knowledge that he had evidently consulted his lawyers about their situation before she had even left his home chilled her to the marrow.

'Nonetheless, I will not leave you destitute. That would be unpardonable,' Lorenzo bit out in a fierce undertone. 'You have done nothing wrong. In your role as Brooke's lookalike you may have innocently contributed to the mistaken identification that was made but your life has been disrupted as much as mine by what happened. It's my responsibility to ensure that you don't suffer for that.'

Milly was already suffering, and she didn't want to hear that he still viewed her as his responsibility, not when he was in the act of casting her off like an old shoe. Her stomach lurched again and she crossed her arms defensively. She said nothing while she watched him from below her lashes, committing every beloved feature to memory. Those beautiful lustrous dark eyes of his were hard and dark without even a redeeming hint of gold. Yet he still looked amazing, sleek and dark and devastatingly handsome. And even the thought made her feel guilty because she was lusting after her sister's husband, wasn't she?

Instead she opted to wonder what his precious lawyers had told him to do. Handle her with kid gloves? Give her no cause for complaint or any excuse to run to the press and tell all? Even after all they had shared, did he still think so little of her that he could believe that she would betray him like that? And what did it matter what he thought of her now when everything was over?

Topsy on her lap, she sat still long after he had departed. She had a new life to plan now, she told herself urgently. She didn't want to return to being a waitress. Living Brooke's life had made her more ambitious, just as the long struggle to recover from the accident and handle living with amnesia had made her stronger. She would look into other jobs and work out if she could qualify for a training course and take it from there. She might feel as if losing her sister for ever and then losing Lorenzo as well had left her with a giant black hole inside her chest, but she couldn't afford to give way to such feelings or they would eat her alive.

Right now, she was at rock bottom but, from here on in, her life could only improve…

CHAPTER NINE

THE NEXT MONTH passed painfully slowly for Milly.

She had no contact whatsoever from Lorenzo, but she received more than one visit from his lawyers, seeking affidavits and signatures to documents while also persuading her to consent to a DNA test. They kept her informed of her legal position and of what would happen next. And it being the law, it moved at a leisurely pace but, finally, the day of Brooke's funeral arrived.

The media storm that had erupted at the news of Brooke's death, and the half-sister who had mistakenly been identified as her, had died surprisingly swiftly, firstly because Brooke had become old news, and secondly because they could neither find Milly to ask her to tell her story nor identify the woman who was Brooke's half-sister.

Milly had lived very quietly, walking miles through the streets with Topsy to keep herself busy while struggling to suppress her memories of the time she had spent with Lorenzo. There was no point looking back to a relationship that should never have happened in the first place, she told herself sternly. He wasn't hers, never had been hers, and never would be hers again.

All the same, even in the midst of her grief there came a day when she could no longer close her eyes to the complication that had developed: she was pregnant with Lorenzo's baby. And a joy that laced her with guilt filled her almost to overflowing at a development that only *she* was likely to welcome. For too long, she had ignored her symptoms, and by the time she went to a doctor to have her pregnancy confirmed, she had already done a home test and had fully come to terms with the reality of her condition.

And that she had fallen pregnant really wasn't that surprising, she reasoned ruefully. She had had sex with Lorenzo countless times and no precautions had been taken. Lorenzo had believed she had an IUD fitted because at the time he had believed that she was Brooke and she hadn't had the knowledge to contradict him.

He would be upset when she told him, and Milly knew that eventually she would *have* to tell him. How could she not? He had a right to know his child— even if the woman carrying his child wasn't the one he would have chosen for the role.

Even when he had believed she was Brooke he had said, *'The last complication we need now is a child.'*

But she wasn't the same person she had been on the day of the crash, she recognised wryly. Her recuperation and dealing with life as an amnesiac in a rocky marriage had taught her that she was far more mentally and physically robust than she had ever dreamt. Neither of them were to blame for her pregnancy. She was happy about her child, even excited about her future. Lorenzo could hurt her, she conceded ruefully, but he wouldn't *break* her.

Those were the thoughts on her mind as she dressed for her sister's funeral, bundling her hair below a hat, doing her utmost to ensure that nobody would notice her and catch on to the powerful resemblance between her and Brooke. The lawyers had assured her that nobody expected her to attend. For nobody, she had read Lorenzo, and she had grimaced and had said that of course she would attend her sister's reburial.

A car picked her up at ten. The church was almost empty, there being few mourners this long after Brooke's demise but the paparazzi were out in force outside the church, peering suspiciously at everyone, in search of the half-sister they had heard about but had not yet contrived to identify. Her head bent, her slender body shrouded in a deliberately unfashionable black coat, Milly dropped into a pew at the back of the church, listening to the service while striving not to stare at the back of Lorenzo's arrogant dark head.

How could she think of him as the father of her baby when it wasn't even acceptable to approach him at the funeral, lest someone snatch a photo of them together? At the graveside, tears burning at the backs of her eyes for the sister who was gone and for the sibling affection she had never managed to ignite, she stole a fleeting glance at Lorenzo. He dealt her a faint nod of acknowledgement. His lean, strong face had a tougher, harder edge. He had lost weight. But then Milly had lost weight as well. She felt nauseous much of the day and it was an effort to remember to eat as one day drifted into another. Usually she tried to eat when she was feeding Topsy.

Lorenzo studied Milly from the other side of the cemetery. He hadn't wanted her to attend. He had needed her to stay in the background and out of sight, had assured himself over and over again that that was the only sensible solution. But there she stood, lost in the folds of a voluminous coat, her incredible hair hidden below a trilby hat, her delicate face shadowed by the brim and barely recognisable. She looked thinner, younger, but naturally she looked younger because she *was* years younger than Brooke had been. Milly would only be twenty-three on her next birthday he reminded himself doggedly. It was all over, *finally* over, the whole distasteful business of his marriage to Brooke, done and dusted, he reflected, fighting to block memories of his time in Italy with Milly: long golden days lazily drifting past, the scent and the taste of her, the sound of her laughter and the readiness of her smile.

It would do him no good to dwell on the past. He had married Brooke and it had been a disaster from start to finish. And Milly was Brooke's half-sister and by acting as her unofficial stand-in had knowingly engaged with Brooke in an unsavoury deception to fool innocent people. Evidently, she had seen nothing wrong with that kind of behaviour. In other words, the same thread of dishonesty that had run through his late wife like poison had an echo in Milly as well. But she could learn to do better with his guidance, he reasoned squarely. After all, nobody was perfect. And after the ordeal of living with Brooke, he wasn't perfect either because he found it very hard to trust a woman again. He had needed time away from Milly to recover from the fallout of his failed marriage and the drama of discovering that he had been living with another woman.

He remembered Milly cooking for him, remembered her giving him pleasure as he had never known, and his teeth gritted. It was done: the connection had to remain broken for the moment, lest the paparazzi go into a feeding frenzy over Milly's very existence. Hopefully, their interest in identifying her wouldn't last much longer. But were they to discover her and place her within his life, they would tear her apart, implying this, implying that, *hurting* her as she did not deserve to be hurt.

When the vicar had finished, Milly watched Lorenzo swing on his heel and walk away, wide strong shoulders straight as girders beneath his black cashmere overcoat, his back even straighter, and suddenly she couldn't bear it. In fact, her temper soared. So much remained unsaid between them and she didn't even have his phone number! What had she done that was so bad that he was treating her as though she didn't exist? And she *had* to tell him about the baby. She had no choice on that score. There was no way she was prepared to ring his lawyers and tell *them*! He owed her a hearing, didn't he?

'Lorenzo!' she exclaimed, darting frantically in his wake, her face heating with embarrassment at being forced to abandon her hard-won dignity.

Lorenzo wheeled to a sudden halt and turned back to face her.

'I need to see you to talk about something,' she told him in an angry rush. 'Do you think you could call round this evening?'

'Tomorrow evening. If I must,' Lorenzo gritted, his glorious dark golden eyes locked to her with an intensity that brought her out in goose bumps.

'You *must*,' Milly declared with bold emphasis. 'I wouldn't ask to see you if I didn't have a good reason for it.'

'Around eight, then,' Lorenzo confirmed coolly. 'Are you sure it isn't something my lawyers could handle?'

'No, it's too personal for that,' Milly retorted in a tight tone of annoyance, her colour higher than ever at being required to make that distinction.

'We'll talk over dinner. I'll pick you up at eight.'

Lorenzo strode towards his limousine, enraged at the shot of adrenalin now coursing through his veins and the undeniable sense of anticipation that powered it. He had been trying to stay away from her for weeks and she had just made that impossible, looking up at him with those haunting violet eyes. Of course, he could get through one dinner with her and behave! And go home *alone*? What was too personal? What the hell could she be referring to? Lorenzo did not like to meet anyone without knowing beforehand exactly what he would be dealing with. His strong jawline clenched hard.

He couldn't fault her behaviour, though, since she had moved out. She had asked for nothing from him and she hadn't gone to the press. She hadn't contacted him, hadn't clung, had, in short, done exactly as he had supposedly wanted. To all intents and purposes, they were finished. Only, it hadn't taken more than a day for Lorenzo to register that while he had acted in the shocked conviction that he didn't have a choice, absence wasn't what he wanted or needed from Milly.

He had told himself that he was free again, had wondered why he was so angry and why the knowledge that he was free wasn't the relief that he had expected it to be. And now he knew. Milly was looking skinny and that tore him up. Her fine-boned face was downright thin now and her ankles seemed too delicate to support her. In terms of weight there hadn't been much of her to begin with, he reasoned…but *was* she looking after herself properly? The idea that she might not be now that he was no longer around to watch over her welfare nagged at him and made him decide that a dinner was a very good idea because he could check her out without making a production out of it. And to hell with the paparazzi!

CHAPTER TEN

THE NEXT DAY Milly rushed round the apartment, feeding Topsy and tidying up. She hadn't slept well the night before, haunted as she had been by memories of her sister and the guilty strain of finally laying those memories to rest. Perhaps had she had more time with Brooke or more in common with her, they would have become closer.

Late afternoon, she took Topsy out for a walk and then let her out onto the roof terrace where she liked to wander among the potted plants. That done, she hurried into the bathroom and had a shower.

Why was she fussing about her appearance simply because Lorenzo would be taking her out to dinner? For goodness' sake, it wasn't a date! She would put on jeans and a sweater, she told herself, so that he could see that she had no silly expectations.

After the shower, she put on her smartest jeans and a simple top, but it was a heck of a struggle to get the zip done up on her jeans. Inexorably her shape was changing and, although she had got thinner, her breasts were still larger, her waist was expanding and her stomach was developing a definite outward curve. There was nothing she could do about any of that, she scolded herself as she examined her reflection and winced at the biting tightness of her jeans. She could tell that the need for maternity wear was only just round the corner.

Five minutes later, she tore off the jeans and the top and pulled out a dress instead, the pretty red dress she had bought when she was living with Lorenzo, only, unhappily for her, the dress was now much too tight over her boobs. In a feverish surge of activity she dragged out her entire wardrobe, trying on outfit after outfit until she found a sundress with a looser cut that was reasonably presentable even if it was a little odd to be wearing a sundress when winter was on the horizon. Lorenzo probably wouldn't even notice what she was wearing. He had hardly looked at her at the cemetery, after all, and once she told him about the baby, he would have much more important things to focus on.

At that point her nervous tension and worries threatened to overwhelm her. The discovery that she was pregnant had made a nonsense of her tentative plans for a better future in which she had planned to work while studying. There were so many things she wouldn't be able to do with a child dependent on her. She had hoped to move out of the apartment and sever her last ties to Lorenzo but how could she do that when she needed somewhere to live while she was pregnant?

The lawyers had assured her that, as William Jackson's younger daughter and Brooke's sibling, she was entitled to inherit Brooke's estate because Lorenzo had refused to accept it. But in her heart, Milly suspected that her half-sister would not have wanted *her* to benefit and that made her squirm. Brooke hadn't been fond enough of her and that made it even more difficult for Milly to contemplate being enriched by her sister's demise. She didn't feel entitled to Brooke's trust fund yet how could she refuse it when she had a baby on the way and desperately needed that security? As for taking any more money from Lorenzo, that was out of the question. Baby or not, she wasn't planning to hang on his sleeve for ever!

Lorenzo worked late at the bank and then headed straight to the apartment. That enervating word, 'personal', had played on his mind throughout the day. Did she still believe that she loved him? She had never mentioned love again after that first time when he had failed to reciprocate. Back then he had been relieved by that silence because he had still been planning to divorce her. After all, leopards didn't change their spots. He had never doubted that they would end up divorced and discovering that Brooke was, in fact, *Milly* had simply set him free sooner and more quickly than he had expected.

The dream scenario, his most senior lawyer had commented cheerfully, and Lorenzo had felt like punching him because the past month had been anything but a dream for him.

Milly opened the door with a fast-beating heart.

Knowing that he was coming up in the lift had simply increased her nerves about what she was going to say. Lorenzo would be completely unprepared for her announcement and yet shouldn't he have become aware of the risk he had run with her the minute he had realised that she wasn't Brooke? Had that contraceptive oversight completely escaped his attention? She supposed it had, just as it had initially escaped her attention in the emotional turmoil of their break-up.

Lorenzo strolled through the door in a charcoal-grey pinstriped suit, blue-black stubble accentuating his wide mobile mouth and hard masculine jawline, imbuing his dark good looks with an even tougher edge. 'I can't work out what you could have to say that falls into the category of personal,' he admitted coolly.

'Believe me, it's very personal to both of us,' Milly retorted, annoyed by his continuing determination to keep her at a distance. 'I wouldn't have asked you here otherwise.'

Lorenzo gazed at her, dark eyes narrowed and shrewd, his attention lingering on the blue and white dress, which he remembered all too well. He remembered it best in a heap on the bedroom floor. He remembered taking it off to reveal her curvy little body. He remembered persuading her out of its concealing folds at a picnic and convincing her that they would not be seen in the shelter of the trees. Indeed, seeing her *wearing* it rather than seeing himself stripping it off her was a novelty, a novelty and a reminder that his libido didn't need. He clenched his teeth as a pulsing wave of arousal assailed his groin.

'Let's go to dinner and talk,' he urged thickly before he let himself down and just grabbed her and carried her back to his cave like a Neanderthal who hadn't seen a woman in years.

The soft blue cashmere stole she had put round her shoulders kept the chill of the evening air off her skin.

Lorenzo remembered buying that for her in Florence when he saw her shiver one evening. Indeed, he seemed to have an extraordinarily photographic memory for everything she had ever worn and everything he had taken off. The limo didn't have to travel very far before they arrived at a small bistro where they were immediately escorted to a dimly lit corner booth.

Lorenzo sank gracefully down. 'There's something I need to say first…'

'Go ahead,' she encouraged as she opened her menu.

'When you regained your memory, we needed a complete break from each other for a while,' he breathed tautly. 'You needed peace to come to terms with everything that had happened. I had to accept that Brooke was gone and deal with that appropriately. I couldn't have done that with you still living with me and I was keen to keep the press out of our relationship.'

'Yes,' Milly conceded uneasily. 'But, perhaps now you can accept that I have no desire to talk to the press *or* embarrass you in any way?'

'If you didn't crave publicity exposure, why did you agree to act as Brooke's stand-in and deceive people?' Lorenzo asked with unnerving suddenness, his disapproval of her behaviour obvious to her for the first time.

Milly flushed because she hadn't yet confronted the embarrassing fact that he viewed her actions as Brooke's stand-in as a form of deception. 'I didn't crave the publicity but it *was* exciting for me to wear her expensive outfits and to be greeted by people as if I was *somebody* for the first time in my life,' she admitted, mortified at having to make that lowering admission. 'But mainly I agreed to do it because I wanted to please her and help her out. It made me feel needed and I truly believed that it would make her fonder of me.'

Disconcerted by that honesty, Lorenzo frowned. 'Then you were very naïve. Brooke didn't like other women. She saw them as rivals and she didn't trust them. Did she pay you for your services?'

Milly reddened even more uneasily. 'She promised that she would but she never actually did. I was missing work and I couldn't afford to and still pay my rent. I once lost a job over it and had to move,' she confessed awkwardly. 'I didn't like to ask her for money and bring our relationship down to that level. I didn't want to be someone she paid like hired help. I wanted to be a sister coming to her aid and I hoped she would eventually appreciate that...'

As Milly fell silent to take note of the waiter hovering, Lorenzo frowned and voiced their selections while also ordering wine.

'How many times did you stand in for her?' he asked bluntly when they were alone again.

'The day of the accident would have been the fifth time but a couple of the times she used me it was simply a matter of me being seen entering or leaving a shop she was publicising,' Milly revealed, worrying anxiously at her lower lip with her teeth. 'But the last time? That was a big deal for me because I was to stay hidden in the hotel room she had booked for six days, which meant that I had to quit my job.'

'I've since learned where she was planning to go,' Lorenzo volunteered as the first course was delivered to the table. 'Brooke was flying to Argentina.'

'Argentina?' Milly gaped. 'Why Argentina?'

'Presumably to meet up with Scott Lansdale, because he was filming on location there,' Lorenzo supplied very drily.

'Scott Lansdale the *movie star*?' Milly whispered in a feverish hiss, both incredulous and ironically impressed by that famous name. 'But he's a married man!'

'She was having an affair with him, probably in the belief that he would put her name forward for a part in his next film,' Lorenzo explained flatly. 'Brooke didn't sleep with men out of love or lust. She picked men she expected to advance her career. If they didn't deliver, she moved on.'

'You say that as if it happened more than once during your marriage,' Milly muttered with a frown, pushing away her glass when the wine arrived and opting instead for water.

'It did. Sex was only another weapon in her arsenal. After the first time I caught her out and she lied about it, I never slept with her again. We were living entirely separate lives by the time I started the divorce,' he completed.

'So, the rumours about other men weren't just gossipy stories like you first said they were?' she pressed in dismay.

'No, they weren't,' he confirmed steadily. 'At the time I didn't want to upset you by telling you the truth about our marriage...well, about my marriage with Brooke.'

Milly dropped her head, suddenly understanding so much more about Lorenzo. He had gone for a divorce as soon as he saw that his marriage was beyond saving. She could easily understand why he had initially steered clear of any further intimacy with her. 'Why on earth did Brooke marry you in the first place?' she pressed.

'Her trust fund didn't run to the designer clothes she adored and my wealth gave her unlimited spending power. Our marriage also propelled her up the social ladder, which gave her more opportunities to meet influential people in the film and television world.'

Milly swallowed hard. 'You think that she never loved you, that she just used you for what you could provide?'

Lorenzo shrugged and thrust his big shoulders back into a more relaxed position. As he shifted lithely his jacket fell back from his chest and the edges parted to display lean muscles rippling below the fine shirt and Milly's mouth ran dry as dust. 'She betrayed me so early in our marriage that she couldn't possibly have loved me. I never saw anything in her that made me think otherwise. I have to be truthful with you on that score. I didn't hate her, I certainly didn't wish her dead, but by the end of the first year when the marriage had died, I had few illusions about her character.'

As the main course was delivered, Milly breathed in slow and deep and thought of the way Lorenzo had looked after her after the accident, refusing to allow his own feelings to influence his attitude. That had taken an immense force of will and self-discipline that in retrospect shook her. But his strength and protectiveness had been powered purely by the mistaken conviction that she was his wife and deserving of his care.

'I'm glad that you felt that you could finally tell me the truth,' she confessed, wondering how the heck they had strayed so far from her intent to tell him that she was carrying his child. However, she didn't believe a public setting was suitable for such a revelation and resolved to tell him only when he had taken her home again.

'Hopefully that's cleared the air. Now, perhaps you'll tell me what was too *personal* to discuss with my lawyers,' Lorenzo murmured smoothly.

Her heart started beating very fast inside her chest, depriving her of breath, but she shook her head vehemently. 'I'll tell you as soon as I get home.'

His ebony brows pleated. 'Why the secrecy?'

'I don't want you to feel constrained by our surroundings,' she admitted stiffly.

When they stepped out of the restaurant, immediately flashbulbs burst all around them, blinding and startling her. As shouted questions were aimed at them like bullets by the paparazzi, Lorenzo curved a protective hand to her spine and urged her unhurriedly in the direction of the car.

'For goodness' sake, we shouldn't have come out together in public!' Milly gasped, stricken, in the back of the limousine. 'Why did you risk it? Before you know it, I'll have been identified.'

'And so what if you are?' Lorenzo incised impatiently between clenched teeth. 'Neither of us has done anything wrong and nobody knows what happened between us. It's nobody else's business either. But I do believe that it's past time for this relationship to come out of the closet and be seen.'

Taken aback by that far-reaching statement that suggested that they still *had* a relationship, Milly climbed breathlessly out of the limo and accompanied him into the lift. He leant back against the wall, all lean, sinuous male, his beautiful dark golden eyes intent on her, and desire clenched low in her pelvis, dismaying her because she had believed that she had better control than that.

'I'm not used to you keeping secrets from me,' he confessed. 'You were always very open.'

Milly recalled how she had told him that she loved him and barely restrained a wince at the recollection of how trustingly naïve she had been in those early days. 'I haven't changed but maybe I've learned a little more discretion,' she parried.

They emerged from the lift into the shadowy foyer of the apartment. Lorenzo strode ahead of her to hit the lights. Milly forged on into the lounge, leaving him to follow.

'So now...' Lorenzo drawled with wry amusement. 'I gather it's finally time for *the big reveal*.'

Milly breathed in so deep that she felt dizzy as she exhaled again and she braced her hands on the back of a sofa, reckoning that hint of amusement would be short-lived. 'I'm pregnant,' she informed him apprehensively.

Lorenzo did a complete double take, his dark head jerking up and back, his dark eyes gleaming sharp as rapier blades. *'Pregnant?'* he emphasised in astonishment.

Milly sighed as she sank wearily down on the sofa. 'I'm almost three months along because *I* wasn't using any birth control while we were together and *you* didn't take any precautions,' she reminded him.

Lorenzo hovered with an incredulous look stamped on his lean, strong face, his dark eyes glittering like polar stars. *'Pregnant?'* he repeated a second time as if he could not comprehend such a development. 'By...*me*?'

'Oh...are you infertile? You never mentioned it,' Milly shot back at him to punish him for that inexcusable second question, her colour warmer than ever.

Unexpectedly, Lorenzo dropped down fluidly into

the seat opposite her, lustrous vibrant eyes fringed by black lashes pinned to her. Hurriedly she looked away, wishing he weren't quite so spectacularly handsome that he distracted her every time she looked at him. On some level her eyes were in love with those hard, chiselled features of his. But she needed to be cool, calm and collected, not tied in emotional and physical knots by her memories of her time with him, she reminded herself doggedly.

'I *could* be infertile,' Lorenzo mused almost conversationally. 'I don't know. Unprotected sex is a risk I've never taken with a woman…you're the single exception.' The instant he was forced to concede that point, he was plunged back into shock and the colour slowly leached from below his bronzed skin as her first words finally sank in. He stared at her, his dense black lashes framing his bemused gaze. *Pregnant?* How was that possible? But he now accepted that it was perfectly possible, even if he had not foreseen that possibility and that knowledge silenced him.

'But as you said, it's a risk you took many times with me,' Milly reminded him shakily, her courage beginning to flag because he still looked absolutely stunned. 'I'm not Brooke. I didn't have the IUD you assumed I still had, and you didn't protect me.'

'No, I didn't,' Lorenzo acknowledged in a low, driven undertone. 'I just assumed it would be safe.'

'And I took your word for it.' Milly sighed.

'*Madre di Dio,*' Lorenzo groaned. 'I've always wanted a child but not like this.'

'I feel the same,' Milly admitted heavily. 'I've always wanted to be a mother, but this is hardly an ideal situation. Even so, I still plan to make the best of it. I won't be considering termination or adoption or any other way out of this situation. I *want* my baby.'

'I wouldn't have suggested those options,' Lorenzo asserted in stark reproof.

'Yet only minutes ago you were quite happy to suggest that this baby might not be yours,' Milly reminded him curtly. 'That was very offensive.'

'How am I to know who you might have been with in recent weeks?' Lorenzo countered in a driven undertone. 'The idea that you could be out there seeing other men has driven me crazy over the past month!'

Milly stared back at him in wonderment. 'I haven't *ever* been with anyone but you!' she told him with a decided edge of bitterness. 'I was a virgin but *you* didn't notice…and although it hurt like hell I just thought it was a question of it having been too long since I'd last had sex, so I didn't say anything about it at the time.'

Lorenzo vaulted upright. 'You were a virgin?' he breathed rawly.

'Yes. And I was planning to stay that way until I was in a serious relationship,' she admitted with spirit.

Lorenzo raked long brown fingers through his ruffled blue-black hair. '*Dio mio…* I'm sorry. You should've told me that I'd hurt you.'

'I didn't want to spoil the moment…engaged as I foolishly was in trying to save my rocky marriage…

the marriage that didn't actually exist,' she completed tightly.

'This…*us*…it is an unholy mess!' Lorenzo growled in sudden frustration.

'Well, I've told you now. Perhaps you would have preferred me to approach your lawyers with this little problem.'

'No. Not with anything that relates to our baby and, by the way, our baby is *not* and will never be a problem,' Lorenzo declared, moving restively about the room, obviously too shaken up by her news to settle again.

Our baby was a label that warmed Milly's heart and she hastily looked away from him, telling herself that she was simply relieved that he wasn't angry or resentful. He *wanted* their child. That was a more positive response than she had even dared to hope for. 'I'll make tea. I'm afraid I don't have any alcohol.'

Lorenzo flashed her a sudden unexpected smile that radiated charisma. 'May I have coffee instead?'

'Of course, you can,' Milly told him cheerfully as she jumped up, a sense of reprieve making her body feel shaky as she walked into the sleek kitchen.

'I want you to come home with me tonight,' Lorenzo announced with staggering abruptness from the doorway.

Wide-eyed with astonishment, Milly whirled round to face him where he lounged gracefully against the frame. 'Why the heck would I do that?'

'You're expecting my child,' Lorenzo countered evenly, as if her question was a surprising one. 'And you've lost a lot of weight. I don't want you living here alone.'

Her facial muscles locking tight with self-discipline, Milly turned away again to put the kettle on, grateful to have something to do with her hands. 'You threw me out, Lorenzo. I'm not coming back.'

'I didn't *throw* you out,' he argued vehemently.

'It's not worth fighting about,' Milly parried quickly. 'You were right when you said our relationship was an unholy mess. So, let's not dig ourselves into a deeper hole. Leave things as they are.'

'But I don't *like* how things are,' Lorenzo framed without apology. 'This child will be my child as well and I want him or her to have my full attention from the start. I can't achieve that if we're living apart.'

Milly's slight shoulders sagged wearily. 'I'm not sure I'd have told you if I'd known you were going to make this much fuss. I'm pregnant…deal with it,' she advised. 'And once you've thought us over, you'll appreciate that we were an accident that should never have happened. But that doesn't mean that we can't still respect each other and maintain a civil relationship for the sake of our child.'

Lorenzo's sculpted features had shadowed and set hard. 'I strongly disagree with everything you just said,' he responded in unambiguous challenge. 'I don't think we were an accident and nor is our baby. I want more than a *civil* relationship with the mother of my child. I'm a traditional man. I want my child's mother to be my wife.'

The mug in Milly's hand dropped from her nerveless fingers and smashed into a million pieces on the tiled floor. She jerked back a step to avoid being splashed by the hot liquid and then gasped as a tiny flying piece of china stung her leg, before stooping down in an automatic movement to pick up the broken china.

Lorenzo's hands closed over hers and yanked her upright again. 'Are you burned?'

'No,' she said limply.

'But your leg's bleeding,' Lorenzo pointed out, bending down to lift her unresisting body up and settle her down on the kitchen counter out of harm's way.

'It's only a little cut!' she protested.

Lorenzo yanked the first-aid box off the wall and broke it open while frowning down at the blood trickling down her leg. Milly sucked in oxygen to steady herself, but she couldn't get her whirling thoughts under her control. All she could hear was Lorenzo saying, 'I want my child's mother to be my wife.' Had that been a marriage proposal? Surely not? That would be crazy. She blinked rapidly, wincing as he tugged the tiny sliver of china from her calf with tweezers and cleaned her up, covering the cut with a plaster as though she were a kid.

'Thanks,' she said as she watched him gathering up the broken china and cleaning up the mess she had made. Slowly, carefully, she slid back down to the floor and poured him a cup of coffee, extending it silently when he had finished.

'Yes, I *meant* what I said,' Lorenzo breathed in a

raw undertone before she could speak again. 'I want us to get married as soon as possible.'

'You're not in a fit state to marry anyone, least of all me,' Milly told him roundly. 'A year and a half ago you were getting a divorce. Then your principles forced you into staying married and pretending. You got tangled up with me but that was only a sexual thing and clearly very casual when it all went wrong. Now you're single again. You need to start again with someone fresh. You've already walked away from me.'

'And look how that turned out for me!' Lorenzo urged impatiently. 'I'm back and I'm not leaving you again. And what we had *wasn't* casual and it *wasn't* just sex.'

'Maybe not on my side, *then*,' she specified with precision. 'But I was working blind in a marriage that was already dead, only I didn't know that. I assumed that I had married you because I loved you. Now I know that I was never married to you at all… and, Lorenzo, no offence intended, but I don't *want* to be married to a man who's only marrying me because I'm pregnant.'

'Well, at least I know you don't want me for my money,' Lorenzo replied with a wry smile. 'But you *know* that I want you and I want our child as well.'

'You can't buy me like a package deal. I won't come cheap or easy,' Milly responded, tilting her chin at him before walking back towards the lounge with her tea. 'Amazing sex isn't enough to base a marriage on.'

'Was I amazing?' Lorenzo probed huskily behind her and she almost dropped a second mug at the same time as an involuntary smile tilted her lips.

'You know you were…but then I don't have anyone to compare you to yet, so—' she protested jerkily.

'Yet?' he queried, removing the mug from her hand to press her down into a seat, setting the tea down on the coffee table in front of her. Glittering dark eyes pierced her. 'If I can't have you, no other man can.'

'I'm afraid it doesn't work like that.' Milly sighed. 'We are both free agents now.'

'You're not free while you've got my baby inside you,' Lorenzo shot at her, his lean bronzed face fierce and forbidding.

'When you've finished your coffee, you should leave. I'm sorry but I'm very tired. Between the exhaustion and the morning sickness, I tend to go to bed early most nights,' she confided. 'I'm not in the mood to argue with you—'

'I'm not trying to argue. I'm trying to make you see sense.'

'You're not getting any further with me than I got with you. You said you wanted to marry me, but I don't think you've thought it through,' Milly said anxiously. 'There's a lot more to marriage than sex and having a child together.'

'I know. I love you,' Lorenzo confessed without the smallest warning. 'I was going to wait another month before approaching you again. I suppose I was trying to be a better man than I am. I didn't want the newspapers writing stuff about you and upsetting you. I thought that if I waited long enough, they would lose interest in us both. But I can't *live* another month without you, so here I am being bloody selfish and weak!'

Milly heard only the first half of that speech and his claim that he loved her knocked her for six. 'You *can't* love me,' she told him weakly.

'I began to fall in love with you the day you awakened from the coma. I fell deeper in love with every visit. At first, I told myself it was just sexual attraction even though it had been years since I'd been physically attracted to Brooke. I assumed that once you recovered your memory you would switch back into being the Brooke I remembered, and I knew I would continue the divorce eventually.'

'But before we went to Italy, you said we'd see how things went for us.'

'By that stage, I was secretly hoping that you would *never* recover your memory and, to be frank, I really didn't have a proper game plan,' Lorenzo confided grimly. 'I only knew that I couldn't face letting you go. I had fallen head over heels in love with a woman who was kind and compassionate and loving and I was revelling in every moment of the experience.' A smile slashed his lean dark features. 'I was extremely happy with you and I want that back. But I want to do everything the right way round this time. I want you to be my wife.'

'Oh…' was all Milly could bleat at that moment.

'You're not saying a flat no any more?' Lorenzo was quick to recognise that she was weakening.

'I'm thinking it over,' Milly muttered, her cheeks colouring. 'Why didn't you at least phone me while we were apart?'

'I was trying to be strong for both of us and I thought we were safer from press intrusion if nobody, including you, knew how I felt about you,' he admitted grimly. 'But I found it very hard to cope without you. I buried myself in work. It didn't help. I came home at night and I couldn't sleep and the house didn't feel like home any longer without you in it.'

Milly began slowly to smile, and her hand crept up to frame one high cheekbone in a tender caress. 'I love you, Lorenzo. I've missed you so much.'

Lorenzo tugged her gently into his arms and held her close. 'How can you still love me after the mess I made of things?'

Milly jerked her head back playfully, a foam of silvery blonde ringlets falling against one cheekbone. 'If you were perfect, you'd be boring. But you must stop hiding stuff from me in the belief that I have to be protected from every adverse event. I'm more resilient than I look,' she told him firmly. 'Yes, there would've been unpleasant stuff in the tabloids if it got out that we were together but we could have got through it. We are stronger together than we are apart.'

His ebony brows pleated. 'I didn't think of that angle.'

'I know. Your glass is always half empty while mine is always half full,' she teased, her violet eyes sparkling as she gazed up at him. 'Let's not care what anyone says or thinks about us. I learned how to do that at school. You must've been more protected than I was. I was always the kid in the unfashionable shoes, who got free lunches because she was the poor foster kid…'

Lean brown hands framed her animated face. 'And now you're going to be the wife of a billionaire.'

Her nose wrinkled. 'It just goes to show…you *can* sleep your way to the top!' she joked.

'*Madre di Dio…* I love you so much, *cara mia*,' Lorenzo husked, his mouth crashing down on hers with all the hunger he had fought to suppress for weeks giving her the strongest message yet that he needed her.

They stood there kissing, urgently entwined, too long separated to bear the idea of being apart even for a moment, both of them studiously ignoring Topsy, who was barking at their feet. She backed him up against the window, wrenching at his tie while he claimed urgent little biting kisses from her luscious mouth.

'I gather I'm staying,' Lorenzo pronounced with a wicked grin.

'Wait until you're invited,' Milly told him, waited a heartbeat. 'You're invited.'

He carried her into the all-white bedroom and dropped down on the side of the bed, holding her between his spread masculine thighs. He made a production out of sliding down one strap on her shoulder and then the other, pushing them gently down her arms to her wrists so that the dress slid down baring the full swell of her breasts cupped in a strapless bra. He undid the bra, let it drop away, studying her ripe curves with reverent intensity. 'You are perfect,' he breathed.

'You are not in the mood to be critical,' Milly laughed, taking in his arousal clearly outlined by the fine fabric of his trousers.

'Perfect,' Lorenzo repeated aggressively as he splayed the gentle fingers of one large hand across her stomach. 'You've got my baby in there…and that means the world to me.'

'And me,' she agreed as the dress fluttered to her feet and he gathered her into his arms and settled her down on the bed.

For a long time afterwards, there was nothing but the sheer urgency of the passion they had feared they might never experience again together, and then, in the tranquil aftermath, the real world intruded again.

Lorenzo fanned her tumbled hair back from her face and stared down at her with an adoring glow in his intense scrutiny. 'We start again fresh from this moment with no ghosts from the past between us,' he murmured sibilantly. 'The house has already been cleared. I had mementoes put aside for you, photos and scrapbooks and such, but I donated the contents of the dressing room and the jewellery I bought her to a charity auction. It's all gone.'

Milly nodded uncertainly, surprised and relieved and sad all at the same time. 'We wouldn't have met but for Brooke,' she reminded him gently.

'I can't stand to think of a world in which I might

not have met you,' Lorenzo confessed. 'So that is something to be grateful to her for.'

'If her trust fund does come to me, I'd like to donate it to a good cause because I would never feel it was mine,' Milly admitted ruefully. 'I mean, our father never acknowledged me and neither did she really. She never once made me feel that she accepted me as an actual sister. It wouldn't be right for me to keep it.'

'As you wish. Just don't let the past poison anything that we share,' Lorenzo urged her anxiously.

Tender fingers stroked his roughened jawline. 'I love you too much, Lorenzo Tassini, to ever let that happen,' she whispered.

'I hope that means that you love me enough to get married soon,' he murmured softly, dropping a kiss down onto her reddened mouth.

Her eyes widened. 'How soon?'

'A couple of weeks?'

'No, that's far too soon,' she told him firmly.

'Well, if I had my choice it would be tomorrow,' Lorenzo admitted unrepentantly.

'Could we get married in Italy?' she asked wistfully. 'I'd love that.'

Lorenzo smiled. 'I think that could be arranged and still give you time to find a beautiful white dress.'

'I can't wear white. I'm pregnant!' Milly gasped with a wince.

'That's an old-fashioned concept,' Lorenzo overruled. 'You deserve to wear white and if I have anything to do with the decision, you will.'

Milly lifted her nose, knowing how bossy he was,

resolved not to let him have anything to do with that
decision. 'We'll see.'

'Is that you placating me?' Lorenzo asked suspiciously.

'Possibly.' Milly looked up at him, her whole face
wreathed with happiness. 'I love you. I can't think of
anything else right now.'

His dark eyes shimmered pure gold. 'Why should
you think of anything else? I love you too, more than
I ever thought I could love anyone, *bellezza mia*.'

Milly slipped into a dreamy sleep. Lorenzo lay
awake planning the wedding and Topsy, suspecting
that she wouldn't be welcomed into her usual spot in
the bed, went for a nap underneath it.

Two months later, Milly adjusted her short veil and
looked in the cheval mirror with a wide contented
smile.

Her dress was a dream. Sheer lace encased her
arms while a Bardot neckline exposed her shoulders
and the fitted lace bodice drew attention away from
the swell of her pregnant stomach, the tulle and or-
ganza layered skirt tumbling softly to the floor. Milly
hadn't needed to hide her bump to feel presentable.
She was proud to be carrying her little girl. It was
only a few weeks since they had learned that they
were to have a daughter and they both liked the name
Liona. While Lorenzo was hopeful that Liona would
inherit her mother's colouring, Milly was hopeful that
she would inherit her father's.

Clutching her beautiful bouquet of wildflowers,

she stepped into the car that would whisk her up the hill to the village church where they would take their vows. Lorenzo's senior lawyer had offered to lead her into the church and down the aisle. As they had become well acquainted during the proceedings that had established her sister's death and her own survival, she had laughed and agreed, especially after he had unbent sufficiently to admit that they had been taking bets in the office about how long it would take Lorenzo to admit that he had fallen madly in love.

Her eyes were intent only on Lorenzo when she entered the crowded church. A large number of Lorenzo's friends had chosen to accept their invitations and fly out for an autumn weekend in Tuscany. Many of them had already met her because once she had moved back in with Lorenzo he had begun entertaining again for the first time in several years. Initially her resemblance to Brooke had unsettled people, but once they had got talking to her and realised how friendly and unassuming she was that unease had melted away. In fact, for the first time ever, now settled and secure and confident in the happiness she had found, Milly was making friends.

Sunlight slanted through the stained-glass windows of the chapel, illuminating the man at the altar, who was very tall beside the small, rounded priest. His hair gleamed blue black in strong light, his eyes gilded to gold in his lean dark face and he was smiling at his bride and she grinned back, barely able now to dredge up the recollection of the forbidding, reserved and very serious man he had once appeared to be. He covered her hand with his. 'You look radiant,' he told her proudly.

And the ceremony began, short and sweet and with no flourishes, because neither of them needed anything fancier than the love they had for each other and the child that was on the way to make them into a family. A slender platinum ring was slid onto her finger and then one to his. Lorenzo kissed his bride without a second's hesitation, and they walked out into the sunlight smiling and united.

The reception was held in the village hall where the earlier civil ceremony had taken place. It was merry and fun-filled and utterly informal, very much in the bride's style. Lorenzo had bought a yacht, an uncharacteristic act of conspicuous consumption that had attracted a lot of flak from his colleagues, and in a day or two they planned to cruise the Caribbean for their honeymoon. That first night of their marriage, though, they returned to the peaceful farmhouse in the hills and ate by candlelight on the terrace with the stars twinkling above them before retiring for the night.

'Happy now?' she teased him as he helped unhook her from her dress.

Lorenzo spread the parted edges of the dress back and kissed a trail across her smooth pale shoulders. 'Yes, now you're officially mine. I feel safer being happy.'

'Nobody's going to take our happiness away from us,' she soothed, spinning round as the gown dipped dangerously low over her full breasts to fall to her waist as she slowly extracted her arms from the tight lace sleeves. 'We worked hard for it, and you earned it every week that you watched over me when I was in a coma.'

'I still don't deserve you,' Lorenzo breathed gruffly, trying without success to drag his attention from her truly magnificent cleavage.

Milly let the dress fall to her feet and stepped out of it. 'Yes, you do. You deserve your happy ending just like everyone else. And I'm going to be it.'

'No complaints here.' Lorenzo laughed, lifting her gently to set her down on the bed, stroking the firm mound of her stomach with a possessive hand. 'Are you tired?'

'More elated now that we've finally got here, where we wanted to be,' she confided quietly. 'It was a glorious day, exactly what I dreamt of.'

'I wanted it to be really special for you, *bellezza mia*,' Lorenzo confided.

'Believe me, it was,' Milly assured him, running her fingertips lazily through his luxuriant black hair, a shiver of sensual awareness quivering through her as his stubbled jaw rubbed across her nape. 'Oh, do *that* again,' she urged helplessly.

Her unashamed enthusiasm made Lorenzo laugh. 'I love you to pieces, Milly.'

'I love you too…'

'And that little girl you're giving us will be as special as you are,' he told her.

And Liona *was*, coming into the world with all her mother's zest for life.

Two years later, she was followed by Pietro, as dark in colouring as his sister was fair, and rather more serious in nature.

Four years beyond that, when their parents naively thought their family was complete, fate surprised them with Cara, blonde with dark eyes, a little elf of a child with a mischievous smile. And together they were the family that both Lorenzo and Milly had always dreamt of having.

* * * * *

HIS GREEK
WEDDING NIGHT
DEBT

MICHELLE SMART

CHAPTER ONE

HELENA ARMSTRONG GAVE her appearance one final look-over.

Mascara and eyeliner intact and unsmudged? Check.

Nude lipstick on the lips and not the teeth? Check.

Thick chestnut hair secured in a professional bun at the base of the neck without any stray distracting strands? Check.

Silver and blue swirl tailored A-line skirt clean and un-creased? Check.

Black blouse clean and uncreased and no gapping around the bust? Check.

Black tights ladder free? Check.

Black heels clean if not easy to walk in? Check.

Thick-framed spectacles fingerprint free? Check.

Drawing tube ready to grab hold of? Check.

Heartbeat under vague semblance of control…? Oh, well, a girl couldn't have everything.

Helena was as ready and prepared as she could be. It was time to make her first major pitch to a client. The blueprints she'd spent a month toiling over were ready to be unveiled to the mystery client who'd driven them all to distraction.

The mystery client, who'd used lawyers up to this point to remain under the cloak of anonymity—which in itself had led to fevered speculation within the firm as to who he or she could be—had invited their firm and four others to pitch for the opportunity to design a house for him. Or her. This would be no ordinary house, nor even an ordinary mansion. The successful lead architect would be flown to a Greek island, name still to be revealed, and tasked with designing a thousand-square-metre villa in traditional Cycladic style from scratch. Each firm was to put forward an architect with an understanding of the Greek language and a leaning towards classical European architecture to pitch. Helena, who had a Greek mother and an adoration of classical architecture, fitted the bill perfectly for her firm. Her father's cruel manner in forcing the Greek language on her had finally paid off.

She'd swallowed her unease at the thought of having to work on an island that was part of the country she'd spent three years actively avoiding, and thrown herself into the pitch. She hadn't fooled herself into thinking she had a chance of winning as no doubt she would be the youngest and least experienced but it was good practice and the successful pitch would be rewarded with a prize unlike any other. Not only would the successful firm make a good sum from it, but also the lead architect would receive a hefty signing-on bonus and a completion bonus, which together would enable Helena to write off her mountain of debt and have a little spare. All she'd been tasked to do for the pitch was show how she would turn an old Greek school into a trio of luxury holiday-let apartments.

Helena headed through the open-plan layout to the boardroom with murmurs of 'good luck' ringing in her ears. The majority of the staff had watched her develop and mature from a naïve twenty-one-year-old graduate to a twenty-six-year-old architect.

When she walked through the boardroom door, she was

fortified to meet Stanley's eye and be on the receiving end of an encouraging wink. She wanted desperately to make the architect who'd taken her under his wing five years ago proud. She'd worked under him for a year when she'd first graduated and he'd then made himself available whenever she needed him during her masters and ensured there was a place within his firm for her last year of work experience before she took her final exam. Stanley had been the one to create a permanent role for her when, after seven years of toil, she became a bona fide architect in her own right.

Along with Stanley were the two other senior partners, a PA and the mystery client, whose back was to the door and who made no effort to turn and greet her.

Her first thought was that the mystery client was a man.

Her second thought was that the staff backing the mystery client's being a celebrity were on the money because, even with his back turned, recognition flashed through her.

Helena hurried to her designated seat opposite him, a warm, welcoming smile on her lips, and finally saw his face.

And that was the moment all her thoughts turned to dust as her brain froze.

The man sitting opposite her in the mystery client's chair was Theo Nikolaidis. The same Theo Nikolaidis she'd jilted three years ago, twenty-four hours before they'd been due to marry.

Theo didn't bother hiding the wide grin that formed on his lips.

This moment, when he wiped the smile off Helena Armstrong's face, was a moment to savour, a moment deserving of a glass of fine wine and, if he were a man for exquisite canapés, a plateful of them. As it was, Theo was a man who preferred hearty food but a huge bowl of his grandmother's *kokkinisto* didn't quite fit this picture-perfect moment.

He rose to his feet and stretched out a hand, tilting his head expectantly. 'Good morning, Helena,' he said with an even wider smile and was rewarded by Helena's beautiful face turning the colour of a sun-ripened tomato. 'It is a pleasure to see you again.'

He was quite sure he heard a collective intake of breath from the others in the room.

If he had it in him to feel sympathy for the woman who'd made him a laughing stock, he was sure he could conjure some, but her panicking eyes darting from his gaze to his outstretched hand was another wonderful response to relish.

After a pause that would be deemed impolite by anyone's standards, a small, milky-white hand with short but shapely nails extended towards him. Her fingers wrapped around his for approximately a tenth of a second before she snatched them away. 'Mr Nikolaidis,' she murmured, taking her seat and putting her bag on the floor and the long tube on the table without looking at him.

'You two know each other?' The question came from one of the partners, a man who had to be old enough to be Helena's father but who was looking at her with a stare that made Theo want to cause him bodily harm.

Instead of allowing his hands to do the talking—Theo had learned to control that side of himself before he'd reached double digits—he smiled again and was rewarded by the older man paling. 'Helena and I are old friends. Aren't we, *agapi mou*?'

That made her look at him. Her naturally plump lips were drawn into a tight line, her dark brown eyes sparking with fury.

She thought she was angry now? This was only the beginning.

Jerking her head into the semblance of a nod, she unscrewed the end of the tube and said, 'Shall we get on with this?'

Theo spread his hands. 'Yes. Show me your designs. Let me see if you are as talented as I have been led to believe.'

Her eyes narrowed before she finally plastered a wide, fake smile to her face. 'You will have to be your own judge of that.'

'Believe me, *agapi mou*, I learned the hard way that reputations are as deceptive as appearances.' Helena was the root of that hardness. Easily the most beautiful woman he'd ever set eyes on, he'd met her on his home island of Agon. At an unexpected loose end for a few hours, he'd decided to pay a visit to his good friend Theseus Kalliakis, an Agon prince who, at the time, had lived in the palace. As it had been a beautiful day and Theo was a man who enjoyed the feel of the sun on his face, he'd decided to walk through the palace gardens to reach Theseus's private residence. In the garden he'd spotted a young woman sitting on a bench beside a statue of the goddess Artemis with an open book on her lap and a pencil in hand. Crouched forward as she'd been, her dark chestnut hair had fallen like a sheet over her face and slender shoulders. She'd absentmindedly swiped it away and tucked it behind her ear, revealing a face that, even behind the largest pair of spectacles he'd ever seen, could in itself have been worshipped as a goddess.

He'd sucked in the longest breath of his life and stared. And stared some more.

Curiosity piqued as to what she was doing, he'd sneaked up behind her to peer over her shoulder. On an A4 sheet of paper was an intricately drawn study of the palace. It was beautiful. Using nothing but a set of graphite pencils, she'd brought the palace to life. She'd even managed to convey light bouncing off some of the windows!

No wonder he'd been so smitten. A woman with beauty, talent *and* brains? He'd put her straight onto a pedestal and worshipped her as his countrymen had worshipped Artemis all those millennia ago.

What a shame he'd forgotten scruples and honour were also wise things to select in the woman you intended to make your wife. He should have taken the statue who'd witnessed their first meeting as a warning sign. Artemis, one of the most revered of the ancient deities, had, according to legend, sworn never to marry.

Unlike Artemis, Helena had failed to mention her aversion to matrimony until the day before they'd been due to exchange their nuptials in Agon's cathedral. Fool that he was, he hadn't believed her, thought her words were shouted in nerves and anger. Of *course* she'd be at the cathedral!

Now, when Theo thought back on that time when Helena had broken his ego, he often thought he should thank her. He could have spent the past three years living a boring, settled life instead of re-embracing the hedonistic party lifestyle he'd been prepared to abandon for her. Truth be told, Helena's jilting had set him free and he had made every moment of his freedom count…but only up to a point.

Three years on from his public humiliation, he was still to bed another woman. God alone knew he'd tried but his usually voracious libido had gone into obstinate hibernation. He, the man who could have any woman he wanted, had lost all interest in the opposite sex. He still dated— any excuse to rub Helena's nose in what she was missing out on—but bedding his dates was impossible.

What had begun as a minor annoyance had become a serious problem. He didn't want another relationship. Relationships were for naïve fools. They involved trust and emotions, neither of which he would allow himself to experience again, but he was only thirty-three, far too young to contemplate a life spent with the sex-life of a monk.

Then, six months ago, he'd seen a notice in the architectural magazine he subscribed to announcing the firm Staffords had given the newly qualified architect Helena Armstrong a permanent contract. Accompanying it had been a grainy photograph of her. The next morning he'd woken with his first erection since she'd left him. Relief that his manhood had awoken had been short-lived. A party that night on a friend's yacht with a bevy of scantily clad nubile women and his manhood couldn't even be bothered to wave hello. Not until he'd been alone in his bed and closed his eyes to remember Helena naked. It had sprung up like a jack-in-a-box.

And just like that, the reason for his impotence had become clear and so had the solution to cure it. Try as he might to forget about her, Helena had become like Japanese knotweed in his head, her roots dug so deep they smothered the normal functions of his masculinity. He needed to sever the roots and burn them. To accomplish that he needed Helena back in his life. This time he would bed her as he should have done three years ago. He would make her fall in love with him again. And then he would be the one to jilt and humiliate her.

And then he could, finally, forget about her and move on with his life.

Helena would never know how she made it through the next hour. Later that evening, on her journey home on the

Tube, travelling so late she found a seat easily, she put her head back and closed her eyes.

Had she dreamt it all?

Had Theodoros Nikolaidis really been the mystery client who'd kept them on their toes these past two months?

Somehow she'd managed to pull herself together and deliver the pitch. She'd known every word she spoke was wasted air, but pride would not allow her to do anything less than her best. When Theo passed her over for a different architect in a different firm, at least her colleagues wouldn't be able to say her professionalism had let her or them down.

And Theo would never know that under her calm, professional exterior had beat a crying heart.

His face had been poker straight when she'd finished her presentation. He hadn't asked a single question. He'd merely looked at his watch, risen to his feet, thanked them all for their efforts, winked at Helena then swept out of the boardroom without a backward glance, leaving five mouths open with astonishment in his wake.

Neither Helena, the senior partners nor the other staff needed to vocalise it but the subdued atmosphere in the aftermath had told its own story. All the work Helena had put in for the pitch, all the help and support her colleagues had given her…it had all been for nothing.

She breathed in deeply, needing oxygen so badly she didn't care that it was the lingering stale body odour of other commuters filling her lungs.

Seeing Theo again after all that time…

Don't think about him.

She could no more stop her memory box opening than a child could resist a bag of sweets. Despite her best endeavours, Helena found herself thrown back over three years to a time when her heart had been intact and her body a flower primed and ready to bloom for the sun.

The sun had appeared in the form of the sexiest man she had ever set eyes on.

It was only on a whim that she'd gone to the palace that day. Needing a break after the first year of slogging for her master's degree, she'd decided to visit her mother's family in Agon. The sun always shone in Agon and life always felt freer. Simpler. Even her father relaxed enough to stop fault-finding every five minutes when he was there.

On her third morning, she'd woken early and decided to visit the palace she'd loved as a child.

Armed with nothing but her sketchbook, drawing pencils, a bottle of water and a picnic lunch, she'd parked her bottom on a bench and drawn her favourite building in the world.

After five hours of stillness cocooned in her own head, tuning out the hordes of tourists drifting around her, she'd suddenly become aware of being watched. She'd looked up at the same moment a voice had spoken behind her ear. 'That is some talent you have there, lady. Name your price.'

She'd turned her head sharply and found herself face to face with a man who'd immediately made her heart swell. Tall—he had to be at least a foot taller than her own five-foot-one frame—and muscular, he'd had messy, short brown hair, the tips highlighted by the sun, and a deep tan that suggested a life spent enjoying the great outdoors. When she'd met the ice-blue eyes surrounded by laughter lines, her swelling heart had set off at a canter.

Over three years later and she'd had the exact same re-action to seeing him again.

Over three years later and Helena was still paying the price for that impulsive visit to the palace.

She'd reached her station. Hooking her bag over her

shoulder, she trudged off the Tube and up the steep escalators. The sun had been setting when she'd begun her commute home but when she left the long, wide tunnel that brought her back out into the world, rain lashed the night sky. So much for the light cloud the forecasters had promised. Naturally, the first thing she did was step into a puddle that immediately soaked through the flat canvas shoe she'd changed into after the disastrous pitch.

Marvellous. All she needed was to be hit by a bus and her day would be complete.

By the time she reached her basement flat, the rest of her body was as soaked to the bone as her left foot.

Her flat was freezing and, shivering, she chided herself for believing that early May would bring glorious sunshine.

She'd turned the heating on, stripped off her soaking clothes and put on a thick towelling robe, and was running herself a hot bath when her doorbell rang.

Helena sighed, removed her glasses and covered her face with her hands. All the energy had been sapped out of her.

When the bell rang again, she turned the taps off and shoved her glasses back on. In the three years she'd rented her little breadcrumb of London she'd had one unannounced visitor: a delivery man hoping she'd take in a parcel for the couple in the flat upstairs.

She padded to the front door and, out of precautionary habit, put her eye to the spy hole…and immediately reared back in fright.

How the hell had he found her?

The bell rang again.

Heart thumping, she backed away. Unless Theo had developed X-ray vision, he couldn't know she was in. She would slip back to the bathroom…

The bell that rang out this time was continuous, as if a

Greek man famed for his impatience had decided to keep his finger on it until he'd annoyed every resident who lived in the building.

The infuriating, egotistical, sneaky little… She couldn't think of a name to call him that wouldn't earn her a slap from her grandmother.

The shock that had cloaked her since she'd come face to face with him in the boardroom lifted and a spike of furious energy shot through her veins, making her legs stride to the front door and her hands remove the three chains, deadlock and ordinary lock to fling the door open.

And there he stood, in a black shirt and black trousers, rain lashing down on him, black overcoat billowing in the growing wind, the widest grin on his face that could have been mistaken for rapture had she not seen the danger sparking from his ice-blue eyes.

Raising his hands and spreading them palm up, Theo tilted his head. 'Surprise!'

CHAPTER TWO

THEO ALLOWED HIMSELF a moment to savour the angry shock on Helena's face before brushing past her and into the pleasant warmth of her home. That this should never have been her home was something he would not allow himself to dwell on.

He wiped the rain off his face with his hands while wiping his feet on the doormat.

'Nice place you have here,' he commented as he stepped over a threadbare rug covering hardwood flooring. An estate agent would call her flat cosy. A lay person would describe it as fit for dormice.

Helena closed the door and stood with her back against it. 'What are you doing here?'

He faced her and placed a hand to his chest in a wounded fashion. 'You don't seem happy to see me, *agapi mou*.'

'Dysentery would be a more welcome visitor. For cripes' sake, Theo, it's been three years. You turn up at my place of work all cloak and dagger and then you turn up at my *home*? What's going on?'

'I thought you would like to know in person that you won.'

Her forehead creased. 'Won what?'

'The job.' He flashed the widest smile he could spread his mouth into. *Theos*, he was enjoying this. 'Congratulations. You are the architect of choice for my new home.'

But her beautiful face only became blanker.

'Why don't you open a bottle of wine for us while we talk details?' He peered round the nearest door and found a kitchen of a size a toddler would struggle to party in.

'What are you talking about?'

He spun back round to face her and clicked his finger and thumb together. 'Details. They are important, do you not agree?'

'Well…yes…'

'And alcohol always makes tedious detail go down easier.' He strode to the fridge and opened it. He tutted and sighed theatrically at the sparsity of its contents. 'No white wine. Where do you keep the red?'

'I haven't got any.'

'None? Anything alcoholic at all?'

'No…'

He pulled his phone out of his pocket and winked as he pressed his thumbprint to it. 'Easily rectified.'

'Hold on.' Suspicion suddenly replaced the disbelieving gormless look.

'Nai, agapi mou?'

'You're telling me I've won the pitch?'

'Nai. You have won. Congratulations.' He raised a hand palm up and waggled his fingers jazz-hands-style.

Her brows drew together in increased suspicion.

'You're allowed to smile, you know.' Goading her was something to relish in itself.

She crossed her arms tightly over her chest, eyes not leaving his face. 'I'll smile when you tell me why you've come to my home to deliver the news instead of using the proper channels, and, now I'm thinking about it, who gave you my address? And will you *stop* going through my cupboards and drawers?'

'The contents of a kitchen are a good indication of a person's character,' he chided playfully, opening another drawer that contained precisely a roll of cooking foil, a roll of Clingfilm and two tea towels.

'And the failure to stop rifling through said kitchen when the owner has requested it is an equally good indicator.'

With another theatrical sigh, he closed the drawer. Judging by the contents of what he'd seen so far, Helena was as averse to cooking now as she'd been three years ago.

'Have you eaten?' he asked.

'N… Yes.'

Laughing at her blatant lie, he pulled his phone back out. 'What would you like?'

'For you to stop mucking about like a hyperactive child, get to the ruddy point and get the hell out of my flat.'

Now Theo's forehead creased and he waggled a finger at her before tapping the screen of his phone. 'Is that any way to speak to the man who is going to make you rich?'

'If I cared anything for riches I would have married you.'

He put his hand to his chest again and pretended to double over. '*Ouch.* I see you have been sharpening your tongue in recent years.'

'And you've been dulling your hearing. For the last time, answer my question.'

'Which one? There have been so many.'

A growl escaped her slender throat. Theo laughed to finally get a proper reaction out of her. Her shock had been transparent in their earlier meeting but she had recovered beautifully, making her pitch with controlled precision. A stranger meeting her for the first time could be forgiven for thinking her controlled persona defined her, but the stranger would be wrong. Helena kept her passion, be it anger or desire, tightly hidden beneath prim clothing, but when it was unleashed…whoa! She *scorched*. He could hardly wait to feel her burn.

'You can start with how you got my address,' she bit out with barely concealed exasperation.

'Your mother gave it to me.' A photograph on the kitchen wall by the door caught his attention. It was a picture of Helena cuddling a cute toddler. He touched the glass frame beside the child's face. 'Who is that?'

She ignored his question. 'You've seen my mother?'

'I wanted to find you, *agapi mou*. Who better to help than your mother?'

He felt her dumbfounded stare on his skin but deliberately kept his gaze from hers.

This was a scene Theo had played out in his mind many times since formulating his plan. So far only two things had marred his picture-perfect fantasy: arriving at Helena's home soaked from the three-metre walk from his car to her front door, and Helena wearing a grey towelling bathrobe. If she'd been psychically attuned to his picture-perfect fantasies, she would have worn a silk kimono that caressed her wonderful curves, not the shapeless thing that covered her from neck to ankle. Sexiness must have been the last thing on her mind when she'd bought it. It didn't stop him from wanting to pull the ugly robe apart—she could have worn a sackcloth and he'd still have wanted her—but he still vowed to burn the ugly thing at the first opportunity.

'When did you see her?' she asked tightly.

'Three months ago. Who is the child?'

'Stop changing the subject.' Her teeth were well and truly gritted. She hadn't moved from the threshold of the kitchen door but the room was so small that if she entered it, she would have to touch him. He knew perfectly well that at that moment, Helena would rather stroke a tarantula than touch him. 'My mother never said anything about seeing you.'

Theo grinned. He was enjoying this. The entire day had been one of unremitting joy. 'I asked her not to.'

The pretty face shaped like a diamond, and which glowed like a diamond under the sun, tightened. 'Why?'

'I will tell you that when you tell me who the child in the photo is.' It couldn't be hers. Firstly, her mother would have mentioned it. Secondly, this apartment wasn't big enough for Helena, let alone Helena, a child and, presumably, the child's father…who would be Helena's lover.

He didn't care what lovers she'd had. Okay, he *did* care. A little. But only in the kicking-himself-for-not-having-her-himself sense. Helena had wanted them to make love. She'd tried every trick in the book to weaken his resolve. It had been *torturous*. Thoughts of making love to her had fuelled his every waking moment but he'd been determined to do things properly. He'd believed himself in love with her. He'd believed they would be together for ever. He'd loved her and he would show that love by respecting her virginity and waiting until they were husband and wife before making love to her. After all, he'd reasoned, they had their whole lives to spend making love. So they had stuck to doing 'everything but' and then she'd jilted him at the last moment, leaving his ego battered and his desire unfulfilled. Was it any wonder he'd been unable to rise to the occasion since?

Just being here and sharing the same air as her proved his plan was going to be a winner. Energy flowed through his veins, his skin tingled and arousal…for once he was having to squash it rather than futilely coax it.

Helena scowled at Theo's profile while he was still studiously examining the photos she'd hung on the wall. 'She's my boss's granddaughter. Now stop looking at my photos and tell me why you've been bothering my mother.' Her poor mother, trained to obey the word of a man, would have told Theo anything he wanted to know and made any promise he asked of her.

No wonder she'd been jumpier than normal during their recent secret get-togethers. She would have wanted to warn Helena that Theo was back on the scene but been unable to say a word. Her mother knew too well the consequences of going against a man who held power.

'I already told you.' He winked again. 'I wanted to find you.'

'You better not have upset her.'

'Why would I have done that?' he asked mildly. 'I like your mother.'

'What about my father? Was he there? Is he in on it too?' She thought it unlikely—if her father thought there was any way Helena and Theo could get back together he was quite likely to kidnap and hand-deliver her to him—but she needed to be sure.

He shrugged. 'He wasn't there when I visited. I don't know if your mother told him.'

Her tight lungs loosened a fraction. 'Well, you've succeeded in your quest to find me. Congratulations. Now you can go.'

He bestowed her with a look that made her feel as though the blood could burst from her veins and she wished she could say it would be entirely due to anger. Theo had always been his own life-force, a man who thrummed with infectious energy. Although far from traditionally handsome, he had a magnetism that ensured every eye in the vicinity was drawn to him, and an affable charm and wit that could make a complete stranger feel they'd just met their new best friend.

For three incredible months Helena had been at the centre of his life-force. He'd treated her like a princess. There was nothing he wouldn't have done for her. If she'd asked for the moon he would have got a lasso and pulled it down to her. If she'd married him she would have wanted for nothing...apart from her own autonomy. Because the flip side of Theo's magnetic energy was a spoilt, entitled, controlling, easily bored ego who thought the world revolved around him. And in Theo's world, everything *did* revolve around him.

The secret fears that had built up in her as their wedding approached had crystallised during the fateful lunch with her parents the day before they'd been due to exchange their vows. Her future had flashed before her, a future that would see her become a clone of her mother, a once vivacious woman turned into a timid mouse under the weight of her husband's misogyny; browbeaten into giving up her dreams and becoming as dependent as a child.

Yanking herself out of Theo's world and far from his orbit had been the hardest thing Helena had ever done but she'd never regretted it. If her heart fisted into a knot whenever she saw a picture of him with yet another walking clothes horse on his arm it was only the residue of her old love making a dying flicker.

To find herself standing only feet away from him, the laser stare penetrating her from the ice-blue eyes that should have made her feel cold but warmed her far more effectively than the bath she'd run for herself... Cells in her body that had been dormant all these years were flickering back to life and, with a burst of fearful clarity, she realised these flickers needed extinguishing immediately.

Turning on her heel, Helena stormed to the front door and yanked it open. 'Get out.'

This was her home. Her sanctuary. Her flat, tiny but usually plentiful enough for her, now, with Theo's hulking body sucking out all its oxygen, felt as if its proportions had shrunk to the size of a playpen. She wanted him gone right now, before she gave in to the urge to punch the arrogance right off his smug face, or, worse, burst into tears or, even worse than that, flung her arms around him.

He moved out of the kitchen but no further than its door, shaking his head sadly. 'But we have not yet discussed the details of the project or answered the other questions we have of each other.'

That blasted voice. She hated it. All gravelly and throaty and capable of penetrating her skin and seeping into her bloodstream.

'I don't care,' she snapped. 'I told you three years ago that I never wanted to see you again. If I'd known you were our mystery client I would never have pitched for the job.'

'I know.' Another wink. 'That's why I kept my identity hidden and asked your mother to keep her mouth shut.'

She didn't know if it was the gust of wind that blew over her through the open front door or Theo's words that made her skin chill. 'You...you hid your identity on *purpose*?'

He winked again and clicked his finger and thumb together. 'Details, *agapi mou*. One must always take care of the details. I needed to get to this position, to where we are right at this precise moment. All the details came from that end game.'

She closed the door slowly as the penny dropped with equal slowness. 'This was a set-up?'

He looked at her pityingly. Or with something that resembled pity mixed with a dollop of glee. If he'd winked again she might just have slapped him. 'The pitch was created for you.'

'No.' She shook her head to clear the ringing in her ears. 'It couldn't have been. I wasn't asked to pitch personally...'

'Details,' he reminded her with another wink. 'I needed you to bite without raising your suspicions.'

'I was always going to win?'

He pulled a musing face. 'Unless your pitch was terrible, in which case I'd have given the job to a Greek firm, but I knew it wouldn't be. I knew it would be fantastic. I knew you were the right woman for the job.'

'So all those other architects who wasted their time...?'

'The only other firms invited to pitch do not have Greek speakers on their books. If they were stupid enough to draw up plans when the stipulation of having a Greek speaker had been made clear then the wasted time is their own doing.' He raised his shoulders in a fashion that reminded her strongly of the stance the naughty boys in her primary school had given when trying to convince the teacher that the culprit wasn't them even with the evidence right at their feet. 'This is a plan I set in motion a long time ago.'

It took a few beats for Helena's brain to compute.

This was revenge. She didn't know how Theo's commissioning her to design a house for him could be a form of revenge but she knew it was.

She'd unwittingly humiliated him. She'd only learned after the fact that he'd stood at the cathedral's altar for an hour before telling their guests the wedding was off. His colossal ego meant he hadn't believed she no longer wanted to marry him until he could no longer deny it.

'I'm not doing it.'

'Yes, you are.'

'No.' She shook her head for emphasis. 'I'm not. No

amount of money is worth the grief working for you would give me.'

His hand went to his chest again and he blinked his eyes in puppy-dog fashion. 'You keep wounding me, *agapi mou*. I am offering you the olive branch but you throw it back at me.'

She snorted. 'Oh, please.' She emphasised the P. 'I never wanted an olive branch and even if I did, this isn't one. This is some Machiavellian scheme you've dreamed up. I'm not stupid. You've gone to an awful lot of trouble…'

'Remember those plans we made when we were on Sidiro? When I inherited the peninsula you would design the home for it, the home in which we would raise our children?'

Sidiro was the tiny Greek island she'd spent the most magical month of her life on. She'd spent three years trying to forget its existence. To remember always made her heart feel as if it were being shredded.

'Well, my sweet temptress,' he continued, 'the peninsula is mine.'

There was a piercing in her heart at the realisation that this meant his grandmother had died. Another loss for a man who'd lost both his parents within three months of each other at the tender age of eighteen.

Helena pulled at her hair and tried desperately to get air into her lungs, trying even harder to stop the room spinning around her as another thought struck her.

If he planned to build a house on the peninsula then it must mean he planned to marry. The peninsula meant too much to him for it to be used for anything else.

So that was how he intended to get his revenge. By getting his ex-fiancée to design the home he would share with his future wife.

CHAPTER THREE

THEO'S ENGAGEMENT MUST have been a whirlwind romance the way theirs had been. Only a month ago Helena had seen a photo of him and his newest clothes horse attending one of those glamorous society parties he enjoyed so much, his famous luxury-underwear model lover not wearing much in the way of actual clothes, thus guaranteeing them front-page coverage on most of the tabloids.

She supposed it had been inevitable that he'd fall for one of the many, many women he'd cavorted with these past three years. She hoped the poor woman knew what she was letting herself in for.

As for Helena...

She knew exactly what she'd be letting herself in for if she took the commission.

'I'm sorry about your grandmother,' she said in as clear a voice as she could manage.

'What are you sorry about?'

That stumped her. Theo must have read her mind, for his eyes gleamed. 'Have no worries there, *agapi mou*. My grandmother is alive and kicking.'

'Good.' Her relief was instant. She'd only met Theo's grandmother a couple of times but had liked her very much.

'She's gifted the peninsula to me.'

'Good for you but I'm not taking the job.'

'Do I have to remind you that it's not just you who will benefit financially?'

Helena pressed her back against the front door, the change in his tone sending needles digging into her skin and making her limbs shaky.

'Staffords,' he added casually, referring to the company she worked for. 'I have seen the accounts. Your company is struggling for commissions.'

'That's not true.'

'It's struggling for commissions worth anything. Your offices are expensive. There have been whispers about redundancies.' He tilted his head. 'I think your job will be safe for now. The other junior architect and the clerical staff though…' He made a tutting sound. 'They will be gone by the end of the summer. If things continue as they are, the company will fold by Christmas and you will be out of a job.'

Feeling faint, she pressed herself harder against the door. 'How do you know all this?'

Every word he'd said was true. Staffords was in serious trouble. If they went under, she would go under too—Helena had debts up to her eyeballs and lived payday to payday.

He winked. 'Details.'

'If you wink at me again I'm going to slap you.'

His eyes gleamed. 'Promises, promises. Take the commission and you can slap me whenever you want.'

'Your face would be swollen by the end of the first day.'

'Then it will match another part of my anatomy.'

How could he utter such innuendoes when he was going to marry someone else?

But then, Theo had always been a flirt, she remembered bitterly. It had driven her mad the way women threw themselves at him. He'd taken their attention as his due. She'd had no cause to think he'd cheated on her—in the three months they were together he'd never let her out of his sight—but deep down had lived the fear that if she let him out of *her* sight, he would happily avail himself of one of them. Her fears had played out when, mere weeks after she'd left him, he'd taken up with his first model. The first of many. All identikit. All tall, skinny as rakes, blonde, beautiful and accomplished in the art of draping themselves over him. The total opposite of her: short, buxom, dark haired, with average looks and averse to public displays of affection.

Oblivious to her dark thoughts and not giving her the chance to retort, he continued. 'Take the commission, and both you and the company that supported you throughout your training will be richly rewarded. The prestige of designing a home for me—and let us be clear, this will be no ordinary home; I want something *spectacular*— will in itself lead to coverage that's usually reserved for Pellegrinis.'

Pellegrinis was an international multi-award-winning architectural firm that scooped up commissions with an ease that left everyone else breathless.

The doorbell rang, making her virtually jump out of her skin.

'That will be our food,' Theo said cheerfully, striding towards the door. Striding towards her...

Helena only just managed to move from the door and squash herself against the wall before Theo reached it, but her hallway was so narrow that he still brushed against her.

A blast of cold air swept into the flat, but if Theo felt its embrace he didn't show it. With his usual bonhomie, he took the large box from the young delivery driver and pressed a note into his hand with his thanks.

And then he closed the door and swept past her again, shouting over his shoulder as he opened the door to her living room, 'If you get the plates and cutlery I'll put this on the table.'

A strangled noise ripped from Helena's throat, but before she could articulate anything Theo came straight back out of the living room and opened her bathroom door, then looked at her with his brow creased. 'Where's your dining room?'

'I don't have one.'

He looked at her as if she'd admitted to having a major drug problem. 'Then where do you eat?'

'Off a tray on my lap… Why are you even here still? I told you to go. Get out. I have no interest in eating with you.'

'I remember you once had great interest in eating me, but I guess that's a reminiscence for another time.' And then he had the audacity to wink at her again. 'Okay, then trays it shall be.'

'I only have one…' But then she realised what he'd just alluded to and her words died on her tongue as her cheeks flamed with humiliation. She would have been talking to thin air anyway, for Theo had bustled back into the kitchen. She heard the distinct sound of cupboards and drawers being flung open.

'Do you want red or white wine?' he called.

Gritting her teeth so tightly she was lucky her jaw didn't shatter, Helena followed him into the cramped space.

'Where are your wine glasses?' he asked before she could get a word in, another perplexed expression on his face.

'I've already told you I don't have any wine, and even if I did, I wouldn't share it with you. For the last time, get out of my flat or—'

'You know what your problem is?' he said, speaking over her as he pulled her half-sized dishwasher open and removed two dirty tall glasses. 'You're too uptight. We will spend much time together in the coming months. It will pass more smoothly if you can learn to loosen up a bit.'

'Loosen up? Are you *kidding* me?'

Placing the glasses under the tap, he ran water into them. 'Fear not, *agapi mou*, once we have eaten our dinner and made our plans, I will leave you in peace.'

'You're taking a lot for granted here. I haven't agreed to anything.'

'But you will.' He raised a hefty shoulder. 'Or you live with the consequences and hope a miracle occurs to save your firm from liquidation and save you from losing your home and independence.'

Helena, Theo had discovered, had accrued thousands of pounds of debt during her studies. Half her monthly salary went on rent for her miniscule flat. The rest went on debt repayment, other household bills, food and transport costs. She would be lucky to survive a month without a job before handing back the keys to the flat and having to go crawling to Mummy and Daddy. It didn't surprise him that she hadn't tapped them up for help with her debt— Helena's middle name should be Independent—but the debt itself did surprise him. Her parents had always been generous with their only child. He guessed she'd severed her financial dependency on them as part of her great strides towards complete independence.

Glasses clean, Theo opened the box, first removing the two bottles of wine and then lifting out the foil cartons. 'I ordered Thai.'

Thai food was Helena's absolute favourite.

'I'm not hungry.'

He shrugged. 'Suit yourself. Me, I'm starving.'

Another strangled sound came from her throat before she bit out, 'Seeing as you're as cloth-eared as you always were and not budging, I'm going to get changed.'

The glare emanating behind her spectacles from her sultry eyes suggested he would be pushing his luck if he suggested she change into something revealing.

'Cloth-eared? Is that a compliment?'

'No, thickhead, it was an insult. And so was that.' And then she stalked out of the room before he could quip a retort.

A door slammed shut. The walls of the flat were so thin the tall glasses drying by the sink rattled from the force.

Alone, Theo opened the bottle of white and poured them both a glass. After taking a hefty slug of his, he rubbed the nape of his neck and closed his eyes.

Had she stripped that ugly robe thing off? Was she, at that very moment, naked?

He remembered every inch of Helena's delicious body, from the small mole above her left breast to the scar on her right hip from a childhood accident involving a bicycle and barbed wire. There was nothing about Helena Armstrong he hadn't committed to memory. He'd spent six months planning this day and had made contingency plans—in his favour, of course—for every eventuality.

Time had not dulled his memories of the woman he'd once worshipped. Goading her and teasing her, watching her cheeks flame with angry colour, heightened the charge racing gloriously through his veins, reminding him vividly of the way her cheeks had flamed with passion when he'd brought her to orgasm with his tongue or his hand.

He straightened his back and breathed deeply to quell the ache in his loins and rid himself of Helena's heady, musky scent suddenly playing like an old forgotten ghost on his senses. He would have that taste again soon, but until such time he thought it best not to walk around her flat with obvious arousal. The mood she was in, she was likely to karate-chop it.

He took their glasses and the wine bottle into the living room, which consisted of a two-seater sofa and single armchair crammed around a low coffee table, then went back to the kitchen and served their food onto chipped plates, found the cutlery and carried it into the living room too. Making one last trip to the kitchen, he found her solitary tray rammed behind the microwave then returned to the living room and sat on the two-seater sofa. The sofa was so old that the springs had gone. No sooner had his backside landed inches from the floor than Helena appeared in the doorway. She'd changed from the ugly robe thing into an equally ugly red T-shirt and even uglier black and white checked workout leggings. He just *knew* she'd selected the vilest items of clothing she possessed especially for him. He doubted she realised that, as gross as the items were, they clung to her hourglass figure like a dream.

'I see you've found your level,' she said with an evil smile.

Theo responded with a suggestive smile of his own. 'You know me, I like to go down low.'

She hit him with a thousand-yard stare but he was rewarded with a deep stain of colour across her beautiful cheeks.

Figuring the floor had to be more comfortable than this excuse for a sofa, Theo heaved himself up then shifted the coffee table until it was placed where he could unfold his legs beneath it.

When he was uncomfortably settled on the threadbare carpet he took his first mouthful of *phat kaphrao*, a street food he'd discovered during his backpacking days on his first visit to Bangkok and which he could eat until the sun came up. This particular *phat kaphrao* didn't quite have the fresh chilli kick he so enjoyed but it was a decent effort.

Helena waited until Theo's big mouth was full of food before saying primly, 'Let us get one thing straight. If—and it's a big if—I take the job, there will be no flirting. I know it's second nature to you but it's inappropriate.'

The sparkle in his eyes as he swallowed his food let her know she'd missed her mark even before he shook his head. 'I wish very much I could make that assurance but my mother always told me never to make a promise I couldn't keep.'

'That's my condition.'

'It's a condition I can't meet. You should eat before your food gets cold.'

'I've already told you, I'm not hungry.' She wouldn't even look at her plate. If she did, her empty belly might start rumbling.

Damn him, since the food delivery she'd had to block her nose off from breathing in his horrible cologne *and* the scent of her favourite food. She couldn't believe he remembered she liked Thai. She thought, after all the women he'd had since she left, she'd have become nothing but a blur, a face amongst many. She was surprised he remembered her name.

Helena wished she'd been able to forget his face. She wished she'd been able to forget everything she'd felt for him.

She wouldn't eat his food but she would drink his wine, she decided. Theo only bought the best, so she was certain the wine would be delicious. Leaning over, she took her glass from the table and brought it to her lips. Theo's dancing ice-blue eyes watched her every move.

The wine slipped down her throat like nectar and she had to resist closing her eyes to savour it.

'Back to my condition,' she said briskly.

'A condition I will not meet.' Another huge forkful of chicken, chilli and basil disappeared into his mouth.

She narrowed her eyes, wishing she could fire lasers from them. 'Flirting with an employee isn't just inappropriate, it's unprofessional and can be construed as sexual harassment.'

He washed his mouthful down with a large drink of wine and grinned. 'You will be a contractor, not an employee.'

'I don't imagine your fiancée will care about the difference if she catches you flirting with me.'

His eyebrows drew together. Heaping another pile of food onto his fork, he laughed, 'What fiancée?'

'The fiancée you're building the house for.'

'You must be mistaking me for someone else. I'm not getting married.'

Her heart jolted so hard at this she had to keep her bottom rooted to the armchair to stop herself springing out of it.

'My apologies,' she said stiffly. 'When you said you were building on the peninsula I made an assumption.'

He shook his head in a chiding fashion. 'First rule of business: never make assumptions. I have no intention of ever marrying, so rest easy, *agapi mou*, I can flirt with you all day every day.'

'What about your girlfriend's feelings?'

His laughter was even louder. 'What girlfriend?'

Having far too much pride to admit to reading any article about him even inadvertently, she arranged her face into a mask of nonchalance. 'Are you saying you don't have one?'

The sparkle in his eyes deepened. 'Would it bother you if I did?'

'Don't be ridiculous,' she spluttered. 'I just think it's cruel to commit to one person and then flirt with another.'

'I've only committed myself to one person before and she left me.' Theo raised his glass and winked, enjoying the latest stain of colour on Helena's face. 'I never make the same mistake twice.'

She clamped her lips together.

'But, seeing as my love-life is on your mind, I am of the same opinion as you.' He smiled. 'It *is* cruel to string lovers along. Honesty is always best, do you not agree?'

He watched her absorb the barbed sting he'd just launched, satisfaction filling him. If Helena had been honest with him from the beginning and not strung him along, he would never have been fool enough to propose, let alone go to all the trouble and expense of preparing an elaborate wedding. He would never have suffered the humiliation of standing at an altar waiting for a bride who would never turn up.

Theo swallowed his last mouthful of food, finished his wine and then hoisted himself to his feet. 'I need to use the bathroom.'

Not waiting for a reply, he strolled out of the cramped living room and took the two steps to the door he'd opened earlier when looking for a dining room.

There was no lock on the door, he noted before spotting the bath filled with water and the few straggling bubbles that had yet to evaporate.

Sitting on the bath's edge, Theo covered his face and took the ten breaths he needed to regain his equilibrium. It was a trick his mother had taught him in childhood when she'd determined his temper would get him into trouble if he didn't learn to curb it, and he credited it with helping him through the worst of the nightmare days after his parents' death. It was a trick he'd employed again when Helena had left him.

By the time he'd reached number ten, the angst knotting in his stomach had eased and he could examine her poky bathroom without wanting to sweep all her stuff onto the floor and crush it under his feet.

But there wasn't much to sweep and crush even if he wanted to. The small wall cabinet contained a handful of cosmetics, make-up remover, day cream, night cream and a spare tube of toothpaste.

There was no discernible reason why the sparsity of her possessions should make him feel so cramped inside.

There was no discernible reason why Helena's tiny flat as a whole should make him feel so disquieted. How she chose to live was none of his business. That she'd suffered financially these last few years was none of his business either.

Leaving the bathroom, he went back to the living room.

Helena was still curled up on the armchair, hugging a cushion. She didn't look at him.

'I'm leaving,' he informed her.

That made her look. There was a vulnerability to her stare that threatened to constrict his throat but he fought through it successfully before it could take root.

He picked up his coat from the back of the sofa and shrugged his arms into it. 'My PA will be in touch tomorrow about the contract and to make the arrangements.'

She pushed her glasses up her nose with a trembling hand and turned her face away. ''Bye, then.'

'Kalinikta, agapi mou.'

Theo walked the narrow hallway, doing up the buttons of his overcoat as he went. When he reached the front door, soft footsteps followed in his wake.

Helena stood behind him. 'Why are you doing this?' she asked.

He closed the gap between them and stared at the up-turned face. The beautiful face he'd fallen in love with all those years ago… Incredibly, time had only made it more exquisite. He stroked a finger along a high cheekbone, relishing the tiny quiver she wasn't quick enough to disguise. 'You promised to design me a house for my peninsula,' he murmured. And then he leaned down to whisper into her ear. 'And you still owe me a wedding night.'

CHAPTER FOUR

WHEN THE JET touched down on the Agon runway, Helena squeezed her eyes shut. If she didn't look out of the window she could pretend she was still in London and that the nightmare she'd just flown into wasn't real.

The last leg of her journey to the island went as smoothly as the first leg had. She was escorted off Theo's private plane and whisked into an ultra-sleek, ultra-expensive car, which in turn whisked her to the harbour, where she was escorted onto an ultra-sleek and ultra-expensive yacht. Before she even had time to blink, the yacht was slicing through the Mediterranean.

An hour after they set sail, land appeared on the horizon.

Sidiro. The most magical island in the world.

Heart thumping and memories assailing her, Helena sucked in a large breath and was glad of her phone vibrating, distracting her. She had two messages. The first was from her mother, wishing her luck. They'd managed only a short get-together at a coffee shop since Theo had waltzed into Helena's flat. She'd confided everything to her, reassuring her mother that she had nothing to be sorry about—if she hadn't given him Helena's address he would have got it another way. Privately, Helena had come to the conclusion that getting her address from her mother had been a fishing expedition for Theo. Her mother, her eyes sad, had made her promise to be careful. In return, Helena had made her promise to think, again, about leaving her father. She didn't hold out much hope but she had to try. She'd given her mother a key to her flat the day she moved in, hoping that one day she would use it. Her hopes had so far been forlorn.

The other message was from Stanley, asking how the journey had gone. His kindness squeezed her heart, as it always did. How different would her life be—would *she* be—if she'd grown up with a man like Stanley as a father? To have a father whose only objective in parenting was his child's well-being and happiness rather than someone whose only objective was to mould his child as he'd moulded his wife into his version of perfection?

But it was as pointless wishing for a different father as it was wishing to erase other aspects of her past.

Three weeks of maniacal planning for this had allowed her to shove from her mind exactly where she was going. Whenever a snapshot of her time on Sidiro had flitted into her mind she'd simply taken a deep breath to counteract the lance of pain and blinked the memory away.

An isolated, horseshoe-shaped, hilly island that would be fortunate to be named in the top one hundred Greek islands by the general public and even then only for its cheese, Sidiro was a tiny dot on the map with a population barely touching two thousand. The majority of said population were involved in the business of tending goats and making and exporting cheese.

However, Sidiro had a secret. Its isolation, along with its pristine white sandy beaches, iron-filled rocks that glowed orange under the sun and from which the island got its name, turquoise waters and spectacular sunsets, had seen it become a mecca for wealthy but discerning party-lovers who found the raucous nightlife of Europe's more notorious nightspots unsavoury. For two months each summer, rich, young, beautiful people sailed across the globe to party in their own secret paradise. One of those partygoers and a founder of this party scene was none other than Theo Nikolaidis, whose mother had been born on the island.

Just a few weeks after they'd met, Theo had taken Helena to Sidiro for a long weekend that had stretched to a month.

It had been on this paradise that he'd first mentioned his dream of turning the three-kilometre-square peninsula off Sidiro's eastern tip, long cut off from Sidiro itself and reached by a five-minute boat ride or a very long swim, into a home to raise a family. The peninsula had many years ago been abandoned by his mother's family, who'd moved to Agon in search of better opportunities, but the now derelict land itself remained in the family.

She remembered exploring the peninsula with him. He'd taken her to an old abandoned shepherd's hut nestled in the most perfect spot, giving a spectacular view of the Mediterranean and shelter from the worst of the elements. This was the spot, Theo had decreed, where they would build their home and raise their family.

More memories flooded her and, to Helena's distress, hot tears stung the backs of her eyes.

How could the afternoon sun blaze so brightly in the perfect blue sky? It should be hidden by thick, dark grey clouds like the ones that had hung over her these past three weeks.

It felt as if she were sailing into a long-forgotten dream.

She supposed that technically that was what she was doing. Once, she had shared the same dream for them. Dreams, she now knew, were whispers and impressions. Dreams were not real. They had no substance.

The peninsula had a small harbour and that was where Helena's first sailing adventure in three years came to an end. There was a flurry of activity as her cases and work equipment were loaded onto a golf cart, the only vehicular transport allowed on the island other than taxis and deliveries from the twice-weekly ferry. As she watched her possessions disappear from view, a growing speck in the distance caused the hairs on the nape of her neck to lift.

Heart rising up her throat, she kept her gaze fixed on the approaching scooter.

Theo brought the scooter to a halt with a flourish and grinned. He'd watched Helena's arrival from the hilltop with a mixture of emotions coursing through his blood. The strongest had been understandable satisfaction, followed closely by unfathomable bitterness. He'd never told her that his grandmother, thrilled at the thought of her only grandson making a life on the island of her birth, had signed over the deeds for the peninsula to him as a wedding present. He'd wanted to surprise Helena with it on their wedding day.

His grandmother was delighted he was finally building on it. She'd adored Helena and had been devastated when she'd jilted him, something else he would never forgive Helena for.

But he didn't want to learn about forgiveness. He wanted that most American concept of closure.

He had not anticipated how greatly seeing Helena again would affect him. Not on an emotional level, of course, but on a physical level, as if inhaling her perfume had retuned his senses to a greater pitch that heightened his every waking moment. He felt like the man he'd been before the jilting and it felt great. There was a zing in his veins, a strut in his walk, a greater appetite for food and stimulation whilst his boredom threshold had increased and he'd had to fight his own mind not to keep wandering off track. Theo employed a great team who were perfectly capable of keeping his many and varied businesses and interests going for a short while without him, but when he was present they looked to him for leadership. He'd had to drink a lot of caffeine to keep himself sharp and stop his wandering mind going off on too many tangents. But really, it was too delicious to imagine Helena going stir crazy as she made the arrangements needed for her trip back into his life.

He knew how badly she'd wanted to say no to the commission and keep the door slammed on him for good.

A flash of their final argument suddenly played in his head. It had come on the heels of a lunch with her parents, a lunch that was supposed to be the last meal they shared before separating for the night to avoid the bad luck that plagued newlyweds foolish enough to see each other before exchanging their vows. If he caught so much as a glimpse of Helena after the sun rose and before they stood before the bishop, they would be cursed with a plague of locusts or some other such nonsense. It was a tradition he'd been willing to honour because Helena had wanted it.

She'd returned to the house with him to get her overnight bag and, he'd thought, for a few minutes of privacy before they separated for the night. Her wedding dress had been sent directly to the hotel Helena and her family were staying at that night. Theo had booked the whole top floor for them.

Instead of the loving words and promises he'd anticipated, she'd turned on him about an innocuous comment he'd made to her father about babies. Theo had taught Helena to argue in their time together and to begin with he'd enjoyed watching his usually possessed fiancée unravel.

'You want me to quit work! You want me barefoot and pregnant in a kitchen…'

The imagery had provoked a burst of wild laughter from him. Helena? In a kitchen? As if that would ever happen, pregnant or otherwise.

'You think that's funny?' she'd shrieked. 'None of this is funny! I thought you were supportive of my career.'

'I am!' he'd shouted back, blissfully unaware that it was his relationship as well as his fiancée unravelling around him. Hadn't he framed that first picture of the palace he'd so admired? Hadn't he told her he wanted her to design their home when the peninsula became his? Hadn't he found all the information needed so she could finish her masters in Greece? Hadn't he found the perfect firm at which to do her final year's placement in Agon? How much more supportive could he be?

'Then why tell my father that as soon as I get my qualifications, you'll have me pregnant and under your watch all the time? I *heard* you!'

'Of course you heard me—I winked at you when I said it. I was joking,' he reiterated for the fourth time. 'It was a clumsy effort to bond with your father. I wish I hadn't bothered.'

'I wish you hadn't bothered too. Many a true word is said in jest and that was a jest too far. I'm not ready for children.'

'You said you wanted them!'

'And maybe I will in the future, but not yet. I'm too young, there's too much I want to—'

'So it's all about you, is it? What about the plans we've already made?'

'The plans *you've* made, you mean! You keep steam-rollering me—'

'I consult you on everything—'

'*After* the fact! You only hear what you want to hear. When I said I wanted children I never said I wanted them straight away.'

'Not straight away, *matia mou*,' he'd pounced, spotting the opening needed to placate her, 'but once you have your qualifications.' See how reasonable he could be? 'We can enjoy each other for two more years and then we can—'

'And then *I* can be under your thumb and under your control.'

The rest of the argument was a blur in his mind but he remembered with utter clarity the moment she'd pulled her engagement ring off her finger and thrown it at him.

'I thought you were different,' Helena had screamed. She'd been unreachable. He remembered the colour of her face, the wildness in her eyes… 'But you're not. You're just like my father and I will not marry a man who wants to control me and make decisions for me. You can shove this engagement where the sun doesn't shine. I quit! And do *not* follow me. I never want to see you again!'

He'd laughed at her. He'd even shut the car door that had driven her away and waved her off for good measure. Not for a second had he thought she was serious. He'd expected her to stew for a few hours then come to her senses. He'd carried her engagement ring in his pocket to the cathedral, ready to slip it back into its rightful place when she joined him at the altar.

He'd never dreamt that the throwing of her ring at his chest would be the last direct contact between them in three years.

The most enjoyable part of these past few weeks had been lying in his bed at night knowing that Helena had been lying in her bed thinking about him. Whether she liked it or not, he'd gatecrashed his way back into her thoughts and thrown her orderly life into the chaos she so detested.

Now she wouldn't be able to leave until *he* said so. Now Theo was the one who held the power, and he intended to have as much fun as he could extract from it.

He looked her up and down, taking in the sensible, businesslike knee-length skirt and scrupulously buttoned black shirt that must be boiling her alive. He smiled. Poor Helena—she'd obviously dressed like a governess to repel him, but it didn't matter what she wore, she would always look good enough to eat. Just remembering her taste sent a charge careering through his veins. What he wouldn't give to peel those goody-goody clothes off and rediscover the creamy-textured golden skin and all her other hidden surprises.

'Good trip?' he asked when he'd feasted his eyes on her for long enough.

Eyes narrowing and cheeks burning under the weight of his blatant approval, she shrugged. 'It could have been worse.'

He laughed at this understatement and patted the space behind him. 'You know what to do.'

Her face darkened further. 'I'm not riding on that thing.'

'You never minded before.'

'I was young and stupid then,' she retorted.

'Maturity is an overrated quality.'

'If you say so. I'm not getting on it without a helmet.'

He suppressed another burst of laughter that he'd correctly anticipated that particular argument from her. 'There's one in the box.'

'Are there leathers for me to change into?'

'There's no traffic and the scooter whines if I push it to more than twenty kilometres an hour.'

'I'll take that as a no, then.' She sniffed and folded

her arms across her chest. 'I'll wait for the golf buggy to come back.'

He shook his head regretfully. 'It isn't coming back.'

Her eyes narrowed into slits. 'Fine. I'll walk.'

He looked at her feet. 'In those shoes?' Helena was wearing a pair of black heels that were about as useful and appropriate for walking distances as an ice cube.

Her chin jutted. 'Yes.'

He let her obstinacy hang for a moment before pointing at the white dwelling with the blue roof far in the distance on the hilltop. 'That's where you need to walk to.'

Her eyes widened a fraction but she managed a brittle smile. 'That's fine. I'll meet you there.'

'Sure you don't want a ride?'

'Perfectly sure.'

'Okay. Enjoy your walk.' Thus saying, he turned the engine back on and did a U-turn on the single track.

'You should wear a helmet,' Helena suddenly shouted at his retreating form. 'Mind you, if you were to fall, it might knock some sense into your thick head.'

His laughter as he rode away swirled into the dust his acceleration created.

Cursing under her breath, Helena put one foot in front of the other and followed the trail left by Theo's scooter.

If she'd known she was going to have to walk she'd have grabbed her trainers from her suitcase before it was whipped away. She'd have taken her sunhat too and applied more sunscreen.

It was late afternoon but the sun still blazed down. She could feel its rays penetrating her scalp and thought what an excellent start to her stay sunstroke would be.

Minutes later she'd folded her skirt up at the waist, undone the top three buttons of her shirt, tied the bottom into a knot around her belly and rolled the sleeves up, yet she still felt as if she'd been placed in a boil-in-the-bag.

She was still cursing both her own stubbornness and Theo's deviousness under her shortening breath ten minutes later when she heard the scooter's distinctive engine nearing.

Theo stopped in front of her again. She was quite sure she looked exactly as she felt—like she was melting from the inside out—while Theo looked as fresh as if he'd just showered and dressed. The black shorts and khaki polo shirt he wore didn't have a speck of road dust on them.

After a long silence he tilted his head and fixed her with a stare that suggested she was behaving like a recalcitrant child. 'Ready to accept a lift now? Or should I do another lap of the peninsula first?'

Helena's feet were killing her. She'd been on the verge of kicking off her stupid shoes and walking barefoot. Her throat was parched. All the moisture in her body had seeped out and clung to her skin.

But she really, really, *really* didn't want to get on the back of that scooter.

Three years ago they had spent a month on this island travelling everywhere by scooter, her face pressed against Theo's back, arms wrapped tightly around his waist. She had loved every minute of it.

'Last chance,' he warned with a raised brow.

She shifted her stance and winced as her shoe inadvertently rubbed against the brand-new blister on the heel of her right foot.

Theo saw the wince, tutted and shook his head sadly. 'It is incredible how the most intelligent people are always the most stubborn.'

'Your IQ must be sky high,' she muttered.

He grinned broadly. 'I thank you for the compliment.'

'It wasn't a…' She sighed, filling her lungs with yet more hot air, which dried her throat that little bit more.

She gave up.

Glaring at him one more time for luck, Helena stepped out of her shoes and swapped them for the helmet in the box. Only when the helmet was secure on her head did she attempt to get on the back of the scooter.

Why had she chosen to wear such a tight skirt? The only way to get her legs to part enough to climb on was to hitch it up to her hips.

'Can you look away, please?' she asked stiffly.

Amusement danced in his eyes but he did as she asked.

Cheeks burning with humiliation, Helena quickly yanked her skirt up and hopped on with a flexibility that took her by surprise. She'd forgotten how nimble she used to be.

But getting onto the back of the scooter was only the first challenge. The second challenge was how to hold on without touching Theo.

The blasted man read her mind. 'You need to hold on to me, *agapi mou*, just as you used to do.'

Gritting her teeth, she placed her hands gingerly on his waist.

'I don't bite,' he said, then lowered his gravelly voice to add at the exact same time that she tightened her hold a fraction, 'Not unless you ask me very nicely.'

There was no time for her to jump off or make a retort for Theo squeezed the throttle and they were off. The motion made her lose her balance and, frightened of being thrown off, she pressed herself into his back and clung on tightly.

He drove them over the narrow tracks, expertly avoiding potholes and other hazards such as random goats. Helena closed her eyes and tried to trick her mind into ignoring the broad back her face was pressed against.

He steered the scooter to the left. She leaned in with him, her thighs squeezing automatically against his. His back muscles bunched against her cheek.

When had she joined her hands together across his hard, flat stomach? It wasn't possible for her to hold on any tighter.

She forgot to breathe through her mouth. The scent of laundry soap from his T-shirt and his cologne coiled into her airways. It was a woody smell that always evoked thoughts of deep forests.

She squeezed her eyes shut even tighter and tried to block out everything, but it had become impossible. The vibrations of the scooter and the solidity and warmth of Theo had transported her back in time to the summer when she'd…

'You can let go now.'

Theo's gravelly voice cut through her desperate, futile mind-block.

Helena opened one eye cautiously.

They'd arrived at the dwelling he'd pointed to earlier.

And she was still pressed against him.

A burst of panic crashed through her. Yanking her hands away from his waist, she swung her left leg in a backward arch and virtually threw herself off the scooter. She would undoubtedly have face-planted the ground had Theo not caught hold of her arm at the last second.

Falling would almost have been preferable.

The impact of Theo's touch was immediate. The pads of four fingers and a thumb holding her forearm sent what felt like a thousand volts of pure electricity charging through her skin and firing into her veins, making her heart accelerate and her breathing shorten.

And then she was caught in his ice-blue stare. Her accelerating heart and shallow breaths froze in suspended animation. Time itself became suspended.

She couldn't break away from the trap of his stare, and in that suspended moment had no desire to break from it, her eyes suddenly thirsty to drink in the face of the man she had once loved with all her heart. There was that groove in his forehead, indented with both laughter and his childhood bicycle accident, which had been practically identical to her own, only the resulting injuries being different. There was his wide mouth, always curved upwards and never far from making a quip, which had flattened into a straight line. His nostrils flared, the pupils of his ice-blue eyes dilated and pulsed…

CHAPTER FIVE

IT WAS THE tingling between her legs that brought Helena to her senses, a damp ache she hadn't felt for so long that she'd forgotten she'd ever experienced it. A frisson of it had shot through her when he'd whispered in her ear that stupid quip about her owing him a wedding night—as *if*—but she'd shoved it aside, refused to acknowledge it, refused to give him the satisfaction of responding to his mind-games.

She had to keep a sane head on her shoulders. Theo was dangerous. For all his convivial, amusing persona, he had a ruthless streak that would make Machiavelli proud. His actions bringing her here proved that better than anything.

Wrenching her stare from his, she shook his hand off her arm, took a step back and cleared her parched throat. 'Is this my base?' Theo's PA had confirmed Helena would be staying in a newly built staffed lodge on the peninsula for the duration. Further lodgings would be built in the coming months to accommodate the team who would build the mansion that would rise like a monolith on the site.

It mattered not what best practice was, Theo wanted Helena living and working on the site. His deep pockets ensured that whatever Theo wanted, Theo got.

'It is.' He climbed off the scooter and stretched his back. 'I'll show you around.'

Inside, she found the lodgings to be much more luxurious than she'd anticipated. The scent of fresh paint permeated the air.

'Let me introduce you to my housekeepers, Elli and Natassa.' He steamed ahead through the wide reception room and led her to a large, hi-tech kitchen.

Helena wished she could feel an ounce of surprise to find the housekeepers were two stunning women of around her age. Theo liked variety, she thought bitterly, and he loved to be loved. His ego demanded it. What better way to dig the knife into his ex than to employ two beautiful, glamorous women to look after her? Which one was he sleeping with? The blonde? The redhead? Both?

Forcing a smile and then fighting to hold it as well as keeping down the nausea roiling in her stomach, she shook hands with them both.

In no time at all, a tall glass of water with ice and fresh lemon slices in it was thrust into her hand and a plate of sweet Greek pastries extended.

'They look lovely,' she said politely. She would not be rude to these women nor allow herself to harbour bad feelings for them. It wasn't their fault Theo had brought them here and was using them in his sadistic mind-games. 'But would you mind if I go to my room before I eat? I could do with freshening up.' And she could really do with some time away from Theo. With any luck, he would leave soon for his home in Athens or, most likely, his home in Agon.

'I'll show you to it,' Theo said before either of the housekeepers could answer. He strode out of the kitchen and through the main living area to the back of the lodge, forcing her to walk double-quick to keep up. He paused to push a door open. 'This is your office. You can arrange it to your liking tomorrow.' She'd barely caught a glimpse of it before he steamed on through an archway.

'Our living quarters,' he said casually.

There were two doors here, facing each other.

'Our?' she asked a beat later.

He met her stare. A knowing, lazy smile tugged at his mouth. *'Nai, agapi mou.* Our living quarters.' Eyes glimmering, he nodded at the right-hand door. 'Your room…' His head turned to the left-hand door. 'My room.'

Temporarily dumbstruck, she had to force herself to speak. 'You're staying here too?'

'But of course,' Theo purred. 'This way I am here and available any time you need me…' He let his words hang before adding, 'Day *or* night.'

Her silent fury was magnificent to behold. Her face was practically contorted with the weight of it. It was a long time before she said, 'I was under the impression I would be staying here with only your staff.'

'I know you were.' He winked and opened her door. 'I was being considerate.'

She snorted her disbelief.

He strode into the bedroom he'd had designed with Helena in mind. 'I thought you had enough to think about. If you knew I was staying here too it would have put you under additional pressure.'

'Or seen me pulling out.' She glared at him from the threshold, making no attempt to cross it.

He shook his head sadly. 'You had too much to lose for that to happen.' And even more to lose if she called it quits now. He'd paid Staffords and Helena the promised substantial down payment. In return they'd signed a watertight contract which tied Helena to him until he deemed the architectural plans complete. If she attempted to leave before that time, Staffords and Helena would be liable to repay the down payment plus interest.

He had her over a barrel, exactly where he wanted her. And, from the fire blazing in her eyes, she knew it too.

He waited with eager anticipation for her fury to boil over.

He was to be disappointed. Speaking through clearly gritted teeth, she said, 'If we have to share a roof, then fine, but I tell you now, I will not be sharing a bed with you.'

'Did I say anything about us sharing a bed?' he asked with mock innocence. 'But, seeing as you're the one thinking it, I tell *you* now that you're welcome to share my bed any time you like.'

'Not in a million years,' she spluttered.

He laughed. 'Is that a challenge?'

'It's a statement of fact. I'm here to work, not be cheap entertainment for you.'

'No one could ever call you cheap, *agapi mou*.'

She finally stepped into the room and stood before him, arms folded over the wonderful breasts he remembered as clearly as if he'd looked at them that morning. 'This is my bedroom, yes?'

He folded his arms in mimicry. 'All yours.'

'Then you will respect that this is my personal space. You do not enter unless invited, got it?'

'So you are already thinking of inviting me in?'

'No!' Her hands clenched beside her breasts and she inhaled deeply before muttering, 'You're impossible.'

'Another compliment,' he said with a wink, knowing perfectly well she meant it as nothing of the sort.

'Is there a pharmacist on the island?'

'Of course.' The randomness of the question bemused him.

'Good.'

'What do you need?'

'Some painkillers. You're giving me a headache.'

Throwing his head back, Theo roared with laughter. Since his parents' death, Helena was the one person other than his grandparents who had never taken his crap. Her insouciance had delighted him. It *still* delighted him.

He noted her lips twitching and when he caught her eye he saw the sparkle in it before she turned her face away. His mirth grew. Helena was trying to conceal her own amusement, the minx.

'I will leave you to settle in. You should have everything you need but if there's anything missing, let Natassa or Elli know and they will sort it out for you.'

Helena tightened her towel around her chest and, for the third time, rifled through her huge walk-in wardrobe hoping that something different would have magically appeared. Eventually she settled on a dark green skirt and a cream top, the least businesslike of her clothing. Unfortunately she, in her stubborn wisdom, had packed only business clothes and a few items to wear for lounging around in the evenings. She'd selected her clothes blissfully unaware she would be sharing a roof with Mr Ego for the duration. Blissfully unaware because he'd designed it that way. The fiend. Her intention to work seven days a week to get the plans drawn up only strengthened.

She could kill Theo. Happily kill him. The vast majority of the three hours Helena had been hiding out in her room had been spent imagining the variety of ways in which she could bump him off. She would write a list, she decided, and let him choose for himself.

Thoughts of murder had to wait while she got ready. Natassa had checked in on her to ask for her approval over dinner, which would be served shortly.

It was only when Helena was checking her make-up for smudges that she realised she'd even applied it. She hurriedly wiped it all off. Theo and his humungous ego would think she'd dolled herself up for him, which was absolutely not the case. Not in the slightest. To make that point even clearer, she tipped her head upside down and shook her hair until it resembled a messy beehive.

Et voila!

One last look in the mirror assured her she looked dreadful.

If this didn't repel him and make clear that she'd rather get intimate with a corpse than him, nothing would.

Natassa greeted her in the kitchen with a wide smile. 'Good timing. Your starter is ready. We have set the table for you on the terrace—is that okay, or would you prefer to eat inside?'

'Outside would be great, thanks...assuming Theo's okay with that?' There was no reason on earth that Helena uttering his name should make her heart skip a beat.

The slightest crease marred Natassa's beautiful brow. 'Why would he not be okay with that?'

'Because he might prefer to eat indoors.'

'He isn't here. He took the yacht back to Agon.' The crease in her brow deepened. 'I think he's gone to a party. Wherever he is, he will be back tomorrow. Lunchtime. I think.'

'You think?'

A shrug. 'He was vague about timings. I am not paid to question him.'

Helena wasn't being paid to question him either, or care that he'd left her on her first night so he could go out and party, something she kept reminding herself as she ate her meal on the terrace with only the crickets for company.

Helena didn't care about eating alone. She was *used* to eating alone. A solo three-course meal that would be worthy of a Michelin-starred restaurant was nothing to complain about. She'd left her flat that morning expecting to eat every meal alone for the foreseeable future. The food and accommodation were a hundred times better than expected, but in the being-left-alone stakes she'd been right.

Theo must have been winding her up about his staying at the lodge with her. Playing another of his little mind-games.

Let him play. She didn't care.

She didn't care at all. She especially didn't care that he was, at that moment, partying hard, no doubt with some clothes horse draped all over him and that he most definitely would not be alone when he awoke.

When she released her clenched fists, she resolutely ignored the indentations left by her fingernails in her palms.

'Triple-aspect windows for the master suite?' Helena clarified. To her great relief, she was able to utter the words 'master suite' without her voice catching.

This first on-site discussion about Theo's requirements and wishes for his new home had been much harder than she'd envisaged. Three years ago, before the top of the hill they were standing on had been flattened in preparation for the monolith that would be built on it, the dream had been for this to be *their* home.

Heads pressed together, they had whispered in the dark for hours, night after night, about the home they'd build. They'd planned the layout, teasing each other about who should have the biggest office and the biggest dressing room. Theo had teased her over the extent of her leisure-use wishes, Helena wanting only a steam room, while he wanted a full-blown gym, two swimming pools, a tennis court, a cinema room and a sprawling games room with its own bar.

Were her memories playing her false or was everything Theo was describing in that expansive way of his exactly as they had whispered during those late-night plotting sessions?

The master suite, with his-and-hers bathrooms and his-and-hers dressing rooms and triple-aspect windows giving an unblemished view of the Mediterranean, had been exactly as they had dreamed up together.

'*Nai*, floor-to-ceiling windows and doors that open up to my private balcony.' He turned his head to face her, amusement dancing on his mesmerising features. 'I will make sure to check for boats on the horizon before going out on it naked—I don't want to be responsible for a surge in blood-pressure conditions.'

A shimmering tendril raced up Helena's spine both at the sudden unbidden image of Theo naked and at the feel of his stare from behind his shades.

He gazed right at her a moment longer before turning his stare back to the area of levelled ground where his bedroom would be situated. His voice dropped to a murmur. 'Do you still find the thought of being pressed naked against a window while being taken from behind erotic?'

His question was so unexpected that it took a few moments for the words to sink in, but when they did and provoked the accompanying imagery…

Her whole being became suffused with sticky heat that sucked all the air from her lungs.

'That,' she hissed when she found her voice, 'is completely inappropriate.'

And cruel. That was another thing whispered during those long nights: seductive discussions about where they wanted to make love in their imaginary future home. The prudish woman he'd met in the Agon palace garden had, under Theo's tutelage, discovered her sensual side, one she'd never suspected existed. He'd opened her mind and set her imagination free and it had been headily joyous. In truth, they had tortured each other with those seductive talks, Helena because she'd been desperate for Theo to forgo his ridiculous pledge to wait until they were married before making love to her and Theo torturing himself in turn by his inability to allow anyone to best him at anything, even his fiancée at erotic fantasies.

The man who saw any woman with a pulse as fair game for bedding had been ruthless about keeping their genitalia apart, whereas she, the strait-laced, hard-working virgin, had been desperate to experience his lovemaking. His willpower had been stronger than her desperation.

Helena swallowed hard and forced the conversation back to the job at hand. 'What about guest rooms? Are they all to be *en suite*?'

'Of course. Each to have its own bath and walk-in shower.'

She nodded and unnecessarily wrote it in her notebook. She hadn't needed to take any notes but would rather hurl herself into the sea than admit she remembered it all.

She forced her features to remain neutral just as she had a few hours ago when he'd finally deigned to return to the peninsula as lunch was being served, looking like a man about to embark on a yachting holiday. Helena, dressed in her usual uniform of A-line skirt and blouse, had resisted the impulse to throw her salad at him. Now she resisted the impulse to throw her notebook at him.

'If you don't mind, I'd like to return to the lodge,' she said with all the politeness she could muster. She would keep her professionalism even if it killed her. Which it probably would.

'You have enough to get going on the designs?'

'I've enough to make a start but that's not the reason I want to return to the lodge.' She stared hard at him, trying to meet his eyes behind the double barrier of their shades, but failing. 'I'm not used to such heat.'

'You're half-Greek.'

'Born and raised in England, which I haven't left in three years. It would be better if we make site visits early, rather than in the afternoon when the sun is at its highest.'

His wide lips twitched, the corners lifting in what could be regarded as a smirk. 'Do I detect a rebuke?'

'You're the client. It's not my place to rebuke you. I'm just pointing out that it's easier to concentrate when my brain isn't being boiled by the sun.'

More lip-twitching. 'Point taken.'

'Thank you. Can we come back after breakfast?'

'If I'm back.'

'Back?' She didn't mean for it to come out so sharply but Theo had, again, caught her off-guard.

'I have a function to attend in Athens this evening.' Even through his shades Theo could see the colour rise on Helena's face. 'A preview exhibition at an art gallery.'

'Then you must want to get going,' she said stiffly, striding away from him. Unfortunately for Helena, her legs were so short it took him only three of his own strides to catch up with her.

'Come with me?'

She gave him a look that could strip paint.

'Is that a no?'

'I am not here for a social life, I'm here to work.'

'You have been working all day.'

'Actually, no. I couldn't start work this morning as you didn't get here until lunch.'

'That must have been torture for you.' Helena was nothing if not dedicated to her career. It had meant far more to her than he ever had. 'How *did* you pass the time?'

Her nose rose. 'By familiarising myself with the computers in my office.'

'You had a morning to yourself on the most beautiful island on Earth and spent it playing with your computer?'

'I wasn't playing.'

'How *has* your social life been?' he asked pointedly, revelling in her growing fury. He could sense her clinging to her professionalism by a thread, using it as a cloak to hide behind. He wanted the Helena he remembered to throw the cloak and all its shackles aside and emerge in her full, seductive glory, and he had no qualms about using whatever weapons he had at his disposal to achieve it.

'That is none of your business.'

'I'm just making conversation. You've made friends?' Helena was the only person he'd ever met who could count her friends on the fingers of one hand, the thumb surplus to requirements. This solitude was alien to him, a man who enjoyed a healthy social life with a vast network of friends.

'Yes, Theo, I have friends.'

'Any friends under the age of fifty? A boyfriend?' He nudged her teasingly with his elbow. 'A lover?'

She stepped out of his reach and accelerated her pace.

'Definitely a lover,' he said knowingly, then was unable to resist adding, 'Does he turn you on as much as I do?'

She came to a sudden stop. Slowly, she twisted to face him and cast him with a look of pure disdain. And then she laughed. 'Do you really want me to answer that? Do you think your ego can take it?' They'd reached the lodge. She smiled serenely and said airily, 'Enjoy your evening, Theo. I'll see you in the morning—in a professional capacity. I trust you'll be able to find your professionalism then too.'

Theo let her go inside. His heart was thudding at the dawning realisation that Helena really *had* taken a lover in the intervening years. It had always been in the back of his mind that she had no reason to hold on to her virginity, but until that moment he'd never believed it had happened. Theo had been unable to move on, but Helena…

She had thrived without him.

She'd had lovers.

He couldn't believe how heavy and twisted it made his guts feel.

CHAPTER SIX

THE OFFICE HELENA had been appointed by Theo was, she had to admit, perfect. He'd provided her with everything she'd requested and as a result she had a humungous rectangular table on which to spread out her plans and display 3D models of her designs, a ginormous desk with three brand-new desktop computers and two brand-new laptops, all with the specified software installed. She also had a 3D printer, an ordinary printer and enough of the specific stationery she used to keep her going for the next year.

She had no intention of being here for even a quarter of a year. Once the designs were approved, she was out of here. A Greek project manager would take over the day-to-day running of the build and liaise with officials. To get to that point, though, was going to take a lot of hard work. Greek planning law was a whole new area for her and, while she'd crammed the subject every spare minute this past month, she was quite sure there were many areas she could trip herself up on if she didn't give it due diligence.

The five days she'd already spent here had gone much better than anticipated, mostly because Theo had stopped flirting with her. Her parting shot at the end of their first site visit must have worked, for he'd turned into the epitome of professionalism. Or had it been her insinuation that she'd had lovers? Whatever the cause, she was glad he'd stopped tormenting her. She *was*.

If it weren't for the sparks that played beneath her skin, working with him would be easy. Theo, she was learning, had a keen but relaxed approach to business that stopped her second-guessing herself and tying herself in knots about meeting his approval. If she suggested something he didn't agree with he would dismiss it, but not in a way that made her feel foolish for broaching the subject. The suggestions he did agree with, he had a way of approving them that made her feel as if she'd grown wings.

It was the nights she struggled with. Her five nights here had been spent with her own company. Theo disappeared the moment business hours finished, sailing away on his yacht to wherever he planned to enjoy his evening. He invited her to join him every time and every time she refused. Each refusal was met with a nonchalant shrug before he strolled off.

So much for him being available to her day and night, but she was in no position to complain, not when he'd complied with all her requests. Since that first day, he'd made sure to be back and ready to work by the time she'd finished breakfast. All their site visits had been done before the sun blazed hot enough to chargrill them.

Last night, for the first time, he'd arrived back before the sun rose. Helena hadn't been listening out for him or anything, but sleep had been slow to arrive since she'd been on the peninsula. She could only have been dozing when she heard footsteps, then his bedroom door close. Whose bed had he crept out of before returning?

Every time she'd closed her eyes after that she'd been plagued by images of Theo and a faceless woman entwined.

It shouldn't bother her whom he spent his time with or

what they did together. Theo was never going to live like a monk and it was unreasonable for her to expect him to curb his lust just because she was working for him. It was unreasonable for her to feel irritated by Theo being Theo.

And the definition of feeling irritated shouldn't need to be changed to mean the flares of burning, twisting violence in Helena's chest and stomach whenever the images taunted her. She'd spent three years seeing real-life images of Theo and his conveyor belt of women without feeling anything apart from the occasional flash of fury that ended the moment she'd scrunched the offending picture into a ball or shredded it into tiny pieces.

In the early hours of the morning, afraid to close her eyes, waiting for the sun to rise and announce the new day, she felt a violence in her stomach that had made her feel capable of ripping someone's head from their shoulders.

It was a violence of emotion that frightened her and that not even an extra-long shower had washed out of her.

To make her frazzled nerves worse, her cumulative lack of sleep had left her looking awful. It was one thing to look dreadful deliberately, but when it came naturally and involved puffy eyes, lank hair and dry skin as side-effects, her vanity cringed every time she caught her reflection. The icing on the cake had come in the form of Theo strolling into the dining room for breakfast with a spring in his step, looking as if he'd had a full eight hours of sleep. Again, he was dressed for the sun in shorts and polo shirt while Helena was dressed in her uniform of skirt and blouse. He hadn't shaved but still looked and smelled as fresh as the morning sun.

It wasn't fair. Theo had everything. He'd always had everything—a life of luxury, his choice of women, unlimited funds…

But he'd known tragedy. His mother's death from cancer, followed three months later by his father's fatal heart attack not long after he'd turned eighteen, had devastated him. He'd been as close to them as a son and his parents could be. Being an only child, he'd inherited the lot, become a multimillionaire while still in his teens. Using that inheritance, he'd quickly established himself as a party animal, then just as quickly established himself as a maverick businessman. Within five years he'd turned those millions into billions.

The sound of approaching footsteps brought Helena up short from her reverie and she blinked herself back into focus, pushed her glasses up her nose and poised herself over her paperwork.

Theo, huge mug of black coffee in his hand, stepped into Helena's office. It took a few moments for her to acknowledge his presence but one look at the colour on her face and the tucking of hair behind both ears proved how flustered his appearance made her.

'How are you getting on?' he asked, closing the door behind him.

Cheeks flaming, she somehow managed to find yet more hair to tuck. 'Fine. I have more things to discuss if you have five minutes.' Her words came out in a rush.

'Of course.' He propped himself on her desk beside her, making sure not to sit close enough for complaint but close enough to disturb her equilibrium a little. This was a balancing act he'd been playing all week to great success.

She reached forward for her notepad, her blouse loosening a touch around the top of her breasts. His vantage point gave him the briefest glimpse of creamy cleavage but it was as tantalising as if she'd left the blouse undone.

Speaking briskly, she said, 'The first thing I wanted to

discuss is the location of the outdoor swimming pool. My advice would be to change it.'

Theo forced his attention away from her breasts. Helena made some excellent points about privacy from passing boats and yachts that hadn't occurred to him and resulted in them settling on the pool's location elsewhere, followed by a brief discussion about the location of the summer house—also to be designed by Helena—that was to be built close by. Theo loved to host parties and his pool and summer house and all the space in between would be the perfect party location. The grounds surrounding the house would all flow from the swimming pool and he admired the fact that she'd picked up on that and understood what he wanted to create. Their late-night talks when they'd dreamed up their perfect house had only been about the interior. It took much effort not to mention sunbathing naked, just to have the pleasure of watching her squirm, but, after their first site visit, he'd decided to change tactics. If Helena wanted him to keep a cool, professional distance in working hours then that was what he'd give her.

Her initial perplexity when he failed to deliver any *double entendres*, even when a subject was crying out for it, or when he restrained himself from making any salacious comment whatsoever had amused him greatly. Every evening, without fail, he politely asked if she would like to sail away with him for some fun. He never spelt out what that fun would entail—Helena's imagination was perfectly capable of dreaming that up itself—which meant he got the pleasure of watching her cheeks flush and her eyes pulse as she fought her own longing to say yes.

Did she realise that every time she spoke to him, she tilted towards him? Did she realise that she fidgeted her way through every conversation? Was she aware that her breath hitched whenever he walked past her? Was she aware that at that very moment her hands trembled?

'The next thing I wanted to discuss is the kitchen,' she said, moving the conversation on.

'What about it?' he asked lightly.

She tugged at the sheets of paper he'd placed his backside on. 'You're sitting on my notes.'

'My apologies.' Sliding smoothly off the desk, he went and sat on the chair on the other side of her desk. 'Is this better?' But she didn't respond. Her eyes were on his, wide and stark, her fidgety body suddenly frozen. 'Helena?'

She blinked at the mention of her name and quickly looked down at her freed notes.

'Yes. The kitchen.' Despite Helena's best efforts, her voice sounded all wrong.

It had been hard enough to breathe with Theo propped on her desk beside her—when he'd first perched himself there she'd feared her heart would explode out of her chest—but when he'd moved off she'd had to fist her hands to stop them from grabbing hold of him. Now he was sitting opposite her and she'd caught a sudden glimpse of his golden chest beneath the collar of his polo shirt, and in the breath of a moment her insides had turned to mush.

It shouldn't be like this, she thought despairingly. She'd spent three months under Theo's intoxicating spell, riding the rollercoaster of her life. He'd had the ability to make her forget everything that mattered. Under his spell she'd believed all she needed was Theo in her life to be happy. She was sure her mother had once believed the same thing before she'd sold her soul to a monster. Theo wasn't a monster like Helena's father but his power over Helena had been just as strong.

How could she still react so strongly to him? She'd believed the sudden detonation of their relationship had killed her feelings for him but she saw now that she'd been hiding them, hiding them so deep inside that she'd forgotten how powerful they were until one look at him in the Staffords boardroom had seen them poke their heads out from dormancy. Now the old feelings were slapping her in the face, taunting her, and it was getting harder and harder to fight them.

Eyes now determinedly fixed on the papers on her desk, she rubbed the nape of her neck, cleared her throat and tried again. 'We need to discuss the kitchen's layout. Do you still want to consult a professional chef about it?'

She knew the moment she said it that she'd made a mistake.

Something sparked in his eyes. He leaned forwards a little, a satisfied smile spreading over his face. 'You *do* remember.'

'Only that neither of us can cook.' She quickly fixed her gaze back on her notes, aware her face was flaming with colour.

'But you asked—specifically—if I *still* wanted to consult a chef about the kitchen… What else do you remember?'

She tucked her hair behind her ear and wrote something nonsensical on her notepad. 'Have you a chef in mind to consult?'

'Answer my question.'

Her hand was shaking too much to write anything else.

'Helena.'

'What?' Helena intended for her one-syllable question to come out as a challenge. She might have succeeded if her voice hadn't cracked.

'Look at me,' he commanded.

Heart thrashing wildly, she breathed deeply before slowly raising her face. 'What?'

His voice dropped to a murmur. 'What do you remember?'

Trapped in his stare, she found herself unable to lie. 'Everything. Now can we move on?'

A weekend at his Agon home gave Theo the perfect backdrop to glory in the fact that he was not alone in remembering everything he and Helena had shared. It had bothered him more than he'd admitted to himself that he might be the only one who remembered every detail.

Leaving her to her own devices for her first weekend on the peninsula was as calculated a move as leaving her to her own devices every night had been. He knew his nightly absences would drive her crazy. Let her think he was respecting her request for professionalism by day, but let his absence unleash her imagination by night. Helena had an incredible imagination. She'd shown it in so many ways. Her increasingly inventive imaginings of lovemaking. The riddles set as poems she'd loved to write for him. Her ability to imagine he'd slept with every woman they'd come across…

He planned to torture her slowly, keep her guessing and slowly reel her back into his snare. And it was working! Every casual invitation to join him for an evening of fun was met with a refusal that sounded less emphatic than the last.

And now he had proof their time together *had* left its mark on her too.

For three years he'd kept distant tabs on her career. Part of him willed everything she touched to turn to gold, the other half hoped everything she touched turned to dust. During those years he'd never listened to a voicemail without first thinking it might be Helena, having come to her senses and begging him to take her back. He had his response ready for this eventuality: a deep chuckle followed by a firm, 'No,' and then him terminating the call.

In his heart he'd known his fantasies weren't worth the effort he put into making them. Helena wasn't sitting around pining for him and regretting her foolishness in throwing their future away. She was working hard and living her focused life. The hidden side of her that had bloomed for Theo had been packed away again, unwanted. She'd packed the love she'd once held for him away with it.

But she did remember!

The tight control she'd kept herself under was on the verge of unravelling. All it would take was a little tug and the veneer of control would be gone…and Helena would be his for the taking.

Helena knew the gentle knock on her office door belonged to one of the housekeepers rather than Theo. For a start, Theo never knocked, and if he did she was quite sure it would be with the force of a battering ram.

'Come in,' she called.

Elli poked her head around the door. 'Are you ready for lunch?'

She forced a rueful smile. 'Thanks, but I'm not hungry.' Not quite a lie. It wasn't that she wasn't hungry but that her stomach was so knotted she didn't think she'd be able to get any food into it.

Where was he?

'You are sure?'

'I had a massive breakfast.' That was true. She'd woken after a welcome good night's sleep with a real spring in her step. She had no idea why she'd woken in such a good mood but it felt as if the sun's rays had penetrated her heart. She'd been ravenous too and eaten everything Elli and Natassa had offered.

The sunrays beaming in her heart had slowly seeped away as the morning stretched out.

'Okay. Well, if you get hungry, just call.'

'Thank you.' Then, because she *had* to ask, 'Have you heard from Theo?'

'No, but I wouldn't expect to. He only tells me when he won't want an evening meal.'

Which had been every night since Helena's arrival.

When he'd sauntered off for his weekend sailing, or whatever he was doing, he'd thrown a casual, 'See you Monday morning,' over his shoulder. He was yet to return.

Alone again, Helena removed her glasses and rubbed her eyes. She supposed she should have called Elli over to look at the draft plans she'd created for the kitchen. After that excruciating moment where she'd admitted remembering everything, she'd looked away from him and broken the brief silence to ask, again, if he had a chef in mind to consult about the kitchen. She'd been afraid to look at him, the memory of them laughing in agreement that the odds of either of them using the kitchen to cook food being pretty much zero, surprisingly painful.

His reply had been to consult Elli and Natassa, which she had done over a shared lunch with them during the weekend.

His beautiful housekeepers, who both cooked as if they'd been sprinkled with angel dust, were staying. When the house was complete, they would move from the small purpose-built studio they shared at the back of the lodge into the lodge itself.

Helena hoped the acid burning her stomach at this hadn't reflected on her face, especially as the two Greek women were so excited about it. She'd learned over the weekend that they were both artists. Sharing the roles of live-in housekeeper and chef gave them a roof over their heads, an income and the time and space to produce their art. She supposed it was possible that Theo hadn't noticed their physical attributes when deciding to employ them. It was also possible that pigs really did fly.

Where was he?

Had he had an accident? He should be here.

She closed her eyes and took five long breaths, but it didn't quell the rolling in her stomach or the growing tightness in her chest. When she put her glasses back on she had to blink a number of times for her vision to clear. Her concentration remained shot.

A vision of his yacht capsizing flashed through her mind.

Removing her glasses again, she put a hand to her heavy heart and took another five breaths, assuring herself he was fine, of *course* he was fine. She mustered some dark humour to think that he'd better have had an accident or she would kill him for his lazy unprofessionalism…

Her office door opened and he strolled in, a grin on his gorgeous face. 'Good afternoon, *agapi mou*. How was your weekend?'

She shot up from her seat, suddenly light-headed. Without her glasses her vision was atrocious, but even so she could see the stubble on his unshaved face and the mussed hair. For once he was wearing an actual suit, an expensive, hand-tailored navy blue one with an open-necked white shirt, the tie removed.

As he neared her, she caught the scent of feminine perfume clinging to him, intermingling with his woody cologne.

'Helena?'

She stared at him, clenching her teeth, the relief that he

was alive and well already fading as the horrible perfume filled her airways, almost making her gag.

He tilted his head. 'Why are you looking like you want to stab me?'

She hadn't realised her temper was hanging by a thread until it snapped. 'Where the hell have you been?'

CHAPTER SEVEN

THEO OPENED HIS mouth but Helena was in no mood to let him answer. She was perilously close to retching. 'Don't bother. I can smell where you've been. You said you'd be back before breakfast. It's already lunch time! I've a million things to run by you, but while I've been sitting here twiddling my thumbs waiting for you to turn up, you've been off shagging.'

He raised a brow. 'Shagging?'

'You know—that thing you're an expert at. Quite frankly, I couldn't care less who you shared a bed with last night—from the look and smell of you, I'd be surprised if you even bothered with a bed—but I will not tolerate your hedonism impacting on *my* time. You stroll in four hours after the working day's begun without a care in the world and have the cheek to ask why I look like I want to stab you? I don't want to stab you, you selfish arse. I want to punch your selfish face.'

There was a glimmer in his eyes as he contemplated her before saying silkily, 'You sound jealous.'

His observation acted like a red rag to a bull. 'You *wish*. Either you find the decency to keep your hedonism outside of working hours or I'm going home.'

He moved closer to the side of her desk, his voice dropping to a murmur. 'You think?'

She glared at him with all the venom she could muster. 'Don't think my signing the contract means you get everything your way. There are employment laws, you know, whatever you might think.'

'If you want to take your chances with the law, then go ahead. I won't try to stop you. But if you want to prove that you're not the little girl who ran away any more and prove that you've matured into a woman, then that means dropping the prudish, indignant act.'

Outraged, Helena shoved her chair back and stormed over to him. 'You patronising, sexist—'

'Cut the outrage. It's boring.' But he didn't look bored. Quite the opposite.

'The only thing that's boring is your endless procession of women,' she spat. 'Don't you have any—?'

But whatever she was about to shout at him evaporated from her mind and died on her tongue when an arm suddenly wrapped around her waist and pulled her to him.

Legs weakening on impact, heart hammering in her throat, she gazed up at the face of the only man on this earth with the potential to make her laugh like a drain and cry like a baby. The only man on this earth who made her feel *anything*.

The back of a long, tapered finger brushed down her cheekbone, sending shivers dancing over and through her skin. The wide mouth curved at the corner, a spark of light in the ice-blue eyes. 'Hello, Helena,' he murmured. 'It's good to have you back.' And then the wide mouth covered hers.

The impact of his lips pressed against hers was immediate. Every cell in her body gave a collective sigh as long-forgotten sensations ignited and pulsed through her in an instantaneous rush. Resistance didn't cross her mind. Her lips parted and, hooking an arm around his neck, she raised herself onto her toes, closed her eyes and sank into the warmth of his coffee-scented mouth and hard body. Her breasts were crushed deliciously against his chest as he tightened the embrace, holding her so securely that she didn't need her legs, weakened further by the surge of molten heat between them that fired into being as the hard ridge in his trousers pressed against her abdomen, to keep her upright.

In the breath of a second the kiss turned into something wet and savage. Hands flattened and swept possessively over her back, sending sensation careering over her skin, her greedy fingers scraping over his nape and into the soft bristles of his hair.

Dragging her mouth from his, suddenly hungry to taste his skin, she grazed her lips and tongue across the stubbled jaw and down to the hard column of his neck…

And was immediately assailed by the cloying scent of another woman's perfume.

Sanity returned with the same rapidity with which it had been lost.

'No!' Frightened at how quickly and immediately she had fallen back into the Theo sickness that had once controlled her, she shoved his chest for good measure.

Backing away, she didn't dare look at him, but even in the periphery of her blurred vision she saw the rapid rise and fall of his chest. She could hear the raggedness of his breaths.

'I am not a cheap toy hired for you to play with.' She tried to spit the words out with venom but her voice cracked. Terrified she was going to cry, she turned to the perpetually filled coffee pot. She poured herself a mug but her hands were shaking so hard that much of it slopped over the rim and spilled onto the floor.

The feel of his gaze on her was almost as potent as his touch and she held onto the mug for dear life.

'On the contrary,' he drawled. 'Your services do not come cheap.' Before she could respond, in outrage or otherwise, he continued. 'I've brought the director of the construction firm I'll be employing to build the house over to meet you—she's waiting in the dining room. You might want to straighten your clothes before meeting her.' Then, striding to the door, he called over his shoulder, 'And, Helena, the next time you want to know the details of my sex-life, just ask.'

Theo suppressed the amusement bubbling inside him to see his green-eyed monster's reaction to the flamboyant director. Savina Mercouri was older than his mother would be if she were alive, had flowing, colourful fabrics draped around her rotund body and wore a perfume that could easily be mistaken for toilet cleaner. She was also the director of one of Greece's most respected construction companies, with a reputation for completing builds on time and within budget, and a knack for sourcing material from around the world with ease. She was also a tactile hugger.

If he'd known that all it would take to get Helena to lose her temper was to walk into her office with the scent of another woman's perfume clinging to his suit, he would have bought a bottle and drenched himself in it.

Finally, his beautiful goddess had cracked.

Helena's jealousy, he'd learned during their relationship, was something that had frightened her far more than it had bothered him. In truth, he'd *liked* it. It was different to the sulky pouting displayed by former lovers if he spoke to another woman for more than two minutes, the lover not realising this childish petulance was the kiss of death for a man who did not like to feel trapped. Theo liked his

freedom. He needed it. Helena was the only woman he'd
wanted to be trapped with. She was the only woman he'd
discovered his own jealous streak with. To witness her
bursts of possessiveness had fed his need for proof that
her love was as strong as his.

He'd seen the relief on her face when he'd walked into
the office. She'd been worried about him. Fear had turned
to anger, which in turn had become a diatribe that had
delighted him. *This* was the Helena he remembered. The
woman with passion in her soul. The woman who had discarded her inhibitions and embraced whatever emotions
were racing through her blood.

It wouldn't take much more to tempt her into his bed.
The passion with which she had kissed him back told him
louder than any subtle cue from her body language how
much she still wanted him. The chemistry that had once
driven them both to the brink of madness still lived in
her veins as much as in his. That he still evoked jealousy
in her too…

She *did* still feel something for him.

Gazing at her now, speaking hesitant, unpractised Greek
to Savina, he wondered idly how deep her feelings for him
still ran. His feelings for her had, of course, died when,
after he'd waited an hour for Helena's arrival at the cathedral, the cold truth had finally washed through his denial.
She wasn't coming. Helena had gone for good.

There he'd stood, in front of family—his and hers—
and friends and business contacts…everyone he knew including royalty, there to witness Theo pledging himself
to the love of his life. Instead, they'd borne witness to his
humiliation. Sure, he'd plastered a smile to his face when
he'd turned to the two-hundred-strong congregation in
Agon's cathedral and announced that the wedding was off.
He wasn't stupid enough to think it had fooled them any

more than his jovial invitation for them all to join him to celebrate his lucky escape at what should have been his wedding reception.

The Lucky Escape party had gone on until the sun had come up the next morning, but no matter how hard he'd partied or how much alcohol he'd tried to numb himself with, bitter humiliation had run deep. When his grandfather, in a moment of reflection a few days later, had kindly told him that his heart would one day mend, Theo had laughed loudly. His heart was just fine. Had he not survived the death of both his parents within three months of each other? Now, *that* had been pain. Excruciating, unbearable pain. The only blow Helena had inflicted on him had been to his ego. That it had felt as unbearable as his parents' deaths he was not prepared to admit…

Helena had killed his love for her. In hindsight, he should be grateful she had severed it so neatly, without the protracted falling out of love so many couples had to suffer.

But he had trusted her. He had thought he would grow old with her. She had sworn that she loved him, trusted him and wanted to grow old with him. It had been a harsh, humiliating lesson but he *had* learned from it. Trust no one. Love no one. Keep control of the heart and never be vulnerable to hurt again.

'Still working?' Theo asked later that evening when a search for Helena found her holed up at her desk.

'Still here?' she responded, not looking at him.

'You get me to yourself for the whole week.'

'Lucky me,' she muttered under her breath.

'No, *agapi mou*, lucky me. Time to stop what you're doing—dinner's ready.'

'I've told Natassa I'll eat in here.'

'It's eight o'clock.'

She raised a shoulder and tapped something on her keyboard with one hand while pushing her glasses up her nose with the other. 'I'm in the middle of something.'

'The middle of avoiding me?'

'Don't flatter yourself.'

'Then look at me.'

He saw her eyes close briefly behind the large frames before she fixed her gaze on him, her beautiful face unreadable…except for the clenching of her jaw. Helena was in no way as nonchalant as she pretended to be. Since their kiss earlier, she had avoided looking him in the eye. She had spoken to him only when she had to. The carefully put-together appearance that had had an air of dishevelment earlier had deteriorated.

It was time to go for the kill.

'Tomorrow morning, we are going to Agon.'

She tucked a lock of hair behind her ear. 'We? What for?'

'To meet the magician creating the sculptures for my garden. We'll sail after breakfast.'

'I don't need to meet the sculptor.'

'I disagree and, as I am paying for your time and effort, I'm not going to take no for an answer. Enjoy your meal at your desk—if you decide to leave your office to smell the fresh air and share a drink with me, you'll find me on the terrace.'

Her face pinched in on itself. 'I'll bear that in mind.'

'Do.' Then, unable to resist a parting shot he knew would get a wonderful rise out of her, he added, 'And if I'm not on the terrace then I will be in bed. You are more than welcome to join me there too.'

The rise he'd hoped for didn't materialise verbally but he noted the tremor of her shoulders and the shaking of her hand as she tucked another lock of hair behind her pretty ear and pretended to ignore him.

Whistling jauntily, he left her to her own lonely company.

Helena dried herself off from her shower and slipped her nightshirt over her head. The spring she'd woken up with that morning had rusted and broken. She was exhausted. Her eyes hurt as much as her brain from concentrating so hard on her work and from trying to forget the kiss.

She might have succeeded in pushing the kiss from her mind but her body had not allowed her to forget. The beats of her heart had become totally erratic. Her lips tingled. Her skin felt as if electrodes had been placed under the surface. And, now that she had no computer screen to distract her, she could not stop reliving every glorious, hateful second of it.

Why had she responded that way? she wondered with clawing desperation as she turned her bedroom's air-conditioning unit off and opened the window. Sitting herself on the windowsill, she inhaled sweet-scented fresh air into her lungs, praying it would help clear her mind.

It had always been like this, she thought miserably. Theo had been like a drug to her. One touch had always been enough to make her lose her mind. It destroyed her to know that nothing had changed. She was still a slave to his touch.

Distant laughter tinkled through the open window. She thought it sounded like Elli. Natassa took life very seriously but Elli had a lightness of spirit Helena envied. As a child she'd longed to be someone fun, a girl the other children would gravitate towards, but she'd found it impossible. She didn't know how to be fun or tell the jokes that made others laugh. Laughter was not something often found in the Armstrong home, not with a stern, elderly English father who ruled the household with an iron fist and a mother forbidden to work or have anything that resembled independence.

In recent years, Helena had asked her mother many times why she stayed in such a marriage. The answer was always a stoical, 'I made my vows.'

She tried to understand. Her mother had been nineteen and just finishing her first year at an English university when she'd been swept off her feet by one of the university's dashing professors thirty years her senior. Six months later they were married and her mother's university life was over as she was remodelled into the perfect wife. Her father entertained his colleagues and star students frequently and expected the house always to be immaculate and the food served to be perfect.

Helena remembered asking her mother once what she'd wanted to be as a child. Her mother had looked away before wistfully saying the life she had was the life she'd always wanted.

Her mother, she'd been certain, had been lying, not to Helena but to herself, a certainty that had crystallised through the years as she'd realised that the way her father ran their household was not normal and hadn't been normal for at least a hundred years. On the rare occasions they'd travelled to Agon without him, her mother became a different woman, the woman Helena was sure her father had first fallen in love with. Why marry someone with such vivacity only to snuff all the life out of them?

The day before she'd been due to marry Theo, they'd had lunch with her parents. Helena had watched her mother sit silently while her father and Theo demolished a bottle of wine. The two men's raucous laughter about a woman's role in marriage alongside her mother's downcast face had been the spurs for the fateful conversation that had broken them. Helena had been halfway into falling into the same trap. She'd let Theo make all the decisions and have his own way on everything, including his insistence that they marry as soon as possible. She'd been a little lamb following its master.

If she'd married Theo, everything she was and everything she could be would have been subsumed by him, just as her mother had allowed the essence of herself to be subsumed by her father... If she'd married Theo *then*.

But back then was not now. The past didn't live in the present. The Helena of then was not the Helena of now.

Another rumble of laughter filtered through the window, closely followed by more tinkling laughter from two feminine sources.

Theo was on the terrace enjoying his evening with Elli and Natassa. She imagined them drinking cold white wine and eating delicious homemade nibbles, Theo holding court as he always did with his irreverent, often indiscreet, humour. A sudden yearning to be out there with them on this clear, balmy evening rippled through her. It had been a long time since she'd loosened up enough to simply enjoy an evening of good company. Three years. Not since Theo.

For all his faults, no one made her laugh the way he did. An evening with him flew by. A night with him...

She closed her eyes.

Lying in Theo's arms night after night was the closest to heaven she had ever been.

What would it feel like to lie in his arms after making love properly...?

When more laughter, much louder this time, filtered

into her room, Helena closed her window and climbed into bed.

Staring at the ceiling, she put a hand to her racing heart and thought again of the inbuilt inhibitions that had made her such a loner until Theo had torn them down.

CHAPTER EIGHT

'THE SCULPTOR LIVES HERE?' Helena's nose wrinkled with incredulity as she soaked in the sprawling beachside villa with its own private jetty at which the captain had moored the yacht. He must be one rich sculptor.

'No, *agapi mou.* I live here.'

She faced him. 'Since when?'

He grinned. 'Since I bought it.'

A male member of Theo's household staff appeared from one of the villa's many rear doors. Theo did like his comforts. Thinking about it, it wasn't surprising that he'd chosen to spend his evenings and nights in the luxury to which he was accustomed. The lodge he'd had built for her was huge compared to her flat, but compared to this...

It was like comparing a Chihuahua with a Great Dane on steroids.

The gangway lowered. Theo stepped on it and beckoned for her to follow.

Holding her laptop bag securely to her stomach, Helena stepped onto the jetty and did as she was bid. The mid-morning sun already blazed down and she rued, again, her lack of foresight in packing only professional outfits. It didn't matter when she was in the air-conditioned lodge or on Theo's air-conditioned yacht, but the moment she stepped outside perspiration broke out on her skin and her brain felt roasted. She hadn't even had the nous to tie her hair back.

'My chef's prepared refreshments for us,' Theo said casually as they left the soft golden sand of the beach and climbed the steps of the extensive grounds.

'When did you buy this?' she asked again.

'Two and a half years ago.'

'And your parents' home?' When she'd been with Theo, his main residence had been the magnificent townhouse he'd inherited from his parents. It made no sense that he'd bought another property in Agon less than twenty miles from the original one but Theo had always had more money than sense. He collected properties the way other people collected ornaments.

It was still strange though. For all his vast portfolio, Agon was his home. One of the reasons he'd wanted to build on Sidiro's peninsula had been its close proximity to it.

There was the slightest tightening of his jawline before he answered. 'I sold it.'

'Why?' Not only did it hold all his childhood memories within its walls, but it had also been the perfect location for a man who loved nothing more than to party.

'It was time for a change.' Then his mood visibly lifted as he bestowed on her a beaming smile. 'Come, I'll show you around.'

'Have we got time?' Her curiosity to see the villa was, she assured herself stubbornly, for professional reasons and nothing to do with wanting to see how Theo lived.

'There is always time,' he answered enigmatically.

She would not fall into the trap of asking 'Time for what?'

Her attention was caught again by the man she'd seen emerge from the villa and who now stood at the top of the steps waiting for them. The nearer they got, the sharper into focus he became. It was Dion, the middle-aged butler Theo had inherited from his parents along with their house.

'Miss Armstrong,' he said in slow Greek, a twinkle in his eye. 'It is a pleasure to see you again.'

Touched that he remembered her and that he remembered her Greek was a beat slower than someone raised here, she smiled and resisted the urge to throw her arms around him. Dion had broken protocol and given her a shoulder to cry on when he'd found her packing her bags and sobbing the day she'd known her relationship with Theo was over. He'd quietly and discreetly taken care of her, and she had never forgotten his kindness.

'It's lovely to see you again too, Dion. How have you been?'

'Very well, thank you. You look like you need to escape from the heat.'

'That obvious, is it?' she said with a grin as she walked through the door he opened for her.

He smiled back. 'I got the chef to make a jug of the pink lemonade you always liked. That should help cool you down.'

'The air conditioning in here has done it already.' She rubbed her suddenly cold arms as she took in the reception room they walked through. 'Did someone set it to freezing?'

'When you're settled in I will work on the controls for your room so it's not as cold for you,' he promised.

'My room?'

Theo, who'd held back while the unanticipated reunion took place, stepped in. 'Please have our refreshments taken to the sun room. We will be there shortly.'

Dion bowed his head and bustled off, leaving Theo with Helena, who was gazing at him with justifiable suspicion.

'*My* room?' she repeated.

'We are meeting with the sculptor in the morning,' he confessed without an ounce of guilt. 'Today is a day for leisure.'

'Absolutely not…'

'You have worked for me for over a week. You are yet to take any time off—you need a break. Seeing as you won't take one, I'm going to force it.'

'You can't do that.'

He took a step closer to her. 'I just have.'

She folded her arms across her ample chest. 'I'll get the captain to take me back to Sidiro.'

'Sorry, *agapi mou*,' he said with a sad shake of his head, 'but he only takes orders from me. If you find another means of returning to Sidiro, then I'm afraid I will be forced to reject your first set of plans for the house, even if they're perfect. And the second,' he added for good measure.

'You'd be that petty?'

'For sure.' Another step closer. 'And if I find you working on your laptop, I will cut the internet off.'

The glare she threw him was undermined by the flare of amusement ringing in her eyes that her humungous spectacles couldn't disguise. Theo tilted his head to soak in her luminescent beauty from a different angle.

Something new flared in those eyes, a something that had him leaning even closer. He inhaled the clean fruitiness of her shampoo and murmured, 'You are going to take the day off whether you like it or not. We will have our refreshments and then I'm taking you shopping.'

'But…'

He put a finger to her perfect lips. 'Arguing with me is now officially banned. What I say goes.'

Her breathing deepened. She grabbed the finger and held it tightly. 'That's not fair.'

'You can be in charge next time.'

'There won't be a next time.'

'And that is exactly why you need this break. You're too uptight. You need to relax and enjoy the sunshine. And if you argue with me one more time, I'll keep you here until the weekend.'

She stared at him a beat too long then seemed to realise she still had hold of his finger and hastily dropped it. 'You're impossible.'

'Thank you. Now, let us enjoy our refreshments and then we can work on loosening you up a little.' With another wink, he sauntered off to the sun room, leaving Helena no choice but to hurry after him.

Helena had no idea how Theo managed to talk her into entering the exclusive boutique hidden up a narrow back-street in Agon's capital, Resina, when there was no way she could afford any of the garments. Actually, she *did* know—by using the force of his personality and the good humour that always lurked behind it. And she, as she'd done all those years ago, had succumbed.

Well, not succumbed exactly. More that she'd realised arguing would get her nowhere. The next ferry to Sidiro wasn't until Friday, so unless she wanted to charter a boat to sail back, she was stuck with Theo in Agon for the next twenty-four hours. She had no doubt his threat to extend their time here until the weekend was something he would happily stick to. It was a threat the old, hedonistic Helena, the Helena Theo had recognised just before he kissed her, kept whispering that she needed to test.

As the day had gone on, she'd felt the Helena that had once emerged like a butterfly for Theo growing in strength. She'd locked it back in its cage three years ago but it had fluttered its wings with joy when she'd come face to face with Theo in the Staffords boardroom and refused to calm down since.

Theo was just too...*everything*. He made her feel everything. He had an innate energy, a zest for life that was as infectious as it was irresistible. He didn't just get under her skin, it was more that her skin rose to welcome him into its confines. Every breath she took, every step she walked, every word she uttered, it was all done with a heart that felt as if it had grown too large for her chest.

Why was she fighting it? He wanted her, she wanted him. They were both adults. She'd already proven to herself that she wasn't the same little lamb for him any more. If she felt the need to take the lead in something, she went ahead and did it without a second thought.

He'd turned his nose up at the first shop they'd gone into—an international brand that sold fashionable, affordable clothing—but he'd followed her inside and been happy to wait while she tried on dozens of outfits, half of which she'd had no intention of buying but used as a form of revenge against a man who got itchy feet if he had to stand still for longer than a second. When she'd held up a summer dress she'd instinctively known he would hate, he'd pulled a face of such deliberate horror that she'd burst into laughter and added it to her to-buy pile.

She'd been too quick for him at the counter and had handed her debit card to the cashier before he'd realised she'd paid for her own stuff.

She had to admit, it felt wonderful to be spending money on herself again. She'd paid a chunk of her debt off with Theo's signing-on payment and for the first time in three years had a little cash to spare. It had been a long time since she'd bought anything but work outfits. Now that she knew what debt felt like, she would never allow herself to be in that position again.

She had to admit, too, that it felt wonderful to change out of her stuffy work clothes into a pair of loose, breathable cream tapered trousers, a pretty cami-top with embroidered pink and purple flowers and a pair of flat sandals. A quick visit to a chemist for some sunscreen and a hair band…and now, with her hair tied in a knot at the back of her head, she felt wonderfully cool.

Having disappeared when they entered the store to chat with the boutique's manageress—an old friend, by the looks of it—Theo suddenly appeared at her side and grabbed hold of her hand. 'Come look at this dress.'

He stopped in front of a mannequin wearing a retro fifties-style dress. 'What do you think? Is it not perfect for you?'

The dress consisted of a strapless black bodice that met a flaring white skirt with black leaf prints at the waist that fell to below the knee. It was elegant and pretty and exactly the kind of dress she would buy if she could afford it. The chances of her being able to afford it were nil. This was a boutique without price tags.

Suddenly she realised Theo was still holding her hand. Not just holding it—at some point their fingers had become entwined.

They were holding hands as they'd used to do. And it felt every bit as necessary and right as it had all those years ago.

Clearing her throat, Helena tugged her hand free and gently ran her trembling fingers over the silk skirt of the dress. Her heart sighed with pleasure. 'It's beautiful.'

'I *knew* you'd like it,' he said smugly.

'It's beautiful, but I'm not buying it,' she said firmly. 'I've spent enough money for one day and now I need coffee.' She needed to get out into the air and clear her lungs of the woody scent filling her senses before she threw herself into Theo's arms, buried her face in his neck and inhaled his scent right from the source.

To her relief, Theo didn't argue. 'There's a coffee shop around the corner that sells amazing baklava.'

Their eyes locked. Her swollen heart pulsed painfully against her ribs.

Baklava was her absolute favourite sweet food. He remembered...

He remembered the style of clothes she liked to wear. He remembered the food she liked. He remembered everything. Just as she did.

Helena hurried out of the boutique.

The shade of the narrow street saved her from the worst of the afternoon heat. Waiting for Theo to catch her up, she pressed her hand to her aching chest and took some long breaths.

It would be too easy to trick her mind that what they were sharing that lazy day was a repeat of a scene that had once filled her with so much joy she'd struggled to breathe.

She'd experienced more happiness in her three months with Theo than she had the rest of her life combined.

She smelt his cologne before she felt the nudge on her arm and was immediately thrown back to the passionate insanity of the kiss they had shared and the preceding fear that had coiled inside her at his lateness, which had twisted into a jealous rage when she'd smelt Savina's perfume on him.

This was what he did. He set the impulsive, hedonistic side of her free and all the heady, terrifying emotions that came with it until her entire being, every thought, every breath, and every emotion had been consumed by Theo and she'd lost all sight of herself.

But just because she'd been a slave for him before did not mean she had to be a slave to him now, did it? She was older and wiser.

She *liked* Theo, she realised. Liked him as a person. Were it not for their history she would be thrilled to spend time in his company. She'd enjoyed shopping with him; enjoyed winding him up, enjoyed putting him in his place when needed, enjoyed his irreverence, even enjoyed the battle of wills.

She had the tools to stand up to him now. She had the tools to separate her emotions from the hedonism that he wanted to unleash in her.

Theo had been honest from the start. He saw her as unfinished business. He wanted to bed her, not marry her.

And she wanted…oh, *how* she wanted…to make love to him too. Just once. Just to see if it was everything she had dreamed it would be. One night spent as if tomorrow didn't exist.

Where was the harm?

Maybe if she let him take her to bed she could put behind her the ghost of her past and move on with her life in more than a professional capacity. Maybe then she'd be able to go on a date and not cringe merely at the thought of kissing someone else.

For the first time since Theo had exploded back into her life, Helena looked at him and openly stared at the gorgeous, devilish face.

His eyes narrowed slightly under her scrutiny.

She smiled lazily. 'Shall we get that coffee now?'

Theo watched Helena bite into her baklava slice and suppressed a groan.

Theos, he loved to watch her eat. Helena loathed cooking but she was an enthusiastic eater. He'd never known her turn her nose up at anything; the perfect dinner guest.

The perfect woman…

He blinked sharply at the stray thought and took a drink of his melon mojito. He'd ordered a jug of it with their coffees and been mildly surprised to find Helena drinking the glass he'd poured for her with enthusiasm. She'd read the surprise on his face and smiled. 'If I'm going to have a day off work, I might as well make the most of it.'

Had he misinterpreted the suggestiveness behind that smile? Was it mere wishful thinking that detected a marked change in Helena's attitude towards him?

A passing waiter asked how the baklava was. A small crease appeared on Helena's brow before comprehension shone in her eyes and she stuck her thumb up in the affirmative.

'Why has your Greek become so rusty?' Theo asked. Although not as fluent as a native speaker, Helena had never needed to think before translating in her head.

She shrugged and popped the final piece of baklava into her mouth. Lucky baklava.

He waited patiently for her to swallow it.

'Well?' he queried.

She shrugged again and, eyes holding his, sucked on the cocktail straw.

There was no mistaking the suggestiveness behind that action.

'I haven't spoken it in years,' she said, placing her glass back on the table.

He dragged his thoughts away from her provocative gesture to the conversation in hand. 'But I thought that's all you spoke with your mother?'

She raised an eyebrow. 'And I thought you'd seen my mother.'

'I did.'

'She didn't tell you?'

'Tell me what?'

'That I'm estranged from them…well, estranged from my father.'

'She never mentioned it.' But then, he hadn't hung around for conversation. He'd gone to Helena's childhood home with the express purpose of getting her current address. As soon as he had it he'd left.

She pulled a rueful face. 'It's painful for her. We have to meet in secret.'

'Why?'

'Because my father would be furious if he knew.'

'So what? You're her daughter. She shouldn't have to see you in secret.'

'She's the one who has to live with the consequences.'

His eyes narrowed. 'What kind of consequences?'

She stared at him for what felt like a long time. 'When he found out she'd spoken to me on the phone he stopped her pocket money.'

He laughed uncertainly. 'Children get pocket money.'

'My father treats her like a child.' She pressed the pad of her forefinger to the crumbs on her plate and popped it in her mouth.

Theo found himself suppressing another groan.

She pushed her plate to one side. When she next spoke, her voice contained a hardness he'd never heard from her lips before. 'I've told you many times that he's a misogynistic dinosaur. He controls and pays for everything. He gives her a small monthly cash payment to spend on personal necessities. She has to provide receipts to account for every penny spent. Everything's in his name, including her phone. All her calls are itemised and he scrutinises them, which is how he found out she'd gone against his word and spoken to me. He stopped her pocket money for a month. That might not sound like a long time to you but try and imagine it—she couldn't even buy herself shampoo when her bottle ran out.'

Theo stared hard at her, looking for a sign that she was exaggerating. Helena was a terrible liar. She'd lied to him twice, the first time when he'd asked if she liked the shirt he'd chosen to wear on a night out and she'd cut eye contact and nodded vigorously while tucking her hair maniacally behind her ears. The second time had been later that same night when they'd been on their way back to his Agon home after partying in a nightclub and he'd asked what she thought of his friends. She'd turned her head away to look out of the window while replying, 'They're great,' in such an unnatural voice that he'd immediately known she was lying. He'd made her promise after that never to spare his feelings, a promise he came to rue when she'd taken him at his word in their last, fateful argument.

Her gaze didn't drop. She spoke the truth.

'What caused the estrangement?' He'd never given much thought to her dismissive description of her father as a dinosaur and her childhood as old-fashioned. He'd been too busy plotting their future to think much about her past.

He should have given it more thought. He should have asked more questions.

She took another sip of her cocktail, loosened her shoulders and sank back into her seat. For all the weight of the subject matter, the Helena sharing a table with him was the most relaxed he'd seen her since he'd brought her back to the peninsula. 'My father was furious that I changed my mind about marrying you. If he could have dragged me down the aisle by my hair he would have.'

'He hardly knew me.'

'But he knew your wealth and status,' she pointed out.

'He'd boasted to all his eminent friends and colleagues about his daughter marrying one of Europe's wealthiest men. My actions humiliated him. My refusal to change my mind…' She shook her head. 'I've never seen him so angry. He kicked me out. He said if I was going to throw away a life of riches then I didn't deserve his money, so he cut off his financial support too.'

Sharp needles dug into Theo's skin. Pieces of a puzzle he hadn't realised he'd been trying to solve were falling into place. Helena's debt. Her screamed words that he was *just like her father*…

Her eyes remained steady on his. 'Anyway, that's why my Greek's gone a little rusty—I haven't needed to speak it in three years.'

Theo shook his head in an effort to clear the buzzing in his ears. 'Forgive me, *agapi mou*, but I fail to see the link. I thought you said you still saw your mother secretly?'

'We only spoke Greek together because my father insisted on it. I've not been allowed to speak English under their roof since my seventh birthday. He banned me from speaking English in his presence. My mother had to translate.'

'I thought you were raised as bilingual?'

'Not until I turned seven. Up to then I could name the days of the week and count to fifteen in Greek but my father decided that wasn't good enough.'

'You were banned from speaking *any* English?' he clarified, the buzzing in his ears louder than ever.

'At home, yes.'

'But that must have been impossible for you.' To suddenly have it enforced that she could only speak a language she barely understood must have been torturous.

'I wanted to please him,' she admitted with a sudden wistfulness that pierced him. 'My father had never taken much interest in me up to that point. He's from the school of thought that children should be seen and not heard.'

'And that wives should do as they're told?' he asked, already knowing the answer.

'Yes. My mother's been indoctrinated into believing his word is law.' And then she gave a smile of such beatification her whole face lit up. 'When we get together it's an illicit thrill to speak only English.'

'How do you meet without your father finding out?'

'I bought her a pay-as-you-go phone to call me on. She hides it in the kitchen cleaning cupboard.' At Theo's puzzled expression, Helena added, 'It's the one place in the whole house he actively avoids.'

She waited for him to laugh, to make an action or say a word to lighten the darkness that had permeated the atmosphere between them.

He rubbed his hair. 'Why does she stay with him?'

'She seems to think that because he's not physically abusive she has nothing to complain about. I think—and this is just an educated guess—that she's scared. She's been with him since she was nineteen. She has no money of her own and doesn't believe she has the tools to support herself.' She sighed. 'I just wish she'd stand up to him. Find some courage. She could live with me. We'd cope. But every time I suggest it she refuses and tells me I'm making too much of it. She *made her vows.*'

She could see how disturbed Theo was at her description of her parents' marriage. He couldn't know that she'd only realised how wrong and abusive it was when she'd been on the verge of marrying him, and the fear that she could end up like her mother had almost paralysed her.

She'd been as guilty as her mother at burying her head in the sand. Until she'd spent those blissful three months with Theo, the longest she'd been away from home had been a week. Until she'd spent those blissful three months with Theo, she'd continued to obey her father. At the age of twenty-three she'd still asked to be excused from the dinner table. She'd still lived under a curfew.

With a sharp pang, Helena realised that had she not met him she would never have had the courage to face her father down at his fury over her failed nuptials. That was one good thing Theo had done for her. He'd made her brave.

She'd been so frightened of becoming like her mother that she hadn't appreciated all the good ways his influence had rubbed off on her.

Theo had freed her in more ways than he could know.

As all these thoughts rushed through her head, Theo's throat moved and his chest rose sharply before he broke the charged air between them to look at his watch. 'We need to go soon.'

Checking her own watch, she was amazed to see they'd been in the café for over an hour. 'I thought we were having a lazy day?' And it was a lazy day she didn't want to end…

The familiar knowing twinkle returned to his eyes. 'I never said we were having a lazy evening.'

Her heart skipped but she feigned nonchalance. 'Oh?'

He folded his arms across his chest and tilted his head. 'We are going out tonight.'

Folding her own arms in mimicry and leaning forward, closer to him, thrills of excitement zinging through her body, she raised a brow. 'Are we?'

A smile tugged at his lips. 'We are.'

'Where?'

'That, *agapi mou*, is a surprise.'

CHAPTER NINE

HELENA DID A full slow-motion pirouette, wonder filling her heart. Theo had given her a room a princess would be thrilled to call her own. She could hardly take it all in: the raised four-poster bed with the muslin curtains, the crystal chandelier that hung from the frescoed ceiling, the thick carpet her toes sank into...

'You like?' The velvet undertone of Theo's deep, gravelly voice coiled into her overloaded senses. She closed her eyes and let it fill her.

'I get why you moved.' Not only was her bedroom fit for a princess but it also had the most wonderful view of the sea.

'Do you?'

'You need the elements.'

His brow creased.

Tucking hair behind her ear, she tried to explain what she meant, but it was hard speaking coherently. There had been a palpable charge between them on the drive back to his villa. For once, conversation had been stilted, not just from her but from Theo too. Every second of every mile had been spent with awareness thrumming through her skin. 'You're a free spirit, Theo. Living in a city is too restrictive for you. You need to be able to throw yourself into the sea or climb a mountain when the urge takes you. Here, and on Sidiro too, you can do that.'

Theo's heart caught in his throat at this unexpected observation. And at the softness of her tone.

Sometimes he forgot that Helena had once known him as well as he'd known her. He'd opened himself to her as he'd never opened himself to anyone. And then she'd left him.

Had she really left because she'd feared a marriage like her parents'? It had sounded ludicrous when she'd shouted it at him three years ago, and he'd told her so. He hadn't believed she was serious. And now he had to contend with the knowledge that she thought him the same as a man who was, by any sane person's definition, an emotional abuser.

He'd known Helena's childhood had been different from his, but in the euphoria of falling in love he'd never appreciated just *how* different it had been. He'd been lucky with his parents. His childhood had been idyllic. He'd been given the best of everything, indulged in every way, and smothered with so much love that he'd assumed all the wonderful things in life were his due.

The death of his mother and father, especially coming so closely together, had taught him pain. Helena leaving him had taught him that non-parental love could be broken as quickly as it had formed. Both had served to strengthen him and harden him.

He didn't want to feel himself softening towards her.

He'd bought this villa when he could no longer bear to walk the rooms and hallways of the townhouse Helena had once walked and where he could still hear the echo of her laughter. That laughter had echoed louder than the childhood memories stored in its walls.

When she left this home, her ghost would not haunt it. He would have exorcised it.

The time for exorcism was getting closer and closer. He

could feel it. He could taste it. Anticipation laced the air and it tasted sweeter than the purest honey.

She tucked her hair behind her ear and cleared her throat. 'So…where are we going tonight?'

'To the palace for a champagne reception, followed by a concert at the royal amphitheatre.'

Her eyes widened. 'You're joking.'

This was a reaction he liked. Helena had a fascination with the palace. It was the place they had met. She'd been wide-eyed with wonder when Theo had shown her their hand-delivered invitation to attend King Helios's wedding. But, of course, she'd left before the wedding had occurred.

He stepped closer to her. 'It is all arranged. A stylist will be here in an hour to assist you.'

Her mouth opened and closed. 'But I have nothing…'

'To wear?' he supplied. He took another step towards her and lowered his head to whisper in her ear. 'Look in your dressing room, *agapi mou*.'

If he wasn't so attuned to her he'd have missed the tiny tremor that ran through her as his words brushed against her skin. It barely distracted from the tremor that ran through his own body as his senses soaked in her fragrance.

Moving like a sleepwalker, Helena went to the dressing room and stared in at a space that was larger than the bedroom in her flat. It was like looking into a hall of mirrors.

And then she saw it, at the far end, hanging beside a beautiful, feminine, antique dressing table.

The dress from the boutique.

'How…?' But that was all she could croak. Theo was standing right behind her. Not a part of him touched her but she felt him as acutely as if he'd wound his arms about her…

The air around her shifted. Warm breath threaded through her hair, seeping through the roots. The hair on the nape of her neck lifted.

She couldn't move. She didn't *want* to move. She didn't want to fight the feelings thrumming through her a moment longer.

A hard body pressed against her. A muscular arm hooked around her waist. Theo's breath grew hotter against her scalp. Flames flickered to feel his arousal press into the small of her back. Every nerve and every cell in her body throbbed a dance.

There was no resistance when he slowly twisted her round. Only more thrills.

Trying to breathe, she looked up into eyes that had turned a deeper shade of blue. It was a shade she recognised and, as she saw it, the flames inside her grew. The burn they gave was agony. Delicious, terrifying, exhilarating agony.

Breathing deeply, his nostrils flaring, he put his hands to her face and removed her glasses.

The world became a blur, yet somehow Theo remained solid.

As desperately as she had tried to forget him, he'd always remained solid in her mind. In her dreams.

This was her last chance to back away and put a stop to this madness…

But there was no turning back. Not for her. Theo was a devil built of fire and passion. Broken dreams lay smashed between them, but this was one dream she didn't need or want to deny.

She placed a hand to his chest. The strong thud of his heart pounded against her palm. Helena filled her lungs with the woody scent that had always delighted her senses so much.

Placing her other hand against his strong neck, she closed her eyes and stepped into Theo's fire.

Later, she would forget whose lips claimed whose first. She would forget everything but the shock of heat that crashed through her to find their lips locked together, because at that first kiss she dissolved.

Her senses went into full-blown overload. Her mouth filled with Theo's dark taste, her airways filled with his scent, her ears soaked in every swipe of their ravenous tongues and every crackle of fabric from their groping hands as they tore at each other's clothes.

Buttons popped, buckles snapped, zips purred…every sound filled her as much as the furnace of heat firing through her veins and bones.

His mouth broke from her lips, swept over her cheeks and down to her neck, sending sensation dancing over her skin. He tugged her trousers and underwear down, then lowered himself to his knees. Catching the hem of her cami-top, he raised it over her breasts and slid a hand round her back to unclasp her bra. Helena took care of the rest, throwing the top over her head and impatiently shrugging the bra off, then almost lost control of her limbs when he greedily covered one of her breasts with his mouth. She gasped his name and cradled his head tightly, savouring every lick and every suck of attention to her sensitised flesh.

When he abandoned her aching breasts and moved lower to kiss her belly, memories flooded her of all the times he'd pleasured her with his mouth. He'd brought her to orgasm so many times…but never in the way she'd craved. She'd wanted Theo inside her. She'd wanted it more than she'd ever wanted anything.

Digging her fingers into his cheeks, she stopped him

just as his mouth reached the top of her pubis, and sank to her knees.

Questions rang from his pulsating eyes. She answered by covering his mouth and kissing him hard, fusing their torsos together again so her naked breasts were crushed against his chest…

He still had his top on.

This time, Helena broke the kiss and pulled at his polo shirt. She wanted to see him naked. She wanted to feel the hardness of his body beneath her fingertips and mouth. He raised his arms, enabling her to pull the shirt off.

The wildness that had become such an intrinsic part of her when they'd been in love scratched beneath her skin for release. Too far gone for caution, she set it free.

In a tumble of arms, they fell onto the thick, soft carpet, mouths fused, both of them tugging at his shorts. Legs kicked, feet scraped and soon Theo was as naked as she. How she'd loved to inhale the scent of his wonderful hard, muscular chest and run her fingers through the smattering of dark hair that surrounded his navel. It felt as if she'd waited a lifetime to touch and smell him again, waited a lifetime for this moment.

There was a fever in Theo's blood he'd never known before. This was beyond sanity. All those nights he'd held off from making love to Helena, all those nights after regretting his chivalry…and still something inside him, a ghost of the Theo who had worshipped the ground this woman walked on, urged him to hold back.

Hold back for what? This was everything he wanted, right here, right now in Helena's arms, melting into her soft curves, the weight of her generous breasts pressed against him.

This was the moment dreams were made of and he was not going to be so foolish as to let it go, not when the hunger in Helena's eyes, her kisses, her touch matched the hunger thrumming through him.

In one sudden movement, he rolled her onto her back and gazed down at her beautiful face as he positioned himself between her legs.

She stared back at him, her eyes as molten as the blood in his veins.

The breaths coming from her kiss-bruised lips were ragged. Desire coloured her high cheekbones.

There was nothing—*nothing*—to stop him giving her what she wanted…and what he wanted.

Still gazing into her eyes, he placed his hands on her thighs and parted them, allowing his arousal access right where it needed to be.

Theos, she was trembling. *He* was trembling.

Bowing his head to ravage her mouth, he closed his eyes and drove himself as deep as he could go inside her. *Theos*, she was tighter than he'd envisaged…

But, as a pleasure he'd never known before suffused him, a part of his brain woke up, needling him that something was wrong. It took a beat to understand what that something was.

It was the suck of air Helena had taken when he'd driven into her. The slight resistance…

Surely not?

But then she shifted beneath him, her lips found his, her warm hands cradled his head and she was urging him with her body to finish what he'd started and all his thoughts flew away as he succumbed to the pleasure of making love to this ravishing woman.

Helena felt as if she was dancing in Theo's flames. The flames licked through her, stoking the furnace of pleasure, reducing to ashes the small sting of pain she'd felt when he'd first entered her.

The chemistry between them had always been so strong that she'd known making love would be wonderful but she'd never known it would be like this, that he would fill her so completely or that the strokes he made as he thrust deeply inside her would bring to life so many new sensations. Pulses of sunshine careered through her, a pleasure she felt from the tips of her fingers to the pads of her toes.

Finally, she understood why making love to Theo had been so important to her. She'd been a virgin but she'd known instinctively that this would be the ultimate act of closeness between them, a fusion of two bodies, a fusion between herself and the man she loved...

She didn't want it to end but the pleasure was just too new and intense to hold back. She was climbing a roller coaster and the exhilarating plunge was in sight. Raising her thighs higher to allow him even deeper penetration, she hooked her ankles around Theo's pounding, tight buttocks, gasping his name over and over until the roller coaster ran out of track and suddenly she wasn't plunging but soaring, flying like a bird over the clouds. She grasped at Theo's sweat-slicked skin and damp hair, his velvet groans soaking her ears and increasing the pleasure until she reached the rainbow and burst through it right at the moment he made one final thrust and, with a long, strangled noise, collapsed on top of her.

The loud beats of his heart thudded in his ears and tremors racked his body. Theo tried desperately to reach for something concrete, anything that would pull him back to a reality that felt as distant as his childhood. But, even as the strength of his orgasm abated, his senses remained filled with Helena. That was her neck his face was buried in, her sweet, soft skin beneath his mouth, the blood of her life a pulse beating against his cheek. That was her heart thudding so heavily against the beat of his own battered heart. Those were her fingers making soft swirls over his back, her mouth pressed against the top of his head. And that was her slick warmth he was buried so deep inside. He wanted to stay right there and savour this most incredible moment for ever.

Never in his life had he felt such closeness to another person. Never had he been unsure where he ended and another began.

Theos, he had known it would be good between them, but this…

His eyes snapped open as he remembered the sensations and the notion that had entered his head as he had first entered her.

It took more effort than he would have believed to raise himself onto an elbow so he could stare into her dark eyes. There was a dazed quality to them he knew must be mimicked in his own.

He cleared his throat, but before he could speak his phone rang, the ring tone telling him it was Dion.

Swearing under his breath, Theo rolled off her and groped for his shorts. He answered it just before it went to voicemail.

'Nai?' he said shortly. *Theos*, he was having difficulty catching his breath.

He forced his drumming ears to listen closely then disconnected the call.

Running his hands through his hair, he took another deep breath and got to his feet.

'The stylist is here,' he said, not looking at Helena, who sat up and backed herself against the wall as he stepped into his shorts. 'Do you want to shower?'

'What?' she croaked.

'Do you want to take a shower before I send the stylist to you?'

She blinked a number of times. Her glasses were on the floor where he'd unthinkingly discarded them. Theo picked them up and handed them to her.

'Thank you,' she whispered. She made no effort to put them on.

'And the shower?'

She nodded in answer.

'I will have her sent up in twenty minutes. Let Dion or any other member of staff know if you need anything.'

Dazed eyes still held his. He'd never believed Helena could look more beautiful, but with the stain of their lovemaking still high on her cheeks, her lips bruised like an overripe strawberry and her hair mussed, his heart bloomed as if he were gazing at a masterpiece.

A thought occurred to him that immediately sent ice up his spine. He had to clear his throat to vocalise it. 'Protection. We didn't…'

'I'm still on the pill,' she said in the same whisper.

He closed his eyes and nodded. Helena had put herself on the pill days before he'd taken her to Sidiro, laughingly saying that when she tempted him into making love to her, they would be protected.

Even then, so early in their relationship, he'd found the woman he wanted to bear his children.

The compulsion to haul her to her feet, carry her to the bed and then hold her so tightly in his arms that they became fused as one again was so strong that he took a step back.

He was not supposed to feel like this. This was supposed to be a moment of great satisfaction, the fulfilment of his fantasies, the first act in shedding the cloak of humiliation he'd worn since he'd been forced to tell their hundreds of guests that the wedding was off.

This was not how he'd envisaged making love to her

for the first time. In his old fantasies, when he'd believed their first time would be the first of a lifetime of lovemaking, he'd dreamed of taking it so slowly that when the moment came for him to take possession of her she would feel nothing but exquisite pleasure. Later, after their relationship had detonated, his fantasies evolved. Knowing that, should they come true, he would no longer be her first, he wouldn't have to take things gently. He would still take it slowly though. Oh, yes, in his fantasies he would still make her putty in his hands and have her begging for him to take her before finally sinking deep inside her and eradicating the thought of every man who'd come before him from her mind. But not like this. Not as a wild frenzy on the bedroom floor. *He* wasn't supposed to lose control of himself.

Desperate to get air into his constricted lungs, Theo strode to the door. Before leaving, he looked one more time at the ravishing beauty now standing by the bathroom door.

Naked as she was, she could be Artemis. But Artemis would not be looking at him with a wary vulnerability that made his heart ache.

Softening his voice, he said, 'I will see you soon, *matia mou*.'

The wary vulnerability lifted. Smiling in response, she entered the bathroom and closed the door behind her.

Theo's smile had never been further away than on the walk he took to his swimming pool.

A swim would clear his mind. A long swim during which he could rearrange his shattered thoughts and try to make sense of what he knew to be a truth.

That, until they had made love on her bedroom floor, Helena had still been a virgin.

CHAPTER TEN

HELENA LEFT HER bedroom feeling as if she'd slipped into a dream.

There had been little time to reflect on the explosion of passion that had consumed them. No sooner had she taken a hurried shower than the stylist and her two assistants had arrived to turn her into a princess for the evening.

The thrum of their lovemaking had still been there in her veins while she'd been pampered and preened. She'd longed to send the women away and have the luxury of composing her thoughts before she had to face Theo again.

All those years ago she'd longed for the complete fulfilment she'd known could only come from his lovemaking. It had been beautiful. It had been everything she'd dreamed it could be.

She had not an ounce of regret.

It was Theo's reaction that played on her mind.

She'd expected him to crow, not in a nasty way but in a Theo way, in a way that involved him making quips about his own prowess and implying without any subtlety whatsoever that this was what she'd been missing out on all these years.

She hadn't expected him to just…leave. Not a single comment, not a solitary wink. He hadn't even strutted out of the room.

He'd looked as dazed as she'd felt.

Helena supposed she should be thankful the stylists were there to distract her, otherwise she'd have her knickers in a twist about where they were going. The palace!

If Theo had planned this in advance, he'd been wise to keep it a secret. Not only was he taking her to her favourite place on earth but, as this was a VIP thing, many of his friends would be there too. She'd always felt gauche in their company. They were all so sophisticated, especially the women, all of whom she'd wondered if they'd shared Theo's bed. She'd sensed the antipathy towards her, from his friends of both sexes. Theo had playfully accused her of being insecure, which *had* accounted for some of her feelings, she knew, but she'd also known it had run deeper than that. Whether his friends saw her as a threat who was going to steal the life and soul of the party from them or if they merely disapproved of a non-socialite joining the gang, she'd never been able to discern.

That was why she'd loved their time on Sidiro so much, she remembered wistfully. There, for a whole glorious month, it had been just them, the sun and the sea and like-minded people loving life without any airs, graces or fancies.

At the end of the corridor was a full-length mirror. Taking one final look at her reflection, she reminded herself that she was not the same naïve young woman who'd felt so out of her depth before. She was strong now. She could hold her own. She would not feel intimidated. She had nothing to feel jealous about.

Despite all these tough words to herself, she descended the stairs with her heart in her throat and legs shaking so hard that she clung to the gold bannister to keep herself upright.

* * *

Theo heard light footsteps nearing the veranda. Every one of his senses immediately set itself on high alert.

Holding his glass of Scotch firmly in his hand, he rose to his feet and braced himself for Helena's appearance.

His own appearance had taken him thirty minutes to master. It had entailed a shower, a shave of his neck—he'd decided to grow his beard—the donning of a dapper suit and the artful mussing of his hair. The rest of his time had been spent reading his PA's business report, a daily briefing she sent at the end of every working day. Usually he would fire back observations or instructions to be carried out, but he'd had a hard enough time concentrating on the report, having to read it numerous times for the words to sink in, without finding the intelligence needed to reply.

The only place his mind wanted to go was reliving every moment of making love to Helena. The harder he tried not to think about it, the more the images pushed into the forefront of his mind. It was a form of mental torture.

He'd expected it to be explosive between them but there had been a part of him expecting it to be anti-climactic. After all, the build-up through the years had taken such weight in his mind that nothing could live up to it. But it had. More than lived up to it.

He could revel in the buzz still alight on his skin were it not for the emotions that had erupted beneath it. Emotions had never been part of the plan.

Damn it, she wasn't supposed to have remained a virgin.

The footsteps grew louder.

He sucked in a breath and braced himself.

With the early evening sun blazing down on her like gold dust, Helena stepped onto the veranda.

Theo sucked in another breath.

She'd foregone her glasses—she had always carried

contact lenses 'just in case'—leaving her beautiful face free from obstruction.

She glowed. Her golden skin had a luminescence he'd never seen before. Her dark hair shone, artfully knotted at the nape of her neck, not a strand displaced. The professionally applied sultry make-up glimmered. The silk of her dress gleamed.

'Well?' she asked shyly, spreading her hands out. 'Will I do?'

He cleared his throat and nodded. 'You look beautiful.'

So beautiful it felt as if his heart had been punched.

Agon's royal palace was an architect's dream, as colourful as the lives of the people who inhabited it. Its influences ranged from Turkish to French, blended to create a vast wonderland that rivalled Buckingham Palace for size. Helena distinctly remembered driving to her grandparents' home from the airport in Agon as a small child, her heart soaring with wonder to see the colourful turrets in the distance. As soon as they'd arrived she'd begged for paper and colouring pencils and immediately set about drawing it. That was her first ever attempt to draw a building and it had ignited a lifelong love of both the palace and the architecture behind it.

The palace interior matched the exterior for opulence, and she kept having to ensure her mouth was closed to stop it hanging open in awe.

Theo at her side, she was taken into a stateroom with around fifty other select guests. There, they were fed all the champagne they could quaff and all the canapés they could fit in their bellies. Naturally, everyone knew Theo, and she was introduced to many people, quite a few of whom she recognised from three years ago.

For a moment she longed to grab hold of Theo's hand

as she'd done back then and feel the solid weight of his support. He'd laughed at her insecurities but had stayed by her side. The times he hadn't was when she'd plucked up the courage to let go of his hand and release him as her life support. That was when everyone would pounce and Helena would find herself pushed to the sidelines, nibbling miserably on any morsel she could get her hands on until Theo extracted himself from whoever was monopolising him and rescued her.

She'd been too inured to a woman being under a male's thumb to realise she should have rescued herself. Her insecurities had not been Theo's fault.

She stared at him now, chatting to a woman she recognised, tall, thin, beautiful, an identikit clothes horse to those he'd hung out with after Helena had left, and swiped a bite-sized chunk of cucumber and avocado artfully rolled into one, and popped it into her mouth. The little devil called Jealousy who lived in her heart rose but she swallowed it down. Theo wasn't flirting. He was exchanging pleasantries. It was her erratic, insecure emotions when they'd been together that had always feared he would look from the beauty at his side to her and realise how wildly unsuitable Helena was for him.

She popped another more substantial canapé into her mouth and chewed absently while making an effort to stop a frown lining her forehead. She remembered complaining to Theo that none of his friends spoke to her unless she was glued to his side. A soft smile had spread over his face and then he'd put his thumbs to her forehead and massaged it gently. 'This is why,' he'd told her sympathetically. 'When you are frightened, you frown. It makes people wary of speaking to you. You look cross.'

'But I'm not cross,' she'd said, dumbfounded that he would say such a thing.

He'd replaced his thumbs with his mouth and wrapped his arms around her. 'I know, *agapi mou*,' he'd whispered. 'I know.'

And he *had* known. And he'd tried to protect her. But even with the best will in the world it was impossible to stay glued to one person for an entire evening.

She helped herself to another canapé. What an insecure, naïve young woman she had been. And as she swallowed the delicious morsel she felt a twinge of sympathy for the clothes horse chewing Theo's ear off. Not only did he look…not bored exactly, more that his attention was elsewhere, but also she must be starving. And cold in the scrap of fabric that barely covered her modesty and was no match for the palace's air-conditioning. When had that woman last had a proper meal? As had been the case three years ago, Helena was the only female guest actually eating. She was too hungry to do anything else. She caught a pencil-thin woman eyeing her and couldn't interpret if the look she was throwing her way was disdain or envy.

Helena raised her champagne glass in salute. The woman quickly looked away.

'Nicely done,' Theo murmured.

His breath whispered in her hair, his cologne enveloping her.

Her heart thumped.

She hadn't noticed him leave the clothes horse's side.

She leaned her face against his and inhaled the musky scent of his skin. The bristles of his fledging beard brushed her cheek. 'I should have learned the art of nonchalance long ago.'

'I don't know, I rather liked the jealous Helena.'

'She wasn't rational.'

'I know.'

Their gazes locked together, lingered…

Then Theo, eyes gleaming, drained his glass of champagne. 'We will be leaving for the amphitheatre soon.' His voice lowered as he leaned in to speak into her ear. 'When we get back home I'm going to strip that dress off and make you come with my tongue.'

A rush of blood to her head almost had her swaying on the spot.

An image of them making love flashed in her vision, sending more heat shooting through her from her pelvis into her dizzy brain.

Helena ground her heeled feet firmly into the antique carpet...

But that only made her think of how she had lost her virginity on her bedroom floor.

Fresh heat burned her cheeks as the monumentality of what they'd shared earlier finally sank in.

They'd had sex. She'd had sex with Theo. On her bedroom floor. And if Theo was to say he wanted to escape this party, take her home and do the things he'd just suggested...

She would go willingly. He wouldn't need to ask twice.

Trying to settle her erratic breaths, she took a sip of her champagne, reminding herself that she was in a royal palace.

But then she looked again into Theo's eyes and saw the gleam ringing in them that suggested he knew his words had had the desired effect. The urge to play him at his own game, to watch him squirm as he'd made her squirm, was irresistible.

Raising herself onto her toes, she placed her mouth to his ear. 'When we get back you'll be able to see for yourself if I'm wearing knickers...or not.' Then she darted her tongue out and licked the lobe of his ear before taking a step back to admire her handiwork.

Theo had stilled. His jaw was clenched, his eyes were hooded and gleaming with a combination of lust and amusement.

Helena smiled knowingly and raised her eyebrows. Nonchalantly, she said, 'How are we getting to the amphitheatre?'

A wide smile spread slowly across his expressive face. He burst into laughter. Wrapping an arm around her waist, he pulled her against him and kissed the top of her head. 'By train, *agapi mou*.' Then he lowered his voice so only she could hear. 'You are in so much trouble, you minx.'

The train transpired to be a brand-new electric transportation system King Helios had had installed earlier that year to traverse the vast palace grounds. With the grounds having been closed to the public for the day, the select guests were transported with the king, his two brothers and the royal wives to the amphitheatre in carriages that evoked thoughts of an age when rail travel had been exotic and luxurious.

Her carriage's window open, Helena closed her eyes and welcomed the refreshing kiss of the breeze on her face. She needed it, especially with Theo sitting so closely beside her. Their thighs were pressed together, his hand clasping hers in a proprietorial manner. She needed the air to blow some sanity into her brain. Here she was, in a carriage with Prince Talos and his beautiful wife, and all she could think about was returning to Theo's villa and enjoying his possession of her body all over again. Indeed, her only thought of the prince was how terrifying he was, easily the biggest man she had ever met. Many men of his size could be referred to as gentle giants. Prince Talos was not one of them…not until Helena caught the softening in his expression whenever he looked at his wife.

An unexpected burn stabbed the backs of her eyes. Theo had used to look at *her* that way...

She didn't want him to look at her that way again, she reminded herself. She'd given Theo possession of her body. Nothing more. Tomorrow they would return to Sidiro's peninsula and she would reset their relationship back to a business footing.

For this one day and night, though, they could fulfil the fantasies that had once driven them to the brink of madness.

Theo stepped into his softly lit villa and took a moment to embrace the silence. A man who usually thrived on noise and chaos, he realised all the noise of the evening had been drowned out by the thuds of his heart pounding in his ears.

He didn't think he'd taken in a single word anyone had said to him during the champagne reception. Apart from Helena. Thinking back on it, he couldn't even remember who he'd spoken to. Apart from Helena. As for the plot of the amphitheatre's show over which the rest of the audience had been in raptures, quite frankly, the entire thing could have been conducted in Swahili for all he'd got of it.

How could a man concentrate on such things when the scent of the most ravishing woman in the world skipped continually into his aroused senses? When she kept throwing him those come-to-bed eyes?

When the show finished, he'd stared into her eyes and in that moment he'd known he would cancel attending Prince Talos's private after-party. Who cared about showing the world that he'd won back the woman who'd jilted him when he could take her home and devour her all over again?

Who could think of revenge when burning desire consumed your every movement? When the soft skin of the object of your revenge as well as of your desire kept brushing against your arm? When her soft hands held yours as tightly as you held hers?

But now they were back, he knew he needed a moment to gather himself together.

'Drink?' he suggested.

He wanted to make love to her so badly, but this time he wanted to take it as slowly as he should have done the first time...*her* first time. Ever.

He led her through to his favourite living area, a vast room that led onto the veranda, separated by a wall of glass. He pressed the button to open the wall then went to his bar. 'What do you want?'

She smiled softly then headed through the gap that had opened onto the veranda, saying over her shoulder, 'Whatever you're having.'

I'm having you, he thought as he opened a bottle of ouzo, poured a large measure of it into a cocktail shaker, then did the same with the vodka. Then he added the juice of a lemon, some orange juice and, remembering to add them only at the last moment, chunks of ice. Then he gave it a good shake before straining it into two tall glasses.

He carried their drinks outside, where he found her barefoot on the lawn below the veranda, staring out at the black sea before her, the moonlight illuminating her pale face.

'Here,' he said.

She took it from him with a smile and sipped it through the straw. Her eyes flickered. 'A Greek Doctor?'

He grinned. 'You remember?'

A mischievous glint sparkled in her eyes. 'I remember getting my first hangover on these. And my last.'

'Still?' That was a night he'd never forgotten. Helena, unused to drinking more than the odd glass of wine, had devoured more than her share of the cocktail one night early on during their stay on Sidiro. He'd had to carry her back to the small hotel room. She'd alternated between clinging to him like a limpet throughout the night to retching over the side of the bed. In the morning she'd clutched her head tightly and vowed never to drink so much again. In all their time together after that, she never had.

She took another sip and nodded. 'I learned my lesson.' Eyes holding his, she swirled the contents of her glass. 'I always learn my lessons.'

He contemplated her. 'Are you trying to tell me something?'

'Only that you and I... I don't want you getting the wrong idea.'

'What wrong idea would that be?'

'That we're getting back together. We're not. When we go back to Sidiro, our relationship goes back to being purely professional.'

CHAPTER ELEVEN

HELENA HELD HER breath while she waited for Theo to respond.

She hadn't intended to put it so bluntly, but Theo was not a man for subtlety. It was best to spell things out, otherwise he would deliberately misconstrue it for his own advantage.

'But you *have* thought of us getting back together,' he said with a gleam in his eye.

'I've been thinking about us a lot,' she admitted. 'Time tends to blur the past. It makes us nostalgic.'

'You are nostalgic for me?'

She had to laugh. 'Nostalgic for your insatiable ego.'

'You're blaming my ego for you running away?'

'I didn't run away. I left.'

'You ran away from me.'

'Are you suffering from selective memory or something? I never ran away from you. I left you and you know perfectly well why I did, and they are reasons that haven't changed even if nostalgia has blunted the edges.'

He shook his head sardonically and raised his glass. 'As I remember it, you decided I was going to be a terrible husband and father and—'

'I never said that,' she cut in, startled. For all his teasing tones, there was a biting message. This conversation was going in a direction she had not anticipated. In her head, she'd envisaged making it clear to Theo that any intimacy between them was to be confined to this villa and Theo immediately agreeing with her—although no doubt with his fingers crossed behind his back—and then whisking her off to bed to make love. Because this was just unfinished business, she'd realised while trying to watch the show. Theo had that right. If he'd dropped his ridiculous insistence that they wait until they were married before making love and they had actually done the deed all that time ago, the itch would have been scratched. The unknown would have been known.

He took a long drink of his cocktail. 'You certainly implied it.'

'No, you interpreted it that way. I didn't mean you would be a bad husband for anyone, just a bad husband for me—out there in this big wide world is a woman you would be perfect for.'

That was *not* a ripple of jealousy streaming through her at the thought of Theo settling down. She would not allow that, not tonight.

He winked. 'You're saying I'm perfect?'

She only just held back from giving his arm a playful slap. Some intimacies must not be allowed back out. 'For someone else, yes. And I definitely did not say you'd be a bad father because I actually think you'd be a great one.'

'How?'

'I don't know…' She thought wildly. 'You're fun. You're generous. You're protective. You're easy to talk to. You don't judge.' Everything her father wasn't.

'All the wonderful qualities you ran away from.'

'I didn't run, I walked, and I would walk again because the flip side is that you're a control freak.'

Her assertion was so offensive that for a moment Theo's mind went blank. 'I am not.'

'Theo, you wanted to control everything. Look at my career—you took it on yourself to arrange for me to finish my studies at Agon University and arranged a placement with an Agon architecture business for my final year. Your insistence that we marry immediately, your wish for me to start popping babies out...even down to when we would make love for the first time. You knew best. You always think you know best.'

He took a long moment to compose himself against the violent emotions coursing through him at this outrageous rewrite of history. Speaking through gritted teeth, he said, 'You let me believe you wanted to live in Agon with me and have babies. If I overstepped the mark in trying to make that happen then I'm sorry...no, I'm *not* sorry.' Absolutely not. That would imply an acceptance of blame. 'I never forced you to do anything you didn't want to. I hated the thought of you going back to England to finish your studies but I would have moved heaven and earth to make the distance between us work if it had come to it. I only got the information together for you because you told me that was what you wanted.'

'I *did* want it,' she admitted softly. 'But you were like a whirlwind without a stop button. You just went ahead and arranged everything.'

'You never once complained.' Not by word or gesture.

She dropped her stare. 'I know. I should have done. I should have told you to let me sort things out for myself.'

'Why didn't you?'

'I was scared.'

Shocked, he had to take another moment to compose himself. 'Scared of *me*?'

'No...' She looked back at him, her face scrunched up.

'Sorry, scared is the wrong word. It just felt like I was being controlled.'

While there was relief that she hadn't been scared of him—he would rather have died than ever make Helena feel unsafe—her words landed like a blow, the implications immediately, nauseatingly clear. 'In the same way your father controls your mother?'

She nodded. 'And the same way he controlled me. That's what scared me. I was too young and unworldly to see that I needed to stand up for myself and just tell you to back off and slow down.'

Theo could feel the pulse in his jaw throbbing to match the throb in his heart.

If she'd confided the truth about her parents' marriage and her fears about what she perceived as his controlling behaviour, he would never have gone full blazes into arranging everything so they wouldn't have to be parted. He would have slowed down and held off, if only she had voiced her fears.

She hadn't trusted him enough to confide her fears. He'd taught her how to let her hair down and unbutton herself and he'd taught her the joy of arguing—he was Greek; his compatriots had turned shouting into an art form—but the arguments they'd had up to that final one had been arguments over trivial matters, like whether or not Brunelleschi was the greatest architect of the Renaissance. Helena was for yes; Theo was for no. Their arguments had never been of a personal nature against each other. When Helena had thrown her engagement ring in his face and screamed that she never wanted to see him again it had never crossed his mind that she meant it.

And now it was too late. All too late. This was a conversation they should have had three years ago.

The past was written and nothing either of them did or

said now could change it. The love that had bound them together had been irrevocably broken...

But the passion hadn't. Their passion still blazed brightly. Their passion was the only thing that mattered now. His passion for her and her passion for him.

Breathing deeply, filling his lungs with her scent, he adopted a silky tone. 'I seem to remember you wanted things to happen faster in the bedroom. You didn't want me to back off there.'

'But that's another thing I felt controlled over,' she said, failing to grasp the opportunity to switch the conversation to a lighter tempo. 'I was desperate for us to make love.'

'You should have told me.'

'I did!'

'You should have told me you felt controlled,' he clarified.

'I didn't feel controlled at the start of our relationship, but after you proposed and everything suddenly started moving at breakneck speed I was too indoctrinated into a believing a man's word is law to say we needed to slow down, and then as the wedding got closer my anxieties crept up on me. When my parents joined us...it was as though all my fears that I would end up with a marriage like theirs crystallised, and I panicked.'

'Are they the same fears that stopped you forming another relationship?'

Startled eyes met his. 'What do you mean?'

'You stayed a virgin.' He looked her squarely in the eye. 'Or am I wrong?'

He didn't know if he wanted to be wrong. Or right. If he was right then Helena had spent the past three years without a warm body beside her, just as he had, but their reasons would be very different. He hadn't had a choice. He'd been unable to move on, not with Helena lodged in his psyche, preventing him from finding desire for another.

If Helena had stayed single, then it would have been a deliberate choice.

'Shall I take your silence as an admission?' He drained his cocktail. 'You should have told me.'

Helena would rather have shaved off her hair than tell him. It would have been tantamount to admitting she'd spent the past three years pining for him, which she hadn't, of course, but Theo would definitely have spotted an opportunity.

'It wasn't important.'

'I disagree. If I'd known you were a virgin I would have taken more care. I could have hurt you.'

'But you didn't.' He would never hurt her.

His huge shoulders rose in a shrug. He looked away from her, out into the distance. 'You really did go back into your shell, didn't you?'

'What do you mean?'

'You left me because you wanted to be free.' He looked sharply back at her with a distinct flash of anger in his eyes. 'What the hell have you been doing? I never expected you to turn into a wild party animal, but *this*...?'

He shook his head and made a grunt-like laugh. 'I have believed these past years that you were living a boring life with a boring accountant or a boring teacher, having boring sex, everything boring but for you perfect.'

'Are you saying I'm boring?' she said, trying to turn it into a joke but shrivelling inside at the acuteness of Theo's observation. She had tried dating when she'd completed her masters. She'd had dinner with two accountants and one maths teacher. On paper they'd each been perfect for her. None of them would have controlled her or interfered with her career. She'd had a strong suspicion the maths teacher would have been delighted to become a house husband and raise any children, should the opportunity arise.

The opportunity had not arisen, not least because each date ended the same way, with Helena paying her share of the bill, politely thanking them for a lovely evening and then getting the nearest public transport home, never to see them again.

It shamed her that, as lovely and as perfect as these men were, they'd bored her rigid. They were so *earnest*, so right-on…

She should have snapped one of them up. They might be boring but wasn't that what she wanted? None of them would have steamrollered her into anything by dint of their personality. Mainly because none of them had *had* a personality.

In short, none of them had been Theo…

He laughed. 'You are the least boring person I know but you're like a frightened bird, terrified to leave the nest and embrace life. You've had all the opportunity in the world to explore the different sides that make you Helena and explore them on *your* terms away from your father's control and influence, and you've squandered them. You haven't even tried.'

'That's not fair,' she said, stung. She *had* tried! Those three disastrous dates proved that.

He grimaced before placing his glass on a curved bench close to them, then stood before her and gently cupped her face.

He gazed into her eyes for the longest time. Under the moonlight, his eyes had a silver hue and they danced with the energy that was always in them whatever colour shone out.

He pressed his lips to hers for a moment and breathed her in. 'You, *agapi mou*, are beautiful. There is not a heterosexual man alive who wouldn't want you. You also have a deeply…' he brushed his lips from her mouth to her ear, sending tiny shivers of delight pirouetting over her skin '… sensual side. I have seen it. I have tasted it. The wildness that lives in you…you have locked it back in its box when it needs its freedom. You hide yourself away…'

She forced her mind out of the stupor into which the velvet of his low voice was pulling her. Why had she gone on those disastrous dates? Because the week she'd started her final year of training, she'd gone into a newsagent's and seen Theo's broad face smiling at her from the magazine rack. The shock at seeing him had landed like a punch in her throat just as it had every time before. But that time had been different and she'd known she had to do something to help her speed up the healing process.

The dates hadn't worked.

In the three years since she'd left Theo she hadn't met a single man who made her feel anything. She couldn't even imagine kissing another man without shuddering.

She mustn't let Theo suspect the truth. She couldn't bear for him to think she had spent the intervening years pining for him.

'We don't all have the time or money to go out partying with a new supermodel every weekend like you.' She put her hands to his chest and pushed. 'You have the cheek to ask me what *I've* been doing since we parted? I could ask the same of you—in fact, I will. Where do you get off making judgements about my sex life when you can't stay with one woman for more than five minutes before your eyes stray to her replacement?'

Under the moonlight, she saw a tick pulse on his jaw. But then he smiled and reclaimed the space between them. He traced a finger across her cheek. 'How do you know so much about my sex life, *agapi mou*?'

Fear and pride had her retort come without hesitation. 'It's hard to miss when it's always splattered over the news.'

Reading about him had become an addiction. It was almost as if he'd taunted her from the pages of the glossy magazines, as if he knew she would seek news of him and chose the greatest weapon at his disposal to get back at her: her jealousy.

Theo watched all the emotions blazing over Helena's face and tilted his head, waiting for the burst of satisfaction to know she *had* followed his life, just as he'd followed hers.

The Helena he'd known had not been interested in current affairs, be it gossip or serious news articles.

She would never know those women had been mere window dressing, a panacea to show the world—and Helena—that his humiliation at being jilted had been a mere flesh wound.

She would never know that the desire burning in him only burned for her. By the time he was finished with her, all the desire would be sated and he would be able to move on.

He traced his fingers lightly to her graceful neck and drifted them down to her bare shoulders, murmuring, 'You need to stop hiding yourself away and stop pretending.'

'I don't—'

'You chain yourself to your work and pretend it counts as a social life. We made love this afternoon and already you're demanding we go back to Sidiro and pretend that nothing happened. I will go along with it and pretend too, if that is what you really want, but we both know it will be a lie.' He dipped his face and nuzzled into her neck. Her skin felt fevered. 'I will still want you. I will be with you in your office and in my head I will be reliving every moment of our lovemaking.'

Her breath hitched.

'I always imagine us together. I watch you work on

your computer and I imagine you taking off your sensible shirt for me in the seductive way you used to strip yourself when you were desperate to tempt me into making love to you.' He flattened a hand over her breasts. Her nipples were as hard as her skin was hot. 'I watch you working at the big table on the blueprints and I imagine myself bending you over and—'

'Stop,' she moaned, but her cheek rubbed into his head and her fingers groped at his shirt.

'Am I turning you on?' He found her mouth and kissed her savagely. 'Remember when you used to talk to me like this? When you told me all the ways you wanted me to make love to you and all the ways you wanted to make love to me?' He found the pins holding her hair together and pulled them free. Her hair tumbled like a fragrant cloud. 'What's holding you back from acting all your fantasies out now? If you have your way, this will be our only night together.'

Taking hold of her hand, he placed it on his throbbing excitement. 'Do you feel that? Tell me it's not the same for you. Tell me you don't ache for me as I ache for you.'

Her eyes were wide, her breaths little pants. For a long time she did nothing but stare at him. And then she bunched the long skirt of her dress up to her thigh, took hold of his hand and placed it at the heart of her femininity. The heat he found there was hot enough to burn. And it told him better than any verbal response that it was the same for her too.

With more strength than even he realised he possessed, Theo swept her into his arms. Moving swiftly, he carried her to his bedroom. By the time he placed her on the bed, she'd already unbuttoned his shirt.

He made deft work of removing her dress and underwear—she *had* been wearing knickers, the minx—while she scratched and pulled at his clothing to free him too.

Naked, he pressed her down so she lay flat on her back, then began worshipping his goddess. There was not an inch of flesh he didn't kiss or drag his tongue over, not an inch of flesh he didn't inhale. And there was not an inch of flesh on his own body that didn't blaze with the passion consuming him.

Their lovemaking earlier had been too urgent for him to luxuriate in the act. This time he was determined to go slow and bring to life the fantasies he'd been dreaming of for three years. But it was hard to take his time with Helena writhing and moaning beneath him, her sounds and movements firing his passion.

He remembered the first time he'd seen her naked and how painfully shy she had been. She'd covered her breasts with an arm and placed her hand over her pubis to hide it from him. Within weeks she'd lost all her inhibitions. She would prance around naked, revelling in the effect her nakedness had on him. Always she would try to tempt him into making love. The control it had taken to resist performing that ultimate act had been torture defined. If he'd known then that the control he'd exhibited, which had been only because he'd wanted their wedding night to mean something pure and beautiful, would be twisted by Helena into an act of control over *her*, he would have said *to hell with it* and made her his entirely.

Then none of this would have happened. With no Helena-shaped mysteries to unravel, he'd have been able to move on with his life. But if he'd moved on with his life they wouldn't be there now and the pleasure consuming him would never have existed.

And, *Theos*, this was pleasure defined. Hungry, dark, all-consuming pleasure. It almost made his three-year abstinence worth it. Tonight, Helena was his. All his. Exactly as she should be.

At the first touch of Theo's tongue on her swollen nub, Helena closed her eyes and sank into the magic she knew would follow. When his hand dragged upwards over her belly and to her breasts, squeezing the highly sensitised flesh, she moaned and captured his fingers in hers, linking them together.

Oh, but he *knew* what she needed and wanted. He knew better than she.

This was why she'd been unable to find desire for another. It was not possible that she could respond to anyone else in this way, a mass of sensation and so *alive*. Theo made her feel as if she could fly.

The hand not clasped in hers cupped her bottom and gently raised it, slightly changing the angle with which he was pleasuring her. It was all that was needed to send her soaring. Crying his name, Helena rode the tsunami of pulsations that throbbed from her core into every crevice of her body.

She was still floating when he slowly kissed his way up her body. His face over hers, he brushed a lock of hair from her eyes and kissed her. Their lips fused together, he entered her.

Their lovemaking felt as if it were happening in slow motion. Every thrust, every brush of his chest against her breasts, every squeeze of their laced fingers, every dance of their tongues consumed her entirely. Theo consumed her.

When they were finally spent and she was cocooned in the safety of his arms, her cheek on his chest, his heartbeat thrumming beneath her ear, unbidden tears suddenly filled her eyes. She blinked them away. This moment was too special to allow doubts and fears to spoil it.

CHAPTER TWELVE

THE SCULPTOR'S STUDIO was nestled in a remote hillside. Theo drove them there himself in his favourite sports car, roof down, music blaring. Wearing one of her new summer dresses, hair loose and whipping around her face, Helena felt an exhilaration she'd not experienced in so long that she closed her eyes to savour it.

She didn't fight the images that immediately popped to the forefront of her mind. They were images to savour as much as the exhilaration was.

Her body became suffused with heat as she remembered all the ways they'd made love throughout the night.

She pressed her thighs together in a futile effort to counter the thickening and pulsing ache between her legs.

They'd had breakfast on his private balcony. After devouring his food, he'd devoured her.

She should be exhausted but that feeling of being alive still buzzed on her skin. There was a zesty energy in her veins. Her throat kept wanting to expel bursts of laughter.

And beside her sat the man who'd brought all these feelings out of her as effortlessly as he controlled the powerful car.

'I love this song!' Theo suddenly said, pressing the controls on the steering wheel to turn the volume up. It was a jaunty summer tune Helena had never heard before but she soon found her foot tapping along to the beat while Theo massacred the lyrics by tunelessly but enthusiastically singing along.

She'd forgotten singing was the one thing he was useless at, but nothing could stop Theo doing something he enjoyed.

Music, like everything else Theo had introduced her to, had been forgotten when she'd returned to her life in London. The only music system she had was an old radio she'd been given by her grandmother on her fifteenth birthday.

The studio, when they reached it, was a huge white building neatly hidden away on a large plot of land. A diminutive man of around fifty, dressed in ragged jeans and T-shirt nominally protected by a black apron, hurried out of the wide-open doors to meet them.

'Theodoros, it's good to see you again,' he said, speaking so quickly Helena struggled to keep up.

Theo shook his hand and then introduced him to Helena. 'Do you have time to give her a tour of your studio before we get down to business?'

'It would be my pleasure.'

Walking past Titanic-sized slabs of marble, they entered the vast space. The temperature dropped and the noise level increased the moment they stepped over the threshold.

Helena found her eyes struggling not to pop out of her head. The interior more closely resembled a warehouse than anything, an interior filled with a dozen people all turning different-sized slabs of marble into works of art. One wall was lined with shelves containing foot-high marble statuettes of religious themes, while dozens and dozens of marble slabs at least ten feet high were raised on boards and in varying stages of finish. Whatever stage any of the works were at, the one common denominator was that they were exquisite. These were works Donatello would have been proud to create.

Takis, the sculptor whose name they all worked under, introduced her to his newest apprentice, a young English-woman covered in white dust who happily showed her the bust she was working on. Her talent took Helena's breath away. The face appearing in the marble already appeared to pulse with life.

'Don't you get scared?' Helena asked her.

'Of what?'

'Making a wrong mark.' Architecture was as precise as sculpting must be, but creating plans was an evolving process. She didn't draw the first line of a building know-ing that if she got it wrong she would not be able to correct it. If the wrong mark was made on marble, it couldn't be deleted or the marble scrunched up like a piece of paper and another magically produced to start again. She had a luxury this woman didn't have and yet she envied her the nerve she must have to make that first mark. Do or die.

If Helena were the sculptor, she would probably spend a year plucking up the courage. Theo, on the other hand, wouldn't think twice. He'd make the mark in a heartbeat.

The woman smiled, her eyes shining. 'It's terrifying!'

Soon, Helena and Theo were led to Takis's office at the far end of the warehouse. Judging by the mess, it was a room rarely cleaned, but Takis was not in the least embar-rassed by the state of it. He rummaged through a drawer and eventually pulled out a thick sheaf of A4 paper and handed it to Theo.

Theo looked through the sheets one by one, automati-cally passing each one to Helena once he'd finished pe-rusing. They were Takis's designs for all the statues and ornate benches that would eventually adorn Theo's garden.

Each and every design was stunning. She had no doubt

that, once completed, any piece could sit proudly in the Vatican or in the Uffizi Gallery.

'What did you think of Takis?' Theo asked her once they were driving back to the villa.

'A true artist,' she replied, shaking her head reverently. 'Your garden is going to be a work of art.'

'That's the idea.' He cast a quick glance at her before turning his attention back to the open road before them.

Theo had loved watching her reaction to the studio. In many ways, she was an artist like Takis, her imagination creating something out of nothing. The sketches she made freehand, he'd always believed, were works of art in themselves and he felt a sudden twinge of guilt to remember the fate of that first sketch in the palace grounds.

Flushed with happiness at his compliments of her work, she'd given the sketch to him and refused to accept anything in return, which he'd immediately pounced on by insisting he buy her dinner as a thank-you. He'd bought her dinner every night for three months thereafter and he'd treasured the sketch, had it professionally framed and hung on his bedroom wall.

He'd smashed the frame's glass and burned the sketch a fortnight after she jilted him.

His jaw clenched. It didn't relax until they were back at the villa.

He pressed the knob to close the car's roof while Helena undid her seatbelt and then smoothed her hair.

He turned to face her. His throat caught. Her golden skin was flushed from the drive, her eyes alight, a soft expression on her face he hadn't seen for a long time. She still wasn't wearing her glasses…

Neither of them spoke. For the longest time, all they did was gaze into each other's eyes, their individual breaths falling into rhythm together, becoming shallow as the chemistry that had always bound them so tightly coiled around them.

He brought his face to hers and captured a lock of her hair in his fingers.

She shivered lightly and raised her chin. Her lips parted. He brushed his mouth against them then pulled back an inch.

'Do I tell the captain to take us back to Sidiro now or in the morning?' he whispered.

Her eyes flickered with confusion then darkened. She bit her bottom lip, all the while staring deep into his eyes…

And then she wound an arm around his neck and pulled him down into a hot, passionate kiss that answered for her.

Helena stared out of her office window, sipping absently at her coffee. She'd had a chat with Stanley for advice on certain aspects of the plans that had been concerning her. Her mind now at ease, she should be busy working on the plans she hadn't touched in three days, and yet…

She felt Theo's absence acutely. An early morning call from his PA about some business crisis had seen him fly from Agon to Athens with a promise to meet her back at Sidiro later.

She'd spent the sail back to Sidiro with her laptop open but her finger pressed in the exact spot on her lips where his mouth had lingered when he'd kissed her goodbye.

She squeezed her eyes shut. There would be no more kisses. They'd had two nights together. That had to be enough. She'd made it perfectly clear that their return to Sidiro meant a return to their professional relationship.

Scolding herself firmly, she drained her coffee and returned to her stool at the large table, where she was working on the physical blueprint. If she continued at the pace she'd set, she should have the first plans ready to present to him in a fortnight. They would then go through it in detail together and anything Theo wasn't happy with would—

Distinct footsteps snatched her attention away from her work.

The pen in her hand slipped from her fingers. She snatched it back up and wiped her suddenly clammy hands on her skirt.

'You've put your uniform back on, I see.' Theo's voice, as distinct as his footsteps and his scent, soaked into her skin.

Changing into a skirt and blouse had been the first thing she'd done when she'd arrived back on the peninsula. Dressing professionally was like mental armour.

She took a moment to compose herself before twisting her stool round to face him.

Theo was still dressed in the same shirt and tailored trousers he'd left the villa in that morning but had ditched the jacket and tie. Dressed or undressed, her body didn't care. It sang for him regardless. Her heart sang for him too…

She pressed her bottom more firmly into the stool to prevent her legs running over to him.

'Everything sorted?' she asked, relieved her voice sounded relatively normal and not all throaty and breathless.

He shrugged. 'As much as it can be.'

'Oh?'

'Minor problems with a new government directive. We thought we were prepared but one of the legal team discovered not all our systems are equipped to cope with it.'

She had no idea what he was talking about.

Theo must have noticed her expression, for he burst into laughter. Strolling to the coffee pot and grabbing a clean cup, he said, 'Don't worry, *matia mou*, it is every bit as boring as it sounds. Did you miss me?'

How she loved the way *matia mou* rolled off his tongue.

That had been his pet name for her before. She'd had no idea how much she hated him calling her *agapi mou* until he'd switched back to the old endearment. It sounded right. It sounded exactly as things should be...

'Helena?'

She blinked, aware she'd fallen into yet another trance. 'Sorry?'

His eyes sparkled and, cup of coffee in hand, he propped himself against the wall. 'I asked if you missed me.'

'You were only gone for a few hours.'

He looked at his watch. 'Eight hours.'

'I never noticed,' she lied, averting her gaze from his. She twisted her stool back around and straightened the blueprint. 'I'm glad you got the directive thing sorted. I know what a pain it can be keeping up with new legislation. I'm lucky I don't have to enforce anything, just implement it where necessary.'

'Still avoiding my question?'

He read her so easily. Like no one else. But then, he'd been witness to a side of her no one else had seen. She'd let that side slip out a little on Agon, but now they were back she had to return it to where it belonged. To allow anything else would be madness.

'Things are always quiet without you,' she finally answered. After she'd spent forty-eight hours glued to his hip...and groin...the silence had felt more acute than ever. Where there was Theo, there was life. Whatever she was feeling, she would never regret agreeing to a second night with him.

'Excellent avoidance. I'm not ashamed to say I missed you.'

She bowed her head and kept her eyes on the blueprints. The lines she'd drawn thickened and blurred...

'All I could think about was getting back to you and

sweeping you off to bed,' he continued with a sensuous purr. 'But I can't sweep you off to bed, can I? Because it's against your rules.'

She closed her eyes and tried to hold back the wave of heat crashing through her, but it would have been easier for Theo to lasso the moon.

'Do you know what I think about rules?' he whispered into the stark silence that followed.

She could guess.

'That they are made to be broken. Or bent...'

She couldn't stop herself from twisting back around to look at him.

His eyes pulsed and he moved away from the wall and stalked towards her. 'What is to stop us from sharing a bed here too? As professionalism is so important to you, I can promise to keep my hands to myself during office hours.'

She dug her fingers into the table, eyes squeezed shut, suddenly holding on for dear life while his caressing words penetrated her senses.

'But when the night comes...' His words dangled in the air between them and then the air itself shifted.

Helena opened her eyes and found him within arm's reach. He leaned down to look directly at her. 'Or we could sail back to Agon every evening. Elli and Natassa would, I'm sure, be grateful of the extra privacy... As would I.' Then he straightened, a wicked gleam playing in his eyes. 'I'm going to get changed.'

And then he sauntered out of her office before she could unglue her vocal cords enough to speak.

Theo showered briskly and changed into a pair of shorts. And nothing else.

Time to go and torture Helena a little more. He didn't think he could ever tire of making her blush.

There was a fizz in his veins when he walked the short route back to her office, where he found her at her desk once more, working on her computer.

She didn't acknowledge his arrival. But she noticed. He saw it in the way she shifted in her seat and had a large gulp of her coffee.

Smiling to himself, he sat on the sofa closest to her and pressed his phone to check his emails. A fresh batch had recently landed from his American employees, who were just waking up to the new business day. Theo enforced a strict policy within all his companies that, unless specifically trading with different time zones, all work communications were muted from eight p.m. until seven a.m. He'd wanted to enforce it from six p.m. but had been advised it would be unenforceable. There were people out there so desperate to get ahead they would forgo a social life to climb another rung on the corporate ladder. He didn't understand the mentality. His father, a hugely successful entrepreneur, had always made sure to be home to share the evening meal with his family. Weekends were sacrosanct. His father had worked hard and played hard, a policy Theo had wholeheartedly adopted. He paid his staff well and was generous with paid leave and other perks because he was a firm believer that staff with happy, fulfilled personal lives were more productive at work.

It made his stomach knot to know his best work had come in the months after Helena had jilted him, when he'd had to occupy every minute of every hour to stop himself from losing his mind. The inheritance he'd quadrupled in the years after his parents' death had increased by a further five-fold in the three years after she'd left him.

Helena, he would bet, took her work home with her. Her upbringing had been similar to his in that they were only children, both had stay-at-home mothers and both shared their evening meals with their parents, but there the similarities ended. Family meals in the Nikolaidis household had been noisy affairs with plenty of disagreements and shouting, especially if his paternal grandfather joined them. Now in his eighties, he could still win awards for shouting. But those meals had been fun and the thing he had missed the most when his parents died.

Any fun in his life had been forced, he now realised. He'd thrown himself into the party lifestyle in part because he couldn't bear being in the huge house without them. The silence of their absence had been acute. Not until he'd met Helena had he experienced true joy again. She'd seamlessly filled the gaping hole his parents had left in him. Before he'd met her, he hadn't had a night in since his father's great heart had given out. The doctors said an undetected abnormality had been the cause of it but Theo knew better. Nursing his mother through her battle with cancer and then the pain of losing her had caused it. His father had died of a broken heart. Theo, eighteen years old and suddenly the possessor of a great fortune, had found relief from his grief in drink, women, exercise and work— and not necessarily in that order. For years he'd tried to escape the pain, never closing his eyes for sleep unless certain he was exhausted enough or inebriated enough to slip into oblivion.

Helena had stopped the merry-go-round. In her he'd found someone to share his life and raise a family with. His parents' marriage had been strong and he'd been certain he and Helena had the same strength to replicate it. Before he'd met her, he hadn't even known he was searching for her.

Once he'd accepted she had left him for good, his grief had speared him. The hole had ripped back open, far bigger and deeper than before. He'd hidden himself from the pain the only way he knew how: by throwing himself back into his old lifestyle with a vengeance. And vengeance had been on his mind too. All the love he'd lavished on Helena had twisted into something ugly. He'd used it as fuel while biding his time for the perfect moment to strike.

He'd never stopped to think of the pain Helena must have gone through too. It had been too easy to see her as the villainess who'd humiliated him when he should have seen the warning signs. They'd been there. If only he had paused a moment to read them.

He remembered her agitation in the days leading up to her parents' arrival before the wedding. He'd assumed she was worried he would dislike them and so had made an extra effort to get on with them and ingratiate himself with her father. His ego, he now knew, had seen him look at everything from a Theo-centric prism.

She'd relayed snippets of her childhood to which he should have paid closer attention. If he had, he'd have understood what she'd tried to tell him.

Meals in the Armstrong household, from how Helena had matter-of-factly described them, had been conducted in silence unless her father wanted to start a discussion about a particular news item on which he had strong views or a book he wished to critique.

Only now did it occur to him that for Helena to contribute to those lofty discussions, she would have had to contribute in Greek, a difficult language to master for non-native speakers.

Little wonder Helena had kept the light that lived inside of her deeply hidden. To let it out would have met heavy disapproval. He remembered her telling him, also matter-of-factly, that her father had hoped to breed a scholar like himself. Archibald Armstrong had approved of architecture as a career choice for his daughter only because it had the social cache he craved. There had been a number of Archibald's equally highbrow friends in the congregation when Theo had stood before them and merrily announced the wedding was off. Her father would have felt humiliated by his daughter's wilful actions, but to throw her out and cut her off for it…?

How could anyone treat their own flesh and blood so abysmally?

How hard must it have been for Helena to cope? To survive?

His ruminations dissolved when he became aware of being watched.

Lifting his head from his phone—he hadn't read a single one of the emails—he found Helena's dark eyes fixed boldly on him.

The tiniest smile played on her lips but it was a smile that stirred his blood.

She slowly placed her hands to her breasts and cupped them.

Theo blinked, suddenly certain his imagination had gone haywire.

She undid the top button of her shirt. And then the next. And the next until, one by one, all her buttons were undone and she parted the shirt…

Her breasts strained against the plain white bra like succulent marshmallows.

All the moisture in his mouth vanished.

She got to her feet and slowly brought the sleeves down her arms and let the shirt drop to the floor.

He gulped for air.

Eyes still holding his, she put her hands behind her back. A beat later, her skirt fell to the floor. She stepped out of it with a sensuous grace that had him gulping for more air.

Then her hands went behind her back again…

The beautiful breasts sprang free, high, full, cherry-tipped… Perfect. Just like the rest of her.

She took another step towards him. Her fingers plucked the sides of her white knickers.

Was he dreaming? He could pinch himself to be sure but that might mean waking up. He did not want to wake up. If this was a dream, then he would let his fantasies live on…

The knickers slid down her creamy thighs.

A groan escaped his throat.

So much for *him* torturing *her*…

CHAPTER THIRTEEN

HELENA STEPPED OUT of her knickers and took another step towards Theo. Her heartbeats were so heavy she was sure he must be able to hear them. Or see them.

He'd left her office and the whole room had spun around her like a wheel on fire. Her thoughts had been a jumble.

When he'd walked back in, her heart had pounded like a fist against her chest and knocked all the confusion out of her.

How could she think two days of being Theo's lover would be enough?

What was to stop them carrying on with their affair?

She wasn't the same woman she'd been three years ago. Theo had helped rip off the straitjacket of her upbringing and, unwitting though it had been, given her the courage to pursue her career without her parents' support—without anyone's support. He had so much nerve, such energy, such confidence... Was it any surprise she'd taken some of that energy into her own blood? He'd made her brave with her father and given her confidence in her work. What was stopping her from using that bravery and confidence for pleasure without putting a time limit to it?

What was wrong with taking things one day at a time and just enjoying and exploring the closeness of the one man who made her feel so alive? He made her feel like the most desirable woman in the world. He made her smile, made her laugh, made her want to wrap her arms around him and crush her skin against his and inhale nothing but his scent.

The feelings he evoked in her were so powerful that she didn't want to lose them. Not yet. Not ever...

She took another step towards him, relishing the expression in his hooded eyes. His breaths were heavy through his nose. His bare chest rose up and down rapidly.

She did this to him. Just as he did it to her.

Reaching him, she stood before him and let her eyes drift over the magnificent body that Takis himself would struggle to replicate in all its beautiful glory.

Carve Theo in marble and put him on a plinth and she would worship it.

The Theo before her was flesh and bone.

Staring deep into his eyes, she put her hands to his warm face and gently stroked the developing beard and the contrasting smooth skin of his cheekbones.

His throat moved but he made no effort to touch her back.

His Greek Wedding Night Debt His Greek Wedding Night Debt, she drifted her fingers down his neck then spread her hands out on his chest, over the fine hair that covered it, rubbing her thumbs over his flat, brown nipples then moving them down to his hard abdomen, gradually lowering herself to her knees as she went.

Now placed between his legs, she looked back up into his eyes.

Not a word was exchanged. None were needed.

She undid the button of his shorts. The thick, dark hair she was greeted with revealed he'd not bothered with underwear.

In that instant she was thrown back to their original

time on Sidiro when he'd only donned shorts to spare everyone else's blushes. When it was just the two of them, he'd stayed naked. And so had she.

How had he found the strength to keep denying her all those years ago? Denying them both?

He raised his buttocks to allow her to tug the shorts down his hips. The movement was enough to make his erection spring free and reveal itself in all its glory.

After pulling his shorts down to his feet, she took his arousal in her hand. Long, thick and as smooth as velvet... Yes. Glorious.

He was glorious.

He was everything. He always had been.

His breaths shallowed. When she bent her head and licked the tip of his erection, he groaned. It was a sound that only served to stoke the heat building inside her.

She took as much of him into her mouth as she could manage, and revelled to hear her name escape from his lips.

Giving him pleasure had always turned her on as much as his giving her pleasure had. There was something incredible in witnessing the great Theo Nikolaidis lose control and know that loss was because of *her*. To know that everything he made her feel was shared. He felt it all too.

Theo was losing his mind. Helena had turned the tables on him, bringing to life his fantasy and sucker-punching him in the process.

She'd performed this intimacy on him before, many times, but never had it felt like this. Her soft moans as she licked and sucked him were like music vibrating in his senses.

Theos, this was incredible...but it wasn't enough. He wanted to feel her soft skin pressed against his.

Gritting his teeth, he lifted his head and groped for her face.

She looked up at him, colour high on her cheeks, eyes molten.

'I want to be inside you,' he said through ragged breaths.

A dreamy smile spread over her face. 'Not yet.' And then she took him back in her mouth.

'Helena...' But his groan tapered into nothing, for she was cupping his balls and squeezing them, oh, so gently.

Holding off from taking full possession of her three years ago hadn't been this torturous. But then, three years ago he'd never experienced the exquisite pleasure of being inside her, never experienced the closeness and wonder he now craved with every fibre of his being.

Squeezing his eyes shut, Theo fought to hold on, but release fought equally hard. Just as he feared he was losing the battle, Helena moved from his arousal to drag her tongue up over his abdomen and chest and climb up to straddle him.

Hands on his shoulders, her breaths shallow, she gazed into his eyes.

Unable to take any more, Theo wound his hand into her hair and pulled her down for a kiss of such savage passion that when she finally sank onto his length, their moans caught in their tongues.

After a moment of stillness, she began to move.

Hands cradling his head, she teased her breasts against his face. He caught one in his mouth.

Still cradling him tightly, Helena threw her head back and arched her spine. The sensations wrought from his tongue and mouth only added to the fire blazing within her.

His strong arm wrapped around her, he held her securely. When she looked into his eyes she saw such a mixture of emotions reflecting back at her that the sensations deepened, strengthened, until all she could see was Theo, all she could feel was Theo, all she could taste, hear...everything was him.

And, when her orgasm ripped through her and she ground down so tightly on him and held him so closely and felt his own orgasm in response, all she could think was that she'd found heaven.

Theo had unlocked heaven for her and in it she had found only him.

'What are you doing?' Theo asked as he entered his yacht's dining room the next weekend. He'd woken to an empty bed and immediately set off in search of Helena.

Dressed in only a silk kimono—see, dreams *did* come true!—she was sitting with her head bent over an English newspaper he'd picked up for her the day before during a short trip to Athens.

'Nothing,' she said with suspicious innocence.

'Is that a crossword?'

'No...'

'You minx.' He shot an arm out to snatch it from her but she was too quick. She hugged it to her chest with a cackle of laughter.

It was a sound that immediately threw him back three years to a time when one of them would sneak downstairs early to grab the morning paper while the other slept, and dive straight to the crossword. Nothing made either of them smugger than completing it in one sitting before the other woke up. They'd been as bad as each other. Neither was averse to hiding the offending crossword within their clothing to stop the other getting to it, which in itself had led to wrestling, which had then led to peals of laughter, quickly followed by intimacies...

How could something as boring and simple as a *cross-*

word bring such laughter? And who else apart from Helena could he laugh with over a crossword? She'd introduced him to a side of himself he'd never explored before. It was Helena's influence that had made him see art with new eyes, to appreciate it, to seek it, to covet it. The only area her influence had failed was with poetry. It bored him rigid—apart from her own poems, of course. They were mercifully short and always contained a riddle for him to solve. Those poems were a language only the two of them knew.

Theo had brought fun into Helena's life and opened her mind to the pleasure life could give. She had opened his mind in other ways. They had complemented each other perfectly. Together, *they* had been perfect.

When he saw melancholy replace the laughter in her eyes, he knew the same memories were playing in her mind too.

The moment Sidiro appeared on the horizon, the tightness in Theo's chest loosened. His two days in Milan had been productive from a business sense but the loneliness of the evening had been acute. He supposed it was his own fault for crying off the party he'd been invited to so he could spend the evening talking dirty on the phone with Helena.

It was the first time in three years he'd stayed in when he could have gone out.

He doubted he would have enjoyed the party without her by his side.

Their time together was ticking onwards, days turning into weeks as if life had been set to fast-forward. Helena shared his bed every night. They made love constantly. How either of them got any work done he didn't know. Their passion for each other remained undiminished and he was no closer to exorcising her from his blood.

He no longer wanted vengeance. He no longer believed he'd ever wanted it, not the way he'd told himself he did.

He couldn't allow what they'd shared this time around to be turned into something ugly for the sake of petty revenge. It was a realisation that had come to him as if he were a man waking from a long dream. Helena didn't deserve it. She'd never set out to hurt or embarrass him. His humiliation at the cathedral was all on him. He hadn't listened. She'd been a frightened child and he, although older than her, had been an immature fool.

She'd been right about one thing though. When it came to her, he *had* been a control freak. Not in the way her father was, God forbid, but in a possessive, all-consuming way. He'd needed to know where she was every minute of the day for his own peace of mind, to know she was safe. He'd wanted her by his side so he could feed his addiction to her, to always be able to touch her, to look at her, to just *be* with her. His love for her had been obsessive and greedy, and he could sense the old feelings building back up in him. He needed to rein them in before he opened himself up to having the great wound in his heart ripped open again.

Helena looked out of her office window and let Theo concentrate on the first complete set of draft plans in peace. In the distance, across the water separating the peninsula from Sidiro itself, were clifftop homes nestled together. Anyone visiting Sidiro for the first time would be forgiven for thinking these pretty, simple dwellings served only one function. They couldn't know—indeed, only a few did know—that when the sun went down in the months of July and August, the owners of these dwellings threw their doors open, their homes becoming nightclubs, bars, restaurants, cafes and shops. When the sun came up, the partygoers would drift back to their rustic lodgings, the owners would close their doors and the island would doze lazily until the sun went down again. Rinse and repeat.

Today, on this beautiful Friday morning, she watched a large yacht with a batch of revellers sail past the peninsula towards Sidiro's small harbour. The past week had seen more yachts sail to and from the island than usually visited throughout the rest of year. She wondered if tonight the wind would carry the music beating from it in their direction.

To which dwelling had Theo taken her dancing that time she'd drunk too many Greek Doctor cocktails? She hadn't realised the strength of them until she'd been rocking like a madwoman on the makeshift dancefloor. Her top had ridden up her belly, she remembered. Theo, who'd been chatting to a group of other people, had noticed. He'd grinned, danced his way to her and discreetly pulled her top back down.

With a stab of emotion, she remembered how, even through the fog of her own inebriation, she'd known he'd pulled her top down out of pure caring. Theo had known how shy she was about her body—by that stage, she'd lost all shyness with him but in public it was a completely different matter—and he'd known she would be mortified to be flashing her belly like that.

It was a memory Helena hadn't thought about since it had happened. She'd forgotten how many hang-ups she'd had. She'd forgotten how Theo had simply sliced through them. He was doing the same now.

As she was about to turn away from the window, her attention was caught by two figures walking hand in hand down the hillside. Elli and Natassa.

What a blind idiot she'd been not to realise they were a couple. Or, if she was being honest with herself, what a *jealous* idiot she'd been. As she'd learned in the weeks since she and Theo had become lovers, the two women had been together since art school. Elli was an old family friend of the Nikolaidises. Theo had got talking to them at a party and learned Natassa had lost her job teaching art and that they were struggling to pay the rent on their tiny apartment. When he'd offered them the shared job of his housekeeper and the promise of their own art studio when the house was built, they'd practically bitten his hand off to accept.

Another yacht sailed by. If she squinted she could see the partygoers sunbathing on it.

Those partygoers had once been her and Theo.

As she looked back at him, her heart hurt to see the exhaustion lining his face. The new legislation had given him nothing but headaches.

To think she had accused him of being spoilt and lazy. Spoilt still held—how could he be anything else considering the life he'd lived—but lazy? No. That had been an unfair accusation. She'd never appreciated that he'd taken three months off from his business to be with her. Every time she'd questioned him about it back then, he'd kissed the tip of her nose and said he wanted to enjoy their time together before real life had to intrude. She should have had faith that he was telling the truth.

While she'd worked diligently on the plans, Theo had quietly got on with running his business empire from the office next door, jetting off occasionally to meetings around Europe. Only twice had he been unable to make it back to the peninsula. She'd worked until her eyes blurred to pass the time, then panicked and dawdled as the plans got nearer to completion.

From wanting to complete the plans as quickly as she could, she now wanted to draw it out for ever. She'd stressed the plans laid out before him were in draft form and that much more work was still needed.

This was only a partial truth.

If he approved these, the proper plans could be finished in days.

Once Theo signed them off...

Neither of them spoke of what would happen then.

The future was terrifyingly opaque.

'Can we go to the island tonight?' she asked impulsively.

He looked at her speculatively. A quirk curved the left side of his mouth. 'You want to party?'

Only with you.

She gave a dreamy sigh. 'Yes. I want to party.' Other than those two nights of bliss on Agon there had been none of the wild partying of old. Not since their night at the palace had they spent time with any of his social circle. Weekends had been enjoyed on Theo's yacht. They'd sailed to other islands, dined in quaint local *tavernas*, snorkelled, ridden on Theo's jet ski and made love so many times she was surprised she could still walk. Those weekends had been heaven.

His eyes gleamed with appreciation but there was something else underlying it, a something that, just for a moment, sent a needle of unease up her spine. Then he grinned and her unease vanished.

'You're an animal,' he said.

Only for you...

They stayed on Sidiro until the sun went down on Sunday night.

For two blissful days they did nothing but make love, sunbathe, make love, drink, make love, eat delicious food, make love and dance. There were many people Helena remembered from their time on the island before and they welcomed her back like an old friend. The new people, she was sure, would one day feel like friends too.

All the worries left her shoulders just as they had three years ago. No wonder she had agreed to marry Theo and have lots of children with him here on Sidiro. They'd been cocooned in a bubble of happiness. The outside world had seemed too far away to be real.

Theo rowed them back to the peninsula, his muscular arms working the oars as adeptly as he did everything else.

Helena stretched out with her feet on his lap. If they interfered with his oar-stroking, he didn't complain.

'Can we go back next weekend?' She held her breath while she awaited his answer. Theo had not given her his thoughts on the draft plans. If he hated them she would go back to the drawing board. If he liked them…

It could all be over by the end of the week.

Only the emerging stars gave the sea any illumination, but without the moon their radiance was not powerful enough for her to see the expression in Theo's eyes. His pause before answering made her wary. It was a feeling she was becoming all too familiar with. For all the bliss that weekend, there had been a few occasions when she'd caught something in his eye, gone before she could really be sure she'd seen it, but powerful enough to send flutters of alarm off in her belly.

'I thought you were keen to get home,' he answered.

Home?

For someone who'd arrived wishing time would pass at the speed of light, she now wished she could bottle it and hold it in stasis.

Scared at how nauseous the thought of returning to England without him made her feel, she settled on, 'It all feels very far away.'

'What will be the first thing you do when you get back?'

Theo's chest was tight. It had been tight the whole weekend. It had been tight since his return from Milan a week ago but had taken on unbearable proportions when Helena had asked if they could spend the weekend on the island.

He had been about to open his mouth and approve the draft plans.

If he had spoken first, they would already be over.

Call him selfish—Helena had called him that more times than he could count—but the thought of one more weekend with her had been irresistible.

She was silent for a long moment before answering. 'I'll visit my mum and see if I can convince her to leave my father.'

'You've tried that before.'

'It might be different this time.'

Theo felt her eyes on him and sensed she was talking about more than her mother.

He knew he'd changed a great deal from the man Helena had jilted but he also knew the possessive control freak still lurked beneath his skin. It itched to be set free. That man was the last thing she wanted. That man frightened her.

Steadily, he said, 'I wish you luck.'

They'd reached the peninsula. Theo jumped out of the boat, helped Helena to climb out too, then hauled it up the beach out of harm from the tide's reach.

Their footprints left indentations in the sand. Come the morning, they would be gone. There was a metaphor in that somewhere but right then he couldn't think what it could be.

It was time to let Helena go. He'd known it since he'd pored over the draft blueprints in her office and felt a fissure rend his heart.

He should have let her go three years ago.

CHAPTER FOURTEEN

THE SCOOTER WAS where they'd left it. Theo climbed on. Helena followed suit behind him and immediately wrapped her arms around his waist and pressed her cheek into the small of his back. He closed his eyes and savoured the warmth of her body against his. It would be for the last time.

When they reached the lodge he headed straight to the terrace. Elli had left a bottle of ouzo, a jug of iced water, two short glasses and two tall glasses on the table for him, as he'd instructed.

'Drink?'

'Just water for me, please.' She smiled softly as she pulled a chair out and sat on it gracefully. 'I think I've drunk enough alcohol for one weekend.'

Wishing she would look at him with the suspicion and venom she had blasted him with when he'd first brought her back to the peninsula, wishing he'd never embarked on this whole rotten act of vengeance, Theo poured her water then a large measure of ouzo for himself and raised his glass to her.

She clinked her glass to his. 'What are we drinking to?'

'To the successful completion of the plans.'

She blinked slowly. 'Really?'

'*Nai*. Everything is exactly as I envisaged.' It was exactly as they had dreamed together three years ago. The perfect house in which to raise the perfect family in the ultimate luxury.

She put her glass to her mouth then hesitated. Placing it down on the table, she reached for the ouzo and poured herself a measure almost as large as the one Theo had poured for himself.

He watched her take a large sip, close her eyes and grimace. Then her eyes opened and her head shook ever so slightly before her shoulders relaxed a little. 'I'm glad you're pleased with it.'

'You have more than fulfilled your brief. The completion payments will be sent to your account and your company's account in the morning.'

'You haven't signed it off yet. I still need to produce the final draft…'

'The blueprint is perfect. The 3D model you made brings it to life.'

'Yes, but I still need to send them to Savina for—'

'That won't be necessary.' Now he'd set the ball rolling to free her for good, he would not torture himself by prolonging their goodbye. Like a surgical procedure, it was best to sever it cleanly and precisely to prevent collateral damage.

Her brow furrowed. 'It's totally necessary.'

Theo closed his eyes and had a large gulp of his ouzo. 'I've changed my mind. The house will not be built.'

It would never be built. He could never live in it. He couldn't live in it without the woman he loved and he'd been a fool to ever think he could.

He would gift the lodge to Elli and Natassa and build a smaller dwelling for his grandmother to enjoy if she wished.

Time seemed to hang in suspended animation. Helena

did nothing but stare at him, fingers continually squeezing and releasing her glass.

When she finally spoke, the strain in her voice was apparent. 'Are you serious?'

Theo took a deep breath then gave a sharp nod. 'It is too far from my business. It is impractical.'

'Since when do you care if things are practical or not?'

He hooked an ankle over his knee. 'It is a lot of money to spend on a party pad that will rarely be used.'

Her laughter sounded as strained as her voice. 'Since when do you care about wasting money? You own properties you haven't even spent a night in.'

'They are properties that will one day serve a purpose.'

She fell into silence again, putting a finger to the bridge of her nose, another furrow appearing on her brow as her finger found no spectacles to push up. Helena hadn't worn her glasses since they'd returned from his villa on Agon. 'Forgive me for being dense, but I don't get why you've spent all this money on something you've suddenly decided isn't going to happen, and I'm not just talking about the fees you've paid me and my company. The levelling of the land, the sculpture commissions, Savina's fee—you'll have to pay her for her time at the very least or she'll have every right to sue you.'

'Savina will be recompensed.' *Theos*, the thuds of his heart beat like a physical pain. 'No one will suffer financially for my change of mind.'

'Good.' Biting into her bottom lip, she tucked her hair behind her ears then raised confused eyes to his. 'What about your grandmother? How does she feel? Have you told her the house you promised to build on the land she gave you is not going to happen?'

'I will explain the situation. She will understand.' She would be upset, he acknowledged painfully, but his grandmother was not one for making judgements on people's lives. All the same, he knew he'd built her hopes up. Her daughter—his mother—had never had any interest in returning to the island of her birth, so to discover her grandson falling in love with it had delighted her and she'd looked forward to seeing his new home there in all its glory.

'I'm glad you'll make her understand but I'm afraid *I* don't understand. We've spent weeks working on this and now you're saying it was all for nothing?'

'I'm sorry.' How he kept his voice calm when his insides were shredding into tiny pieces he would never know. 'I appreciate it must be disappointing to learn your plans will never come to fruition but you can take pride in the work you produced.' The slightest crack echoed in his voice when he added, 'It's spectacular. You, *matia mou*, have one hell of a career ahead of you.'

Her voice hardly above a whisper, seemingly not having heard his heartfelt compliment, she said, 'What happens now?'

'We'll sail to Agon in the morning. I'll arrange for my flight crew to fly you back to London on my jet. Take the plans and 3D model with you. They're yours. Add them to your portfolio.' He didn't think he could bear to look at them. He didn't think he could look at anything associated with Helena again.

Something flickered in her eyes. 'You're too kind.' She drained her water and put the glass on the table. Then she fixed her stare back on him. 'Perhaps you would be kind enough to tell me if you ever had any intention of building the house.'

'I did.' When he'd been too filled with pain-twisted vengeance to think straight.

She gave a short burst of mirthless laughter. 'And perhaps you would be kind enough to tell me if you want to see me again. Or should I assume your plan to pack me off to London tomorrow means this is goodbye for us?'

'Helena...'

'We're back to calling me Helena, are we?' Another even shorter burst of humourless laughter. 'Well, if that doesn't answer my question, nothing will. But I do have one more question,' she added before he could interject. 'When you hired me, was it your sole intention to seduce me, make me fall for you again and then dump me?'

If she hadn't been watching Theo so closely she might have missed the slight blanching of his features. The coldness that had been creeping through her veins throughout this whole wretched conversation suddenly spread into every cell of her body.

'That's what this has all been about, hasn't it?' she whispered when she managed to unfreeze her vocal cords. 'Revenge for me having the temerity to jilt you.'

There was nothing subtle about his wince this time.

Rubbing her arms madly to try and inject some warmth into them, she stared at his now unreadable face. 'I knew you had an agenda but I thought it was to watch me squirm while I designed the house we had once planned to live in together. I thought you wanted me to have a taste of everything I threw away, but it was more than that, wasn't it?'

Please, she prayed, *don't let it be true. Please, don't let it be true.*

'Yes.'

That one word was enough to make her stomach plummet to the floor.

'Yes?' she echoed.

Dropping his head, he kneaded his forehead with both hands. Then he looked back up. His eyes held hers as he steadily said, 'Yes. Everything you said is correct. I brought you back here for revenge. I wanted to seduce you into falling in love with me again, display you on my arm to the world and then dump you.'

Her head swimming, she rubbed her arms even harder. She couldn't remember ever feeling so cold. 'I never realised you hated me so much.'

'I thought I hated you.' His features were stark. 'One minute we were going to marry, the next you were gone. You cut me out of your life like I was nothing, like I'd never meant anything to you.'

'And you didn't cut me out of yours?' Anger rose like a snake inside her. 'You didn't call me once. You were in another woman's bed within weeks. While I was going out of my mind missing you, you were getting on with your life like I'd never been a part of it. You go to all this trouble for your petty revenge and for what? You never loved me. *How* could you have loved me if you were happy to sleep with other women so soon after I'd left? Dear God, I couldn't even bring myself to *kiss* another man, not in all the years since I left you.'

'You think *I* moved on?' There was anguish in the gravelly tones. 'I never moved on. God knows I tried but it was impossible. You were like a ghost in my head.'

'And this is your exorcism?' She couldn't believe how blind she'd been, how *stupid* she'd been. 'Make me fall in love with you again and then drop me from a great height for better impact?'

His throat moved. 'Yes. I'm sorry. I've been cruel…'

'That's one way of putting it. Life's just one big game to you, isn't it?' She was shaking so hard that when she got to her feet and put her hands on the table, the tremors shook it. 'I thought you'd changed but you're still the same spoilt bastard you always were. Everything has to be your way and you hate losing at anything. Well, congratulations. You've *won*!'

'I have won nothing,' he bit back, a spark of anger rising in his voice and glowing in his eyes. 'I know I deserve your anger but you leaving me…it destroyed me. You weren't marrying a statue. You were marrying a man who loved you and wanted only to make you happy. You threw that away, Helena. Not me. And for what?' He shook his head in despair. 'All I see is a lonely existence with a computer for company when there is so much more to you…'

'Don't you dare think I want advice on how to live my life from a charlatan like you,' she spat.

Theo stared at her and felt his thimble of anger die. Helena was as unreachable as she'd been the day she jilted him.

There was far more than humiliation and rage flowing from her. There was pain there too. A lot of pain. And he was the cause of it.

'I promise you cannot hate me more than I hate myself,' he said bleakly.

'Hate doesn't begin to describe how I feel. You set out to seduce me and make me fall for you just so you could publicly dump me!' There was a flash of confusion in her dark eyes. 'Why are you ending things like this? Where's the grand finale you planned? You had me where you wanted me. You could have strung me along a few more days, taken me to a couple more high-profile places and really got your pound of flesh. Did you get a fit of conscience? Or did you figure out that my love for you was punishment enough?'

'Helena—'

'Don't *ever* speak my name again,' she suddenly screamed, her hands flying to her ears. 'Everything has been one big fat lie. You wanted to hurt me and you've succeeded, more than you could ever know. You've also reassured me that I did exactly the right thing in not marrying you, you selfish, narcissistic *bastard*!'

Unable to look at him or breathe the same air as him a second longer, Helena turned on her heel and fled. She needed to get as far away from Theo as quickly as she could and to hell with dignity and pride.

Running as fast as her legs would carry her, she soon left the perimeter of the lodge and the safety of its nightlights and was plunged into darkness. She didn't care. Let the darkness of the moonless night take her where it wanted. Nothing could be worse than the pain she was feeling now.

How could Theo have done this? And for what purpose? *Why?*

Pebbles crunched beneath her feet as she ran the dirt trail that stretched to the small harbour. Wildly, she thought of jumping into the rowing boat and sailing to Sidiro.

Oh, God, please, never let her have to face him again. She couldn't.

Everything they'd shared this past month, all the tenderness that had developed between them, all the laughter, all the joy, it had all been a lie. She had let Theo back into her heart and it had been a lie.

She had no idea how long she'd been running when the burn in her thighs and lungs forced her to stop. Doubling over and putting her hands on her knees to keep herself upright, she tried to catch her breath.

'Helena!' Theo's voice bellowed out of nowhere.

He'd followed her.

Panic pulled her into its grip. She dragged as much air through her ragged throat as she could. She needed to get moving before he caught her...

'Helena!' The bellow was closer. A light emerged

through the darkness. 'Please, *matia mou*, come back. It's too dark. It isn't safe.'

His distinctive footsteps drew nearer. The light got brighter. Either side of the trail were low, prickly bushes and rocks of differing sizes. There was nowhere to hide.

'Leave me *alone*!' she finally managed to croak. Her legs were trembling too hard for her to take another step.

And then, when the light hit her, the footsteps stopped.

His distant form behind it was little more than a shimmer.

'Helena…' His voice was shakier than she had ever heard it. It carried through the night sky. 'I'm sorry. I wish I could say I never intended to hurt you but I did. God forgive me, I wanted to hurt you in exactly the way you hurt me.'

Her legs finally giving up on her, Helena crouched down onto her haunches and covered her ears. His voice still penetrated.

'You think I moved on with my life…' She heard a long intake of breath. 'There has been no one else. I couldn't.' A mirthless laugh. 'I was basically impotent. I blamed you for emasculating me but it was much worse than that. I'd bound my heart to you so tightly my body is incapable of switching on for anyone else. All those women you saw me with…it was all a front. Another lie. I never stopped loving you. I missed you every single minute we were apart.'

She pressed her hands even tighter to her ears. She didn't want to hear this. No more lies. She couldn't bear it.

But still his voice sounded through the barriers of her hands.

'You asked why I didn't go through with my plan to humiliate you. I *couldn't*. It wasn't a change of heart. More an awakening. Much as it pains me to admit this, *matia mou*, you were right to leave me. I *am* a control freak when it comes to you. Even the years we were apart I kept tabs on your career. I told myself it was because I was biding my time for the perfect opportunity to strike, but it was because I needed the reassurance that you were okay.' His voice dropped to a whisper. 'That you were safe.'

Silence stretched out.

Only when his voice rang out again, stronger, did Helena realise she'd lowered her hands.

'You are the only person I've let into my heart since my parents died. I was so scared of losing you like I lost them that I suffocated you. I was so desperate to make you mine and tie you to me for ever that I steamrollered you into the wedding.' Another pained laugh. 'I refused to believe you had gone. I stood at that altar waiting for you even though I knew damn well you were already back in England. I was in complete denial. When the reality of the situation sank in, I lost my mind. I see that now.'

He sighed. 'Please don't think I'm making excuses or putting the blame for my actions on my parents' death because I'm not. Even if they had lived I would be greedy and possessive of you. I take full responsibility. It's all on me. I want you to know all this because you deserve the truth. I owe you that much.' His voice faded into silence.

The flashlight moved in the blackness and was laid on the ground.

'I'm going back to the lodge now,' he said through the blackness. 'I'll leave my phone for you so you can see your way back.'

His footsteps crunched away and then stopped again.

'I have behaved appallingly. I don't expect your forgiveness but I really am sorry, *matia mou*. I promise I will leave you to get on with your life in peace, but please, I beg you, *live* it.'

Only when the crunching of Theo's footsteps faded into nothing did Helena's bottom hit the ground.

Deep inside her, something sharp and acrid roiled violently and rose within her until it reached her throat, escaping from her mouth as a desolate scream.

Curling herself into a ball on the dirt trail, she wept until there were no tears left to cry.

CHAPTER FIFTEEN

THE MOMENT THEO'S eyes opened, memories of the previous night flooded in.

He squeezed them back shut. The memories refused to shift. Nausea washed through him.

Not bothering to shower, he threw on a pair of shorts and a T-shirt without looking at them and staggered to the kitchen for what would be the last time. In approximately twenty minutes he would be on his yacht. He would never come back.

Natassa was removing fresh pastries from the oven. For once he was oblivious to their aroma and made none of his usual effort to pinch one fresh off the baking tray.

Head pounding, he poured himself a coffee. Helena had placed his phone next to the coffee machine.

He pocketed the phone and took a swig of his coffee, uncaring that he scalded his mouth. 'Is Helena up yet?'

Theos, it hurt to say her name.

He'd waited over an hour to hear her footsteps treading quietly through the lodge. He'd listened to the soft closing of her bedroom door and the turn of her lock. Only then, knowing she was safely back, did he strip off his clothes and get into bed. It had taken him hours to fall asleep.

He would keep his distance on the yacht, he decided

bleakly. He would let her settle on it first then find a space far from her.

'She left hours ago,' Natassa replied.

He craned his head round sharply. 'What do you mean, *she left*?'

'She went to the island.'

'Sidiro?'

She nodded, eyes suddenly wary.

'How?'

'I don't know. I assume she took the boat.'

Theo took a moment to compose his features and lower his tone. 'Did she say how long she would be there for?'

'No…' Natassa raised her shoulders. 'She gave me a hug and thanked me for everything. My feeling was that she wouldn't be coming back—she said her work for you was done. Should I have told you? I didn't think. I assumed you knew.'

'It's okay.' He breathed deeply as he attempted to reassure her. He felt light-headed and blinked hard a number of times to regain his focus. 'Her work here is complete.' And Helena had no reason to suffer his company another minute. She had probably decided to get a lift back to Agon from one of the partygoers on the island. 'Where is Elli? I have something to discuss with you both.'

Fifteen minutes later, Theo borrowed Elli's scooter to reach his yacht. He assumed Helena had taken his when she'd made her early morning escape, an assumption confirmed when he reached the small cove he kept the rowing boat in. The boat had gone and his scooter was propped up in its place.

Shading his eyes from the rising sun, he squinted. The sea was calm. There was nothing floating on the water.

It was only a short boat ride to the island. Helena could

have reached it in ten, maybe twenty minutes. She was no-where near as strong as him but she was hardly a weakling.

All the same, he borrowed the captain's binoculars when he boarded his yacht and found he could breathe a little easier when he spotted his rowing boat pulled up high on the beach. She had made it there safe and sound. She had money in her bank account. She had friends on Sidiro. If the worst happened and she couldn't get a lift off the island, she could catch the ferry.

It was time to put into practice what he'd promised and leave her to get on with her life. Maybe one day he'd be able to get on with his too.

Helena looked out of the window of the bedroom she'd taken possession of barely an hour ago. She'd arrived on Sidiro as all the partygoers were off to bed and had been incredibly lucky the room they'd rented that weekend was still free. Even luckier that Marinella, the owner of the house-hotel, allowed her to swap the room for another. She couldn't bring herself to sleep in the bed in which she and Theo had spent practically the whole weekend.

Had it really been only twelve hours since they'd left it?

She'd come to Sidiro on impulse after a sleepless night. She hadn't been able to stomach the thought of travelling back to Agon with Theo on his yacht, so had rowed here intending to spend a night catching up on sleep and then either cadge a lift or get the ferry off the island.

The house-hotel was located high on a hilltop. The only downside with this room was that it faced the peninsula.

About to fall onto the bed and sleep her exhaustion away, she caught a flash of white in the distance.

Theo's yacht.

Her eyes remained fixed on it until it became a distant speck and then faded into nothing.

Theo had gone.

She would never see him again.

Theo drummed his fingers as he read the email that had pinged into his inbox a few minutes ago from Staffords. His phone, switched to silent, vibrated. Seeing it was an old friend no doubt wanting to make plans for a night out, he let it go to voicemail. He'd been home for five days and had only left the villa for business purposes, but now it was Friday and all his friends, neglected since he and Helena had become lovers, were trying to tempt him out.

He rubbed his eyes and reread the generic email. It was an acknowledgement of the payment Theo had made to them. He printed it off and read it again. Reading it somehow made him feel closer to Helena.

Was she, at that moment, sitting in her open-plan London office working on a new project? Had she spoken to her mother? Had she *seen* her mother?

His phone vibrated again. He let it go to voicemail again. Sooner or later his friends would get the message. Theo didn't want to party. He didn't want to go anywhere.

Without Helena, what was the point?

He'd never allowed himself to grieve the first time he'd lost Helena. He'd done everything he could to deny the pain that had ravaged him. This time he would grieve. He would suck it up because all the pain he was feeling was his own fault.

His phone suddenly emitted a short trill, notifying him of a text message.

His heart stopped.

It was the specific tone he'd set for Helena. He'd set the emergency bypass on his phone so he would always hear if she reached out to him on it, even if his phone was on silent. He'd never dared hope it would happen.

His hand shook so much he dropped his phone. It took a few attempts to get his fingers to work enough to open the message.

His first instinct was she'd sent it to the wrong person.

Greek Doctors and golden sand, sunshine and warm sea. A happy place for everyone, find me and together be free.

He read it a number of times, trying to make sense of it.

On impulse, he called Staffords and asked to be put through to Helena.

'I'm sorry, sir,' the disembodied voice politely informed him, 'but Miss Armstrong is on leave.'

He disconnected the call and read the text again, his shuddering heart pounding through his ribs.

He hardly dared believe what he thought it meant.

Helena hit send and then pressed her phone to her chest. She felt giddy.

'Can I get you anything else?'

She looked up at the friendly waitress and smiled. 'No, thank you. Just the bill, please.'

While she waited, Helena gazed out at the blazing orange sunset. Soon, Theo's yacht would appear.

Had she been too subtle with her message to him? Should she have simply put that she was on Sidiro and that she wanted to see him?

She smiled to herself. No. Theo would know. He'd always understood the little poems and riddles she'd liked to write for him. He understood her like no one else. Sending it as a riddle poem felt right.

Being in his arms felt right.

The one night she'd intended to spend on Sidiro had stretched into days. Slowly, the dark cloud of Theo's betrayal had lifted. Everywhere she'd walked on this beautiful island brought back memories. Good memories. Beautiful memories.

She began to see more clearly. Theo's heartfelt words began to echo in her ears. His behaviour had been heinous and there was no excusing it, but as her blinkers came down she began to understand. And she began to forgive.

She understood because love did crazy things to people. She should know.

She'd spent three years adrift without him. They'd been necessary years in which she'd learned to stand on her own two feet, find her voice and gain the confidence to speak her mind about important things without fear of the consequences. But always there had been something missing: Theo.

They were years she would never get back and she didn't want to live any more of them. The frightened bird he'd once described her as had flown free but the only nest it wanted to make was with Theo.

She'd never stopped loving him. She could admit that now. Her heart had bound itself to Theo and never let go.

Her bill paid, she left the beachside bar and joined the throng of partygoers emerging like vampires from their hotels to start the weekend in style. It didn't bother her being there alone. The people who came to party on Sidiro were too warm and friendly to allow anyone to be by themselves unless it was what they wanted. They were people in Theo's own mould.

Theo, still uncertain of his instincts, disembarked from his yacht. He'd barely reached the end of the beach when he was pounced on by friendly familiar faces.

It took a few minutes to extract himself and then he was off, walking the familiar path to the top of the island, where the evenings really came to life. He strolled past dwellings rammed with people dancing, eating, drinking, laughing, past the booths selling mouthwatering street food, past a street magician holding a small child with braids in her hair, enthralled—he'd noticed an increased number of small children here last weekend, the first generation of Sidiro's partygoers bringing their offspring with them.

He didn't dare dream that one day he and Helena would bring their own children here.

He still wasn't convinced he'd interpreted the message correctly.

He should have replied to make sure but his hands had refused to co-operate, too fearful that his fledging hopes would be dashed.

Theo found the dwelling he'd been looking for.

The front door was open. Dance music pumped out. He paid his entry fee and stepped inside. There were only two dozen people in the living area, which had been cleared of furniture for two months and transformed into a nightclub. He scanned the dancing bodies illuminated by the twirling disco lights, unable to exhale until he spotted a curvy figure dressed in frayed denim shorts and a white vest top, her chestnut hair loose and sprawled over her shoulders, dance her way through the doorway separating the dance floor from the makeshift bar. She held a glass of what was unmistakably a Greek Doctor in her hand.

Her eyes locked on to his in seconds. For a moment she stilled. Slowly, a smile spread over her face before she turned and disappeared for a moment. She returned holding a second cocktail. The smile on her face was wider than ever. And then she began to move.

Her body softly swaying, eyes not leaving his, she danced her way through the heaving bodies. When she was only a foot from him she stopped and passed one of the glasses to him. Feeling as if he'd slipped into a dream, Theo chinked his glass to hers. In unison, they drained their cocktails. Helena took his empty glass and put both on a nearby stool. Only then did she take the last step to him.

For a long time she did nothing but stare at him and then a smile of such radiance lit her face that, finally, the kernel of hope nestling inside him since he'd received her message broke to the surface.

Her fingers drifted down his arms and entwined with his. She took a step back into the throng of dancers and tugged him with her.

Hands clasped tightly together, hips gyrating, her hair flicking in all directions, they danced, not speaking, simply as one in a moment that time could never replicate.

More people arrived. The dance floor became crammed. Theo didn't care, not when it forced him to hold Helena even closer, dancing now with their thighs nestled together, her arms looped around his neck, his arms wrapped around the hot curves that were tailor-made for him.

And then she stopped dancing, took hold of his hand again and led him to the bar. There, she shouted for two Greek Doctors. When they had them in their hands, she led Theo through the back door and out onto the small, deserted courtyard.

After the noise and heat of the dance floor, it took a few moments for his ears to adjust to the comparative silence. Only when the freshness of the night air cooled his face did he accept that this was no dream.

Helena had reached out to him and brought him here.

She hauled herself onto a wooden table and turned her face up to the starry sky. He didn't think she'd ever exuded such serenity. She shone brighter than any of the stars above them.

He sat beside her and waited for her to speak.

He didn't have to wait long.

'Can we marry in the chapel here?'

He almost choked on the mouthful of cocktail he'd just swallowed.

Still gazing at the sky, she laughed, a joyous tinkling sound that landed like music in his ears. 'You know you have to marry me, don't you?'

He couldn't speak.

'I think it's the least you deserve.' She spoke matter-of-factly but he could hear the undertones of glee. 'That's going to be your punishment. You have to marry me. And impregnate me.'

'That's a punishment?' he managed to say.

Her bright eyes landed on him. 'Oh, yes, my love. I've decided that killing you is a waste of an excellent lover, so you have to do a lifetime of hard labour in my bed instead.'

If wishes could come true, then all of his had just turned to gold.

Bowing his head, he closed his eyes. 'I would like nothing more than to spend the rest of my life with you...'

'But?' she prompted cheerfully when his voice trailed off.

He met her gaze. 'I'm all wrong for you. You deserve...'

'I deserve retribution for your heinous plot, is that what you were going to say?' Mock innocence rang out of the sparkling eyes. 'I quite agree.'

Before he could speak, she jumped off the table. She appeared to have springs in her feet. Spreading her arms wide, she pirouetted then curtseyed. 'Do you see what you do to me?'

At Theo's furrowed brow, Helena burst into another peal of laughter. She felt as if she could fly. 'You've set me free, my possessive love. You've taught me how to embrace life, and you know what? I'm going to take your advice and live but unfortunately for you that means you have to put up with possessive, jealous little old me.'

The furrow in his brow was now so deep she was quite sure it would lead to a permanent indentation.

'You think you're the only possessive one? My love, since the day I met you, I've wanted to scratch the eyes out of every woman who's looked at you. It's like I have a hot snake living in my belly that strikes whenever a pretty woman is within a twenty-foot radius of you.'

'I've only had eyes for you since the day I met you.'

Fresh happiness bubbled in her. 'I *know*. But three years ago I was a naïve, insecure lamb who was terrified of all the feelings you brought out in me. I was as terrified of losing you as you were of losing me, but I was too immature to understand my feelings. I remember shouting at you that you were just like my father, but the truth is I was terrified that *I* was like him. I couldn't handle the jealousy and the control-freakery I have in me. I never understood what you saw in me. To be honest, I still don't…'

'Sunlight,' he interrupted.

She looked at him.

Finally, a smile played on his lips. 'That's what I see in you. Sunlight.'

She beamed. 'That's much more romantic than the gorgeous devil I see in you.' She stepped to him and hooked her arms around his shoulders and sighed. 'You swept me off my feet when I was still learning to dance. I wasn't ready for you and I definitely wasn't ready for the love I felt for you. It all got too much for me, fears I would become my mother and fears over my possessive feelings for you… I couldn't see straight, so I ran. I spent three years web-searching your name and going green with jealousy over those women but I was powerless to stop. When you brought me back here, all those feelings I'd buried built up in me again…' She shook her head. 'They don't frighten me any more. Your control-freakery doesn't frighten me any more either. I know you love me as much as I love you. I know you're as greedy for me as I am for you. I know what we have is special. We belong together and I know we will both move heaven and earth to make it work. So, my love, I figure you deserve retribution too for all the hurt I caused you and I figured that if you were telling me the truth the other night, then you might settle for me doing hard labour in your bed for the rest of my life to make up for it.'

Staring deep into her eyes, his hands clasped her hips. 'You love me?'

'More than there are stars in the sky.'

'Say it again,' Theo whispered. He brushed his lips over hers and inhaled her warm, sweet breath.

'I love you.'

'Again.'

'I love you.'

He kissed her, then wound his arms around her and crushed her to him. 'I love you, you crazy, beautiful, clever woman. I swear I will spend the rest of my life making up for—'

She interrupted him with a kiss full of such passion that the last cells in his body able to believe that this was happening, that Helena was here, solid, beautiful and declaring her love for him, woke up and joined the party.

'No more apologies,' she whispered when she broke the kiss. 'Let's make this a new beginning for us. No secrets, no lies, just you and me together, loving each other.'

'Always.'

'Always.'

Then their mouths fused in a kiss that sealed their fates together for the rest of their lives.

EPILOGUE

HELENA LOOKED OUT of the kitchen window at her husband holding court in their vast garden and smiled. She finished her glass of water, swiped a canapé from a tray freshly removed from the oven and went out to join their guests, blowing a kiss at Theo's grandmother, who was beaming her joy at the grand home on the peninsula finally built and lived in.

Theo's eyes brightened when he saw her. 'I was about to send a search party out for you.' He hooked an arm around her waist.

'I was only gone for five minutes,' she chided, tapping his nose.

'Takis is here.'

'Right.' She had no idea why this was supposed to mean something to her. All the guests at their housewarming party had already shown their rapture at the sculptures Takis had created.

A gleam flared in his eyes. 'I have a surprise for you.'

She patted her growing belly. 'Bet it's not bigger than this one.'

He laughed and nuzzled his face into her hair. 'Nearly.'

They'd married in the small church on Sidiro two weeks after they'd declared themselves to each other. A month after that, Helena had come off the pill. They'd both been thrilled when she'd fallen pregnant a month later. They'd both been confounded when, four months after Freya's birth, Helena had discovered she was pregnant again.

As she thought of Freya, she quickly scanned for her mother, who was on babysitting duty that day, and found her chatting, Freya on her hip, with her mother's oldest sister. Her mother had come to stay in Agon when Freya was born and had never gone back. Seeing her daughter in a marriage of equals, with love and laughter always in abundance, had been all it took for her to see that the misery of her life would never change if she didn't do something about it. Having since installed her in the guest wing of their new home, Theo and Helena were in the process of building her mother a home of her own, designed by Helena, close to their summer house.

Helena's father continued to live in his city home. He employed a full-time housekeeper to look after him. The irony that her husband now paid someone to do the job she'd been forced to do for free was not lost on her mother. He'd met baby Freya only once. When he'd learned Helena planned to open her own architectural practice and would work from home, sharing an office with Theo—they'd made adjustments to the original design to include a vast office space for the pair of them to share—he'd pulled Theo aside and given him advice on the best ways to neutralise Helena's wanton need for independence. Theo had laughed in his face.

Takis appeared, followed by four strapping young men, all carefully dragging a draped six-foot sculpture on a wheeled pallet. Another three men dragged a plinth on another pallet.

All the guests stopped chatting to watch.

Theo had placed one of the marble benches Takis had made in the vine section of their garden. The men placed the plinth next to it then they raised the other pallet to slide the draped sculpture onto it.

When they were done, Theo winked at her before striding to it. At the same moment, the staff they'd hired for the day—Natassa and Elli were too much like family to them not to be at the party as guests—spread amongst the guests with trays of champagne.

Helena accepted an alcohol-free sparkling wine while wondering what her devious husband had been up to behind her back. This had never been part of the script they'd planned for the day.

Theo called for everyone's attention.

'Thank you all for coming and for the excellent gifts you have given us. We will treasure them.' Now he looked straight at Helena.

She held her breath.

'The person I most want to thank is my wife. You all know I worship the ground she walks on...' a peal of laughter and much nodding of heads '...and I thought it fitting that in this garden she created there should be a monument for me to worship her if ever I lose her for five minutes.'

Another peal of knowing laughter.

Theo nodded at Takis.

Takis pulled the sheet.

There was a collective gasp. The loudest came from Helena.

The statue was identical to the statue of Artemis in the Agon Palace gardens she'd sat beside when she'd first met Theo. But this Artemis had Helena's face.

Tentatively, she placed a hand to it, felt the smooth, cold marble beneath the pads of her fingers.

'What do you think?' Theo whispered, sidling up behind her.

'That you're a sneaky, gorgeous devil and that I love you. It's wonderful.'

'It felt fitting. Like it brings us full circle.'

She turned to wrap her arms around him. 'Thank you. I love it. I love you.'

'I love you too.'

She gazed up at him. 'Do you know what I think?'

He shook his head.

'That if Artemis had met you, she would have forgone her vow never to marry too.'

His eyes gleamed. He smiled. And then he kissed her.

* * * * *

COMING SOON!

We really hope you enjoyed reading this book. If you're looking for more romance, be sure to head to the shops when new books are available on

Thursday 2ⁿᵈ April

To see which titles are coming soon, please visit

millsandboon.co.uk/nextmonth

MILLS & BOON

Coming next month

THE SECRET KEPT FROM THE KING
Clare Connelly

'No.' He held onto her wrist as though he could tell she was about to run from the room. 'Stop.'

Her eyes lifted to his and she jerked on her wrist so she could lift her fingers to her eyes and brush away her tears. Panic was filling her, panic and disbelief at the mess she found herself in.

'How is this upsetting to you?' he asked more gently, pressing his hands to her shoulders, stroking his thumbs over her collarbone. 'We agreed at the hotel that we could only have two nights together, and you were fine with that. I'm offering you three months, on exactly those same terms, and you're acting as though I've asked you to parade naked through the streets of Shajarah.'

'You're ashamed of me,' she said simply. 'In New York we were two people who wanted to be together. What you're proposing turns me into your possession.'

He stared at her, his eyes narrowed. 'The money I will give you is beside the point.'

More tears sparkled on her lashes. 'Not to me it's not.'

'Then don't take the money,' he said, urgently. 'Come to the RKH and be my lover because you want to be with me.'

'I can't.' Tears fell freely down her face now. 'I need that money. I need it.'

A muscle jerked in his jaw. 'So have both.'

'No, you don't understand.'

She was a live wire of panic but she had to tell him, so that he understood why his offer was so revolting to her.

She pulled away from him, pacing towards the windows, looking out on this city she loved. The trees at Bryant Park whistled in the fall breeze and she watched them for a moment, remembering the first time she'd seen them. She'd been a little girl, five, maybe six, and her dad had been performing at the restaurant on the fringes of the park. She'd worn her Very Best dress, and, despite the heat, she'd worn tights that were so uncomfortable she could vividly remember that feeling now. But the park had been beautiful and her dad's music had, as always, filled her heart with pleasure and joy.

Sariq was behind her now, she felt him, but didn't turn to look at him.

'I'm glad you were so honest with me today.' Her voice was hollow. 'It makes it easier for me, in a way, because I know exactly how you feel, how you see me, and what you want from me.' Her voice was hollow, completely devoid of emotion when she had a thousand throbbing inside her.

He said nothing. He didn't try to deny it. Good. Just as she'd said, it was easier when things were black and white.

'I don't want money so I can attend the Juilliard, Your Highness.' It pleased her to use his title, to use that as a point of difference, to put a line between them that neither of them could cross.

Silence. Heavy, loaded with questions. And finally, 'Then what do you need such a sum for?'

She bit down on her lip, her tummy squeezing tight. 'I'm pregnant. And you're the father.'

Continue reading
THE SECRET KEPT FROM THE KING
Clare Connelly

Available next month
www.millsandboon.co.uk

LET'S TALK
Romance

For exclusive extracts, competitions
and special offers, find us online:

 facebook.com/millsandboon

 @MillsandBoon

@MillsandBoonUK

Get in touch on 01413 063232

MILLS & BOON

THE HEART OF ROMANCE

A ROMANCE FOR EVERY KIND OF READER

MODERN

Prepare to be swept off your feet by sophisticated, sexy and seductive heroes, in some of the world's most glamorous and romantic locations, where power and passion collide.
8 stories per month.

HISTORICAL

Escape with historical heroes from time gone by. Whether your passion is for wicked Regency Rakes, muscled Vikings or rugged Highlanders, awaken the romance of the past.
6 stories per month.

MEDICAL

Set your pulse racing with dedicated, delectable doctors in the high-pressure world of medicine, where emotions run high and passion, comfort and love are the best medicine.
6 stories per month.

True Love

Celebrate true love with tender stories of heartfelt romance, the rush of falling in love to the joy a new baby can bring, and focus on the emotional heart of a relationship.
8 stories per month.

Desire

Indulge in secrets and scandal, intense drama and plenty of sizzling hot action with powerful and passionate heroes who have it all: wealth, status, good looks…everything but the right woman.
6 stories per month.

HEROES

Experience all the excitement of a gripping thriller, with an intense romance at its heart. Resourceful, true-to-life women and strong, fearless men face danger and desire - a killer combination!
8 stories per month.

DARE

Sensual love stories featuring smart, sassy heroines you'd want as a best friend, and compelling intense heroes who are worthy of them.
4 stories per month.

To see which titles are coming soon, please visit

millsandboon.co.uk/nextmonth

JOIN US ON SOCIAL MEDIA!

Stay up to date with our latest releases, author news and gossip, special offers and discounts, and all the behind-the-scenes action from Mills & Boon...

 millsandboon

 millsandboonuk

 millsandboon

might just be true love...